"Kristine Kathryn Rusch's *Diving into the Wreck* is exactly what the sf genre needs to get more readers...and to keep the readers the genre already has."
—*Elitist Book Reviews* on *Diving into the Wreck*

"Rusch keeps the science accessible, the cultures intriguing, and the characters engaging. For anyone needing to add to their science fiction library, keep an eye out for this."
—*Speculative Fiction Examiner* on *City of Ruins*

"Rusch's latest addition to her Diving series features a strong, capable female heroine and a vividly imagined far-future universe. Blending fast-paced action with an exploration of the nature of friendship and the ethics of scientific discoveries, this tale should appeal to Rusch's readers and fans of space opera."
—*Library Journal* on *Boneyards*

"Rusch follows *Diving into the Wreck* and *City of Ruins* with another fast-paced novel of the far future... [Rusch's] sensibilities will endear this book to readers looking for a light, quick space adventure with strong female protagonists."
—*Publishers Weekly* on *Boneyards*

"Filled with well-defined characters who confront a variety of ethical and moral dilemmas, Rusch's third Diving novel is classic space opera, with richly detailed worldbuilding and lots of drama."
—*RT Book Reviews* on *Boneyards*

"...a fabulous outer space thriller that rotates perspective between the divers, the Alliance and to a lesser degree the Empire. Action-packed and filled with twists yet allowing the reader to understand the motives of the key players, *Skirmishes* is another intelligent exciting voyage into the Rusch Diving universe."
—*The Midwest Book Review* on *Skirmishes*

The Diving Universe

(Reading Order)

THE CHASE

A DIVING NOVEL

KRISTINE KATHRYN RUSCH

wmg **PUBLISHING**

The Chase

THE CHASE

A DIVING NOVEL

THE CHASE

1

THE *BILATZAILEA* ARRIVED IN THE MIDDLE OF A BATTLE.

Captain Kimi Nyguta stood on the *BilatZailea*'s bridge, hands clasped behind her back. The moment the *BilatZailea* arrived, it received all of the telemetry from the battle, so she spread it across the five holo-screens before her.

Someone had breached Base 20 on Nindowne. Immediately, the Armada Jefatura dispatched a flotilla, but the Jefatura had to have known or suspected something major, something they weren't telling the captains, because that flotilla included the *BilatZailea* and a sister ship, the *EhizTari*. Both were foldspace tracking vessels.

The *EhizTari*'s presence annoyed Nyguta. All the Armada needed in a battle like this one was a single foldspace tracking vessel. Whoever had issued this order had never worked with a foldspace tracking vessel.

Either that, or this battle was more significant than she thought.

It didn't seem that way when she had arrived. The battle was already underway, and it was complicated. Much of it occurred in the space around Nindowne, and seemed to be directed at a single skip.

Skips weren't major threats, especially when faced with Dignity Vessels and Security Class Vessels. An orbiter, properly equipped, could take out a skip—unless the skip was something special.

1

The skip wasn't much to look at. Boxy, with runners along its side, and shuttered portals. It was well-piloted, but if it was like other skips of its kind, it had no real weaponry and inadequate defenses.

She couldn't really believe that a skip was any kind of threat. She'd seen skips like it before—the Armada had repurposed several—and none of them held more than thirty people. Even that was uncomfortable.

She hadn't checked the telemetry, but if she had to guess, the skip probably held ten to twenty at most.

Her team was monitoring the skip. She had instructed them to do so the moment the *BilatZailea* had come out of foldspace. She had made the short trip using the *anacapa* drive, because she needed to arrive quickly—and there was no quickly from where the *BilatZailea* had been deployed.

She also hadn't wanted the *BilatZailea* to be seen by the enemy. At that point, she had had no idea that an entire flotilla had been called to take on a single, small ship. She had thought she would be handling cleanup, chasing dozens of ships into foldspace.

She hadn't wanted the enemy to know that a foldspace tracking vessel was anywhere nearby. The *EhizTari* hadn't been as cautious, which irritated her further. The *EhizTari* hovered around the edges of the battle, looking conspicuous—or maybe she just thought the damn thing was conspicuous.

Which furthered her annoyance at being partnered with another ship on a mission that made partnering difficult—especially since she had never partnered with this vehicle. She didn't even know who the captain of the *EhizTari* was.

She wasn't even going to look that information up, which was probably petty, and she didn't care. She was annoyed, but she tried not to let her annoyance show. She wanted her team to focus on the task at hand, even if the task seemed surprisingly small.

Her bridge team was one of the best she'd ever worked with. They were behind her, their workstations staggering upwards and curved around her, almost as if she stood in the center of an amphitheater.

Screens decorated the walls—screens she normally called useless, because the *BilatZailea* spent most of its time in foldspace, which didn't have relevant views.

Although, she had to admit, she'd been using the screens off and on all day, from the moment she'd arrived. She wanted to see this possible Fleet vessel whose crew had somehow invaded Base 20, and was now under attack from almost all of the Armada vessels in the sector.

The backs of her knees pushed up against the stupidly designed captain's chair. The *BilatZailea* had been designed as a Fleet foldspace search vehicle a long time ago, and modified to become an Armada foldspace tracking vehicle. The engineers had left the stupid captain's chair, with the idea that Nyguta might have to spend days in it while she was working.

Instead, she spent days bumping up against it because she preferred to stand when she was on the bridge.

She watched the fighters stream after the skip. It had left Nindowne's orbit just as she arrived, skating past all the space junk the Armada left in place around the planet, so that ships thought twice before even trying to enter orbit.

The skip was moving at a faster clip than she had expected. Instead of heading away from the flotilla, the skip had headed toward it, confusing the fighters at first.

Then they rallied, and swarmed around it, firing, the shots somehow going wide or missing it entirely. The shots didn't seem to bank off of it, though, so it didn't have unusually great shields.

Apparently, it just had an unusually great pilot.

That skip had to be heading somewhere. She scanned the ships nearby, and saw one she didn't recognized. It had a label in Old Fleet Standard. *Shadow.*

That made her skin crawl. She had no idea how an old Fleet ship got in the middle of a flotilla.

Then the skip vanished.

3

She leaned forward and had her screens refresh the action before her, but even as she did so, she saw—out of the corner of her eye—that some of her team members were doing the same thing.

"Did it just disappear?" she asked, worrying that it had gone into foldspace without opening a foldspace window. No ship that she had ever seen had done that before. Would that make the skip harder to track? Was that why the Jefatura had wanted both the *BilatZailea* and the *EhizTari?* Because the skip had new technology?

Then, before her crew said anything, she looked for the *Shadow.* Instead of a ship called *Shadow,* she saw what had been a Fleet Dignity Vessel, repurposed into an Armada vessel.

She cursed.

"The damn skip was ghosted," she said. Not just the skip, but that other ship as well. The *Shadow.*

"Yes," said Mikai Rockowitz, her second-in-command. He wasn't so much answering her as providing quiet confirmation.

He was a balding, wizened man who never wanted his own command. He reluctantly became her second, only after she begged repeatedly, mostly because he knew as much (or maybe more) about foldspace tracking than she did.

"The actual skip is far from the fighters," he said, as he sent her coordinates for the skip.

She didn't need them. She had already spotted the real skip, trundling forward at a much slower speed than its ghost.

She had been right, though: the pilot of the skip was unusually gifted.

Ghosting was difficult. The pilot, while under attack, created a false image of the ship, and that image had to hold up while the attackers went after it. Usually most ghosts vanished the moment laser weapons fire hit. This ghost ship had survived hundreds of shots, and confused two dozen fighters which were seeing it up close.

And, on top of it, the pilot had ghosted a destination. That took incredible know-how and the ability to work on the fly.

In spite of herself, she was impressed.

But the pilot tipped his hand. His skip wasn't heading toward a base somewhere. The skip was heading toward another ship.

There was no way that destination ship would be near the flotilla. That ship had to be waiting somewhere protected.

If she were hiding a large ship—probably a Dignity Vessel named *Shadow*—she would place it near a moon. Not near Nindowne, though. And there was only one planet with a moon nearby.

She had her equipment scan the area near that planet, and instantly saw the destination ship.

It was an ancient Dignity Vessel ship, but it wasn't called *Shadow*.

It was called the *Ivoire*.

She let out a breath.

The actual skip had sped up. It appeared to be vibrating—either from the speed or maybe some damage sustained earlier. If she had to guess, she would assume that the skip was about to break up.

Given how ragged the skip looked, it might not even make the *Ivoire*.

The fighters realized their error and corrected, and, she noticed on the screens before her, a few ships had finally managed to follow the correct skip.

The fighters fired on it as they closed in. They shot at it, but either the shots went wild or something was protecting it.

The skip propelled itself toward the *Ivoire*, and for a moment, she thought it was going to ram the side. And then she realized what was going to happen.

"Prepare to launch into foldspace," she said to her team.

"Yes, Captain," said Rockowitz. He was probably already prepared, given his tone of voice. She hadn't given that order as much for him as she had for the rest of the team.

Something was niggling at her. Maybe the presence of the *EhizTari* had nothing to do with incompetence. Maybe the presence of the *EhizTari* showed that the Jefatura thought that Base 20 had been breached by Fleet personnel.

All that the Armada had known when Nyguta had received her orders was that the personnel who had entered Base 20 had used Fleet equipment. Those people had some ancient Fleet identification devices.

From there, the Armada had assumed—maybe hoped—that the invaders were actual members of the Fleet.

Nyguta felt a shiver of excitement. For millennia, the Armada had hoped to find the Fleet again, to extract a revenge long in the making.

She wanted that as much as anyone else, but she couldn't let it color her thinking. Not now.

Right now, her best course of action was to ignore the *EhizTari* and do the work as if the *BilatZailea* were the only foldspace tracking vessel in the vicinity.

Besides, the captain of the *EhizTari* hadn't responded to hails, which wasn't that uncommon in this kind of situation. Unnecessary communication was discouraged and, at the moment, neither vessel knew if they were even needed.

Now Nyguta knew: she would be tracking an ancient Fleet-built Dignity Vessel which, more likely than not, had a powerful *anacapa* drive.

The *BilatZailea's anacapa* drive was powerful as well, and in prime condition. The *BilatZailea* might have a problem, though, if the *Ivoire's* drive was as old as the ship herself. Because that drive could malfunction in ways no one completely understood.

Nyguta silently cursed under her breath. The Armada's Legion of Engineers still hadn't completely deciphered all of the secrets of the *anacapa* drive. The Fleet didn't know how the drive worked either— or at least, hadn't known it millennia ago, when they abandoned the Armada's founders.

The Fleet had stolen the *anacapa* drives thousands of years ago, and had been able to replicate them, but not reverse engineer the technology itself.

The Armada had made reverse engineering the *anacapa* technology a major part of its raison d'être, but hadn't yet completely figured out how the tech worked.

If the *Ivoire's anacapa* had brought them to this time period, and they were seeking a way home, then following the *Ivoire* into foldspace was doubly risky. Nyguta had tracked ships that had been displaced in time through foldspace, but that was tricky as well. The key was to find the ship while the crew was still alive, without trapping her crew in the process.

She'd managed, but it hadn't always been easy.

Tracking in real time was different. She wouldn't have a chance to think through the options.

The *Ivoire* fired on the smaller ships around it, and she watched that with trepidation as well. So many things could cause a launch into foldspace to go awry, and getting caught in weapons' fire was one of them, particularly if the *anacapa* drive was activated as a ship got hit.

She had to stay out of the line of fire, monitor the *Ivoire*, and follow it, should it jump. Ideally, the *BilatZailea* should enter foldspace at the exact same point as the *Ivoire* but she wasn't certain if she could do that.

"Contact the *Indarra* and *Hirugarren*," she said to DeMarcus Habibi. He was slender and soft-spoken, and had served on a dozen ships before joining hers nearly a decade before.

As a result, he knew someone on almost every ship, and could reach the right person to help her execute her commands quickly. He had served on the *Indarra*, which was a redesigned Dignity Vessel. He knew the captain of the *Hirugarren*, which had started its existence as a Ready Vessel.

Those two ships had long since been co-opted by the Armada and had more than enough firepower to defend the *BilatZailea*, so Nyguta could concentrate on the foldspace tracking.

Habibi looked up at her, his brown eyes sharp. He probably knew what she was going to say, but he let her say it anyway.

"They'll need to flank us as we approach the *Ivoire*'s position," Nyguta said. "We want to enter foldspace as close to that spot as possible."

"And the *EhizTari?*" Habibi asked.

"We'll let them handle their own journey." She wasn't going to worry about any of the Armada ships. She was going to concentrate on her own.

Her team was tracking telemetry and coordinates and *anacapa* energy. They would know the instant that the *Ivoire* started its transition into foldspace.

In the meantime, she would watch what was happening to the *Ivoire*.

A cargo bay door opened on the side of the *Ivoire*. If Nyguta were in charge of attacking this unknown enemy, she would attack them right now. They had to drop shields to get that skip inside.

The fighters and the other ships had to know that. She expected to see more laser fire, but she didn't see any.

Partly because the skip came in fast and hot, hot enough that unless the *Ivoire* had some kind of plan in place, the skip would ram through interior walls. The cargo bay door slammed shut just as fast, and something winked around the *Ivoire*—most likely the reinstatement of the shield.

"Now," she said to her crew.

The *BilatZailea* sped forward, heading toward the *Ivoire's* position. The *Indarra* and *Hirugarren* flanked her, just as requested.

A foldspace window opened to the *Ivoire's* side, and the *Ivoire* launched itself through.

Then the *EhizTari* zoomed past the *BilatZailea*.

Nyguta muttered, "Idiots," and hoped none of her crew had heard.

Although they probably would agree. The *EhizTari* was trying to enter the same foldspace launch window as the *Ivoire*, a truly dangerous and mostly reckless move.

But the launch window closed, and the *EhizTari* overshot the coordinates. It turned around, creating its own foldspace opening at the exact same moment.

Rockowitz cursed. Habibi said, "We really should warn them—" But stopped himself as the *EhizTari* disappeared into their own foldspace launch window.

"Maybe it'll work," Nyguta said, as much to herself as to her crew.

She couldn't think about the *EhizTari* right now, though. She had to focus on her own mission.

"All right," she said to her team. "The *Ivoire* has gone into foldspace. We have the exact coordinates, right?"

The person responsible for combining everyone's information into one set of coordinates was Jaci Intxausti. She tucked her long silver-and-black hair behind her ears, and frowned.

That frown caught Nyguta. Intxausti usually didn't make faces before answering questions. Perhaps the information contradicted itself. That happened at times, and while Nyguta could program for it, she preferred not to. It was better to use a human eye on it, because the machines were more likely to either use an average or some other formula to choose the most likely set of coordinates.

Relying on the tech for decision-making was what made other foldspace tracking vessels less accurate than the *BilatZailea* was. When Nyguta got conflicting information, she threw it all out and started again.

"Jaci?" Nyguta said, wondering if she had to repeat the question.

"I have the coordinates," Intxausti said. "I was checking to see if there was any unusual *anacapa* energy since that ship we're chasing was reported lost five thousand years ago."

So her team had researched the name. Without a request from her. Which was why this team was the best she'd ever worked with.

The *Ivoire* had been lost in time, probably through foldspace. That made it both less interesting (she had been hoping to find the Fleet) and more interesting.

"Maybe," said Tiberius Kibbuku, one of the researchers. He rarely spoke up, so a "maybe" from him was as powerful as half the sentences the rest of her team spoke. "Maybe it had been lost."

Nyguta was about to follow up, but Intxausti spoke first.

"Less of a maybe than you'd think," Intxausti said. "I investigated the moment I saw the identification. I used several Fleet databases from several time periods. The ship matches every descriptive point, including the name."

Kibbuku looked like he wanted to argue, but Nyguta didn't have time for that. She held up a hand, silencing him and directed her question at Intxausti.

"Problems, then?" Nyguta asked.

"Not that I can tell," Intxausti said, "but I don't have time to do a thorough examination. If the ship is here, it got lost in foldspace like everyone thought."

"Maybe," Kibbuku said again, a bit more forcefully this time.

Nyguta didn't look at him. She wanted to hear Intxausti out.

"And," Intxausti said, "if it did, that means there could be something wrong with the *anacapa*."

She put a slight emphasis on the word "could," which led to Nyguta's question.

"But you don't think so," Nyguta said.

"I wouldn't be going in and out of foldspace if I knew I had a malfunctioning *anacapa* drive, would you?" Intxausti asked.

"That's not definitive," Kibbuku said, and he was right. Intxausti's point was speculative, but the speculation was a good one.

If this was the *Ivoire* and if it was piloted by the same crew that had gotten lost in foldspace, then they wouldn't venture in and out of foldspace easily, even if they were being followed.

But that was a lot of "ifs." For all Nyguta knew, for all her team knew, the *Ivoire* had been abandoned and then stolen by yet another group.

Although that didn't really explain the Fleet signatures that the Jefatura had picked up in the alarms around Base 20.

Figuring out what the *Ivoire* was mattered less than their mission. Which the *EhizTari* was already fulfilling.

"Are you worried about following the *Ivoire* into foldspace?" Nyguta asked.

"I certainly wouldn't have tried to use their foldspace window," Intxausti said, the judgmental tone in her voice matching the one in Nyguta's head.

"Neither would I," Nyguta said. "But are you worried about tracking them?"

Intxausti looked at Kibbuku, not Nyguta, which surprised her. The look was one of consultation, not disagreement.

"There's a lot we don't know," Kibbuku said.

It seemed like he was saying the obvious, but he wasn't that kind of man. Instead, he wanted everyone to make the same logical leaps he did. And sometimes Nyguta wasn't up for it.

"About the *Ivoire?*" she asked.

"About foldspace, *anacapa* drives, and tracking," he said. "If they're malfunctioning, and we get too close, are we in danger?"

He shrugged, not willing to add the last sentence. The one that included *we don't know*.

They didn't know, and they didn't have the luxury to figure it out.

"Well," Nyguta said, "if they are creating something dangerous through their foldspace window, we might not be able to track them at all. Have you thought of that?"

Her question was a bit aggressive. His eyes met hers. She usually didn't talk to her team that way.

"I think we've waited long enough for our own safety's sake," Nyguta said. "Take us to the coordinates, Jaci, and open a foldspace window."

Intxausti didn't respond verbally. Instead, she executed the command.

The *BilatZailea* reached those coordinates in less than a minute, and as it did, a foldspace window opened. Nyguta braced herself, something she normally didn't do when she went into foldspace.

The *BilatZailea* entered the window, vibrating slightly as it did so. Nyguta let out a small sigh. The vibration was normal. The Armada's engineers had managed to tone down the entry—which used to be a lot bumpier and sometimes violent—but still hadn't been able to get rid of the vibration.

No one knew what it was about foldspace that differed from regular space or why entry into (and out of) foldspace caused something akin to turbulence. Nyguta paid attention to the changes, thinking they might have an impact on foldspace tracking, but so far, nothing had made much of a difference.

Something, though, had led her to believe that entering foldspace this time would be more difficult. Maybe the discussion with Intxausti. Maybe a sense.

Everything had been odd on this trip.

She didn't think foldspace would be any different.

2

NYGUTA SHUT OFF THE WALL SCREENS. Seeing the exterior of the *BilatZailea* in real time made no difference now. She had left the battle behind her, and she couldn't see the *EhizTari* at all. Nor could she see the *Ivoire*.

Which was not unusual.

Foldspace tracking wasn't about actually following a vessel through foldspace. She had never done that, except during training. And that had been difficult in a variety of unexpected ways.

She actually preferred to track a vessel through foldspace using instrumentation, *anacapa* energy readings, and good old common sense.

"Clear the signature of the *EhizTari*," she said to her team.

She didn't want the mistakes of the *EhizTari* to contaminate her search and, as far as she was concerned, the *EhizTari* had made mistakes from the moment she tried to enter foldspace with the *Ivoire*.

No one on Nyguta's team responded verbally to her order, but, on her holoscreens, she noted that the *EhizTari's* energy signature vanished. Good.

Now it was time for her entire team to get to work.

Her team knew their jobs. They had tracked through foldspace fifty times before, at minimum, although never so soon after a ship had entered.

Nor had they always had the exact coordinates where the ship had gone into foldspace. Nyguta had some advantages here, although she wasn't sure how she was going to use them—*if* she was going to use them.

Her job was threefold: She needed to monitor what her team was doing; she needed to track the *Ivoire* on her own; and she needed to keep an eye on the goal which, in this case, was finding and possibly subduing the *Ivoire*.

She wasn't going to worry about subduing the *Ivoire* yet. The moment she saw the *Ivoire* again, she would send its coordinates back to the Jefatura, and they would send a ship to that point. Or several ships, depending on how intransigent the *Ivoire* was.

Some ships (especially older ones) needed a bit of time to recover from a foldspace journey, and she wasn't sure if the *Ivoire* was one of those.

This was where she felt the lack of prep time. Usually she had hours, sometimes days, to prepare for a foldspace tracking job. And she had never tracked a ship that didn't belong to the Armada. With Armada ships, she had their histories, their quirks, and usually, she had a theory about why they had disappeared in foldspace.

The *Ivoire* hadn't disappeared. It had fled from the Armada, while under fire. And the *Ivoire* was, in theory, an ancient Fleet ship that had ended up in the wrong time period. Or it had been the subject of a mutiny and vanished from the Fleet's records. Or the ship she saw wasn't even the *Ivoire* that she thought it was, but another old Dignity Vessel with the same name.

She knew next to nothing about the makeup of that model of Dignity Vessel. She didn't even know what its defensive (and offensive) capabilities were.

"Tiberius," she said to Kibbuku. "Put a team on *Ivoire* research. We need to know as much about this ship as we can. Duplicate Intxausti's work. Make sure you can confirm the identity of this ship."

"Already on it," Kibbuku said, in that dry flat way of his. Of course, he had already double-checked Intxausti's work. He double-checked everyone's work when it had an impact on his own.

"I want to know ship specs, if you can find them," Nyguta said. "Otherwise, I want the specs for that Dignity Vessel model. I also want to know if there was a mention of the *Ivoire* after its purported disappearance in any of the Fleet records we've confiscated. Any *Ivoire* sightings, any clue how it got here."

"So far nothing," Kibbuku said, in a way that let her know he was slightly offended she had even given that instruction. He was ahead of her on research. He always was. "I also have three different programs running to check the Scrapheaps we've encountered for any record of the *Ivoire*."

That was a case in point: He thought of a detail she hadn't. If the *Ivoire* had been stored in one of the Scrapheaps and then recovered, that information wouldn't be in standard Fleet record-keeping. It would be a part of the Scrapheap itself.

If the *Ivoire* had been stored in a Scrapheap, then she would know when and where it was recovered, and maybe even who commanded it now.

"Good, thank you," she said.

That took care of the *Ivoire*, at least for the moment. She would have a plan to deal with the *Ivoire* once she found it.

Right now, though, she had to find it.

By isolating the *Ivoire's* energy signature as well as the subtle variations in its *anacapa* drive's energy, she was able to find the path the *Ivoire* left.

She wasn't used to seeing a path that was so strong and so clearly marked. For a few moments, she hesitated, worried that she was seeing some kind of planted trail.

But no ship of the Fleet knew how to track in foldspace—at least, the Fleet hadn't known that centuries ago. Nothing in the Fleet's research files over the millennia led her to believe that the Fleet would develop real-time tracking technology.

Sure, the Fleet had once had foldspace search vessels. The *BilatZailea* had been modified from one. But the Fleet's foldspace search methods were complicated and ineffective.

The Fleet was wasteful. It left ships all over the sectors it passed through. It would abandon its people in foldspace rather than search for them to the bitter end. It would leave entire communities behind at its sector bases, while leaving them little to survive and thrive on.

The Armada wasn't governed by a group of military leaders eager to get to the next sector. The Armada had been built by engineers. Finding and correcting errors was in the Armada's blood. And, in the beginning of their existence, they hadn't had enough personnel to lose.

So anytime someone got trapped or injured or lost, the Armada searched for that person. Searched until the person was rescued or the body was recovered.

In its entire existence, the Armada had never abandoned anyone. The Armada rescued or recovered its people, and it recorded its history. Because it was built by engineers, it valued detail, and it valued those who worked for it.

It also valued time. Searching, using the old Fleet method, was wasteful in time and personnel. Which was why the Legion of Engineers had learned how to track in foldspace. That way, ships didn't lose entire years searching for someone.

Instead, they tracked the lost ship. What got in the way of finding it wasn't the methodology. It was the time slips that happened with a malfunctioning *anacapa* drive.

Replicating those had once been almost impossible. But the Armada had found a way around that as well. It hadn't been able to take its people back along the same track as the injured ship, but it was able to answer questions about what became of that ship and its crew.

At some point, the Armada would learn how to handle the time slips. Only then would it feel like it had completely conquered foldspace.

Nyguta forced herself to concentrate on the *Ivoire's* path. The *Ivoire* wasn't traveling the way she had expected it to.

There was a logic to foldspace, one that took a lot of study to understand. Her entire team understood it though.

If Nyguta had been required to predict where the *Ivoire* would travel, she would have predicted that it would have gone forward from Base 20, past Base 21 and into the areas beyond.

But, it looked like, the *Ivoire* was going backwards, toward Base 15 or maybe even farther back—in distance, anyway.

She had no idea what was back there. She hadn't traveled that far backwards, not even through foldspace.

Most of her trips had been sideways, making rescues that had gone awry, working within the sectors where the Armada currently existed, not the ones where it had existed before.

And there was something about Base 11 or maybe Base 12 that niggled her memory.

"Anastasia," she said to another of her researchers. Anastasia Telli was even quieter than Kibbuku, but she worked faster than any other researcher that Nyguta had.

"Captain." Telli lifted her head. Her slender face was pale and she had deep shadows under her eyes. She hadn't been sleeping again, but that usually wasn't a medical problem with her. It was often a research problem. She would find something she was interested in, and forget to sleep.

Nyguta set aside that thread of worry she always felt when she saw Telli look so pale and tired.

"Do you recall something odd about the bases around 11 or 12?"

Telli nodded and suddenly seemed animated. Information excited her. Imparting information excited her more.

"Yes, sir, I do recall," she said. "We didn't use the sector bases that the Fleet left behind for Base 12 and Base 13."

That was it. Those sector bases were among the few that the Armada hadn't coopted for their own.

"Do you recall why not?" Nyguta moved her holoscreens slightly, so she could observe Telli and keep an eye on the information that flowed across the screens.

"Yes, sir," Telli said. "One base, Base 12, was in hostile territory. We lost fighters in some kind of war, and the Jefatura decided that it wasn't worth our while to try to capture the sector base. It took us too deep into that hostile region."

Nyguta felt a tingle of nerves. She didn't like how this was going. And she hoped she was wrong.

"And Base 13?" she asked.

"The sector base we would have coopted was destroyed long before we ever got near it. Destroyed so thoroughly that there was no point in even trying to salvage it." Telli gave her an uncomfortable smile. "There are a few other bases we didn't use, but they're even farther back. I'd have to research which ones exactly. Base 7, maybe?"

"No need to research that at the moment," Nyguta said. "Thank you."

Her stomach had tightened. Whoever piloted that skip had been brilliant. The skip had arrived at the *Ivoire*, and the launch into fold-space had been nearly perfect. The journey seemed to be pretty consistent as well.

But not in the direction she expected. Backwards. Toward those older bases.

She hoped she had given Telli the correct instruction. She hoped the *Ivoire* wasn't going back as far as Base 7 or Base 6.

Nyguta had made long foldspace journeys before, but she had always prepared for them. And she had never taken the *BilatZailea* or this crew on a journey that long.

If it looked like the journey was going to be long, she was going to have to pursue the *Ivoire* in parts, which the Jefatura wouldn't like. But she wasn't going to risk her crew on a long foldspace journey that was unplanned.

She hoped that the *EhizTari* wouldn't do that either.

But she had a feeling that the *Ivoire* wasn't going all the way back to Bases 6 or 7. Most well-captained ships didn't make long journeys just to escape a bad situation.

Most well-captained ships fled to their own base.

And then she felt that tingle of nerves again. If the base was in territory the Fleet had traveled through millennia ago, and that the Armada had already passed beyond as well, then she wasn't chasing someone from the Fleet. She was chasing someone who was using a Fleet vessel.

Unless whoever captained the *Ivoire* was a brilliant tactician, something she couldn't rule out. Not after what she had seen in that firefight.

The words "hostile territory" kept resounding in her brain.

If she were captaining a lone Dignity Vessel against ships with twice the firepower hers had, more ships than she could ever hope to fight, all she could do was outrun them.

But if she worried about being tracked—and why would a Fleet ship worry about being tracked? She set that question aside for a moment and tried again. If she were worried about being tracked, she would lead the ships that followed her into a trap of some kind.

Or maybe that hostile region was home.

It didn't matter either way. She had to be prepared.

She turned to her team.

"The moment we come out of foldspace, we have to have shields up and weapons at the ready," she said.

"You think a single ship will turn around and attack us?" Rockowitz sounded skeptical.

"I have no idea. But the *Ivoire* knew it was outgunned. It might have assumed ships were going to follow it through foldspace, like the *EhizTari* had. So the *Ivoire* might have gone somewhere it could defend."

Santiago Pereira shifted slightly, something he did when he wanted to speak, but didn't know if he should. He was thinner than most of her team, and shorter as well. But she relied on him, particularly for tactical information.

"Standard practice for the Fleet is—was—to launch into foldspace, and then return hours later, after the fighters cleared out," he said.

She had already thought of that. She wasn't going to argue with him over the words "standard practice." He had already covered the fact that they knew little about the current Fleet with the word "was."

"I wouldn't do that in this instance," she said. "Because of the base and the quick arrival of the other ships."

He nodded. "We can't entirely rule it out," he said. "But I might enact a feint."

"A feint as in go elsewhere, and then return," she said.

He nodded again.

"That presupposes they know we can track them through foldspace," she said.

The Fleet knew nothing about the Armada, but other cultures did. Which led her to believe that the Jefatura was wrong about this. The *Ivoire* might once have been a Fleet vessel, but she doubted it was any longer.

"Even if I knew that my pursuers could track me through foldspace," Pereira said, "I wouldn't do anything elaborate. I would take those pursuers as far from my home base as possible, and then I would cross a bit of regular space, and open a new foldspace window, and head home."

"And hope you weren't tracked again?" Intxausti asked.

"Yes," Pereira said.

Nyguta thought about that for a moment. "I would do something similar. If nothing else, it would buy time. Whoever tracked the ship through foldspace would be looking for a base or other ships or something first, before trying to figure out what happened in regular space."

She let out a breath. She had to be prepared for anything. If the *Ivoire* was heading back to its home base, it would attack anything that came through foldspace. If the *Ivoire* wasn't heading back to its own base, then it would travel through regular space to get to either another launch point or a good attack position.

She wished she could contact the *EhizTari* now. They should have coordinated after all. But the *EhizTari's* enthusiasm and, perhaps, its captain's desire to impress the Jefatura, made that impossible.

The Jefatura would note where the two tracking vessels emerged from foldspace. Both had automated systems that contacted the Armada the moment the ships arrived in a real space location. The messages would be sent across real space, and through a foldspace system, using the communications *anacapa*.

The Armada would figure out, just like she did, that the *Ivoire* had gone backwards, not toward some other base.

"Changes ahead," Rockowitz said.

19

That was internal code for the fact that the energy pattern they were following was growing, the way that it should just before a ship used its *anacapa* to leave foldspace.

"All right," Nyguta said. "Shields, weapons. Battlestations."

She almost never got to say that. It made her nervous. But she was ready—and she hoped she was up to the task.

3

THE *IVOIRE*'S FOLDSPACE TRAIL ENDED ABRUPTLY, not far from the *BilatZailea's* position.

"This is it," Nyguta said, and braced herself again for the *BilatZailea* to exit foldspace.

Her crew was ready, and the ship was on alert. She had no idea what she would face.

As they vibrated their way out of foldspace, something caught her ear. Before she could ask, Rockowitz said, "We're getting a distress signal."

"Sent into foldspace?" Intxausti asked, echoing Nyguta's surprise. She'd had ships send messages through foldspace, but they usually weren't standard distress signals. They targeted the Armada, to keep anyone with foldspace capability away from their disabled ships.

"Yes," Rockowitz said.

Nyguta glanced at the telemetry in front of her. "The *Ivoire*," she said.

Had it been hit in that barrage of laser fire? She thought only the shields had been hit. Or maybe the skip had done some internal damage when it launched itself into the ship.

Why would the *Ivoire* come out of foldspace and ask for help? To bring in its own warships? Some kind of backup?

If so, she was ready.

The *BilatZailea* vibrated a moment longer, then emerged from foldspace right next to a gigantic starbase, tilted, damaged, and seemingly abandoned. If the *BilatZailea* had missed her entry coordinates by just a little, she would have ended up in the middle of that starbase.

Nyguta's heart was pounding. That captain of the *Ivoire* was as smart as she had assumed. That *Ivoire* captain had deliberately exited foldspace in this spot, knowing the abandoned starbase was here.

The starbase looked like it had been built by the Fleet, but she didn't have time to check it, because laser fire was streaking all around her. She used the sensors to see what was going on as the distress message continued blaring around her.

She shut off the message using one of her screens rather than ask someone else to do it. The bridge was suddenly blessedly silent. She moved her screens and brought up the wall screens—

Which showed the *EhizTari* in the middle of a ring of large ships of a type that Nyguta didn't recognize. The *EhizTari* was cratered on one side, and most of her lights were out. Her shields were down, and she was listing.

"Target those ships," Nyguta said to her crew, "and fire."

The laser canons fired almost before she completed the command, their pulses zooming toward the ships surrounding the *EhizTari*. Seven ships. Seven, all larger than the *EhizTari*, all of them armored and shielded.

The laser pulses dissipated along the edges of the larger ships' shields.

"These shields are odd," Pereira said. "They seem to rotate energy and power levels."

"In a predictable way," Rockowitz said.

"More than predictable," Nyguta said. "A known way."

She recognized one of the icons on her screens, although she had only seen that icon once before. The *BilatZailea's* computer recognized the pattern, recognized everything about those ships, and wanted to use a set program.

Normally, Nyguta would have investigated, but she didn't have time. She initiated the program, and immediately the pattern of laser fire from the *BilatZailea* changed.

"Hey!" Pereira said. "I just lost control of the weapons."

"I did that," Nyguta said. "It's all right. I've got this."

And she did. The laser pulses got through the shields on all seven ships, hitting their armored exterior. Each pulse seemed to punch through the exteriors.

"Let me work with the program," Pereira said.

"Not yet," Nyguta said. "It seems to be working. I don't want to mess with it."

"I just want it to target propulsion," Pereira said. "That'll—"

But he didn't even have a chance to finish before the ship closest to the *BilatZailea* exploded. Then the next ship exploded, followed by another, lighting up the entire area.

The ships farthest from the *BilatZailea* spun, clearly about to leave the area. The fourth ship started to follow, but as it spun, a laser pulse caught its side, and the entire ship glowed for a moment before exploding.

The remaining three ships sped up, stuttered a bit, and then seemed to expand.

Nyguta recognized what was happening. Apparently those ships had a nanobit component, and those nanobits were unbonding. The ships were going to come apart.

And just as she had that thought, the ships *did* come apart, but not in a full explosion like the others. More like a slow-motion disassembly, as pieces fell off. The ships stopped moving.

Nyguta's breath caught. She knew what would happen next. She'd seen it before. The ships started coming apart and then the nanobits disassembled something crucial, and that something touched something else, and—

All three ships exploded.

Bits of ship shrapnel spun in all directions, some of it hitting the unprotected *EhizTari*, doing even more damage.

"Contact the *EhizTari*," Nyguta said. "We have to get them out of here. And figure out where here is."

"Already done," Telli said. "Here is something called the Enterran Empire, and that abandoned starbase was what the Fleet called Starbase Kappa."

"So this was where we would have had Base 12, if we decided to use the Fleet's sector base," Nyguta said. Right here, in hostile territory, just like her staff had mentioned.

Apparently the territory was still hostile.

"Base 11, actually," Telli said. "But yes, the Armada has history here."

"The Enterran Empire is a military culture," Intxausti said. "They don't accept defeat easily. They will be back."

None of them doubted that the ships had contacted colleagues before the explosions. How long it would take the messages to get through was anyone's guess. And once those messages arrived, there was no way to know how long it would take for more ships to arrive.

"Any sign of the *Ivoire*?" Nyguta asked.

"None," Rockowitz said. "I'm sure there's an energy signature—"

"But right now, there's too much going on for us to find it." Nyguta shook her head, trying to tamp down the admiration she felt for the *Ivoire's* captain.

She had figured the captain might attack. She had figured that the captain might enter a region and then leave it quickly. But she hadn't expected the captain to use ships from another culture as a diversion to prevent her—or the *EhizTari*—from following the *Ivoire* to its home base.

She would follow it, though. She would find that home base, and she would bring that captain of the *Ivoire*, the ship, and its crew back to the Armada.

But first, she had to deal with the *EhizTari*.

She had to get it out of here before the Enterran Empire ships returned.

Because she no longer had the element of surprise.

4

It only took fifteen minutes for the news of the *Ivoire's* return to the Room of Lost Souls to reach Group Commander Elissa Trekov. It took her another fifteen minutes to assemble ships—one hundred in total—to advance on the *Ivoire's* position.

By the time she had contacted all of the Operations Commanders and ignored her own boss, Flag Commander Janik, another crisis started to unfold.

Seven of the Enterran Empire's ships had arrived at the Room of Lost Souls, ships not directly under her command. They had been drawn by a false emergency request, and all seven had been destroyed.

That news brought a taste of ash to her mouth, and it made her hands ache. Captain Cooper of the *Ivoire* had, yet again, figured out how to destroy Empire vessels, like he had destroyed one of hers.

She stood in the command center on the *Ewing Trekov*, the lumbering ancient flagship named for her great-great-grandfather. Ewing Trekov had ended his career as the Supreme Commander for the Enterran Empire and many people thought she had become a Group Commander because of him.

Only she hadn't known him, and she had risen up the ranks based on her own abilities, not the Trekov name. Considering how the others who held that name had used it, it was amazing she was allowed to serve at all.

She rubbed the back of her right hand, feeling the bones beneath her taut skin. She made herself stop the movement—it was a nervous habit that she couldn't quite shake since Captain Cooper nearly killed her the last time she was at the Room of Lost Souls.

She was not happy about returning, and certainly not happy to be returning because of him.

The command center was mostly quiet. Usually the command center bustled with activity—crew members coming in and out, working on a dozen different projects, while the command center staff handled the day-to-day minutiae of managing the ships under Elissa's command.

But this afternoon was different: the arrival of the *Ivoire* and the almost instantaneous loss of seven ships put the entire Empire's space force on alert. She didn't contact Flag Commander Janik when she heard the news. She just ordered the free ships under her command to head directly toward the Room of Lost Souls, without clearing it with anyone.

She was going to take care of Captain Cooper once and for all.

The dozen people in the command center were coordinating the ships heading toward the Room of Lost Souls. Her own assistant, Sub-Lieutenant Tawhiri Paek, stood to her right, trying to organize the material Elissa had asked for.

Paek was big and muscular. He worked hard to maintain his gravity-built strength. His light-brown skin was covered with tattoos, which were only visible when he dressed down. In his uniform, the tattoos that were visible were the ones that peeked out of the cuffs of his sleeves.

He preferred to work while standing—the chairs in the command center, like the functional chairs throughout the ship, were too small for his bulk.

Elissa always felt tiny beside him—not in height, because theirs was similar, but in bulk. She had maybe half of his.

Part of her wanted to be down on the bridge, commanding the *Ewing Trekov* herself instead of coordinating all one hundred ships that were heading toward the Room of Lost Souls. But the *Trekov's* new commander, Iver Derrida, was one of the most capable commanders in the

Empire—and he trusted her more than he trusted Flag Commander Janik, which meant more than either man knew.

Derrida had been on the border between the Empire and the Nine Planets Alliance the last time Elissa had dealt with Captain Cooper. Her mission had been to breach the Nine Planets, bring more territory into the Empire. She had gone to that border twenty-seven ships strong, thinking she could easily defeat Cooper. He'd faced her with the *Ivoire* which was a Dignity Vessel, as well as with another Dignity Vessel, and a strange amalgam of vessels that didn't deserve the name "ship."

Yet none of those vessels were harmed in the final battle, and Elissa's ship—the *Ewing Trekov*, ironically enough—had only survived because she had retreated against Flag Commander Janik's orders.

The moment Cooper had threatened her with a weapon of his, a weapon she'd now encountered twice, a weapon that she still didn't have a name for, she knew she couldn't defeat him. Not then, and not now. But Janik believed that the Empire never retreated, and it had cost twenty-three ships and hundreds of lives.

It would have cost more lives, but Elissa had encountered that weapon, and she knew its impact. She knew how to run a rescue after ships were disabled from the strange energy shockwave that emanated from the weapon's deployment.

She had known where the most likely survivors had been. And because she was close, she managed to save more of them than later models suggested she would.

Which was why she still held the title of Group Commander and why she still worked from the *Ewing Trekov*.

Force Commander Bik Singh had divided the blame for the loss. She believed that Elissa should have come up with a way to defeat Cooper and the Nine Planets, but Force Commander Singh also believed that Janik should have listened to Elissa's warning.

While Elissa hadn't received a direct punishment for her role in that defeat, Force Commander Singh had made it clear that Elissa's rise in the ranks was most likely over. Elissa had an internal black mark on her record, one that would be difficult to scrub off.

Although—maybe—winning a battle against Cooper would help.

Elissa found herself rubbing the skin on her hands again, and she made herself stop. She needed to focus, but it was hard given the fact that the evidence of her first encounter with Cooper was etched on her body.

She had found him, and the *Ivoire*, at the Room of Lost Souls. At that point she had no idea what his name was or why his people were there. She still wasn't exactly certain why his people had been there.

But she had asked him to leave, and he had, but not before activating some kind of weapon that had destroyed part of the Room itself. The weapon exploded, and then sent out a destructive wave of energy that had destroyed all the systems in her ship as well as all of the technology in the environmental suits and anything else that the Empire crews could use to save themselves.

The wave had spread through the entire area, took out several other ships, and cost six hundred lives. Through some quick thinking, she had managed to save her bridge crew and had nearly died herself.

The incident had destroyed much of the skin on her face and hands—which had been exposed to the cold of space—and she had suffered through several procedures so that she looked more or less normal.

She had been urged by friends to have some cosmetic procedures done, but she had decided against it after Captain Cooper had defeated her a second time.

Because of him, the Empire had not crossed the border into the Nine Planets. Because of him, she remained stuck in a gigantic out-of-date vessel named for a relative she had never known.

Because of Cooper, she was no longer seen as an innovative commander with a lot of potential. She was seen as a once-talented commander who was heading toward the end of her career.

As she stood in the middle of the command center, she was aware that she wanted revenge against Cooper. But she was also aware that he had no reason to venture this deep into Empire territory.

He was a good commander. One who used situations to his advantage, but who wasn't afraid to leave an area when he had nothing to gain from being in that area.

He knew that his presence here, at the Room of Lost Souls—the *Ivoire's* presence here—could be seen as an act of war. The Nine Planets Alliance and the Empire had a truce, negotiated primarily by Elissa and Cooper that kept the borders between the two secure.

For the last year, both sides had abided by the terms of that truce. The Empire had ships stationed at the border between Empire space and the Nine Planets space, and the Nine Planets kept vessels there as well.

They monitored each other, waiting for someone to make a false move. No one—at least no one in the Empire—expected a ship to just appear in the middle of Empire space, far from the border.

And no one, not even her, expected that ship to be the *Ivoire*.

The buoys planted around the Room of Lost Souls had sent her the information about the *Ivoire*. She had added that bit of programming to the buoys before she had faced Captain Cooper a second time. She wondered if he would return to the Room of Lost Souls, but he hadn't—until now.

The Room of Lost Souls had always been an enigma to the Empire. They didn't build it and they didn't know where it had come from. Before Cooper's attack on it, it looked like an abandoned space station.

Over the centuries, ships had docked there for a variety of reasons, but their experiences all ended up the same. Usually at least one of their crew members died hideously at the Room.

The problem got so bad that the Empire put up buoys as warnings, letting any ship that approached the Room know it was dangerous, and they should avoid it at all costs.

Eventually, the buoys ended up with cameras and other monitoring equipment, not just to see who approached the Room, but who survived it. It turned out that people with a specific genetic marker could go in and out of the Room with no ill effect, while those who did not have the marker died.

29

Apparently, everyone on the *Ivoire* had the marker. On his first journey there, Captain Cooper hadn't thought twice about sending his personnel into all of the sections of that abandoned space station.

Elissa had forgotten about those buoys after the confrontation at the border. She had figured that her first impulse about Cooper had been wrong; that he hadn't been interested in the Room per se, but that he had needed something from it, which he retrieved before trying to kill Elissa the first time.

For that reason, she hadn't expected him to come back.

So when she got the notification of his return, she had told Derrida to drop everything. They were taking the *Ewing Trekov* to the Room of Lost Souls.

That was when the report about the seven ships, responding to some kind of massive emergency beacon had come through. And then the ships' destruction.

She had just gotten the footage from those seven ships. They had sent, as part of the rescue mission, all of their transmissions back to command. The information cut off as each ship was destroyed.

She had funneled the information through a program that compiled everything into one big continuous action file. She wanted video first, in two dimensions, so that she could watch it and continue to observe the live telemetry on the monitors all over the command center.

The staff had set up—as they always had—different parts of the center to give information about each grouping of ships, as they headed toward the Room of Lost Souls.

One hundred strong. But the first order of business she had given their commanders was this: She wanted them to watch for a change in the energy signatures near the Room of Lost Souls.

That weapon Captain Cooper used had a similar energy signature to the Empire's own stealth tech, except that Cooper's weapon was twenty times stronger and purer. The wave that went through the ships after he activated the weapon had even more of the stealth tech energy and it was that energy, her engineers had determined, that had destroyed all the tech on every single vessel it touched.

She didn't want her ships to go into another trap. So she had given her ships specific instructions as to how far back to stay should that energy signature be present.

But right now, it didn't look like any of her ships were going to get there ahead of the *Trekov*, and for that, she was grateful.

She bent her head over the imagery, and frowned immediately. The ship hovering outside the Room of Lost Souls was not the *Ivoire*. This ship was fatter and not as sleek. It looked like it was made of the same black material though, material that gleamed in the reflective lights of the Empire vessels.

She glanced at Paek. He was watching the footage with her. She always liked having a second set of eyes on something this complicated.

"Check for me," she said. "Did that ship also call itself the *Ivoire?*"

"I don't know," he said, then set to work over a console near hers, his thick fingers moving deftly on the screen. She was always amazed at how quickly he could work.

She also called up more information, having the system search for the source of the emergency beacon. She found it, through one of the seven ships which had also traced it.

There was an actual beacon near the new ship's position, blaring an emergency message in Standard, over and over again. And the message stated that Empire ships were under attack.

Which was why some Operations Commander had sent in seven ships, thinking they were going to defend some Empire ship against some hostile something or other.

Instead, they had an interchange with that fat ship. Because Elissa was watching in two-dimensions and not listening to the interaction, she wasn't sure exactly what the interchange was. The computer program simply listed it as an audio exchange.

But that cut off quickly, after one of the seven Empire ships fired on the fat ship. The ship tried to defend itself, but its shots went wide.

All seven ships opened fire, targeting the center of the new ship, and cratering a part of the ship she hadn't even seen until the laser fire hit it.

That was the moment a second ship—similar in build and with that same black hull—appeared and fired shots that bounced away harmlessly. The seven ships started firing at the attacking vessel, and it responded again.

Only this time, all of its shots got through the shields, and the seven ships' information feed cut off, almost simultaneously.

Paek let out a breath near her. He had been watching instead of looking at the damaged ship's identification.

"It's almost like they knew how to get through our shields," he said.

Elissa had the same thought, and she didn't like it. More to warn her ships about, depending on what they would find when they arrived at the Room of Lost Souls.

"Is that disabled ship called the *Ivoire?*" she asked.

"It has no discernable ship identification that I could find," he said.

She let out a small breath. She had had the same problem once, when she had encountered the *Ivoire* the very first time.

"Pull up the buoy footage for me, would you?" she asked.

Buoy footage was trickier than footage from ships. The footage wasn't as detailed and it didn't have as much information.

"I was already doing that when we heard about the attack on the ships," he said, bending over his console again. "Give me a minute."

She went back as far as she could on the footage from the seven ships. None of them showed the attacking vessel before it fired on them. Not even a shadow of that ship showed up anywhere.

One of the seven ships had older footage of that first vessel, but not much footage. And what was there simply showed the vessel near the Room of Lost Souls, unmoving, as if lying in wait.

But lying in wait for what?

She took a quick glance at the Room itself. It was quite close to all of this action, closer than she had expected it to be. The Room looked different now, with that landing pad gone. Some of the researchers told her that the Room's measurements changed over time, and she was beginning to believe that, since it looked smaller here than it ever had.

Some of that might have been that the Room's shape was different now, or maybe it was simply because it loomed so very large in her memory and her life.

"Got it," Paek said, referring to the buoy footage. "Remember, it's not very complete—"

"I know," she said.

He waved a hand at the navigation panel, indicating that she should watch there.

"You're not going to put it on the screen?" she asked. She preferred looking at images directly in front of her.

"The footage will just look bigger and grainier," he said. "Trust me, this is easier to see."

She did trust him, which was why he was her assistant. He had footage that clearly came from several buoys because the angles changed as she watched.

The imagery was black and white and gray, with running lines of interference from at least one of the cameras. A time stamp ran along the top, in the center, showing the date and time down to the millisecond.

She mostly ignored that, after noting that the footage Paek had compiled started an hour earlier than she expected.

The footage showed the damaged Room of Lost Souls just at the edge of the navigation screen. Then a small section of space near the Room glowed, just for an instant. If she had to describe it to someone else, she would have said that a window opened.

A ship then appeared where that window had been. The ship got selected by the cameras and identified as Enemy Vessel *Ivoire*. The identification ran in Standard along the bottom, along with a notification to contact Elissa Trekov immediately—which something in the system had.

Her breath caught as she looked at the outlines of that ship. It looked familiar, a sleek Dignity Vessel that she had met in battle twice before.

What had it been doing here?

What do you want? she thought at Captain Cooper, as if their thoughts could touch. *Why are you here?*

The *Ivoire* immediately zoomed away from the Room of Lost Souls. Then the *Ivoire* seemed to pause for a moment before another whiter square appeared. The *Ivoire* disappeared into it, like a person walking from a dark room into a lighted one and then closing the door.

Elissa bit her lower lip, trying to figure out what was going on.

She was about to ask Paek to reverse the footage to the beginning of the incident when that second ship showed up.

And, if her eyes were any judge, that ship showed up exactly where the *Ivoire* had been.

Her heart started pounding hard.

"I want to see a few things," she said to Paek. "How do I control the images?"

"Let me," he said. "It's easier. I made some modifications that are tough to explain."

That was irritating, because she wanted to be hands-on, but she knew better than to argue.

"Take me back to the moment the *Ivoire* appeared, and freeze the footage."

Paek did so. The *Ivoire* seemed almost insubstantial with that weird light behind it.

"Can you open another screen of this footage and freeze it on the moment that second ship arrived?" Elissa asked.

It took Paek a moment of work, but he managed to open another screen of footage. As he scanned for the arrival of the second ship, Elissa continued to study the first ship.

It was the *Ivoire*, at least as she remembered it. If she hadn't added that notification on the buoys, then no one would have even known the *Ivoire* had arrived.

But that emergency beacon guaranteed that local Empire vessels would come to the Room of Lost Souls and find the second ship.

A shiver ran down her back.

"Got it," Paek said.

The second ship wasn't quite in the same position as the *Ivoire*, but close. And that strange window had opened, making the second ship look as flimsy as the *Ivoire* had when it came through.

Elissa said nothing. She just moved the *Ivoire's* footage forward, bit by bit, looking at the ship's side.

And finally she saw it. Or something that could have been it. A little gray oblong shape that could have been the emergency beacon.

She compared the shape of the thing to the shape of the emergency beacon in the footage from the seven ships.

Same shape, same position.

She swore softly.

"What, ma'am?" Paek asked.

She glanced at him, having forgotten he was nearby.

"Cooper," she said. "The man is a brilliant tactician."

"Ma'am?" Paek sounded as confused as he looked.

She tapped the beacon.

"Cooper was being pursued," she said. "He knew those ships weren't far behind him. So he dropped that beacon, and drew us out to fight or maybe capture those ships."

She stared at the information before her. The chill she had felt earlier had grown.

"This wasn't about us," she said. "This is about him. He was trying to escape."

"Escape what, ma'am?" Paek asked.

"That's the question, isn't it?" she said. "That might just be the heart of it all."

5

"CAN YOU HAIL THE *EHIZTARI*?" Nyguta asked. She didn't like repeating herself, but a lot had been happening, and she wasn't certain if her command to contact the *EhizTari* had gotten lost in the skirmish the *BilatZailea* had just fought.

She stood on the *BilatZailea's* bridge, hands still clasped tightly behind her back, staring at the holoscreens.

"They're not responding, Captain," Habibi said.

Nyguta cursed again. She didn't want to send someone over to the *EhizTari* to figure out what was going on. And she needed answers, now.

She tapped one of her holoscreens, bringing up life signs, finding fifty. So, unless the *EhizTari* had more than the usual allotment of crew, no one had died in that assault.

The ship was in bad shape. Maybe bad enough that it couldn't get through foldspace.

"How badly is the hull damaged?" she asked Rockowitz.

"There isn't much of a hull left," he said. "And it looks like both the bridge and engineering were targeted. I don't think they can respond, no matter what we do."

"The *anacapa* drive is intact, though," Habibi said.

That was both good and bad.

Nyguta let out a sigh. She didn't want this job. She hadn't expected it. And she wouldn't have needed to do it, if the *EhizTari's* crew hadn't been so reckless.

The *BilatZailea* had come in properly, ready to take on the *Ivoire*. Apparently the *EhizTari* had simply followed the *Ivoire*, then entered Enterran space without considering that they might have a welcoming committee.

"Get a rescue team over there," Nyguta said. "We'll need to get them off that ship."

"Captain, wouldn't it be better to repair the hull?" Habibi asked. "Maybe augment the nanobits, see if we can make them work faster. The *anacapa* is functional and—"

"Yes, it would be better to repair the hull," Nyguta snapped. "I'd love to. But I don't know when those other ships will be back or what they'll bring with them. I'm not even sure if we have time for a rescue, but we're going to do it. And we're getting the *anacapa* drive off the *EhizTari* as well, so bring a double-reinforced container. I don't want that drive near anything of ours."

Just in case the *anacapa* was slightly damaged. Just in case the readings were ever so slightly off.

She was going to have to take the crew back to Base 20, and that wasn't going to be pretty. Then she would come back here, and see if she could ferret out information about the *Ivoire*, without antagonizing this Enterran Empire any further.

And to think she'd been excited about this job when she first heard of it. She hadn't imagined that by the middle of her day she would be in hostile territory, rescuing the crew of a ship that should have known better.

But she was.

And she had to do it fast.

6

CARLOTTA TOSIDIS PULLED DOWN her environmental suit's hood, and tightened the straps on her wrists. She concentrated on making sure her suit was in good condition, but didn't lose sight of the details around her. Her team was in the rescue ship, preparing, just like she was. She was in charge of the rescue mission for the *EhizTari*, and Captain Nyguta had made the mission very clear: Time was of the essence. If the rescue team couldn't get everyone off the *EhizTari* before the return of the Empire ships, then there might be some acceptable losses.

Tosidis didn't believe in acceptable losses. She was a member of one of the Honored Families which were all original Armada stock, and her family had once been considered an acceptable loss. Only through ingenuity and sheer luck had her ancestors survived.

She wasn't ever going to allow a loss to become acceptable.

For any reason.

She had divided her team into four, with four different rescue vessels heading to various undamaged sections of the *EhizTari*. Her four vessels had more than enough room for fifty survivors.

She had to assume that the *EhizTari's* captain and bridge crew weren't among them, since the bridge had been obliterated.

But her rescue vehicle was heading toward that part of the ship, just in case.

She had brought two different medics with her. The other three rescue vehicles only had one medic each.

The other damaged areas of the *EhizTari* weren't as heavily populated as the bridge.

Tosidis also had the double container for the *anacapa* drive. She was taking on a lot with this mission, but she didn't mind. She liked working hard.

The rescue vessel was small and designed for short trips. There was no cockpit, no galley, no quarters. Just one large rectangular room that the entire crew bunched into. There were two different navigation areas, and the engineering section was in the very center, so that engineering would be harder to destroy.

The vessel had retractable runners for landings on flat surfaces, grapplers to attach to shaky areas, and lots of spacebridges which were essentially tunnels for going from ship to ship.

Since there was a gaping hole in the side of the *EhizTari* where the bridge should be, she figured she'd need grapplers and a spacebridge.

Her small team didn't need any special instructions. One medic would travel with her; the other would remain on board with someone who could act as pilot.

She would take three others with her. They were suited up and ready to go.

This part was always the hardest, because the adrenaline was already flowing. Everyone wanted to move, even when moving was impossible.

The rescue vessel approached the *EhizTari*. The other rescue vessels flanked her. Two would go around the *EhizTari*, and one would go to the damaged area below the bridge. That seemed to be where most of the life signs had congregated.

There were two life signs near the bridge, and they seemed faint. Technically, Tosidis wasn't heading toward them. She was bringing her team to the *anacapa* drive.

Practically, though, she was bringing the team to the bridge to save those two gasping lives first.

Before leaving, Tosidis had scanned the *EhizTari's* hull, and had found what she believed to be four good entry points. Hers was the destroyed area near the bridge.

The collapsed hole would enable her and her team to get to the *anacapa* drive quickly, and had the side benefit of being close to those life signs.

The rescue vessel reached the *EhizTari's* hull. Tosidis released the grapplers. They extended, reaching the edges and digging their claws into the ragged sides. The claws poked through the sides, and nothing else happened.

Tosidis paused for a moment. Normally, the nanobits that made up the hull would have been repairing the side of the *EhizTari*. They would have taken the grappler's claws and either rejected them or incorporated them into the repair.

Neither happened. Which was very odd.

For Tosidis, though, it was a bit of a blessing that the nanobit repair function had shut down. She always hated using a grappler on an area that nanobits were trying to repair. Sometimes the grappler's claws got entangled in the repairs and became part of a damaged ship.

More than once, she'd had to leave bits of her grapplers behind, because the nanobits were too good at doing their job.

She made sure the grappler was secure. Then she released the space-bridge. It would go through the hole and find the nearest door or open space. Then it would attach to that area, and seal tightly. The nanobits would bond with the interior, and then they would add a layer of protection inside the spacebridge, allowing it to create its own environment, if she so commanded.

She hoped she wouldn't be inside the spacebridge long enough to need an environment.

"Ready?" she asked her team as she adjusted her own environmental suit. She checked the hood's attachment and ran a quick diagnostic to make certain the suit had no weak spots, and that the temperature and oxygen mix was just right.

Evgeny Mancuso moved closer to the exit. He was tugging on the fingers of his gloves, as if they bothered him. If Tosidis hadn't worked with him for years, she would have thought he had a suit problem. But the glove-tugging was one of his rituals, and seemed to calm him down before a rescue attempt.

Next to him, Ibrahim Stradel watched the ritual. Tosidis didn't have to see his rather pudgy face to know he was rolling his eyes. Stradel was precise and quick: he had donned his suit in the middle of the trip and had probably already run a diagnostic or two.

She knew that Stradel would double-check her plans, even before she asked him to. Having Stradel on the team made her feel calmer.

The only unknown, Tomika Probihzy, wasn't a true unknown. Tosidis had gone to school with her until their careers diverged. Probihzy headed into medicine, and Tosidis followed the family career—engineering and piloting, hoping to be in charge of a ship one day.

Tosidis had sent her usual medic to one of the other teams, because she wanted a lot of rescue medical experience with all of those life signs. She figured Probihzy, who had just joined rescue medical teams, would be able to handle this one.

Although the way that Probihzy was pacing, it seemed like Tosidis might be wrong. Probihzy was acting nervous—and not in the way that Mancuso had. Or maybe Tosidis was just used to Mancuso, and didn't know how Probihzy acted before a mission.

"Check your suit," Tosidis said to Probihzy as she approached the exit. Probihzy nodded, although Tosidis couldn't tell if that nod was an acknowledgement, as in Probihzy had already done it, or a response to the command.

At this point, Tosidis didn't care. They needed to leave.

She looked for DeLissa Boyé, the remaining member of the team. Boyé should have been next to the exit with the others, but instead, she was standing near one of the navigation panels, her suit hood flopping against her back, her wavy black hair loose.

"Problem, DeLissa?" Tosidis asked with an edge to her tone.

"The nanobits aren't working," Boyé said. "They should have been interacting with the grappler."

"I know," Tosidis said.

"Doesn't that bother you?" Boyé asked.

"We have two fading life signs," Tosidis said. "That bothers me."

Boyé frowned as she tucked her hair into its net, then pulled up her hood. "Let's at least let the *BilatZailea* know about it, okay? Something's really wrong here."

Tosidis hated the statement. Of course something was really wrong, or the team wouldn't be about to go into the *EhizTari*. But she didn't say that, because she knew what Boyé was getting at. The fact that the nanobits weren't responding correctly bothered her too.

"Let Captain Nyguta know," Tosidis said to Kwame Alexander, who was going to act as emergency pilot if the rescue vehicle needed one.

Alexander nodded, and Tosidis had the sense that he had already contacted the *BilatZailea*. That pleased her. Tosidis kept her team as close to her equals as possible, because she found that a team that didn't have to look to one person for all the answers worked better than one that was constantly waiting for instruction.

Tosidis nodded at Alexander and Greggi Causey, the other medic. Causey gave Tosidis a tentative smile. They hadn't worked together either, but Tosidis had heard good things about Causey, and was happy to have her on the team.

"Let's go," Tosidis said again to her team, and swept her arm around. She double-checked the spacebridge, made sure the nanobits were working there, and the entire thing was solid enough to handle her people.

She had the gravity off—there wasn't going to be any environment in the spacebridge at all—but she always worried about the stability of a spacebridge. If she doubted one would work well, she also made sure her team used tethers to go between ships.

The spacebridge was solid and complete, though. She didn't need tethers. Mancuso stepped into the airlock, the first on the mission, just as he was supposed to be. The exit closed behind him, circling, not really taking much time between departures, just the way she had set it up.

Stradel followed, then Boyé, even though Probihzy should've been next.

"Problems, Tomika?" Tosidis asked.

Probihzy shook her head in response and almost dove into the airlock. So, there were problems. Great. Tosidis didn't need that kind of worry on this trip.

Tosidis grabbed the *anacapa* container. It was heavy even without the *anacapa* drive. She strapped the container to her left hand in an excess of caution, then stepped into the airlock herself.

The airlock was tiny, barely big enough for a single person. She had to hold the container vertical while she waited for the exterior door to open.

The exterior door slid open, disappearing into the hull of the rescue vehicle. The gravity in the airlock wasn't enough to hold her, and she rose slowly. Then she pushed off, and floated through the spacebridge.

This spacebridge was smaller than usual, probably so that it could fit into the hole inside the *EhizTari*. Tosidis felt a little cramped. She also floated closer to the floor of the spacebridge than the top of it. She almost felt like she was crawling.

The rest of her team had already disappeared inside the *EhizTari*, and were supposed to be waiting for her. She used her right hand to propel herself forward again, and into the *EhizTari*.

The spacebridge ended at an interior door that apparently led from a storage area into one of the main corridors. The *EhizTari* had a different configuration than the *BilatZailea*. The *EhizTari* was a newer foldspace tracking vehicle, built like an oval with smaller ovals on all four sides.

The difference in design meant that Tosidis had to memorize the ship's layout. She also used the design specs so that she could figure out where she was.

The team was waiting for her on the other side of that door. The environmental system was still working here, so somewhere the *EhizTari* had shut down the damaged sections and protected the humans on the inside. Strange that the damaged sections would be partitioned off, but the nanobits hadn't started repairs. Usually those two functions worked together.

Emergency lighting had come on, just like it always did when the bridge had been compromised. The lighting had changed from a normal sunlike golden to a slightly pale blue, notification to anyone in the Armada that the bridge was no longer functional—without the blare of emergency announcements or flaring warning lights, that would have tipped off enemies to any kind of problem.

Tosidis pulled herself through the door and closed it as she eased her feet to the ground. The gravity felt heavier than usual, but she blamed that on the *anacapa* container. She didn't like carrying something that bulky, but she knew she had to.

"Still have life signs?" she asked Probihzy.

"Faint," Probihzy said.

"This way." Boyé had already figured out the best route to get to the injured.

"You three go," Tosidis said to Boyé, Probihzy, and Stradel. "Evgeny and I will see if we can find the *anacapa* drive."

Boyé swiveled her face toward Tosidis, in what might have been a protest, but didn't say anything. Then she led the other two down a branch in the corridor.

The *anacapa* would have been on or near the bridge. And there was a communications *anacapa* to find as well. Tosidis didn't want to take the time to search for the communications array, but she would if she had to.

"This way," Mancuso said. He too, apparently, had figured out where everything was.

He led her down another fork in the corridor. According to the design specs, it would take her to a storage area off the bridge. She couldn't tell from what she was looking at whether or not that area had been damaged in the attack as well.

"I'm not getting any *anacapa* energy readings," she said.

"Me either," he said.

But they both knew that the drive hadn't been hit. If it had, the entire ship would have blown up.

They rounded a corner. Tosidis actually wished that the environmental system was off, because she could move faster without gravity, especially holding the damn container.

But she didn't dare shut off the environmental system. She wasn't sure if it was too compromised. Anything she did might shut off the system to the entire ship, and that might cost lives.

The lighting in this part of the corridor seemed even paler, and the walls narrower. It took Tosidis a moment to realize that the wall to her right was reinforced with a double shield.

She and Mancuso were hurrying past a part of the ship that had been open to space not that long ago.

She eyeballed the shield. It looked like it was made of nanobits.

"The nanobits are working here," she said to him.

"So it would seem," he said. "It's almost like those ships hit this one with one of our weapons."

That was what bothered her. He was exactly right. The Armada had built weapons that unbonded nanobits. The Armada had spent centuries crafting and perfecting those weapons, always planning to use them against the Fleet—if they ever met the Fleet.

So how had some culture that the Armada had never fought with in its entire history developed the same weapons?

She let out a small breath, then scanned the ship design.

The problem wasn't the weapon that hit the *EhizTari*. It was where the hit had occurred. The section of the ship her vehicle had grappled to had held some of the *EhizTari* backup weaponry.

She pinged the rescue vehicle. "Kwame," she said, "check our grappler. Make sure it's still solid, that the nanobits aren't pulling apart."

"Already figured that out, Carlotta," Alexander said. "And they're fine. Someone on the *EhizTari* shut down the nanobit function in that area, just like we're supposed to in a weapons' malfunction."

Shutting down any nanobit activity usually confused the weapons system. That was a flaw that the Armada hadn't yet fixed. She should have thought of that part of the procedure when she noted that the nanobits were malfunctioning. But she had been thinking about rescue, not weapons.

"Thanks," she said, and continued after Mancuso. The *EhizTari* felt even more vulnerable now than it had a moment ago.

There was no chatter on the comms. Her teams never spoke to each other during a mission unless they needed to coordinate. The silence meant that they were all doing what they had come to do, rescue the people who had suddenly found themselves stranded in this strange sector of space, on a ship that was no longer reliable.

Mancuso stopped, then turned slightly to the left. She lost track of him for a moment. And then she understood why he had stopped.

The wall to their right and now the one directly before them were made of nanobits. A double shield again.

Just a bit of quality emergency engineering between them and space.

Mancuso had stepped into what used to be another corridor but which had become more of an alcove. There was a door, but it opened into that shielded area, which meant that it led nowhere.

There was no marked place on the ship's specs that showed where the *anacapa* drive would be, because the drives were too precious to call attention to them. But layout of the now ruined bridge suggested that the *anacapa* drive would be near here.

Mancuso was using sensors in his gloves to see if he could find any *anacapa* energy. But if the drive had been properly stored and wasn't being used, then it wouldn't give off any energy at all.

Tosidis unstrapped the container from her wrist, then set the container down, feeling a relief she hadn't expected at losing the weight.

Then she pushed her gloves against the wall, hoping to activate a cupboard door behind which she would find the *anacapa* drive. She didn't have to search long.

The wall itself glowed slightly orange, an acknowledgment of her effort. And then, through a channel the Armada only used in emergencies, the *EhizTari* addressed her.

Carlotta Tosidis, we are damaged, but our drive is secure.

Mancuso tilted his head back slightly, clearly surprised by the mechanical voice. Apparently he heard it as well, and just as apparently, he had never encountered anything like it.

"The ship is not," she said through the same channel. "I need both drives."

The communications drive is not secure, the ship told her. *Nor is it on this level. It is where such drives always are, and may be accessed by a qualified engineer.*

On the usual channel, she said to Mancuso, "See if we have an engineer close to the communications array."

Half the Armada—or so it seemed—had background in engineering. But a qualified engineer meant that the engineer could actually serve in the engineering department of an Armada vessel, the most prestigious department in any vessel.

Tosidis was a qualified engineer, but she had never checked to see if anyone else on the rescue team had the word "qualified" before their credentials.

"We have two," Mancuso said. "I sent them in, telling them to take the communications *anacapa* inside its cradle and bring it back to the *BilatZailea.*"

"Well done," Tosidis said, relieved that she wasn't going to have stay on this ship any longer than necessary. "Let's get this one then."

To remove an *anacapa* drive took three layers of security. She had completed the first by letting the ship know who she was. But she had to enter her personal security code, and then she needed to enter the current security numerical protocol.

Her personal code was easy; she used it for half a dozen things. But she had never used the current security protocol. The numbers changed weekly, and while she committed them to memory, she didn't always trust that memory.

She couldn't ask either, because asking would cause the entire system to shut down. She had checked on the numerical code before leaving the *BilatZailea*, but the code was a long one, and she worried about entering it incorrectly.

She would only get one chance at it.

Her personal code was a combination of tiny gestures combined with short words in three different languages, all of which sounded alike. Anyone who tried to replicate that code would probably fail, because they would most likely miss a gesture or mispronounce the word.

She had chosen a subtle personal code. Not everyone did.

Once she entered that, then she entered this week's string of thirty-five numbers, hoping she got them right.

Mancuso stood back. He had looked away when she had enacted her personal code, but he watched as she entered the numerical code. He couldn't coach her. The numbers couldn't be spoken aloud, and only one person could enter them.

If another person helped, the entire system went into alert, thinking that the person entering the code was probably compromised.

Tosidis forced herself to concentrate. Each numerical sequence was made up of patterns, and she usually memorized it with the pattern. She just had never had a reason to test her methodology before.

She went slower than she might normally have, and mouthed the numbers as she pressed them onto the physical pad near her right hand.

When she finished, she brought her hand to her side, just like she was supposed to.

And nothing happened.

No doors opened, no cupboard appeared, no *anacapa* drive flared into life.

She let out a small breath, suddenly terrified she had done it wrong.

But the shutdown sequence hadn't started either, and she took some measure of hope in that.

Mancuso started to open his mouth but she shook her head ever so slightly. Speaking might undo all the work she had already done.

Her heart pounded. She wasn't sure what she would do if this storage area didn't open on its own.

And then the center of the wall slid upward, revealing the cupboard she had hoped she would find. A small emergency light turned on as the door locked into place.

Tosidis opened the *anacapa* container that she had brought. It was two containers merged together, both of them strong enough to contain a working *anacapa* drive's energy.

Mancuso opened the interior door in the cupboard, revealing the *EhizTari's anacapa* drive container. He worked quickly along each side, unhooking the *anacapa* drive's container from the interior of the *EhizTari*.

No alarms went off, and the color of the lighting didn't change. Apparently, the ship had accepted Tosidis fully.

Which she was grateful for. She had seen engineers who tried to pull an *anacapa* drive too quickly get shot with some hidden weapon for their troubles.

The Armada doubly protected its *anacapa* drives, monitoring them and making certain they worked properly. That ancient history which led to the founding of the Armada wouldn't have happened without a malfunctioning *anacapa* drive, and a paucity of good drives.

She waited until Mancuso was done separating the drive's container from the *EhizTari*, then she reached in and pulled the container loose. She moved it to the lip of the cupboard, then pried the edge of the container open.

The *anacapa* drive was long and narrow. It looked like it had been cut from a much bigger drive, because its shape was perfectly rectangular. It glowed golden ever so slightly, the way that an active drive not in use should glow.

She closed the container, and pulled it all the way out of the cupboard. The container was heavier than the container she had brought. The weight would be something to contend with as she headed back to the rescue vehicle.

She eased the container into the container she had brought, hoping it would fit.

It did, which was a relief. She didn't want to pull the *anacapa* drive out and set it into the container she had brought. When she touched an *anacapa* drive, her bones vibrated and her teeth hurt for days afterwards.

She closed the container and sealed it. Then she let out a small sigh.

"Ready?" she asked Mancuso.

He'd been struggling to close the cupboard. She reached past him and touched the edge of the wall, finding the switch that manually operated the door.

Tiny details like that were important, particularly if the Armada lost control of this ship. Tosidis knew that Captain Nyguta would do everything she could to make sure the *EhizTari* was protected, but the fact that they were removing the crew from the disabled ship meant that it would be left behind.

Mancuso helped her lift the *anacapa* container. He grunted as he did so.

"I think we'll both need to carry it," he said.

"I've got it," she said. She wasn't being tough. The container was awkward, and trying to hold it between them would be more difficult than wrestling it back to the rescue vehicle. "As long as you get the doors."

She could see his smile through his hood. He nodded once.

She strapped the container to both wrists, then lifted it by its sides. The weight unbalanced her, and she nearly toppled forward.

It would take work to get the container off the *EhizTari*, but she could do it.

The problem was that she couldn't help the rest of her team with their rescues, which she hoped were going well.

So she staggered down the corridor with the *anacapa* container, hoping she had enough time to get out of here, with all the drives and personnel in place.

7

THE WALL SCREENS AROUND NYGUTA made her feel as if her bridge had moved into the area around that abandoned starbase. The starbase floated on one of the screens to her right, a gigantic half-ruin that listed in the wrong direction.

Some of the shrapnel from the destroyed ships had penetrated one side of that starbase, just adding to the damage. The rest of the shrapnel—the bits that hadn't hit the *EhizTari* or the starbase—floated like wisps of smoke after a damaging fire.

The *EhizTari* took up the entire center screen, the crater where the bridge had been a black hole in her vision. Nyguta couldn't see her people working the ship, but she knew, whenever she looked at that hole, that she had people there, trying to save lives.

From this angle, she could only see one rescue vehicle, even though she knew four had attached themselves to the *EhizTari*. Her people knew what to do. They had rescued thousands of crew members over the years. But never in a situation like this, the remains of an active firefight that the *BilatZailea* had been part of.

Nyguta was using the wall screens more than she ever had before, and they made her uncomfortable. They were like windows on a relaxation vessel, showing parts of space that seemed close enough to touch and yet too far away.

Plus, she didn't like the two-dimensions, so she had activated some holoscreens around her, giving her a tiny view of the entire area in three-dimensions. Little images floated around her main holoscreen, red for the *EhizTari* (because it was in trouble), gold for the rescue vehicles, and a silver-gray for that starbase, which bothered her more than she wanted to say.

She moved slightly, and the damn captain's chair banged the back of her knees. She was going to remove the dumb thing next time she was at a base. She spent half her time on the bridge annoyed by her chair.

No one seemed to notice the grimace she had made, which was good. She needed her team to concentrate, and they were. She had assigned them all different tasks, so she could keep track of this entire mission.

Most of the team was working on the rescue. If she didn't get the *BilatZailea* out of here soon, she would be outnumbered and outgunned.

She had no idea if the Empire had *anacapa* drives, but at the moment, she wasn't going to rule it out. Nor was she going to count on the fact that they couldn't track through foldspace, although she'd never seen any other culture be able to do it.

She just needed to plan for everything. And some of that planning included the *Ivoire*. Intxausti and two of the other researchers were combing through the Fleet's historical records that she had on the *BilatZailea*, looking for any mention of the *Ivoire*. She also had the researchers look through the Armada's records, seeing what had happened when the Armada went through—or avoided—this area of space.

She needed information on the *Ivoire*. It seemed to know this sector of space very well, which meant its captain might know of some good hiding places that prevented any sensors from finding the ship.

And, judging by what she had seen in orbit around Base 20, the *Ivoire* had very good shields, the kind that might actually cloak the ship from any cursory search that the Armada might do.

Nyguta was doing just that kind of cursory search for the *Ivoire* herself. She didn't have time for anything else, not while she was doing two other things.

One of those things was monitoring the rescue taking place on the *EhizTari*. The rescue vehicles were all in the middle of their mission.

A single rescue vehicle had removed its spacebridge and grappler, and was heading back to the *BilatZailea* with ten survivors, most of whom were unharmed. They had been able to get to the rescue vehicle on their own, which was why the vehicle left the *EhizTari* so quickly. The other three rescue vehicles were all still attached to the *EhizTari*.

Nyguta was also watching the telemetry around her, waiting for the Enterran Empire ships to return. She had no idea what kind of warning she would get of their arrival. Nor did she know if the Empire ships she obliterated had managed to let the Empire know that they were under attack, although she had to assume that they had.

Under attack. Such a big phrase for what had happened. Because the Empire wasn't under attack, although the *Ivoire's* captain had set it up so that it would seem that way.

And Nyguta had played right into that captain's hands, although she really had no choice. She had destroyed seven ships to save one of her own. If she didn't get out of here quickly, the *BilatZailea* would truly find itself in some kind of battle, one they weren't really equipped to fight.

The *BilatZailea* was still in battle mode, though. The weapons systems were activated, and her tactical team was ready. She had shields partially down so that the rescue vehicles could return, but she would raise shields the moment she had to.

She had instructed engineering to work on extending the shields around the entire rescue area, something an Armada DV-Class ship could do, but no one had ever thought to build that capability into a foldspace tracking vehicle. And logically, foldspace tracking vehicles needed that perhaps more than a DV-Class ship.

"Captain?" Rockowitz's tone was the kind of measured tone he used when he wanted to sound calm, but really wasn't. "I'm seeing activity that could be a large number of ships."

"Where?" she asked, and she didn't mean *where were the ships?* She meant *what screen?* She was monitoring so many screens, using so many different programs, that she had lost track of which one was his.

He bobbled the holoscreen that mirrored his, briefly blocking her vision of the wall screen showing the side of the *EhizTari* with the caved-in bridge.

She looked at the holoscreen and saw what could be a flotilla of ships heading in the direction of the *BilatZailea*. Of course, that grouping might be something else entirely or have nothing to do with them.

The ships were too far away, at the very edge of sensor range, and they didn't seem to be moving too fast.

Still, her stomach tightened. She had a hunch Rockowitz was right; she had a hunch that she needed to pay attention to those ships.

"Captain." Kibbuku bobbled the holoscreen that mirrored his. "There's more."

She looked at that information, saw more ships coming from a completely different direction, also on the edge of sensor range.

Now she saw the speed at which they were traveling as deliberate, not too slow.

She swallowed hard. She hadn't been given a captaincy because of her fighting skills. She had been promoted to this rank in the foldspace tracking arena because she was the best at what she did.

And what she did did not include any kind of military tactics.

"Let Carlotta know that we need the rescue teams on board now," Nyguta said.

She normally would have contacted Tosidis herself, but Nyguta wanted to see exactly what she was facing.

Nyguta slid her holographic command station closer to her, and tapped in all kinds of commands. She made the *BilatZailea* do a 360-degree scan of the section of space around them, searching for ships.

Of course, she found hundreds of them, mostly alone, mostly traveling on what seemed to be commercial or normal travel routes in the sector.

But she also saw six more ship groupings, all at the edge of her sensor range and all heading toward her, and this strange former Fleet starbase beside her.

She had scanned that base while waiting for her rescue teams to do their jobs. And Kibbuku had pulled what records he could find quickly on the base, which the Fleet had called Starbase Kappa. It had been decommissioned thousands of years ago and from the looks of it, no other culture had commandeered it.

She couldn't find anything on it either, very little tech and no *anacapa* drive, although there was a built-in section of the base that would have housed the drive.

Yet another mystery, and one that wasn't hers to solve. She simply recorded the faint ancient signature of the drive, surprised that it had given off a signature strong enough that she could find it thousands of years later. She made note of that ancient signature, and then ruled it out in the various scans she was running to track down the *Ivoire*.

She kept those scans running, but she stared at those incoming vessels. If they were Empire ships, she couldn't fight them. She couldn't even fight them if she had a flotilla of her own.

"Santiago," she said, "we're going to need to get out of here fast."

"I know." Pereira's voice was calm, not that fake calm that Rockowitz used.

"I want the coordinates locked in so that when I give the order, we head into foldspace immediately." Not that there was an immediately when a ship went into foldspace. There was always a second or two lag. And seconds could be precious.

She glanced at the *Ehiz Tari*. A second rescue vehicle had retracted its spacebridge and was disconnecting the grappler now.

"Are they going to get off that thing soon?" she asked, not sure who she was directing the question to.

"Everyone has loaded the survivors," Rockowitz said. "One team is waiting for the *anacapa* drive before they go."

"How many survivors did we end up with?" Nyguta asked.

"Forty-nine," Rockowitz said. "We also have one body."

"Crew compliment was fifty-six," Kibbuku said. "We're not getting life signs for the others, and there would have been—"

"At least six on the bridge," Nyguta finished for him, her voice soft. She had suspected there might be losses but to have them confirmed hurt.

She took a deep breath. She had no idea who had died. She would probably find out later. She probably knew who they were, although perhaps by name only. Foldspace tracking was a smaller group within the Armada, but not so small that she could keep track of everyone.

"Is the *EhizTari* solid enough for us to attach and bring it through foldspace?" Nyguta asked.

She glanced at those incoming ships again. They were moving steadily, not hurriedly, and that worried her more than ships speeding toward her. That meant these ships would probably follow a plan.

"No, I don't think the *EhizTari* is solid enough for us to pull it through foldspace," Habibi said.

Nyguta made note of that in the records. She had deliberately asked about the *EhizTari's* stability first, because that took some of the liability for its loss away from her.

When she started eyeballing the other ships, she had known, deep in her gut, that the *BilatZailea* wouldn't have the time to set up secure grapplers, and brace the *EhizTari* against the *BilatZailea's* hull.

Taking a disabled ship through foldspace was difficult in the best of circumstances, which these decidedly were not.

But she would have faced an inquisition if she unilaterally decided not to drag the *EhizTari* with her, based on the timing of the incoming ships. However, if the *EhizTari* was too damaged to drag through foldspace, she only had to provide the records of that damage.

"You don't *think* the *EhizTari* is stable enough," Nyguta repeated. "But do we actually have evidence of her instability?"

"Besides the fact that the nanobits don't seem to be repairing the hull?" Habibi seemed a bit put out at the way she had phrased the question. She hated it when he got overly sensitive. "I've been checking with engineering. They advise against using any more grapplers on the *EhizTari*."

"Because…?" she asked, wishing she didn't have to lead him through this. But, then, Habibi was probably thinking about the rescue alone, and not the aftermath.

It was her job to consider the aftermath as well.

He looked up, frowned at her, and then closed his eyes as the actual reason for her question dawned on him.

"Because," he said, "the grapplers we have used have torn into the *EhizTari*. She's not repairing herself, and I worry—and the engineers concur—that we wouldn't be able to pull her through foldspace. We'd lose her, and maybe do some damage to ourselves."

Nyguta nodded. He had given her the report she wanted, as succinctly as possible.

"I don't like leaving the ship behind," Intxausti said. "If we do—"

"I know," Nyguta didn't want to go into all of the problems. What would happen to the *EhizTari* was her decision, not theirs.

"We could try to bring it into foldspace," Habibi said slowly. "I wouldn't recommend it, for all the reasons I mentioned, but we could try…"

"No," Rockowitz said firmly. "It'll slow us down. And not just in foldspace, but as we enter."

The entry point into foldspace would be open much longer to accommodate both ships. It would make both ships vulnerable to outside attack.

If one of those flotillas arrived as the two ships were entering foldspace, and if some ships in that flotilla shot at them, then those shots would have a good chance of harming the *EhizTari* or the *BilatZailea* or both.

Not to mention the fact that the Empire vessels would see the ships disappearing into foldspace and maybe realize that the Armada had some advanced technology that the Empire didn't even know existed.

Nyguta swallowed hard. She was making an assumption that this Empire didn't know about foldspace. But so far, the Armada hadn't discovered any other culture familiar with foldspace—except the Fleet.

And that was the problem.

The Armada had developed many of its systems in opposition to the Fleet. The Armada did not leave personnel behind, and it didn't leave ships scattered around the sectors either. The Armada kept records, and it didn't want those records falling into unfriendly hands.

Nyguta glanced at those incoming vessels. They had gotten a lot closer. They were moving faster than she had initially thought.

"Tell our people to hurry," she said to Habibi. "We need to clear the area around the *EhizTari* as soon as possible."

He nodded, but Pereira gave her a sideways look.

"As soon as the rescue vehicles are all on board," she said, "I want us to return to our original coordinates, the area where we left foldspace, so we can return the way we came."

And not leave more of a trail than necessary, she thought but didn't say. Her team knew that.

"Do as much research as you can on what happened to the *Ivoire*," she said.

"Are we coming back here?" Kibbuku asked, sounding surprised.

"That's not my decision," Nyguta said. "I want to be able to present our alternatives to the Jefatura."

She didn't want to come back. Much as she admired the *Ivoire*'s maneuvers, she doubted the ship was Fleet. Partly because the *Ivoire* knew about this place.

Starbase Kappa dated from the same period in Fleet history as the *Ivoire*. That led her to believe that they were tied together somehow. And since the Fleet dramatically left its past behind, then it wouldn't be lurking around this hostile sector.

"We have at least twenty minutes before the last of the rescue vehicles docks with us," Habibi said.

"Tell them that's unacceptable." Twenty minutes was cutting it very close. Nyguta wanted to be away from this sector of space before the sensors on those Empire vessels could figure out exactly what the *BilatZailea* was doing. "Tell them we need them here now."

"Already done, Captain," Habibi said. "Twenty minutes is as fast as they can go."

She shook her head. She didn't dare leave them behind. That rescue vehicle was the one with the *anacapa* drive. The Jefatura frowned on leaving people behind—it was counter to everything the Armada stood for—but it happened.

But the Jefatura punished anyone who lost control of an *anacapa* drive, particularly one that the Jefatura knew had been recovered. Not that she would have been the kind of captain who would lie and say she left a drive behind when she had not.

Nyguta bit the inside of her lower lip.

She was going to have to wait for them, and risk having their entry into foldspace show up clearly on Empire sensors.

She could only hope that this Empire would see the leap as perhaps a special cloaking device or some kind of faster-than-usual engine.

She didn't want to start something bad for the Armada with this Empire. She wanted to get out and leave almost no trace.

Which was not what the captain of the *Ivoire* wanted. That captain—whoever they were—wanted some kind of conflict between the ships that had been following the *Ivoire* and this Empire.

She didn't want to give the *Ivoire* the satisfaction.

8

"I WANT ALL OF THE SCANS WE HAVE on the Room of Lost Souls," Elissa said to the team in the command center. She knew the *Ewing Trekov* was too far away for any kind of deep space scan to show much, but it might show what vessels were still near the Room.

Paek was working quietly beside her, his fingers moving across his console as he monitored telemetry. He was trying to pull the footage she asked for, but he was using his own method to do so.

The rest of the team in the command center was spread over several consoles. She couldn't monitor what they were doing as easily as she could monitor Paek.

Still, she knew they were working hard. All dozen team members were bent forward, working as the information poured onto their console screens. Each member was responsible for a different grouping of ships heading to the Room of Lost Souls.

Others in the command center, huddled to one side, were monitoring the communications from the space force. So far, no one above her had contacted her. They would eventually, and wonder why she hadn't notified anyone of the incursion in the Empire's space.

With luck, she would have answers by then.

Although she was frustrated by the age of the *Ewing Trekov*. Its command center had been upgraded a dozen times since she had joined the space force, but each upgrade had simply triaged problems that already existed.

Like the ability to do a proper deep space scan. She had served on some ships that would have given her more information than she could get here.

But she would have to make do with what she had. And that frustrated her. She wanted answers now.

From the footage she had seen, the first ship had sustained too much damage to leave quickly. If she got there fast enough so that she could capture both ships, then she might figure out who was after Captain Cooper and why.

She felt slightly breathless. Her great-great-grandfather used to say that enemies who shared a common enemy formed the best alliances. If she could figure out who these new attackers were, and why they were after Cooper, she might be able to ally with them, and defeat that horrid weapon of his.

Which might or might not have something to do with that glowing window of light that had shown up on the scans, and the way ships could appear and disappear. That didn't look like a cloak to her. It looked like a method of transport.

Something to study at a different point. She would order teams to get on it as soon as she could.

She sent a coordinated message to all of the lead ships in the formations heading toward the Room of Lost Souls. She wanted full scans of the entire area as they approached, not just of the ships that they were heading toward, but the seemingly empty space around them.

She also sent the signature of that weapon Cooper had used on her twice, with a warning to all of the ships. They needed to be alert to anything that showed even a hint of that energy signature. If they saw it powering up or gradually appearing, they had to retreat immediately— all ships needed to get as far away from whatever caused that signature as possible.

She even gave them distances to explain what she meant by far away.

I don't want any of you to be heroes, she put in that communique. *I've faced this weapon twice now. I survived it by luck the first time, and by retreat the second. We study it, and live to fight another day.*

Janik would hate that command, but Singh would understand it. Trekov wasn't going to lose a hundred ships because Cooper hid, and then unleashed that weapon again.

If Cooper was even still there. She had a hunch he wasn't and her theory was correct—that he was being pursued.

But she wasn't going to base all of her actions on a single theory. She was going to act as if he were still there.

And if he was afraid of those ships, then maybe they had a similar weapon as well.

Although that begged the question: If they did, why hadn't they used it on the seven Empire ships? The weaponry that had destroyed her ships had been more or less conventional. What had ultimately made the ships explode hadn't been a superior weapon, but a shield failure— on all of the ships.

She sucked in air, and ran that footage in her mind one more time. The second vessel, the attacker vessel, had gone through those shields as if they were paper. But not on the first attack.

On the second.

"We need to alter our shield frequency," she muttered.

"What?" Paek asked. He looked up from his work, and frowned at her.

She was a bit startled he had heard what she had said because she thought she had spoken softly.

"All of the ships," she said, "we need to alter our shield frequencies, continually. That ship that we're heading toward has some kind of pro- gram that enables conventional weapons to cut through our shields. We need to counter that."

"Yes, ma'am," he said, and she sighed ever so slightly. She hadn't been giving him a command. She had been thinking aloud.

But he didn't know that.

He was looking a bit stressed at the thought of having to handle her two rather contradictory requests.

"I'll examine the shield requirements, Sub-Lieutenant," she said. "You get that footage for me. I want to know what, if anything, those two invader ships are doing."

She walked across the command center, to Sub-Lieutenant Fernanda Bahe's station. Bahe was one of the most competent people on the *Ewing Trekov*. Elissa was keeping an eye on her, hoping to promote her to Elissa's personal staff when the time was right.

Bahe was a rather wispy woman with an equally wispy voice. Her skin was a kind of pale whitish gray that some people who spent too much time on ships got. She looked insubstantial, almost sickly, and she was neither.

She was one of the most formidable people on the ship.

Elissa handed Bahe a tablet with the footage from the attack, cued up to the moments before the shields were breached.

"I want you to send this to all the ships heading toward the Room of Lost Souls," she said. "Tell them to develop their own programs that will rotate shield frequency. Each ship needs to be different. Tell the commanders of each vessel that I want them to watch the attack closely, and realize those ships were destroyed because the shields were breached, not because the weapons are powerful."

Bahe's gray eyes opened wide for just a moment, as she absorbed what Elissa had said. Then Bahe nodded.

"I'll make certain they understand, ma'am," she said.

Elissa gave Bahe the tiniest of smiles. Elissa had no doubt that Bahe would do the job as asked, just like Paek would.

The problem was that so few other members of the space force were as competent as they were—even on a ship as renowned as the *Ewing Trekov*.

She returned to the command center.

Paek lifted his head, his dark eyes meeting hers.

"That second ship appears to be mounting a rescue mission," he said.

She crossed behind his console, and looked at the grainy real-time footage.

It took a moment for her eyes to adjust to the flatness of the screen, and the varying tones of gray and black. Both ships remained close to the Room of Lost Souls. Neither ship had moved.

But smaller vessels were covering the distance between the attacking vessel and the damaged ship.

She frowned. Standard Empire procedure would be to attach the damaged ship to the intact ship, and travel out of the area as fast as that arrangement would allow.

But they clearly weren't part of Empire ground or space forces, and on the clearer footage from the seven ships, she hadn't seen any other markings that identified these ships.

She had seen the ship's shapes before, but she had a hunch she had seen them as derelicts, like so many of the abandoned ships floating around this area of space.

She didn't want to compare at the moment, however. She needed to focus on both ships.

A rescue mission meant that they were going to leave the damaged ship behind.

She turned slightly and hit the command console, putting her own codes into it. She looked at the speed at which the *Ewing Trekov* was traveling, hoping she could get Derrida to take it out quicker.

But he couldn't. The *Trekov* was going as fast as it safely could, which meant that all of the ships in their group were going fast.

She looked at the positions of the remaining groups. None of them would get to the Room of Lost Souls in the next forty-five minutes.

Then she expended her area grid search, to see if there were any other ships that happened to be in the area, ships that weren't under her direct command, but ships she could commandeer.

If she got someone there during that rescue mission, she might be able to confiscate both vessels, as well as take prisoners. Prisoners meant that she would learn what these ships were and what the *Ivoire* had been up to.

Her heart beat hard.

She wasn't quite sure what she was up against, but she would figure it out. She threaded her hands together, felt the too-tight skin beneath her fingertips.

These people might hold the answers to the jump in technology that the Nine Planets had taken and to that weapon that had nearly destroyed her as well as her ships.

Most importantly, these people might hold the answer to Captain Cooper. Who he was, where he came from, and where he had learned those tactical skills.

If she knew those things, she might be able to beat him.

She might be able to destroy him, once and for all.

9

Sweat had drenched Tosidis by the time she reached the final door leading out of the *EhizTari*. She hadn't ever carried anything that heavy for a prolonged distance before, and her back, shoulders, and arms ached.

Mancuso offered to take the *anacapa* container from her, but she had shaken him off. He had even less upper body strength than she did. She at least worked out in normal gravity on a regular basis. He preferred playing games in zero-g in his spare time.

Her throat was dry and she was just a little woozy. She stopped in front of the door, her heart pounding hard against her chest.

She indicated the door with her head, because apparently Mancuso thought she was going to open it.

He apologized, then slapped his own glove on the manual door command.

She didn't acknowledge the apology; he should have known better. Afterall, she'd been talking to DeMarcus Habibi back on the *BilatZailea*. He'd been pressing her for an ETA, as if she hadn't known time was of the essence.

But she hadn't realized, until he contacted her, that the entire ship was waiting on her. The rescue of the surviving crew of the *EhizTari* was complete: even her secondary team had brought back their survivors.

It was just taking some time for her to stagger down that corridor, which she had done.

They were almost out of here.

The door slid open, revealing the damaged section of the *EhizTari*. The spacebridge still connected it to the rescue vehicle, and for that, Tosidis let out a tiny, private sigh of relief.

Part of her expected the spacebridge to have retracted and the rescue vehicle to have left. She wouldn't have blamed them. She knew that some ships were bearing down on their position, and the *BilatZailea* wasn't up to any kind of defense.

Mancuso stepped through the door, then turned and helped her, by bracing the bottom of the *anacapa* container. As she stepped into this part of the ship, though, she could feel the gravity lessen. The pressure on her back, shoulder, and arms eased.

Mancuso closed the door behind them, and the gravity got even lighter. It wasn't quite zero-g, not here, but it was close enough.

Tosidis staggered down the spacebridge until she felt light enough to float. She placed one foot in front of the other, bent her knees and pushed herself forward, just like she had been taught. A ground lunge start, which she hadn't done in years.

But her hands were cramped and still clutched around the drive container, so using them to push off the spacebridge's walls would not have been possible. And she didn't want to kick sideways. The spacebridge's walls were thin, and more than once, she'd seen someone's foot go through the wall into space.

Not that it would be a serious problem, but if it happened, it would catch her up, and take even more time.

At least the distance she had to cover was short, and it was so much easier now that she no longer felt the weight of the *anacapa* drive container. When she got to the other side, someone would meet her and take the damn thing from her, or so she hoped.

She made it to the airlock door, and finally unhooked her right hand from the container. It didn't even tilt downward like she expected—which just went to show how deeply that experience with normal gravity had gotten into her head.

She pressed her glove against the exterior of the rescue ship, and the exterior door slid open. She clutched at the container, and pulled it against her.

She awkwardly maneuvered herself into the airlock. The exterior door closed, and the environment resumed enough for her to feel gravity again.

The container seemed even heavier than it had on the *EhizTari*. The container slipped, and she managed to catch it, causing a spasm in her lower back.

Then the interior door opened, and she staggered inside the rescue vehicle, nearly falling. DeLissa Boyé, who was no longer wearing the hood on her environmental suit, caught Tosidis and they both staggered under the weight of the container.

Ibrahim Stradel hurried over, and put his hands underneath the container, bracing it. Tosidis reached across and unhooked the damn thing from her left wrist.

Her wrist jerked upwards, almost like it did in zero-g. But the response here was the opposite of zero-g. Her wrist jerked upward because it no longer bore the weight of that stupid container.

Mancuso burst through the airlock door a moment later. He staggered as well, which seemed odd to Tosidis but she didn't give it a lot of thought.

She waited while the team unhooked her right wrist, which also jerked upwards. The pain in her back and shoulders was sharp and sudden.

She moved away from that stupid container, and toward the navigational controls. Kwame Alexander was moving his hands over a holographic screen.

"I've got this." He sounded tense. And why wouldn't he be? This was the last of the rescue vehicles to get away from the *EhizTari*.

Tosidis pulled down her own environmental hood. Her sweat-soaked hair was plastered against her scalp. The air inside the rescue vehicle was cooler than the interior of her environmental suit.

Her team was unusually quiet. She didn't look at her own holoscreen, which was what she had initially meant to do. Instead, she glanced behind her, then wished she hadn't.

Both medics—Tomika Probihzy and Greggi Causey—were bent over a seat. The seats usually folded into the floor. Tosidis couldn't remember ever using one of the seats on an actual mission.

This seat was completely horizontal, and a person was stretched out on it. Tosidis didn't recognize the boots, which were rather small. But she did recognize the equipment that Probihzy and Causey were using. They had a protective bubble over the person on the seat, and were doing their best to stabilize that person.

Just behind them was a black inflatable body carrier, attached to the wall on one side and the floor on the other. Body carriers were used in a variety of circumstances, usually to get someone injured out of a zero-g environment without using an environmental suit.

But the carriers got their name from their usage in battlefield situations. The Armada tried not to leave anyone behind, and if their bodies could be recovered, they were, so that the families would get closure.

The body carriers also made it easy to move someone who was unconscious from one place to another. The carriers floated in regular gravity, so no one had to lug them, the way Tosidis had just had to lug that stupid container.

Which Mancuso and Boyé were stabilizing just across the vehicle from the body carrier.

Tosidis felt cold. There was another body carrier, deflated and crumpled, next to that raised seat.

Her team had rescued one of the people whose life signs had been fading, but apparently hadn't been able to save the other.

She turned away, only to see Stradel watching her. She let the sadness she felt show on her face. He nodded, but didn't say anything, not that there was anything to say.

Then she turned her attention to the holoscreen near her. Alexander was trying to loosen the grapplers. The spacebridge was already rolled up.

"Just tear through the ship," she said to Alexander.

"I don't want to do more damage," he said. "It's bad enough—"

"There's no one on board, and they had us take the *anacapa*," she said. "No one is worried about the condition of the *EhizTari*."

She sounded harsh, even to her own ears, but he needed to know the truth of it, especially since theirs was the last rescue vehicle. Captain Nyguta had been pressuring her to get back. Nyguta usually wasn't one of those captains who pressured unnecessarily.

"All right," Alexander said. "But I don't like it."

He didn't have to like it. He just had to do it, and he did. The grapplers shredded what was left of that section of the *EhizTari's* hull. Then they retracted, folding in on themselves as they slid back into the rescue vehicle.

"Let's go," Tosidis said. She would take over the piloting, except that her arms were shaking and she was woozy from the effort of getting the *anacapa* drive back here. "Quickly."

Alexander nodded, but didn't respond. He was going as quickly as he could. Tosidis could actually feel the rescue vehicle accelerate.

She leaned against the navigation panel, her entire body aching. No previous mission had ever exhausted her like this before. But then, she'd never had to do anything quite that physical in real gravity before.

And, if she were being honest with herself, the body behind her shook her up more than she wanted to admit. She had never lost anyone, not as a team leader. And she didn't even know who she had lost this time.

That, and the pressure from the incoming ships. That little battle when they arrived had been bad enough. If the *BilatZailea* was delayed because of her, and they got into another battle again…

She shook the thought away. It wasn't productive, and she needed to remain alert until they arrived back with the Armada.

Then she could think about the what-ifs and the might-have-beens. Until then, she just had to survive.

10

THE LAST RESCUE VEHICLE DOCKED WITH THE *BilatZailea*.

Nyguta let out a small breath, relieved that her people were back on her ship. She shifted slightly, and nearly sat in the stupid captain's chair before she caught herself. She didn't have time to sit, no matter how relieved she was.

She adjusted one of the holoscreens, made sure that the rescue vehicle was secure, and then checked on those incoming Empire ships.

Those ships had to be scanning this area. They had to know she was here.

She had no idea how powerful their scanning equipment was, or what they could tell about her ship from the information they were gathering.

But she also knew that staying here much longer was going to guarantee that at least one of those squadrons would see her ship enter foldspace in real time, not just on a distant scan.

She couldn't put off the last part of this assignment any longer, no matter how reluctant she was to complete it.

The *BilatZailea* was already near the coordinates that marked where it had arrived in this hostile sector of space. She just had to give the command and the foldspace window would open. The *BilatZailea* could leave.

But she didn't give the command. She could feel everyone watching her closely, expecting her to say something.

There was nothing to say.

She moved one of the holoscreens directly in front of her. Then she set up the weapons system, and targeted the *EhizTari*.

It looked so vulnerable floating there, its bridge gone and pieces of its hull hanging off the sides like ripped cloth.

In all of her training, she had never targeted a vessel that couldn't target her back. Every simulation had been of a firefight, and the decisions had to be made in the heat of the moment, with too much information coming at her.

Not too little.

It almost felt like she was kicking a corpse.

Which, she supposed, she was.

The *EhizTari* glowed whitely on the target screen, pulsing, as if waiting for her command.

She didn't command. She didn't give her crew an order to do this. She had to do it herself.

She touched the screen, then she launched the laser missiles at an Armada vessel, her stomach clenched, bile in her throat.

She had positioned the screen so that she could see the simulation at the same time as the actual missiles crossing the small distance of space, heading toward the *EhizTari*.

She had targeted all of the remaining propulsion systems, all of the empty crew areas, and she hoped her information was right—that no one had been left on that vessel.

The missiles zoomed toward the *EhizTari*. She kept her fingers over the command screen, half expecting countermeasures. She'd been trained to overcome countermeasures.

But of course, there were none.

The missiles slammed into the *EhizTari*, two underneath, three along the front and two more spinning around the *EhizTari* and hitting crucial systems on the side of the ship that she couldn't see from this angle.

Red laser light coated the *EhizTari* where she was hit. Then the light faded and that section of the *EhizTari* swelled, as if it had gained mass.

The swelling grew and grew and finally burst—only it wasn't really *finally*. It only took seconds, maybe a minute, before the bursts scattered throughout the ship.

The *EhizTari* would explode in a few more seconds, and be no more.

"Get us out of here now, Mikai," she said to Rockowitz.

"Done," he said.

And there was that inevitable wait as a foldspace window opened.

Nyguta dug her fingers into the back of the chair she almost never used, and braced herself for the vibrations that would lead the *BilatZailea* into foldspace.

The *EhizTari* exploded in sections, each section dividing itself into pieces so small that no culture, no matter how technologically advanced it was, could reassemble the ship.

At the same moment, the *BilatZailea* vibrated, and the screens went black. The *BilatZailea* had entered foldspace.

They were heading back to the Armada.

Nyguta sank into the chair. It felt too firm, unused, uncomfortable. Or maybe that was just because she never used it, never had her knees weaken like that before.

She would see the *EhizTari* fall apart in her nightmares. She would be cursed by that ship forever.

But, she had rescued the crew, and their captain had been over-eager, and they wouldn't have been in this situation if they had followed procedure.

The *BilatZailea* would have been the ship in the bad situation.

The *BilatZailea* would have arrived first, would have been the subject of that distress signal, would have had to deal with those Empire ships.

She wasn't sure how she could have done that, especially if the *BilatZailea* had been alone. And if the order had been reversed—if the *BilatZailea* had arrived first, and the *EhizTari* arrived second, Nyguta doubted that the *EhizTari's* captain would have figured out how to save her.

She let out a small sigh. The vibrations inside the *BilatZailea* ceased.

They were safely in foldspace. She supposed she should get up and check to make sure they weren't followed or observed.

But she didn't move.

None of what she thought about the *EhizTari* or her now-dead captain mattered. None of those mistakes really mattered either.

The *EhizTari* was no more, and the *Ivoire* had gotten away.

Both of those things were on Nyguta, and always would be.

11

THE *EWING TREKOV* WAS ALMOST within proper scanning range. Elissa almost willed the *Trekov* to go faster. She wanted to see what was going on at the Room of Lost Souls through all the various data sources, not just the limited visual information that was coming from the buoys.

She had taken to pacing around the command center. The workstations took up half the deck, so she had plenty of room to pace. She could stop and look at wall screens if she wanted, but mostly she didn't want to.

She did stop and peered at the work of her team, seeing numbers scroll on screens, blurry images coming from the buoys, clearer footage from the ships that those two vessels had destroyed. Everyone stiffened almost imperceptibly when she stopped beside them, but they continued working, just like they were trained to do.

Only Paek gave her a sideways look when she stopped beside him a second time. He raised his eyebrows, and half-smiled at her, as if he understood her impatience.

So far, Flag Commander Janik hadn't contacted her, so either he approved of what she was doing or he didn't know.

The incoming information was making her nervous, based on what she could see from the buoys. For a while, the smaller enemy vessels—black blobs along the grayness of space—appeared to be attached to the damaged ship.

But one by one, those blobs were returning to the attacking vessel. And if they all docked before the *Trekov* got to the Room of Lost Souls, then there was a good chance the attacking vessel would leave.

She would get the damaged ship, and it would most likely be scrubbed. The Empire's engineers would be able to glean some information from it, but that would take time.

She would rather have humans under her control, people she could talk to, people she could interrogate and learn from and maybe ally with, if they were out to get Captain Cooper.

"How soon until we're within proper scanning range?" she asked Paek.

She supposed she could look it up herself, but didn't want to take the time. She was still monitoring the flat footage off the buoys, staring at those tiny ship blobs. Only one remained on that damaged vessel.

Only one.

"We'll be able to accurately scan in maybe half an hour," Paek said.

Elissa clenched her right fist, then slowly unclenched it, one finger at a time, feeling the skin pull. Her ships wouldn't get to the Room of Lost Souls in time. She would have to track the enemy ship, while taking possession of the other, which she really didn't want to do.

She wanted to capture the active enemy vessel, the one with the crew of both ships on board. She wanted to talk with her prisoners, learn what they knew, figure out how to use them.

Figure out who they were.

But the circumstances were what they were. She had to work within what she could do, not with what she wanted to do.

"The moment we are able to do an accurate deep scan," she said, "I want it to start. I want it to measure everything from the ship movement to the energy readings to the readings in the area. I even want to monitor the Room of Lost Souls, in case the *Ivoire* placed someone there. Are we clear?"

"Yes, ma'am," Paek said. His stubby fingers immediately started putting in commands, making certain that her orders would be carried out.

She stared at that last blob, and as she did, it wobbled, then dislodged from the disabled vehicle.

She silently cursed. She had hoped that whatever the last little vessel had been doing would take a significant amount of time.

Clearly, it hadn't.

"Making sure we're tracking the intact enemy ship," she said to Paek.

"We're doing the best we can with the buoy information," he said formally, which meant that she had finally irritated him. He had, apparently, been doing what she asked before she even asked about it.

The last little vessel wobbled its way back to the attacking ship. Once the blob arrived, there was no movement for a good minute or two.

Then the attacking enemy ship moved away from the Room of Lost Souls, just like she had expected.

Elissa's heart sank. She made herself breathe and look at the positive side. That derelict ship was more than she had had when she had gotten out of bed that morning.

She was one step closer to regaining the territory she had lost to Cooper.

Then, as she watched, one of those light windows opened right near the side of the attacking enemy vessel. The attacking enemy vessel seemed to move into that window, but it hovered there for a moment, as if it couldn't quite get inside.

She let out a breath, that was irritation and elation combined. Irritation that she wouldn't be able to capture the attacking enemy vessel, but elation that she had just learned the attacker and the other ship had the same technology that the *Ivoire* did.

Which meant that the Empire's engineers could reverse engineer whatever was on that vessel, and figure out—

Light appeared around the damaged vessel, light that was the same color as the light in that window still etched around the attacking vessel.

Elissa's mouth opened. She knew, without knowing how, what was going to happen next.

The damaged ship seemed to expand, the light making the ship seem bigger than it was.

And then, the light absorbed into it. And the damaged ship seemed to vanish.

"What the—?" Paek asked.

She didn't say anything. Instead, she watched the remaining window, willing to bet on what was going to happen next.

And sure enough, what happened next was that the attacking enemy vessel moved deeper into that window. The window closed, and the attacking enemy vessel vanished.

Elissa's elation vanished as well. Her irritation turned into full-blown anger. She wanted that damaged vessel. She had been counting on it.

"Adjust the imagery from those buoys," she said to Paek. "I want to see that ship."

"There's no ship to see, ma'am." The voice didn't belong to Paek. It belonged to Bahe, from the other side of the command center. "The ship has been obliterated."

"Are you certain?" Elissa asked. After all, they didn't have proper data. Only the weak telemetry and visuals sent by the buoys.

"Yes," Bahe said. "I can enhance if you want."

Elissa shook her head. She could see, as well as anyone else, that the black and gray imagery had shifted. There was no black blob at all anymore.

And the fact that the damaged ship had exploded explained the rescue mission. No one was going to survive on that ship, because the ship was too damaged to survive.

Or was it?

"I want to see what happened again," she said to Paek.

He reversed the imagery, and she stared at the light appearing around the ship. That light seemed to start the moment that the attacking enemy vessel had made it to the window part of space.

"Did the intact ship fire on the damaged ship?" she asked.

"I'll see," Paek said as Bahe said, "Yes. I have the buoy footage from a different angle. I'll send it to your screen."

"No need," Elissa said. She needed to move. She had gone through too many emotions in the space of the past few hours. Hope that she would catch Cooper after all, maybe even defeat him. Worry that she wasn't moving fast enough. Concern that she hadn't seen the *Ivoire* after all. Fury that seven of the Empire's ships had been destroyed. Elation that she might actually learn what the *Ivoire*'s weapon was.

And now this.

She wasn't sure how to feel about this. Hence the restlessness.

She walked to Bahe's station, watched as a white light streamed from the attacking enemy vessel to the damaged vessel. There appeared to be other white lights as well, but she wasn't certain about it.

Damn the lack of deep scan.

They had information. Just not enough.

Then she was hailed by Derrida on the bridge.

"It appears that the vessels we were in pursuit of are gone," he said. Apparently he had been monitoring the buoy footage. "Shall we return to normal business?"

That was a cheeky question of him, and showed he hadn't liked this assignment in the first place.

"No," Elissa said. "We lost seven ships and a lot of lives. We'll need to investigate."

"Beg pardon, ma'am, but a hundred strong?"

"Those ships all appeared and disappeared out of nowhere," she said. "Can you guarantee that there aren't other ships nearby, about to attack more Empire vessels?"

There must have been a bit of an edge to her voice, more of an edge than she realized, because his initial response was quiet.

Then he said, "No, ma'am, I can't."

"We proceed as if those ships are still at the Room of Lost Souls," she said. "And we will approach that way as well."

"Yes, ma'am," he said, and signed off.

No one in command central spoke either. They all appeared to be staring at their consoles.

Her order wasn't out of line, so she had no idea why they all seemed tense. They had no qualms about approaching two ships with a hundred vessels, but the moment those ships seemingly vanished, they all wanted to retreat.

She wasn't ready to. She might send the other ships back as the deep scans showed an empty region of space, but no matter what the *Ewing Trekov* would get to the Room of Lost Souls.

She was going to mine whatever information she could from the area.

And she was going to pursue the *Ivoire* for violating Empire space.

She just wasn't yet sure how to go about it.

ARRIVALS

12

THE LIGHTS IN HIS BEDROOM were at full brightness. An irritating ping echoed through the room. The communications wristband he had taken to wearing to bed vibrated gently, but the vibrations were becoming more insistent.

Jonathon "Coop" Cooper flung his right arm over his eyes, then scrunched his pillows against the headboard. His mouth tasted of old socks and sour peaches, and there was a dull ache near the bridge of his nose.

The vibration on his left arm grew stronger, the pinging more insistent, and the lights became even brighter. He wasn't commanding anything right now, so technically, he didn't need to wake up quickly, but someone was trying to reach him, and the contact was urgent.

He leaned over and hit the comm button on the fake wood nightstand he hadn't yet changed out for something that was black and sleek, like the nightstand in his captain's quarters on the *Ivoire*.

This room still felt unfamiliar, even though he had lived in this apartment on the Lost Souls Corporation starbase for nearly a year now. He used to sleep in his captain's quarters on the *Ivoire* more often than not, but after his discussion with Yash last night, he wanted to stay on the starbase.

He was beginning to think of Lost Souls as home, not the *Ivoire*. He had talked with Yash about that. He had talked with her about many things, from the loss of Dix, to the fact that Coop was ready now to face the future. *This* future, in this timeline, as a citizen of this universe, not the one he'd left behind when the *Ivoire* time-traveled five thousand years away from everything they'd ever known.

He licked his lips before saying anything into the comm. His tongue felt thick and his eyes ached with the light.

It took him a moment to realize what was happening: he wasn't uncomfortable in this bedroom and the light wasn't too bright. He was hungover.

He hadn't gotten drunk like that, especially on sweet liquor, since he tried to prove that the crew of the *Arama* that he didn't deserve the nickname "Lieutenant Tightass." He half-smiled at the memory, then set it aside.

He had no idea how he looked, so he set the comm on audio only. Then he took a deep breath and answered.

"Oh, good, Captain, I was about to send someone to find you." The voice belonged to Ilona Blake, who ran the entire Lost Souls Corporation. She had never contacted him in the middle of the night, about anything.

He was instantly awake—the kind of awake that he had perfected when he was on active duty.

"What's going on?" he asked, his tone military crisp.

"The *Sove* returned about fifteen minutes ago. Unscheduled. There are problems. Salvador Ahidjo is in command. He says he will confer with us once they disembark. He's being very cagey, Coop."

Coop blinked, running through the staff of the *Sove* in his mind. The *Sove* had gone to the Boneyard, with Boss, to dive DV vessels. The *Sove* had been there for months, and had sent back several ships.

Ahidjo shouldn't be in charge. Ahidjo was a good man, but not someone Boss would choose to run the ship. If anyone ran the *Sove* when Boss was diving, it was Zaria Diaz. Coop knew Diaz was at the Boneyard, because he had spoken with her before he left on that mission to go to Sector Base E-2. He had wanted to bring as many of the original *Ivoire* crew as he could on that mission, but he ran into snags. Some of

the original crew members left service altogether, preferring to move to a landbound life or to work solely in the workshops here at Lost Souls.

A handful of members of the original crew liked working with Boss, which he only slightly understood. Much as he cared about her, he found her work methods capricious and haphazard. Neither Diaz nor Gustav Denby seemed to, though. They were in the Boneyard.

Or they were supposed to be.

And either one of them would have been better at captaining the *Sove* than Ahidjo.

Not to mention Boss herself. Technically, she and her usual crew should've been running the *Sove*.

Coop's heart constricted, and he made himself breathe again. Boss could take care of herself.

But she had nearly died on this last run, and he'd hoped she would return to Lost Souls after that. She hadn't, of course. Near-death experiences didn't scare her, any more than they scared him. Except, of course, when they involved someone he cared about.

"Any clue as to what's going on?" he asked Blake.

"None," she said. "But I need you in the conference room off Docking Bay 5 in fifteen minutes."

Fifteen minutes. That was fast. This space station was larger than the other one that the Lost Souls Corporation had been using. Blake had expanded the entire corporation this past year. Two space stations, an extra maintenance station, and now she had started negotiating for some manufacturing space on the nearby planet, Odite.

As one of the founders of Lost Souls, he'd been given this apartment, and it was in prime real estate on the space station. Far from the docking rings in an area that would become more residential, or so Blake wanted.

Coop hadn't given the location much thought, until now.

"I'll be there," he said to Blake, and signed off.

He signed off, and swung his legs out of bed, feeling a bit dizzy and disoriented. He wasn't supposed to be the person who got notified that the people he cared about were in trouble.

He was supposed to be the person who was risking his life, not drinking too much and sleeping.

Not that the drinking was normal for him. If it was, he probably would have moved faster when the notice came in.

He ran a hand through his thick black hair, grabbed some clothes out of his closet, and headed for the bathroom. By the time he got there, the headache was forgotten.

Something bad had happened at the Boneyard, and he needed to know exactly what that something was.

13

THE CONFERENCE ROOM OFF DOCKING BAY 5 was an afterthought. Smaller than most conference rooms on the station, squeezed into a narrow corridor near what had once been the service entrance into the docking bay, the conference room didn't even have windows overlooking the corridor.

Coop had been to this conference room precisely once, when Ilona Blake was thinking of buying the then-abandoned space station for an unholy amount of money. He had walked through every part of the station, looking for problems or flawed designs, looking for reasons—as she had said to him—to knock down the price or send her looking for another station altogether.

He remembered this conference room, and another like it near Docking Bay 9. He thought, someday, the Lost Souls Corporation would repurpose the entire area, and make it usable.

Right now, it wasn't usable. Not really. Lost Souls didn't have the personnel to staff all of the docking bays. Most of this space station was a ghost station, filled with empty corridors and unused maintenance rooms, set up for people who hadn't been hired yet, and maybe never would be.

The entire corridor smelled a little musty as if the environmental system here needed a good cleaning. It probably did. The automated cleaning bots could only do so much, and they were as old as the station itself.

At some point, Blake would have to spring for upgrades or shut down parts of the station she didn't plan to use. She had asked him if he wanted to help her run this thing, and he had said no. He was glad now that he had.

He pushed the conference room door open, surprised to find Blake and Salvador Ahidjo already inside. Blake stood at the head of an old conference table, one that looked like it didn't recess into the floor. The table had scratches on the surface, and the chairs alongside it were mismatched. The top was covered with half a dozen tablets, some of them Fleet issued, some of them not.

Blake had pulled her chair back, and was standing between it and the table, her fingertips resting on the top of the table, as if they helped her keep her balance. Her long black hair was piled on top of her head, giving her some added height. Even with the hair up, she was still the shortest person in the room.

Ahidjo stood on the far side of the room, hands in the pocket of the long white robe he wore. His silver-black hair stuck out all over the place. He had clearly just gone through decontamination, and he hadn't properly dried his hair. Nor had he stopped for proper clothing at his rooms here on the station.

He had come directly from the *Sove*.

Both he and Blake turned as Coop entered. "Yash on her way?" Ahidjo asked Coop.

Coop looked at Blake. Coop hadn't contacted Yash, so Blake must have.

Blake nodded. "I thought she'd be here by now."

"I don't think we can wait," Ahidjo said. He picked up one of the Fleet-issued tablets, holding it tightly in his meaty hand.

In all the years Coop had worked with Ahidjo—and that included every year Coop had spent on the *Ivoire*—he had never seen the man so agitated. Usually, Ahidjo, who was older than Coop, was unflappable.

At that moment, the door opened wider, and Yash Zarlengo pushed in. She gave Coop a sideways glance.

"This doesn't look good," she said.

She didn't look as tired as he felt. Only her red-rimmed eyes showed the effect of a lack of sleep and too much drink. She frowned at the entire room, as if everyone in it had displeased her.

She moved to the far side of the table, across from Blake.

Yash was an interesting choice to be here. She was the *Ivoire's* chief engineer, and she'd been working hard with Blake on revamping old technologies and developing new ones.

In fact, it was Yash's vision that had fueled a lot of the innovation that was making Lost Souls one of the wealthiest corporations in the sector.

Ahidjo hadn't watched Yash enter. He had picked up one of the Fleet-made tablets, and was poking at it.

His expression grew even more grim.

"All right, Salvador," Coop said. "What's going on?"

He was going to ask more questions—*Where's Boss? What happened back there?*—but he would save those until Ahidjo had a chance to explain himself.

"Boss sent the *Sove* back here." Ahidjo's fingers played with the edge of the tablet he had just set down. "We were about to dive one of the DV vessels we hoped to bring here when she let us know we had leave immediately."

"You make it sound like she wasn't on the ship," Coop said.

"She wasn't." Ahidjo glanced at Blake, then back at Coop. "She was in the SC-Class vessel, the *Veilig*. Along with her team, and Zaria."

Coop glanced at Blake, who was chewing on her lower lip. It was a nervous habit, one he wasn't even sure she knew about.

Blake knew something about Boss, something she hadn't told Coop.

But Coop wasn't going to deal with that yet. He was going to find out what was happening, and he knew if he quizzed Ahidjo, he'd get the answers he wanted, without Blake getting in the way.

Yash's frown had grown deeper. "She was doing something she shouldn't have been, wasn't she?" Yash asked.

"She owns the corporation," Blake said, and her tone was defensive. "She's the one running the Boneyards mission. She—"

"What the hell did she need an SC-Class vessel for?" Yash asked.

"It doesn't matter." Ahidjo raised his voice. Coop wasn't sure he had ever heard Ahidjo yell. "They should have been right behind us."

Coop's stomach twisted.

"From the beginning, Salvador," Coop said.

"We don't have time for that," Ahidjo said. "Here's what I know. We were getting ready to dive the ship when Boss contacted me. She didn't sound panicked but she…"

He glanced at Yash, as if he wanted to say something else, and then changed his mind.

"She was businesslike, crisp. I'd never heard her like that before," he said.

Coop had. On a couple of missions. Boss had an internal place that shut off all panic and made her very clear-thinking. She went there in an emergency. She was very logical and cold, and sometimes quite harsh.

"She said that there were five ships outside of the Boneyard, and they had destroyed our buoys." Ahidjo picked up the tablet again. "I checked. She was right. The five ships—they were mostly DV-Class vessels, but of a kind I'd never seen before."

"Mostly?" Blake asked.

Coop waved a hand. He wasn't going to let this conversation go sideways again.

"Then what happened, Salvador?" he asked.

"She told us to leave immediately. To make sure everyone was on board and get the hell out of the Boneyard, to come here."

"To get help?" Blake asked.

Coop shot her an annoyed look. This wasn't the time for her to establish that she was in charge. When it came to any kind of crisis, especially one that might need real military intervention, he was the person who needed to be in charge.

He would discuss that with her later.

"That's what I asked her," Ahidjo said. "You want us to bring back help? And Boss got mad and told me to get the hell out of there right then. She said she'd be right behind us. But she's not here yet."

Coop's heart started to pound hard. Boss lost in foldspace in an unfamiliar vehicle was the last thing he wanted her to experience. But he didn't need to get ahead of himself here.

"And," Ahidjo said, looking at Coop, "there are two more things you need to know, maybe three."

Coop stiffened ever so slightly. He didn't like the sound of that.

"As we left the Boneyard," Ahidjo said, "there was all kinds of activity. Ships were…I don't know how to say it. Activating? I'm not sure, exactly. We have some of it in our database, but I haven't looked it over yet."

"Activating," Yash muttered.

Coop took one deep breath, calming himself. He needed to get to that same internal place Boss had gone to before she sent Ahidjo away. He needed to be calm, logical, thoughtful.

He would consider the implications of an active Boneyard in a minute.

"Ilona," he said, "you'll need to activate Lost Souls' defensives."

"I will," she said.

"*Now*," he said.

She glared at him, and for a moment, it looked like she was going to say something about being the person in charge of Lost Souls. Then she nodded, moved away from the table, and headed into the corridor.

Another strike against this damn old station. It apparently didn't have a good communication system in the conference rooms.

"What was Boss doing in that ship?" Coop asked.

Ahidjo's lips thinned. He clutched the tablet so hard his knuckles turned white. "She found a protected area inside the Boneyard. Another forcefield."

"And she was looking into it," Coop said. Because he knew her. Because something like that would be the kind of temptation she couldn't resist.

"The system destroyed a few probes," Ahidjo said, "and just before those ships showed up, that forcefield blew up a runabout."

Yash leaned forward, clearly startled. "With someone on it?" she asked.

"Deliberately empty," Ahidjo said.

"Boss was trying to check system response," Coop said.

"More or less." Ahidjo swallowed. "But what you have to know, one of the things I was going to tell you, is that there were ships behind that forcefield. Hundreds, maybe a thousand ships."

"There are ships all over the Boneyard," Yash said before Coop could speak. "So what?"

"These ships are intact," Ahidjo said. "And I'd never seen any like them before. We were able to get a look, thanks to a probe, and the ships—well, our databases say they're some kind of warship...?"

Coop let out a breath. "Fleet?" he asked.

"Yes," Ahidjo said.

Warships. He knew about them, had even been offered a track to work them, not long after he returned from serving on the *Arama*. But he'd been married at that point, and one of the requirements was that he would take himself out of the standard Fleet and into the secret Ready Ship program.

He would have to leave his family behind. He only had Mae, but at that point, they were thinking about children, and she was a linguist, not a job that would have traveled to the warship program.

So he passed.

He thought about that sometimes. Because if he hadn't married her so young, he might have taken the other path. And if he had, he wouldn't have ended up here, five thousand years in his own future.

His silence must have been noticeable. Yash shot a glance at him before saying, "You think the Boneyard attacked Boss's ship because she was trying to breach that forcefield?"

"I have no idea," Ahidjo said. He was poking at the tablet again. "But she's not here yet, and I expected her to be right behind me."

"Boss doesn't always do what you expect," Coop said.

"And foldspace doesn't always work the way you want it to," Yash said quietly.

Both Coop and Ahidjo looked at her. She shrugged ever so slightly, as if to say, *You both know what I mean.* And they did.

So Yash was thinking something similar to what Coop was thinking.

He didn't like the ideas that they both had.

The door opened, and Blake came back in. "We're setting up the defenses now. But I want you to look at it, Coop. We're using conventional defenses. I worry about setting up too much, if Boss is coming back. She—"

"She's here!" Ahidjo said. He was staring at the tablet. Apparently, he saw the *Veilig*'s arrival.

Coop wanted to snatch the tablet from Ahidjo's hands. It took all of Coop's self-control not to do that.

"Is she being followed?" Coop asked, and then cursed. Enough of this guessing. He didn't need it, and he wasn't the kind of person who could handle it.

He waved a hand—and not even he was sure what he meant by that gesture. Goodbye? Never mind? All of the above?—as he pivoted and headed for the door.

The Docking Bay held two DV-Class vessels. One of them, the *Madxaf*, was a fairly new rebuild. Lynda Rooney had captained it to the Boneyard. The *Madxaf* was as up to date as a ship got around here, and Coop was going to use that.

He sprinted down the narrow corridor, and flung open the service door into the Docking Bay. If Boss was coming out of foldspace now, and if some Fleet vessel—or some other vessel—was following her, it would arrive only a few minutes later.

Docking Bay 5 looked unbelievably empty. It was set up for dozens of large ships, permanent vessels, not the ones that would attach to the docking ring outside the space station.

But there were still very few vessels in Lost Souls. They'd been gathering some, but not too many large ships. The corporation did not have the personnel to man all these large ships, and what people they did have didn't always have the right training.

The cavernous space seemed to go on for miles, but Coop knew that was a result of the emptiness. The light-gray floors reflected the gray walls, which barely absorbed the dark catwalks and equipment that waited for ships to dock near them.

He leapt onto one of the catwalks that should have gone around some of the vessels, but for the moment just hung into space. His footsteps echoed as he ran across the metal surface.

Then he realized that the noise was odd, more than an echo. He didn't have to turn to know who was behind him.

Yash.

But he turned anyway, and saw that it wasn't just Yash, but Ahidjo. His robe was tangling around his legs, and his sandaled feet weren't really clad for this kind of effort.

But he seemed to be making some really good time, just like Coop and Yash were. Ahidjo split away from Coop and Yash, and headed back to the *Sove* where, presumably, his crew was still inside, going through arrival procedures.

Ahidjo understood the urgency as well. If Boss wasn't alone, then all of Lost Souls was in danger.

The *Madxaf* was on the opposite side of the docking bay from the *Sove*. Ahidjo looked like a small berobed religious leader as he scurried across the catwalks to his ship.

Coop ran toward the *Madxaf*, which got larger and larger the closer he came. He reached the front of the vessel, waved his hand with its identification so that a ramp would slide out of the nearest entrance, and sure enough, one did.

He sprinted up it, and shouted, "Emergency procedures. Captain Jonathon Cooper," and rattled off his identification password, opened his eyes as wide as he could, and hoped the ship could do a physical screening while he was moving.

Sometimes the Fleet tech didn't properly survive the upgrades.

"Yash Zarlengo," she called from behind him, reciting her password, and holding up her hand.

Backup, then, which they desperately needed.

The entrance door slid up. He bolted inside. The interior airlock door slid into the pocket to its left, opening the hallway. The ship knew it was in dry dock, and didn't make them go through extra procedures.

The door opened onto deck three of the *Madxaf*, which was far enough from the bridge that Coop decided to go for one of the backup command consoles rather than run to the bridge. If the interior layout remained the same as it had when this ship was brought to Lost Souls, he was closest to the captain's mess.

He took the right fork in the corridor ahead of him, hurried down one of the ramps to the recreational deck, and sprinted past the regular mess, which still smelled faintly of coffee.

The officer's mess was closed and locked, and the captain's mess, just beyond it, wasn't even visible. Coop's throat constricted for just a moment, wondering if the haters of hierarchy here at Lost Souls had done away with the captain's mess altogether.

Then he remembered that when a DV-Class vessel was shut down, the captain's mess wasn't visible to the naked eye.

He stopped where the door should be and slammed his palm against the nearest wall. It warmed beneath his touch and then, in a sultry female voice, said, "Welcome, Captain Cooper. We'll—"

"Just let me in," he snapped, and the door slid open, revealing a dark nearly empty space.

He didn't care that the tables were recessed or the lighting was set at dim. He didn't care that there were no food smells here at all and no food stations either.

He just wanted the tertiary command center, and if he was right it would be—

"Over here." Yash was at the far wall, and he had no idea how she had gotten there without him seeing her. "You have to open the damn thing. I'm not listed as flight engineer for the *Madxaf*."

He wasn't listed as captain either, and he hoped that wouldn't be a problem. But he snapped, "Emergency procedures, Captain Jonathon Cooper—"

And before he even got to the password the tertiary command center door slid upward, revealing a narrow room with two stools and a control console that had just started to boot up.

He hurried inside, took the stool farthest from the door, and surrounded himself with holoscreens. He programmed the screens to show the entire 360-degree view around every part of Lost Souls, including this space station, and the small base that they had used from the beginning. On another screen he called up the view from the border between the Empire and the Nine Planets, just in case something strange was happening there.

The screens showed him the forcefield that Blake had set up around the space station and her docking ring, as well as the forcefield around the old base. The forcefields were new. They hadn't been tested.

Yash had put together a team after the battle at the border with the Empire to use Fleet technology to form a forcefield around the entire Lost Souls Corporation. But Yash hadn't worked on the forcefield; she had supervised it while helping him find out what was going on with the Fleet.

Now, he regretted pulling her from the forcefield project. He didn't have faith in the ability of engineers he didn't know, hired to cobble together Fleet tech with old tech from one of the Nine Planets.

Besides, if Boss's ship—the *Veilig*—got through those forcefields, then some ship (or ships) following her through foldspace would get through as well.

Coop checked the weapons system built into the old base. Jason Xilvii had used that system to good effect against ships from the Empire about ten months ago—before the forcefields were installed.

Coop cursed at himself. He had stopped thinking about Lost Souls defenses while he was focused on searching for the Fleet. He had fallen down on a very important job.

"What?" Yash asked. She was sitting on the stool next to him, her narrow face barely visible through the holoscreens he had surrounded himself in.

"We haven't tested our damn defenses," he said. "I have no idea if all this tech is compatible with any of the other tech."

She cursed, a lot longer and more creatively than he had. "I'm being pulled in too many directions," she said.

"I'm not blaming you, Yash," he said, searching for Boss's ship in the area around Lost Souls.

"You don't have to blame me," she said. "I'm doing a good enough job for both of us."

Her hands were moving on the screens between them, some gold and red colors from the screens she had called up reflecting on her face. Seen through layers of holograms, her face seemed insubstantial. She looked like a ghost of herself as she worked.

"Blake's talking to her," Yash said.

Coop cursed. He didn't want Boss distracted. He wanted her to bring the damn ship, whatever it was, into Lost Souls, and then he would power up the old defenses as well.

Something crackled, and then Blake's voice echoed overhead: … *have a debrief in a few hours. That should give you time to go through all of the arrival procedures.*

Blake wasn't thinking clearly either, but then, she wasn't a military commander. She ran a corporation.

Coop scanned all of his screens searching for the new arrival. He searched, not quite sure what kind of ship he was dealing with.

"Found her," Yash said, and pushed the image of an SC-Class vessel toward him, along with the coordinates.

All right. Boss's voice filled the tiny narrow room. Coop's heart jumped. *I can't wait to see you all.*

He couldn't wait to see her either. But he had to make sure she—and Lost Souls—was safe first.

The image Yash had sent him was on a holoscreen that knifed through two other screens so that it could float in front of him. The ship Boss was traveling in was, as advertised, an SC-Class vessel, but not of a kind he had served in.

It was rounder than the older models, and it glimmered with rebuilt newness. Even though lights were on throughout the ship, many of them were dim, letting someone who knew Fleet procedure know that the ship was understaffed.

Judging by those dim lights, the ship had almost no staffing at all. Which matched what Ahidjo had told him. SC-Class vessels held roughly five hundred people. This thing—the *Veilig*—probably had less than twenty.

Coop scanned the area around the *Veilig*, but saw nothing.

"Do you know where they came in?" Coop asked.

"Yeah," Yash said. "I've found the foldspace window coordinates. I'm monitoring them. I'm also doing as deep a scan as I can to see if something arrived before the *Veilig*."

He half-smiled. He never had to tell Yash what to do. She was always five steps ahead of him.

He opened a channel to the *Veilig*. "Hey," he said, following his practice of not calling her "Boss" like everyone else did. "It's great to hear your voice."

"Captain Cooper," Boss said, sounding pleased. "My comm says you're on the *Madxaf*. What's that about?"

"Making sure you weren't followed," he said. "I need you to come to Docking Bay 5. I'm sending coordinates now."

"I know where Docking Bay 5 is," Boss said. "Or rather, Zaria does. I don't think I've seen that part of the space station."

She barely toured the main parts of it before she headed off to the Boneyard. She had no interest in anything permanent, not sector bases, not land-based cities, not starbases or, apparently, space stations bought with money her corporation had earned.

"I need you here now," Coop said. "We need your ship secured immediately."

"Okay, Captain!" Boss laughed. "See you in a few minutes."

It would take longer than a few minutes to get to Docking Bay 5. More proof that she didn't know the entire layout.

"Does she sound odd to you?" Yash asked.

He nodded. He had gotten so caught up in the sound of her voice that he had missed her tone.

It was upbeat, almost giddy. Something had excited her. Something had pleased her.

And, knowing Boss, that something wasn't predictable. It was something she discovered or something that she had learned or something that required a whole lot of work to recover.

Whatever he had expected from his mad run to the docking bay, giddiness on the part of Boss wasn't it.

"What do you think she found?" Yash asked. Yash didn't know Boss as well as he did, but Yash knew her, and Yash knew how to parse moods.

"I have no idea," Coop said. "But I think we're about to find out."

14

THE BRIDGE OF THE *VEILIG* IS ODDLY SILENT. I would have thought everyone would be relieved to be at the Lost Souls Corporation, but I'm not sensing relief. I'm sensing concern.

The bridge curves downward, with consoles and the exit behind me. The captain's chair is to my left—I've moved aside so that Zaria Diaz can access the captain's command center. I want her to dock the ship with the space station.

Diaz is small and her dark hair is mussed, which is unusual for her. But she's been working for nearly twenty-four hours straight. Her belongings were on the *Sove*. She had initially come to the *Veilig* to help us with some work in the Boneyard.

She did not expect to ride all the way back to Lost Souls with us.

She isn't paying a lot of attention to me, or to anyone else. She has a small frown on her face, and she's moving her hands rapidly along the navigation screen, trying to get us to the Docking Bay.

I haven't ever docked an SC-Class vessel in a space station—any space station—and I'm not all that interested in learning how. Now that we're back at Lost Souls, I'm ready to do some research, figure out what just happened, and talk to Coop.

He sounded stressed when he contacted us, and his mood seems to have infected the entire team. Mikk has called up an extra holoscreen, his bald head bent forward as he goes over the telemetry.

Orlando is leaning to his right, watching Diaz work. Roderick and Tamaz are whispering, something about telemetry. Fahd has moved beside Denby, and they are discussing weapons.

Only Nyssa meets my gaze, and hers is filled with concern. She's still standing near the exit, so she looks taller than she actually is. Her dark hair is tangled as well, even though it's shorter than Diaz's.

We all look like we've been through an emergency. I'm sure my hair is spiked upwards. I tend to run my hands through it when I'm not paying attention.

"Coop seems to think we might have been followed," I say to the entire team. "Let's double-check."

We had checked twice before—right after we went into foldspace, and then as we were traveling through it. But double-checking doesn't hurt.

"I thought we were in the clear." That's Nyssa, who still has a thread of panic in her voice.

If we were followed, we might have been followed by a group of vessels that I greatly expect are affiliated with the Fleet. The real Fleet.

The modern Fleet.

The one Coop has been searching for since he arrived in his own future.

"We didn't see anyone," Denby says to Nyssa. He half turns toward her, his posture perfect. That's a sign of his Fleet training. Everyone who served on the *Ivoire* and came to their own future with Coop has that perfect posture.

Nyssa gives Denby an uncomfortable smile, but he doesn't smile in return.

He adds, "The fact that we didn't see anyone doesn't always mean anything."

And there's a subtext to his words.

I keep forgetting about the ways that foldspace can mess with time. Even though the very first thing we did when we arrived back here at Lost Souls was to make sure that our timeline corresponded with the one being broadcast from the station itself. Diaz told me, rather breathlessly, we hadn't lost time.

But any ship that followed us into foldspace might have lost time. Each ship's experience in foldspace is different from every other ship's.

I understand foldspace even less than the officers of the Fleet do. They, at least, have studied foldspace since their days at the academy. The engineers seem to know it best of all—even though no one in the Fleet really understands it either.

I should be upset that we're traveling long distances using technology that no one seems to understand fully, but I'm not. I've messed with technology I don't understand from the very beginning of my career. Half of my early dives have been to explore ancient tech and old ships, and occasionally I activated those ships, not entirely understanding what I was doing.

That is, in essence, what I was doing in the Boneyard.

I'm still not sure whether or not that has backfired on us.

"You're watching for any arrivals out of foldspace, right?" I ask Fahd. He raises his dark eyes toward me for just a moment, his lips thin.

He's as worried about this as Coop seems to be. And Fahd is a member of my team. He's never been stuck in foldspace, or pursued by enemy vessels—that I know of. Although he was part of the group that had to flee Vaycehn quickly years ago.

The week we met Coop.

So much to worry about, and yet, I'm not as worried as everyone around me. Sometimes that's a problem. And it's on me. I get too excited about what I'm doing.

I let out a breath, and watch the screens around us as Diaz guides the *Veilig* toward the space station. It still doesn't quite compute in my head that Lost Souls owns both the space station and the base in this region of space.

I own them, since Lost Souls is mine. Ilona Blake tells me I'm fabulously wealthy, and I don't care. A number of people, Ilona included, tell me I should pay more attention to the money so that no one steals it from me, but I can't think of something I'm less interested in. It's not so much that I trust Ilona as that she's doing all the work I don't care about.

If she doesn't do it, it's not going to get done. I'm diving again, and I adore that. I'm not interested in running a corporation filled with people.

I did that for a few years after we established Lost Souls here at the Nine Planets, and I was never that unhappy before in my entire life.

Although now, maybe, my diving has jeopardized the place that I have built. From my diving.

The *Veilig* travels slower than I would like, crossing the short area between our arrival coordinates and the open bay doors at what I can only assume is Docking Bay Five. Five. Which means there are several more.

I should probably have looked at those specs.

I fold my hands together, trying to ignore my pounding heart. I still have the gids—just a little—and I want them to go away before I talk with Coop.

I've been thinking about what to tell him from the moment the *Veilig* entered foldspace. I have no idea how he's going to react to what happened to us in the Boneyard.

I suspect he'll see the events in the Boneyard like I do—as confirmation that the Fleet still exists. He's been searching for them for nearly six years. He'll probably be pleased.

And that thought makes my heart sink. Because I don't want to lose Coop to the Fleet, especially a Fleet that is five thousand years removed from the one he knew.

I make myself take a deep calming breath. What Coop does with the information I give him is not my problem. Our relationship is based on each one of us living our lives separately and coming together when we can.

We have never promised to spend our lives with each other. Even if the lives we were living accommodated that—and I'm not sure they do—we're not the kind of people who can live up to that kind of promise.

I don't want to make one like that, and I know he doesn't either.

Still, it would break my heart to have him leave Lost Souls.

The *Veilig* enters the docking bay. Landing a large ship inside one of these bays is a trick that requires a finesse I don't have.

I'm a good pilot—with small ships, in space. I can get small ships in and out of almost any situation they find themselves in. I'm an even better diver.

But getting a ship of this size—one that is built for a crew of five hundred—into a space station originally built for thousands, and being converted into some kind of factory/warehouse/manufacturing station is beyond me.

Still, I stand slightly behind Diaz so I can watch her. I've learned over the years that the greater my understanding of skills I don't have, the better off I am. If I understand the principles of something, I can sometimes make that something work—or at least figure out who on my team would be the best at doing that something.

Right now, Diaz is the best for this task. She is using one hand to guide the *Veilig* into the space station, while flipping back and forth between changing telemetry from the bay doors.

She's adjusting them—making them slightly wider to accommodate the ship.

One of the screens to my side shows the bay doors. They look small on the side of the space station, which only shows how vast the station itself is. It's got more levels than I can count from the exterior. When I've approached a space station somewhere else, I've counting the stacked lights, but there aren't a lot of people in this station, so some floors have no lighting at all.

In fact, the station looks slightly creepy. The top and bottom of it—at least from the direction that we're approaching—have no lights at all. So they're outlined by the exterior lights only. The exterior lights show the station's oblong shape, but the upper levels and the lower levels are a ghostly gray.

Only the lights in the middle show any life in the station.

Diaz glides the *Veilig* toward those open doors. The area that we're supposed to enter grows wider as we get closer.

I glance at Orlando, and he knows what I'm asking.

"Not seeing anything yet, Boss," he says.

Nothing coming out of foldspace. We're okay, then.

The *Veilig* enters the bay. Up close, we have a lot of clearance on all sides. But what startles me—and shouldn't—is how much emptiness there is inside that bay.

I've landed on space stations countless times, and they're always filled to the brim with ships and cargo and people.

Here, no other ships are immediately visible. Lighting and coordinates guide Diaz as she moves the ship toward a dock. There are catwalks everywhere, and they look small compared to the *Veilig*.

It's as if we've entered an abandoned space station instead of a working one.

And I suppose that's partially true.

We're modifying the station so that we can build ships here and modify Fleet technology so that we can sell it throughout the Nine Planets. That operation is what Ilona oversees, and what she loves.

That's why I put her in charge, so I don't have to think about any of it.

The ship's movement is so slight that I can't feel it any longer. The only reason that I know it has stopped is because the images I'm seeing through the various screens do not show us hitting catwalks and walls.

I let out a sigh, and immediately the gids leave.

The adventure at the Boneyard is over. We're at Lost Souls now. Lost Souls, which I associate with hard unpleasant work. The moment I get here—even in this space station I barely know—I want to leave.

"Ilona said we have to go through arrival procedures." Mikk's tone is dry, but I know what's beneath it. He doesn't like "procedures" any more than I do. "She means all of it, doesn't she?"

"It is prudent." Diaz is closing screens, as well as making notations on the navigation screen. "We were in that Boneyard and foldspace and we were under attack."

"Yeah." Somehow Mikk made that short word even shorter. "You want us all to stay?"

I'm not sure if he's asking me or Diaz.

"I need one other person," she said. "It probably should be Gustav."

Probably because he had been Fleet and didn't mind regulations. Although I don't ask.

"I've got some data to examine anyway," Denby says. He's not even looking up. "I don't mind."

Mikk raises his eyebrows. The idea of not-minding about regulations is as foreign to him as it is to me.

"I can't go through decontamination for you, though," Denby says.

"I didn't ask you to," Mikk says.

I turn ever so slightly, so that I can see Denby's face. He's half-hidden behind the holoscreens, but there's a small curve to his lips that hadn't been there before.

He's deliberately goading Mikk. That's new. I'd thought their inability to get along was pure Mikk, but apparently it isn't. Apparently, Denby likes to get a rise out of Mikk. And apparently, it doesn't take a lot of effort.

"Thanks, Zaria," I say, then nod at Denby. "Gustav."

"We'll have this wrapped up before the debrief," Diaz says.

"And I'll bring data," Denby says. He lifts his gaze over the edge of one of the holoscreens, and I suddenly understand what he's doing.

He knows his Fleet compatriots better than I do, even after being around them for almost six years.

They're all going to want data. They're going to want to see what happened in the Boneyard for themselves.

They're going to want confirmation of what we already understand.

They're going to want to interpret it their way.

My heart lurches. That down mood which started the moment the doors closed on the docking bay grows darker.

I spent the last half of the mission in the Boneyard feeling angry at Coop. He and Yash had found a shutdown Fleet Sector Base and had visited it without telling me about it, even though they had informed everyone who had served on the *Ivoire*, including Denby and Diaz.

And now I have news for him that I hadn't exactly shared with him either. News that will most likely change everything.

Suddenly, I don't want to leave this ship. We made the right call coming back here, but if I could, I'd leave immediately to dive somewhere else.

Mikk claps a hand on my shoulder, startling me. He peers at me.

"You going to be all right?" he asks quietly.

"We left a lot of mysteries back at that Boneyard," I say.

"We did," he says. "And maybe, if we're lucky, we can go back to them."

If we're lucky.

Which I doubt will be any time soon.

15

THE *VEILIG* DOCKED ON THE OTHER SIDE of the docking bay, about as far from the *Madxaf* as possible. Coop left Yash in the *Madxaf's* tertiary control room, still monitoring for any ship that might arrive out of foldspace. He also contacted Xilvii, who was running the Lost Souls Corporation's defenses, and warned him that there might be vessels following the *Veilig*.

Coop stressed that those vessels all had to go through foldspace, so Xilvii understood: the ships might be coming, but they might be hours delayed.

Coop's heart was pounding hard. He was relieved the *Veilig* had arrived safely, with no ship arriving moments later, but he was also on edge. He needed to talk to Boss and that wouldn't be an easy discussion.

He stepped onto the catwalk outside of the *Madxaf*. The catwalk bounced beneath his feet. The air—colder than it had been an hour before—smelled tangy, the way it often did around a ship that had just arrived from foldspace.

He had no idea what that odor was, but it was comforting to him. He'd been around ships forever, and foldspace just as long, and as unpredictable as it was, it was still something that was familiar, one of the few constants in his life.

He sprinted across the docking bay, knowing it would take time for the crew to disembark. They had to leave and get to decontamination, and if he met up with them, he'd have to go through decontamination too, but he wanted to see Boss before the official meeting with Blake.

Considering all that had happened in the Boneyard—none of which Boss had told him—she might not want to see him unless there was a crowd around. She usually wanted to avoid difficult conversations, and if she couldn't avoid them, she wanted to have them only once.

The *Veilig* gleamed in the dim lighting. That gleam usually meant that a nanobit exterior was resetting itself after a difficult journey through foldspace. Ships like the *Veilig* were built to test their own systems and rebuild what was necessary. Sometimes long journeys like the one the *Veilig* had just taken caused the exterior of the ship to be pockmarked with tiny cracks and holes. The ship's systems always repaired that.

He had just reached the side of the bay with the ship, when a ramp emerged from one of the exterior doors. He wouldn't be able to get to the bottom of that ramp quickly, and he didn't want to miss Boss. So, instead of heading to the *Veilig*, he pivoted and made his way across bouncy catwalks to the closest side door, the one that was flashing a sign saying that decontamination was required.

The first person off the *Veilig* was Nyssa Quinte. She was talking over her shoulder to Fahd Al-Nasir. Behind him, Orlando Rea came down, looking uncomfortable. Tamaz, whose last name Coop had never learned (if he even had one), followed, also looking uncomfortable.

Then Mikk, Boss's right hand on some of these missions, her accomplice on some of the dumber stuff she'd done, stalked down the ramp. He did not look happy.

Coop stood at the exit, arms crossed, as the team headed toward him.

He felt a bit uncomfortable, surprised that Boss hadn't left yet. She usually handed off things like required shut-down protocols to others, and she had two good team members who could handle such fussy requirements—Gustav Denby and Zaria Diaz.

But, just as Coop had that thought, Boss emerged from the door. She looked smaller than he'd ever seen her, as if some of the life had drained from her. She had sounded almost joyful when he talked to her, so he wasn't sure what had changed in the last half hour.

She stopped at the top of the ramp and surveyed the docking bay, as if she'd never seen it before, which she probably hadn't. Then she sighed visibly, and walked down, her back hunched.

Coop started toward her, which caught the attention of the rest of her team. Nyssa smiled at him, and Tamaz nodded. Orlando also nodded—those two were so alike it made Coop uncomfortable—and Fahd touched a finger to his forehead in greeting. Coop nodded at all of them, acknowledging their greetings.

Mikk glared at Coop, and that look sent a shiver through him. Mikk's reaction to him probably presaged Boss's. She was upset with him, and Coop wasn't quite sure why.

He said hello to all of them as he passed.

Boss had stopped at the base of the ramp.

For a moment, Coop wasn't sure if she had seen him. Then she lifted her head and her eyes met his. Her expression seemed guarded, and then she smiled.

The smile lit up her entire face, making her eyes sparkle. She looked younger and prettier every time she smiled like that—which wasn't very often.

He walked faster, smiling in relief. Maybe she wasn't upset with him. Maybe she was just tired.

Or maybe she was scared.

Although he had never seen Boss well and truly scared. Alarmed, worried, overly confident, but never scared.

But he knew that no matter how well a strong person hid their fear, they still experienced it at times. He had tried to keep his at bay when the *Ivoire* got becalmed in foldspace, and confronted it just a bit when he realized he and his crew would be five thousand years in their future, maybe forever.

Boss and her team had left the Boneyard in a hurry. And the situation they had left, from what little he gleaned from Ahidjo, had been a bad one.

Boss didn't come to Coop. She waited for him, and when he arrived at her side, he enveloped her in a hug.

For a moment, he thought she wasn't going to return it. But she slipped her arms around him, and rested her head on his shoulder, sighing ever so softly.

Her body felt unfamiliar. They hadn't seen each other in months. If anything, she seemed smaller than she had before. Thinner, as if she hadn't been eating. And a little brittle, as if he squeezed too hard, he might break her.

He never thought of Boss as breakable before.

They leaned on each other. Coop closed his eyes, realizing how much he missed this, how much he had missed her. They had kept their relationship casual because it suited them, but underneath that lack of defined formality was an intensity he didn't really want to tap.

That intensity could encourage him to make the wrong choices.

Still he pulled her even closer and buried his face in her hair. Her scent, beneath the sharp clean smell of the soap she always used, was both familiar and welcoming.

He had missed her, more than he wanted to admit.

She pulled out of the hug before he did. She put her hands on his biceps, then looked up at him. She had circles under her eyes which, for most people, would signify deep worry, but Boss often lost sleep when she was running dives—not because she was worried about what would happen but because she was so excited about what she might learn.

He smiled a little to soften his words. "You gonna tell me about your adventures in the Boneyard."

She didn't smile back. "If you tell me about your adventures at Sector Base E-2."

So she knew, and she wasn't happy with him. He probably shouldn't have been surprised. He had asked the others who had served on the *Ivoire* not to tell her about that mission, letting them know that he wanted to tell her. But he had put off telling her for weeks about what he and Yash had found in the research, not wanting to distract Boss while she was diving.

And then he put the mission together to go to E-2, thinking he could report to her when he got back. Which was only a few days ago.

He had put that off, by telling himself that he needed to process what he had seen, that they had to go through the data.

But the truth was, he didn't want to tell Boss anything about it, and she knew that. That's probably why her voice had such an edge.

Besides, the present and former crew of the *Ivoire* weren't the only ones who had known he was going.

Blake had known, and she worked for Boss, not him.

Others learned about it as well, only after he and Yash had come back.

"It seems like we have a lot of catching up to do," Coop said to Boss, trying to keep it light.

But she was having none of that. She let her hands drop. "Yeah, it does," she said. "It seems like you found evidence of your Fleet."

"And it sounds like you found the Fleet." His words sounded sharper than he intended.

"Maybe," she said. And then she grinned at him, which surprised him. It was almost as if a joy lived inside her, one she couldn't repress.

She shook her head, the grin still there, her eyes far away.

"You should have seen it, Coop," she said. "The entire Boneyard lit up. Ships all around us, activated."

He didn't see that as a cause for joy, but he knew better than to say so.

"I had no idea they could do that," she said. "They were all empty, but something activated them. I want to know what that is. And the Boneyard itself—it has so many secrets. I want to know what they are as well."

Then her grin faded, and her gaze met his again.

"But I may not get the chance, though, right?" she said. "It's going to be too dangerous."

Her mood was infectious. He felt his mood lift, although—he knew—some of that was from seeing her.

"We don't know," he said. "Right now, they probably thought you were invaders."

"Thieves," she said, "which, technically, I am."

"But we're not," he said. "The Fleet is the Fleet is the Fleet."

Or it was when he was part of it.

"No way to know if that was the Fleet," she said. "Although Fahd believes we can analyze the data we have to figure that out."

"Ships approached you?" Coop asked.

"Ships approached the Boneyard," Boss said. "We saw five before they destroyed the buoys."

"Not pirate ships?" Coop asked. They had run into pirates around that Boneyard before—when they had first found the Boneyard. Then Coop had thought that massive ship graveyard was there because of a war. Once the team started diving it and going through information found on the abandoned ships, he learned that Boneyards—Scrapheaps—had been left all over areas that the Fleet had traveled to.

No one on the *Ivoire* had known about Scrapheaps, though, because apparently, Scrapheaps were need-to-know.

Maybe he would have learned about them if he had taken the warship track, and learned to command Ready Vessels.

"I don't know if they were pirate ships," Boss said. "We're assuming they weren't, because the ships inside the Boneyard acted as one unit. That's why I'm thinking Fleet."

Coop nodded, his emotions tangled. That odd joy was still there, along with confusion. He had just decided after this last trip to accept that his future was here, at Lost Souls. He would build his own fleet, and live out the rest of his days here, guarding this place.

He had accepted the loss of the Fleet, the loss of everything he had known. The remains of Sector Base E-2, taken over by the Not-Fleet, whoever they were, had shown him—in ways that other things hadn't—just how much time had passed.

And now, this. The Fleet—at least what Boss thought was the Fleet—appearing at the Boneyard, defending it.

Which…his Fleet wouldn't have done. Would it?

Boss could see something on his face, because her eyebrows came together in a very small frown.

"Before you make any decisions," she said, "we'll need to talk."

He bristled. They hadn't made claims on each other, so she didn't have a say on his decision-making at all.

Then he made a note of that reaction and set it aside. He needed to listen right now, instead of react. She knew more about what was happening at the Boneyard than he did.

And she had no idea what he or the *Ivoire* had experienced at Sector Base E-2. He would have to explain it to her, show her that there were a lot of other dangers in this part of the universe besides the Empire and some pirates near the Boneyard.

And maybe, the Fleet.

That idea made him breathless.

"Yeah," he said. "We need to talk. We don't even know if you're out of danger yet."

"No one followed us through foldspace," she said.

"That you know of," he said.

"Zaria believes we would have seen them," Boss said.

"Maybe," Coop said. "Foldspace is never straightforward."

Boss nodded. She knew that, but she didn't know it. She had a healthy respect for foldspace, but she hadn't been raised around it, didn't know its intricacies.

Coop didn't know all of them either, but he was used to foldspace and its unpredictability. He was used to the idea that it would surprise him, often when he least expected it.

He held out his hand to her. Boss looked at it for a moment.

"I haven't gone through decontamination yet," she said.

"I've been talking to you long enough that I'll have to go through it too," Coop said.

She laughed then, startling him. "Wow," she said. "Either you really want to know what's going on, or you care more than you've admitted. *I* wouldn't go through decontamination if I didn't have to."

He held out his hand to her. "Some sacrifices are worthwhile," he said. "Some sacrifices are more than worthwhile."

THE ROOM OF LOST SOULS

16

ONE HUNDRED SHIPS CONVERGED on the Room of Lost Souls. The ships lined up in formation, each squadron twenty strong.

They all waited, just out of range of the abandoned space station, until all of the squadrons had arrived. Then they moved toward the station and surrounded it.

Elissa had issued those orders for the arrival. The deep space scans that the *Ewing Trekov* had conducted showed nothing around the station except bits of her seven ships, blown up by a single enemy vessel, and then the remains of another enemy vessel, in pieces too small to register except as foreign matter in a sea of debris.

The space station—the Room of Lost Souls—had no gravity well, and there were no planets nearby. Nothing that gathered and allowed the debris to form a ring or anything more than a cloud of metal and blood and bone.

A lot of lives were lost here just a few hours ago. Too many lives.

Not counting all the lives that had been lost here the first time Elissa had encountered Captain Cooper of the *Ivoire*.

Only this time, he hadn't even stayed for the destruction.

She stood in the command center on the *Ewing Trekov*, the muscles in her back spasming. Some of that was because of the tension this fight had caused, but some of it was just being here. She'd had the required counseling. She'd done the emotional work, even after the losses. She'd even convinced one counselor it was in her best interest to hang onto her scars.

But being here, where she had nearly died, made little shivers run up and down Elissa's spine.

The other ninety-nine ships didn't help. They seemed like potential victims of Cooper, rather than a force that could defeat him.

Elissa knew she was allowing her imagination to gift him with magical powers, and she was going to have to work on that. But not right now.

The team around her hadn't said much as they approached the Room of Lost Souls. They were doing their jobs, scanning, searching, collecting information.

Paek was her voice with the squadrons, assembling them at a safe distance from the Room, and splitting up the search duties.

They all knew this was, at best, a recovery mission. They also knew that there was a chance, however slight, that the enemy ships might still be around.

So all one hundred ships had approached the Room with caution.

Elissa wasn't sure if the area around the Room had ever been so thoroughly scanned. Every inch of it was covered, with probably more than one scanning device.

The search was intense, and it came up dry. There were no enemy ships. There was no *Ivoire*. The Room itself was empty.

All that was left were floating bits and pieces of ships, so recently destroyed.

"I need four different ships doing research," she said now to Paek.

He looked over at her. He was clearly tired, and more than a little stressed. He was probably worried that they would get in trouble for bringing such a large force to an empty region.

She wanted to reassure him, but she didn't. If Flag Commander Janik called her irresponsible or worse, tried to demote her, she would go over his head to Operations Command.

The loss of seven ships was worth the response, and that was without counting this new way of travel that she had discovered—the fact that both the attacking enemy vessel and the *Ivoire* could open a window in space, and disappear inside of it.

She had no idea what that window was. Nor did she know if they were merely camouflaged or if that window took those ships somewhere else.

"I also want the command vessels to modify their scans," she said. "Use techniques we haven't tried in years. Use some other equipment, if they have it available."

"Searching for what?" Paek asked.

"Evidence that the *Ivoire* and that enemy vessel are still nearby," Elissa said.

"We can't see them anymore," someone said from down front. She couldn't see who had said it, and she didn't recognize the person from the voice.

Which was probably good because Elissa wanted to snap at them to shut the hell up.

Paek had noted her instant reaction. He had sucked air in through his teeth, a habit he had whenever he felt she was going to be unreasonable.

He used to follow that sound with words of caution directed at her.

Now he didn't need to.

She shot him a sideways glance, but his gaze was downward. He was looking at the backs of his hands, which were folded together, almost like he was trying to control them.

"Yes," Elissa said, trying to sound reasonable. She wasn't sounding reasonable. She was sounding annoyed. Annoyed was better than furious. "Those ships disappeared into some kind of window. That window could be a shield or a cloak. It could also be an opening that allows instant travel."

Which would explain how the *Ivoire* had eluded her more than once. She knew it, and she would have thought her team would understand it as well.

But they weren't always as quick on the uptake as she was, which also irritated her.

"If it is a cloak or a shield," she said, "we might be able to find them, and see through whatever they're doing."

"If they have that kind of technology," Paek said quietly to her, "what makes you think that we're going to be able to see through it?"

"I don't know," Elissa said, this time letting her irritation through. "I do know if we don't try to investigate, we're not going to learn anything at all."

Heads were bowed all over the control center. The screens showed large images of the Room of Lost Souls, tilted and abandoned and smaller than it had been when she first encountered it.

She walked around consoles and personnel, heading toward that Room. The mysterious Room of Lost Souls, placed here by an unknown race centuries before the Enterran Empire ever began.

"Commander," Paek said. He was fearless in his approach to her, which was why he had been promoted to her assistant when others, whose résumés made them seem more qualified, had not been. "Shouldn't we let the other ships go, maybe leave one squadron?"

That had been the order she had been about to give before she got sidetracked.

"Check first," she said. "See if any of the squadrons brought science vessels here."

She had gathered the squadrons so fast that they wouldn't have time to configure for battle. They would have come to the Room with the ships they were using for whatever mission they had been on when she summoned them.

Some of these squadrons had to have science ships. Maybe more than one.

She continued to stare at the Room, smaller. Tilting. All the things that shouldn't have happened to a stable and abandoned space station but had.

The Room had remained the same for generations, only to change after Cooper had visited.

She had checked on the Room regularly. Janik called her focus on the Room an obsession. And maybe it was.

She let out a long breath. Just thinking about Janik and his reactions made her tense.

And she was tense enough. She had no idea who was on those seven ships, but she had a hunch she knew several of them.

Even if she hadn't, it wouldn't have mattered. Those ships were filled with good people who hadn't deserved to die like that.

At least it had been relatively quick.

Although she didn't always find that as comforting as other people intended it.

The ship that had destroyed them had used laser canons. Those laser pulses had hit the ships' shields, doing no damage, and then, somehow, had broken through the shield frequency remarkably quickly.

Those seven ships had been destroyed in a matter of minutes. Maybe not even with enough time to upload the telemetry of the attack to other ships nearby.

That would be something she had to check. But this enemy vessel chasing Captain Cooper and the *Ivoire*, it had the same capability that the *Ivoire* did, the ability to disappear into one of those windows.

Which might mean that the enemy vessel had had the same kind of massive energy weapon that Cooper had used on Elissa twice—once here at the Room and once on the border between the Empire and the Nine Planets Alliance.

"Commander," Paek said, "I'm checking on the science vessels now. One of the leaders wants to know if the ships need to be fully staffed."

His voice caught her, and almost broke her concentration. But she held it, because she felt like she was on the way to a breakthrough. Which meant she could only give Paek half of her brain at the moment.

"Fully staffed?" she asked.

All ships were usually fully staffed when they were sent into battle. A ship that wasn't shouldn't have joined one of the squadrons. So his comment didn't entirely make sense to her.

And then it did.

"With scientists?" she asked.

"Yes, commander." Somehow Paek made that sound humble, not sarcastic. That was one of the reasons she liked working with him. He knew how to manage her, even when she was distracted.

"Yes," she said, answering his initial question. Or rather, the unknown squadron leader's initial question. "The science ships need to be fully staffed with scientists."

She managed not to sound as annoyed as she felt. Why would she ask for science ships if they weren't properly staffed?

Paek nodded once, and then moved slightly to one side, away from her, as he communicated with whichever squadron leader had contacted him. Or maybe he was contacting all of them. She didn't know, and wasn't sure she cared.

Because the Room itself had reminded her of something. The energy weapon Cooper had used against her twice had a similar signature to the energy that used to exist around the Room of Lost Souls.

Energy that was no longer here.

Or was it?

She slipped into a chair in front of one of the nearby consoles, making a member of the team move to a different chair. The console was on, so clearly that person had been working here, and right now, that wasn't Elissa's concern.

"Commander…?" Paek said again. He had a habit of letting his voice trail off slightly and ending with a question because he thought that was less offensive than asking firmly.

She had to admit that sometimes it was.

"Just a minute," she said without looking at him.

She tapped the console, changed its configuration, and focused narrowly on the Room. She had the energy signature of Cooper's weapon memorized, and she entered the signature now as a search.

The Room was no longer giving off any of that energy. But there were remnants of it all over the area, especially at the coordinates where the enemy vessel had hovered while it was executing its rescue.

She opened another window, called up decades' old readings around the Room of Lost Souls, and saw what she expected to find. That energy signature, altered somewhat, probably with age and decay, but still there, and strong.

It had been there before she ran into Cooper at the Room, but not after.

She leaned back in the chair. Had there been a weapon on the Room of Lost Souls for centuries and no one knew it? Was that what Cooper had initially come to the Room to retrieve?

Did that mean he was connected to the people who had initially built the Room? Or had he encountered Rooms like that before?

Cooper had accessed parts of the Room that the Empire had never been able to. For some reason, the Room had not been as deadly to his people as it had been to most travelers. Did he have some kind of protective equipment that enabled his people to work the Room?

She had asked those questions before, but had been told that they were not relevant.

They were now, especially because Cooper had returned.

She didn't even know how long he had been at the Room and if he had once again removed something from it.

She slapped her hands on the console, startling everyone in the command center. The movement sent pain through her scarred palms, and she didn't care.

She ignored all the expectant faces—all of them, except Paek's.

"Here's what I need," she said to him. "I need at least four science vessels here, as well as research vessels. I want them to conduct several layers of research."

He was frowning at her. He clearly hadn't expected this kind of order.

"I want at least two of those science vessels to figure out what that window those ships created is. I want to know how it was created, and what it did, exactly."

"Commander, I'm not sure we have the ability to—"

"I'm aware that it might not be possible," Elissa said, no longer trying to be nice. "But I want us to gather as much information as we can."

He nodded and, unlike several others in the command center, did not look stressed by her tone.

"I have noted in the past that the signature of that energy weapon the *Ivoire* used on us twice now had a lot in common with the energy that was once given off by the Room of Lost Souls. The Room doesn't give off that signature any longer, but the Room has changed."

Paek frowned as he stared at her. He wasn't quite sure what she meant.

She probably hadn't ever explained it to him. "If you take the Room's measurements now," she said, "they're different than they were five years ago, when I first encountered the *Ivoire*. The Room is smaller, and it seems to be listing more."

Paek licked his lips, almost as if he were holding back on making a comment. She nodded toward him, silently giving him permission to speak.

"I—um…" He shook his head just once, then visibly caught himself. "You think that's because of what the *Ivoire* did?"

"I've monitored the Room since that encounter," she said. "And yes, it's clear if you look at the evidence that all of the changes to the Room happened after I encountered the *Ivoire*. And now, the *Ivoire* has returned."

"Okay." Paek sounded skeptical. "Why would it do that?"

"At first, I thought maybe it was a maneuver," she said. "Which is, you must admit, somewhat brilliant. Cooper—if indeed he's still the one captaining the *Ivoire*—led the other ships here, and let us deal with them while he escaped."

"That's what I thought it was," Paek said.

"But what if it's something more?" she said. "What if he came here to get another weapon?"

Even as she said the words aloud, a spasm ran through her back. She blinked at the pain, hoping it didn't show on her face.

"I don't think he did," that same someone down front said. Elissa squinted at them, unable to make out who it was.

"We don't know that for certain," Elissa said. "We got a proximity alarm and information from the buoys, but I'm not sure that's enough. We need someone to take this battle apart bit by bit. We also need research into the history of the Room. We need to know to know if this shrinkage has happened before. Or if the Room itself is something more than what we think it is."

"What would that be?" Paek asked the question flatly, almost as if it didn't interest him.

She recognized the tone. He used it when he didn't want to antagonize her, when he thought she was being stupid or following the wrong path, but he didn't want to say that to her.

"I don't know," she said, then couldn't help herself. She had to add, "If I knew, I wouldn't ask for the research. But Cooper seems to know what the Room is. He took something from it, and then he prevented us from tracking him by attacking us."

"Made easier by his ability to open that window." Paek no longer sounded disinterested. He actually nodded, as if the very idea of what Cooper had done intrigued him.

"Exactly," she said. "So let's see if we can figure out what he's doing. Let's put people on it."

One more spasm ran through her back. She gripped the edge of the console, willing the pain to go away. She hadn't helped herself by coming here. Apparently, she still had a lot of unresolved issues about this place.

"Let's also figure out where the *Ivoire* has gone," she said. "I'd love to talk with this Cooper."

"Talk with him?" Paek asked.

She nodded.

"But he's working with the Nine Planets," Paek said. "And diplomatically—"

"You don't need to explain that to me, Sub-Lieutenant," she said. "I know the rules. And I'm not certain that this Cooper is part of the Nine Planets. I know he worked with them, but that job might have been mercenary."

She didn't explain farther. She'd kept an eye on the Nine Planets Alliance as well, and she knew they'd been building up their force at the border between the Empire and the Nine Planets. If this Cooper wasn't part of one of the member states of the Nine Planets—and some of what she gleaned over the past several years made her think that—then he was hired to fight the Empire when the Nine Planets didn't have the ability to do so on its own.

"We have some things to figure out," she said.

Paek was watching her, as if he were trying to figure out what her next order would be. The others were watching her as well, but with less intensity. They would be working no matter what she assigned. Sometimes she had the sense that they didn't care a bit for their jobs; they just completed the work because it was their living.

"We need a patrol here at the Room," she said. "I want several ships to guard the science and research ships. I want any information those ships glean to be sent to me unfiltered. I want that information stored off-ship, because we have no idea if the *Ivoire* or any other of these ships will reappear."

"The patrol," Paek said, bringing the focus back to the practical. "Will they be defending the Room or will they only defend themselves?"

It was a good question. He wanted to know if they could shoot first when a possible enemy vessel arrived.

"Neither," she said. "I want them to defend the science and research ships. So if those ships are under threat, then the patrol can use force. Otherwise, we're going to try our hand at diplomacy."

A back spasm shuddered through her again, as if reminding her that diplomacy hadn't worked with Cooper the first time she encountered him.

But the second time, on the border of the Nine Planets and the Empire, he had been somewhat diplomatic with her. He had given her a chance to retreat, to get away from that horrid weapon of his, and she had taken it. She just couldn't convince Janik to let other ships join her.

So diplomacy might work with Cooper. Which meant that she needed to take more time to attempt to find him.

Maybe he would actually talk with her.

Or maybe he would attack again.

He hadn't attacked this time, though. He had that monstrous weapon, and he hadn't waited around to use it on the enemy vessel. Or on her ships.

She had no idea what that meant. She had no idea what any of it meant. But she was going to find out.

THE JEFATURA

17

NYGUTA SAT IN THE ANTEROOM outside the Fourth Judgement Room on the Jefatura's Second Level. She'd been to judgement rooms on several levels, but never higher than the Fifth Level. She had only gone to that Judgement Room as part of a ceremony to acknowledge her new captaincy, years ago.

Now, she felt like a young student being disciplined by a teacher. She sat, because she had no choice. Pacing would make her look like she was guilty of something, which, in her mind, she was. She had lost a ship at the cost of several lives.

In theory, such things were forgivable, particularly in outside attacks, but she didn't feel like she deserved forgiveness, and she knew that was a problem.

She kept her hands clasped on her knees. Every time her fingers tightened, she willed them to loosen. She made herself take in the waiting area, inch by inch, not that the waiting area was that spectacular.

It smelled faintly of old Swiss cheese, which was odd since bringing food and drink here was discouraged. The air was too cold, and it wasn't being recycled as often as she liked, which probably made that smell linger. The chair was solid and square with no padding, about as uncomfortable as a chair could be.

This room was not designed to lull someone into a sense of security while waiting. The room had been designed to keep anyone waiting on edge.

It did not have any entertainment the way that many other waiting areas throughout the Armada did. Usually something played on a screen—a short film about an obscure historical fact, or a hologram that played games with children.

But here there was nothing even smacking of amusement. A few chairs set away from each other to discourage conversation, a couple of matching tables with spaces for the storage of specialized entertainment tablets, but no tablets to be seen. Static signs discouraged conversation as well as barring any "foreign objects" including snacks and beverages. Floating signs, personalized to anyone waiting, told them how long the wait would be.

She was alone in the waiting room, so her sign hovered near her, rousing itself every five minutes to give her an update on the wait time. The number never changed. It always told her she had a ten-minute wait, even though she'd been waiting for twenty minutes now.

She was used to inaccurate wait times whenever she visited the Jefatura. "Jefatura" wasn't the official name of the ship-station she was on, but it was the word everyone used, both for the twelve-person team that ran the Armada and for the ship-station she was on now.

The leadership team was legendary. Each person on the team ran other leadership teams that stretched down through the judgement levels, making certain that all of the rules of the Armada were followed to the letter.

When those rules were broken, for whatever reason, a subset of one of the leadership teams of the appropriate level made certain that the error was justified. If it wasn't, the person who broke that rule would receive some kind of punishment—usually a demotion, although a handful were sent to some form of manual labor or out of the Armada entirely.

No matter what happened at her judgement hearing, she wouldn't get thrown out of the Armada. But she might be facing a demotion.

She hadn't slept the night before, because she kept replaying the events of the attack and rescue over and over again in her mind.

She made herself think of something else on her trip to the ship-station, but she couldn't help feeling overwhelmed as it loomed large ahead of her. She'd taken a bubbleship from the *BilatZailea*, a choice she regretted the moment she left her ship.

She had initially chosen the bubbleship because it was her favorite type of single ship. Usually she liked being able to see everything around her while traveling through space. The bubble itself, modified from the various Fleet specs that the Legion of Engineers had found and stored, was oblong and sleek, not really a bubble per se as the beginning of one, before it found its perfectly round shape.

The bubbleship enveloped its pilot, and made her feel as if she were a protected part of the universe rather than a person traveling alone in space.

She had thought that was going to be comforting, but it wasn't. She had forgotten how big and daunting the ship-station was.

The ship-station's formal name was *Primary: The Official Headquarters of the Jefatura of the Armada*. All of the ship-stations throughout the Armada's history had that name, without a number afterwards. The name had originally been put on a ship, back when the founders of the Armada had been abandoned in a Scrapheap by duplicitous members of the Fleet.

Over the millennia, however, the ship morphed into a traveling space station, the largest vessel she or anyone in the Armada had ever seen. It was larger than the moons of many planets, but smaller than the planets themselves.

But it didn't look like a moon. It wasn't spherical and solid. It was composed of concentric rings that looped into each other. At the center of each ring were fat rounded rectangles that housed most of the life on the ship-station, although some people lived in the rings.

The design was part utility and part history. The rings could split away from the ship-station if need be. Each ring could—and sometimes did—travel on its own, although the central rings hadn't moved from the ship-station in a century or more. Each ring could fit inside a flotilla, and pass for an unusual ship, thus protecting the important people inside. And each ring had its own defensive systems, some of which were different from the defensive systems in the other rings. They all also had weaponry, something that got upgraded often whenever the Legion of Engineers deemed new technology better than the old tech.

Because there was no direct path from one part of the ship-station to another part, it took forever for someone to travel from one ring to another. Most people didn't. They lived and worked within their ring. But the higher up the judgement levels went, the more likely it was that someone important had to travel a distance to arrive at a meeting.

She was clearly waiting for someone important now, which was why that sign was stuck at ten minutes. Usually, the members of a Jefatura Judgment Panel lived near the official rooms of their ring, but maybe that wasn't the case at the Second Level. Maybe the members had to travel from different rings.

Her fingers were gripping her knees tightly. She released the fingertips one by one, making herself concentrate on them. Her heart was beating a little too fast, and she was restless.

She wanted to move. She wasn't used to sitting this long. She never sat this long on the *BilatZailea*. She was always going from one part of the ship to another, or walking around on the bridge as she executed tasks.

Maybe it wasn't just the sitting. It was the lack of a task. She almost always had too much work, and she rarely had idle time. She didn't like idle time.

A bright green light lit up her arms and hands. She glanced at the sign. The green came from new words. *You may enter now.* The words grew large, then became small again, and then grew, and she knew that pattern would continue if she didn't stand up.

Her mouth was dry. She stood, adjusted her uniform, and hoped she looked more composed than she felt. She wiped her hands on her thighs, and squared her shoulders.

She had known this was coming. She could handle it. She was the captain of the *BilatZailea*. She could handle anything.

She approached the big double doors at the far end of the waiting room. She had spent her entire wait time not staring at those doors, and now that she approached them, she realized they had an unusual feature: they had door handles. Big fat rounded rectangles that looked like tiny versions of the fat rounded rectangles in the middle of each ring.

The doors themselves were patterned, covered in rings. The design caught her. She was used to the utilitarian décor of the *BilatZailea*. She hadn't noted any whimsy elsewhere in the ship-station, but she hadn't absorbed the detail of the place on her infrequent visits here.

She reached for the door handles with shaking fingers, only to have the doors open inward, as if she were about to take part in some kind of ceremony. She half expected to be formally announced. But no voice or music accompanied her as she walked down a narrow aisle between a series of rounded seats that—she knew from their design—could be turned into long bench seating.

At the end of the aisle was a raised platform with twelve round seats, all padded, and all filled with Jefatura members, most of whom she did not recognize. Their names floated below them on tiny signs, similar to the sign that hovered near her in the waiting room.

Nyguta only recognized one name: Amyta Crowe. Crowe was a lanky woman with a square face. Her long black hair was pulled into a ponytail that rested across her right shoulder, almost like part of the design of her white tunic. Crowe sat directly in front of the aisle, her black eyes staring intently at Nyguta.

Nyguta willed herself not to stare. She'd seen members of the powerful Crowe family before, but she had never been close to one, and certainly not in front of one who actually ran the entire Armada.

Amyta Crowe wasn't Second Level Jefatura. She was one of the twelve who governed the entire Armada. Her chair was initially an Honored Family Position, but she didn't rest on inherited laurels. She was also the head of the Legion of Engineers, a position that was earned through hard work, political skills and incredible engineering expertise.

Nyguta found Crowe's presence both breathtaking and intimidating.

It took Nyguta a moment to process the remaining eleven members of this judgment panel. Five men, five women, and another who appeared gender neutral.

Nyguta hadn't met any of them. They were all much older than she was. It took time to work their way up to this level at the Jefatura. Time, and a lot of expertise. Unless they were one of the Honored Families.

As she walked forward, she scanned the other names, looking for others belonging to the Honored Families. She saw two others: LaKynnda Atwater and Ahritza Newark. The Newarks were known for their artistry with anything to do with food, hydroponics, and nutrition. So Ahritza Newark, however imposing she looked, wasn't here because of the engineering or even command side of Nyguta's judgment.

But LaKynnda Atwater. She was legendary. Her work with *anacapa* drives built on the Atwater family legacy. She had refined foldspace tracking into an art, and had made foldspace travel safer through protections built around *anacapa* drives.

She had more knowledge of foldspace, *anacapa* drives, and foldspace tracking than Nyguta could hope to learn in a lifetime.

Atwater was seated next to Crowe. Atwater had the family red hair, which had somehow found its way into almost half of the Armada. Unlike many of the Atwaters, her skin was light brown, not as dark as Crowe's but not that weird pale that seemed to crop up every two generations or so in the Atwater family. Atwater did have the trademark green eyes, though, and they were fixed on Nyguta with the same level of intensity as Crowe's eyes were.

Atwater and Crowe weren't here because they were part of the Second Level Jefatura. They were here because they wanted to grill Nyguta themselves.

Her heart triple-hammered against her chest, as if trying to escape. She hadn't been this nervous since she first applied to leadership training.

She folded her hands together, then bowed her head slightly, and bent her knees at the same time in the traditional greeting to the Jefatura. She had practiced that little maneuver the night before as well, because she almost never used it.

"Captain Kimi Nyguta of the *BilatZailea*," Crowe said, her tone deliberately formal. She had a deep rich voice, suited toward that formality. "You are here because of the events that surrounded the loss of the *EhizTari*."

Nyguta raised her head, and straightened her knees. She clasped her hands together before her.

Nyguta wasn't sure if she was supposed to make a verbal response, so she nodded to acknowledge Crowe's remarks. Nyguta had no counsel for this meeting, because none was offered. Usually when a captain faced a demotion, she was offered counsel.

The lack of counsel made her believe that the demotion was already in motion when she was called before this Judgment Panel. A counsel wouldn't have prevented the demotion, but a counsel would have been nice anyway, if only to help Nyguta with the formalities.

"We have reviewed the files," Crowe said, "and interviewed many of the *EhizTari*'s surviving crew. They believe you acted quickly, and in doing so, saved hundreds of lives."

Nyguta's fingers tightened. The words were reassuring, but that formal tone led her to believe that this was just the beginning of the judgment, not the sentencing.

"The footage, from your own ship, bears that out. Your crew also believes that your swift action saved lives on the *EhizTari*." Crowe leaned forward ever so slightly. "No one believes that the *EhizTari* could have been saved."

That was forgiveness. Nyguta recognized it, even in her agitated state. They weren't going to charge her with recklessly or needlessly destroying a ship. They believed she had no other choice.

"However," Crowe continued, "we did not bring you here to discuss the *EhizTari*. We have other questions for you."

Nyguta felt as if someone had shut down gravity only to realize their mistake a second later and quickly re-established it. Her knees felt shaky, almost as if she had slid ever so slightly across the floor.

Her mind was having trouble focusing on what Crowe had said. Nyguta had prepared to defend herself—or maybe not to defend herself—regarding the *EhizTari*. She hadn't considered anything else.

All twelve members of the Jefatura watched her, as if they were trying to read something into her every movement. So she tried not to move at all.

"Here's what we know," Crowe said. "A group of people arrived at Base 20, uninvited, and rather than being repelled by our countermeasures, they were able to enter, using Fleet identification."

Nyguta swallowed hard. She knew only the vaguest of these details.

"Those people, who escaped through some rather impressive maneuvers, came from a DV-Class vessel called the *Ivoire*." Crowe was still leaning ever so slightly forward. "That ship then disappeared into foldspace. You and the *EhizTari* were assigned to track it."

"Yes," Nyguta said. "And we did. That's how we ended up near that lost Fleet starbase."

"Yes, the empty Fleet starbase," Crowe said. "I will get to that in a minute. The *Ivoire* was not at that base when you arrived, am I correct?"

"Yes, you are," Nyguta said. "The *Ivoire* left a standard distress signal, which was what brought in those local vessels."

"Local to something called the Enterran Empire," Crowe said. "It has been based in that region almost since the Fleet left it five thousand years ago."

Nyguta had not known that. Normally, she would have been interested. But she wasn't. She was still trying to figure out what this judgment panel was all about.

"As I understand it," Crowe said, "you had a choice. You could have gone after the *Ivoire* instead of rescuing the crew of the *EhizTari*."

So that was what this was about? Nyguta had to stop herself from shaking her head in surprise. They weren't going to be upset at her for failing to track the *Ivoire*, were they?

Armada regulations were firm: never leave anyone behind. And she would have left an entire vessel's worth of people behind if she had gone after the *Ivoire*. All of those crew members would have been captured, or worse, slaughtered.

"No, ma'am, I couldn't have gone after the *Ivoire*," Nyguta said. "There were ships on the way. The crew of the *EhizTari* would have been captured, and the ship would have as well. It was severely disabled—"

"We are not questioning your actions, Captain," Crowe said. "You followed the highest directive of the Armada. You saved our people. You also had no choice but to destroy our ship. We don't want information from our people to get into enemy hands."

"There is no guarantee that this Empire is an enemy," said the gender-neutral member of the panel. They had an alto voice, just as rich and formal as Crowe's voice. They were thin and almost ethereal, with light blond hair that looked like a halo around their reddish-brown skin.

The name on the sign floating below the panel member was Uri Chawbra, someone that Nyguta had not heard of before.

Newark turned slightly in her chair. Her black hair, cut in a perfect bob, swung with her.

"I'm sure that Empire is our enemy now," she said with a wry smile.

Chawbra inclined their head toward Newark, acknowledging the point. Then Chawbra tented their fingers and frowned at Nyguta.

"Was there a reason you chose not to follow the *Ivoire's* foldspace trail after you rescued the crew of the *EhizTari?*" they asked.

Nyguta had expected that question.

"The captain of the *Ivoire* had already proved quite adept at strategy," she said. "We—well, I—assumed they would guess they were being tracked, and would have yet another trick to play on whomever followed them. I had hundreds of vessels coming toward my position, a rescue to complete, and then double the usual number of crew on my ship, some of whom were injured. I made the decision to let this *Ivoire* vessel go for the time being."

Chawbra tilted their head the other way. "You believe we can still follow their foldspace trail?"

"The *Ivoire's* foldspace trail?" Nyguta asked. She hadn't expected that question either. "It's been days."

"You've tracked ships that have been lost longer," Chawbra said. Apparently, they had looked into her record. Probably the entire judgment panel had.

Nyguta nodded. "I have, but they were exploring areas without a lot of foldspace traffic. Theirs was the only signature. I don't know about this Empire. If they have foldspace technology, I might not be able to track the *Ivoire* at this late date."

"It might be worth a try." Chawbra didn't say that to her. Instead, Chawbra was looking at Atwater.

"Captain Nyguta's right," Atwater said. "We would need to know more about this Empire, and what its technological capabilities are. That old Fleet starbase might create problems of its own, particularly if this Empire uses it. Who knows how well that starbase was decommissioned."

"It doesn't have any *anacapa* capability," Nyguta said. "I checked, because I was worried about the starbase when we arrived. It looks like it might have been subjected to uncontrolled *anacapa* energy."

"Which looks like what?" Newark asked.

Atwater rolled her eyes as she turned away from Newark. Crowe saw the disrespected, and her own eyes narrowed.

"The starbase is in our records," Nyguta said. "Its specs are clear. But the remains of the base are off-kilter, and parts of the base appear to be missing."

"Because they were taken?" Newark asked.

"Because they might be in foldspace," Atwater snapped. "Is this relevant?" She asked that last of Crowe.

"It might be," Crowe said. "If this Empire had access to an *anacapa* drive, they might have some version of the technology."

"In that case," Nyguta said, because she remembered that the question had initially been posed to her, "I wouldn't be able to accurately pinpoint if the trail I was following belonged to the *Ivoire* or one of the Empire ships."

"Looks like we have some questions to answer before we move on," said one of the men. His floating name badge identified him as Dominic Villanueva. He was slight, with the fragile look of someone born and raised in zero-g, a look accented by the fact that he was bald, probably by choice. Many who grew up in zero-g preferred to shave their skulls.

"We have a lot of questions to answer." Crowe answered him, but she was looking at Nyguta. "I need opinions from you, Captain."

"Opinions," Nyguta repeated. She hated it when her superiors asked for opinions. Nyguta dealt better with facts.

"Do you believe that this *Ivoire* ship is from the Fleet?" Crowe asked.

Nyguta swallowed hard. It would be easier to answer opinion questions if the question was clear.

"The vessel itself is Fleet tech," she said cautiously. "It's a DV-Class vessel with a five-thousand-year-old design."

"Yes." Crowe sounded both patient and annoyed at the same time.

Nyguta envied the tone. She would love to use it herself as a captain. As someone currently being judged, though, that tone made her feel deeply uncomfortable.

"We took a lot of readings about that ship near Base 20," Crowe was saying. "It shows a relatively unmodified DV-Class vessel. Some technology that we could see looked unfamiliar to us, but most of it was exactly what you'd expect on a ship of that design. Except, of course, that it was newer."

"Newer?" Nyguta said.

"The nanobots hadn't replicated enough times for five thousand years to have passed. And some of the materials stopped being used in Fleet vessels because the Fleet had moved away from the areas where those materials were made." Crowe folded her hands over her knees.

Nyguta held herself very still. Those facts were new to her. She had scanned the *Ivoire*, but hadn't had time to get anything beside a cursory surface reading.

"So I ask you again, do you believe this ship is Fleet?" Crowe asked.

"Part of the Fleet?" Nyguta asked. "Do you want to know if I think we found the Fleet?"

"Do you?" Crowe asked, maddeningly not answering the direct question that Nyguta had posed.

She swallowed again. Dang the compulsive swallowing. She hadn't done that since she was a cadet.

"I did, at first," she said. "I had hopes."

"And now?" Crowe asked.

Nyguta didn't want to go down this path. She had hoped to avoid it altogether.

She looked at Atwater whose expression was impassive. But if Nyguta was going to be contradicted by anyone, it would be Atwater.

Atwater wasn't going to bail her out though. Apparently, Atwater wanted to hear what Nyguta had to say as much as Crowe did.

Nyguta took a deep breath, and plunged in.

"A lot about the *Ivoire* bothers me," she said. "I didn't know about its age, or anything, but its design did catch my eye. And then there's the fact that it knew about this abandoned base in the middle of what seems like hostile territory. It's clear that whoever was captaining the *Ivoire* knew that its distress signal would get a response, and then that the Empire would react swiftly to the destruction of those seven ships."

"Which is not unusual for a strictly military culture," Chawbra muttered.

Nyguta nodded at them, because she didn't want the twelve to think she wasn't paying attention to what they were saying.

"That's true," she said, "but I wouldn't complete a maneuver based on that."

"I'm not sure it was based," Chawbra said. "The seven ships, yes. But the hundreds of vessels? That seems like overkill to me."

Crowe raised a hand, languidly commanding Chawbra to be quiet.

"I thought of that too," Nyguta said. "I looked at our scans when we returned. There doesn't appear to be anything of value in that abandoned starbase. Which means that the hundreds of ships came either for us, as a response to destroying the seven vessels. Or more likely, they came for the *Ivoire*."

"Why do you say more likely?" This from Atwater. Clearly she hadn't expected that comment.

"Because those hundred ships were already on the way when our scanners picked them up. And it seems—please note that I'm not certain—that they had left the moment the *Ivoire* had arrived at that starbase, not when the seven ships were destroyed."

"Timing," Villanueva said softly to the others. "We'll have to look into that."

Through it all, Atwater was watching Nyguta closely. "You were going to say something else about the *Ivoire*. Something that bothered you."

The fact that Atwater brought Nyguta back to that point seemed curious to Nyguta. It almost felt as if the two of them were having a slightly different conversation than Nyguta was having with everyone else.

She straightened her shoulders. "There's a ship called the *Ivoire* in the Fleet's historical record," she said. "It disappeared into foldspace during a battle, never to be heard from again. The man who captained the *Ivoire* was a well-known tactician who could get in and out of any fight. He also spent a lot of time at Starbase Kappa, which is the abandoned starbase he led our ships to."

Atwater moved her head so slightly that Nyguta wasn't sure she had seen it. It had been a nod, right? But did that mean it was an encouraging nod or not?

"Is that all that you have?" Atwater asked.

"I was going to look deeper," Nyguta said, "and then I got this summons…"

"Why?" Crowe asked. "Do you have something, LaKynnda?"

That tone again. That patient but annoyed tone.

"Actually, I do," Atwater said. "Jonathon Cooper, the captain of the *Ivoire* when it disappeared, was a divisive figure in Fleet history. Captain Nyguta is correct in that he was well known for his command abilities and his creative methods, particularly in a fight, although that did not serve him well in the end."

Nyguta pressed her lips together. She was not sure what this all meant, but she was paying as close attention as she could.

"He had been on a diplomatic mission that went awry," Atwater said. "The locals attacked, and it was in that attack that the *Ivoire*, which went into foldspace, disappeared forever."

Nyguta started to say that she had known that much, but Atwater gave her a cautious look before continuing.

"That diplomatic mission went so poorly," Atwater said, "and the loss of the *Ivoire* caused so much trouble, that relations between that culture and the Fleet put them on a war footing. The Fleet, of course, moved on, as it does, leaving the other culture behind, but permanently changed. That was the beginning of what you all are calling the Enterran Empire."

"I don't see how that's relevant to our current discussion," Crowe said. "We're trying to figure out—"

"Let me finish." Atwater shifted ever so slightly in her chair, so that she could look at Crowe directly. "Cooper was court-martialed in absentia for his role in the creation of the Empire, and for several other things. He is one of those historic figures who could be seen as a great hero or a great villain, depending on your point of view."

"What's your point of view, LaKynnda?" Chawbra asked.

Atwater gave them a small smile. It wasn't quite condescending or maybe it was. Nyguta didn't know her well enough to understand the subtleties of her expressions.

"This creative maneuver—*all* of these creative maneuvers," Atwater said, "are leading me to wonder if the *Ivoire* is Cooper's ship, with him at the helm."

"Five thousand years in his own future?" Villanueva asked. "Is that even possible?"

Atwater gave him a withering glare. "You know that ships can lose time," she said. "You know they can lose years. Why is five thousand harder to believe than five?"

Villanueva looked down at his hands.

Nyguta felt her own shoulders relax. She had wondered if the *Ivoire* she had seen was the lost ship. She had never seen evidence of five thousand years lost to foldspace, but she felt like Atwater did. If losing one year was possible, then losing five thousand was possible as well.

"Well," Crowe said, "there's a lot here we don't know—"

"If," Atwater said, as if Crowe hadn't spoken, "we are dealing with Cooper of the *Ivoire*, then we are not looking at a modern Fleet ship, separated from the Fleet to run a mission in this Empire. We are looking at a lost ship."

"We've found ships from that period," Chawbra said. "Even if this is Cooper, it doesn't matter. He can't give us information that we don't already have."

"Do you think that means we shouldn't go after the *Ivoire*?" Crowe asked.

Nyguta wasn't sure who she was asking. All of them? Just Atwater?

"The codes used at Base 20 were old," Atwater said. "The ship is an old design that looks like it was built in the last fifty years. The maneuvers are signature Cooper, if the historical record is to be believed. And he spent a lot of time at Starbase Kappa. I think we have a lot of evidence of a lost ship, and a man trying to find his way back to his time and his people."

"I don't know how that's relevant," Crowe said, and this time the exasperation was apparent. She clipped the end of the sentence, as if Atwater was wasting all of their time.

"Well, there are two ways it's relevant," Atwater said. "The first is that we should know if ships can lose thousands of years to foldspace. That might make a difference in our searches."

She paused there and gave Nyguta a meaningful look. Maybe Atwater expected her to jump in and say something, but she wasn't going to. And she wasn't sure if it was useful to know if a ship could lose thousands of years. She wasn't sure if she would want to track a ship that had lost so much time. She certainly didn't want to lose that much time herself.

"The second is this," Atwater said, "if the *Ivoire* truly is a lost ship, and Cooper helms her, he won't have Fleet backup. He'll be on his own, which also explains those maneuvers. They're the product of a tactical mind that knows it has only itself to rely on."

"You think we should go after him," Nyguta said, and caught herself. She had just revealed what interpretation of the data she believed.

"I do," Atwater said. "If nothing else, we lie to him, let him believe that we are what the Fleet has become five thousand years in his future, and learn from that incredible tactician's brain."

"We have good tacticians," Crowe said.

"And," Atwater said, "we might be able to use him and his codes to actually find the Fleet."

"How do you figure that?" Chawbra asked.

Atwater leaned back in her chair and folded her hands on her lap. She looked like the picture of innocence, sitting there, except for her sparkling green eyes.

"The Fleet loses its history," Atwater said quietly. "Deliberately loses it. They record less than half, by my estimation, which means that there's a lot of knowledge that we are not finding in these old ships and bases we locate."

No one asked why that knowledge had importance. The Armada believed in knowledge—sometimes too much knowledge.

"You are going to want me to go after the *Ivoire*, aren't you?" Nyguta asked.

"Yes," Atwater said, "we are."

Crowe glared at her. Apparently, Crowe wanted to be the one to make the decisions.

"*If* you go after the *Ivoire*," Crowe said, "you cannot do so alone. You will need ships to guard you and to protect you, should the *Ivoire* attack."

Crowe paused, and everyone looked at Nyguta. Were they waiting for her to say that she could handle the *Ivoire* on her own? Because she wasn't going to say that. She couldn't handle the *Ivoire* on her own. She could handle herself in a battlefield situation, but battles weren't her area of expertise.

Foldspace tracking was.

"I don't like bringing groups of ships into foldspace," she said.

"We'll figure out the logistics later," Crowe said. "Right now, we need to discuss what our plans are."

Nyguta was being dismissed. She wasn't quite sure why she had been brought here. Atwater was the one who claimed that Cooper was still alive, that the *Ivoire* had jumped here from the past. Atwater could have made those claims without Nyguta.

But Nyguta's hesitation, her willingness to consider that option *before* Atwater brought it up, that probably had helped Atwater.

Atwater gave her a small smile and a real nod this time. An acknowledgement. And in that moment, Nyguta knew her hunch was right. She had been brought here to fulfill Atwater's agenda.

Atwater wanted to find the *Ivoire*, and Atwater was willing to use Nyguta to do so.

And Nyguta was willing to go.

RESEARCH

18

THE COMMAND CENTER FOR THE LOST SOULS CORPORATION was in the exact center of the main space station—which was not how the Fleet designed its starbases. Command and control on Fleet starbases was scattered, with different systems in different sections of the base. Only the main command—where the defense team met in emergencies—was in the center of the starbase.

Every time Coop had gone into Lost Soul's command and control center, he felt blind, even though he wasn't. Blind and claustrophobic, unable to see, with the weight of the entire station bearing down on him.

He hurried through the corridor, stunned, as always, at how wide it was. Space stations in this region were built for a crush of inhabitants. Some of the space stations he'd visited in the Nine Planets had double or maybe triple the recommended number of people on board at any one time. Going through the corridors was a master class in avoiding contact, especially if someone was in a hurry.

This station was understaffed, like everything else at Lost Souls. And the station didn't have the rotating number of visitors, like most space stations or starbases. Blake didn't want that. She wanted this to be a working station, where everyone and everything had a purpose—and that purpose was building the corporation, not providing respite for travelers.

Sometimes he liked to blame his discomfort here on that design, but he couldn't do that today. Today, he had to acknowledge his own carelessness.

Try as he might, he never thought in terms of starbases or space stations, sector bases or plants that were planetside. He thought about ships. Sometimes in groupings, but mostly *his* ship, the *Ivoire*. Her defenses were topnotch, even now. He had felt confident taking her to Sector Base E-2, because he knew she could defend herself.

He had no real idea if Lost Souls could defend itself.

He had assigned Jason Xilvii to running the station defenses a year ago, and Xilvii had brought in half the team from the *Ivoire*, mostly junior officers who'd been technicians on the ship.

None of them had ever built starbase defenses. None of them had that kind of training. The Fleet—Coop's Fleet, from five thousand years ago—believed in separating the training: People who worked on ships received shipwide training; people who worked on starbases received starbase-specific training; and people who worked on sector bases received sector base training.

They all had theory, of course. They knew how each division worked with every other division. But other than that, they didn't know much at all.

He let out an exasperated breath as he rounded a corner. And that had been an excuse, at least for him. Because anything to do with starbases or sector bases did not interest him.

He stopped outside the large double doors leading into the command center, and wiped a hand over his face. He was off-balance, not just because he was in the middle of the space station. Not just because he was berating himself. Not just because this entire station—all of Lost Souls, really—needed work.

But because of Boss's news.

His thoughts kept returning to those five ships she had seen. Five ships that had destroyed her buoys and had powered up ships inside the Boneyard.

It wasn't proof that she had found the Fleet—or, more accurately, that the Fleet had found her—but it was the most hopeful news that he had had since arriving in this time period.

And yet, now that he had the hopeful news, part of him wanted to ignore it.

He had wanted so desperately to find the Fleet, but something had changed these past five years. And it had really changed in the past four days.

That sector base—E-2—had solidified something for him. That base had been in his future, a base he would never have seen if he had stayed in his own timeline. It would have been a base for his great-grandchildren or even later.

But he found it, and it had been abandoned, then its remains commandeered by the Not-Fleet, whoever they were.

Maybe this all should have registered with him when he arrived at Sector Base V, so far in his future that the base was abandoned and forgotten, left in ruins so old that the entire city that had once housed Fleet personnel didn't even know a base existed beneath the mountains.

But he'd been newly arrived and incredulous, trying to cope with his entire crew's reaction to being five thousand years in their future. Trying to get his feet underneath him, while figuring out a new language, a new universe—a place where everything he had ever known, everything he had understood, was not just gone: it had devolved into legend and rumor and ghost ships and abandoned starbases.

It had become somewhere (somewhen) he did not recognize.

Now, he knew, that even if Boss had found the Fleet, it would not be his Fleet. Nothing would.

He knew that in his bones.

Boss's debrief had been odd. It was rushed, because everyone expected the Fleet to show up out of foldspace at any moment. Boss had been short on concrete details, although she had a lot of footage and assumptions, just like Ahidjo had. They knew what they thought had happened, but they weren't sure who had done it.

They didn't know who was behind anything, and Boss, in particular, was careful to say she had no idea if they had faced the Fleet or not.

She seemed more excited by the warships she had found—if, indeed, that was what she had found.

He had to admit, he was confused by the misdirection inside the Boneyard itself. The hidden star maps, the starscape, the forcefields. All of that suggested the Fleet had become something different as it moved out here, because his Fleet wouldn't have used those techniques.

But the Fleet did grow and change: he knew that. He also knew that its core fundamentally remained the same.

And that was what he had counted on in his early years in this time-line, that whenever he found the Fleet, it would be recognizable, it would have the same core as the Fleet he had left.

He wasn't sure of that now.

And he was worried that Boss had touched off something which could destroy Lost Souls. He had to shore up and redesign the defenses here. He had angered the Empire four days ago, and even though he believed they wouldn't realize it was him, he had to plan for that as well.

So he needed to handle the defenses.

After scanning the footage and telemetry that Boss had brought back, he left it all to Yash. She would search it, and do her best to understand it. She would work with Boss and maybe they would be able to figure out what they were facing.

Coop wanted to do that, but he was needed here first. He didn't trust anyone else to handle putting Lost Souls defenses into place.

Which was a lie to make himself feel better. Because, for the past year, he had trusted others to handle Lost Souls defenses.

He shoved open the double doors with the heels of his hands, using a bit more force than necessary. He caught himself a half-second too late; it wasn't like him to let his emotions overtake any of his actions.

He stepped inside, expecting the command center to look like he had last seen it, months ago—a lot of equipment, most of it unused, and three bored attendants, monitoring the function.

Instead, he found a large, warm, vibrant room, with blinking lights and control panels he didn't recognize, holoimages of the exterior of Lost Souls, and lots of employees, most of whom were standing and comparing information on their tablets.

The conversational hum was dense and loud, covering the occasional rhythmic beep that was designed as an audio alarm to show everything on the perimeter of Lost Souls was functioning properly.

Xilvii stood in the middle of an almost-circular console, covered with more equipment than Coop had ever seen in a working command center. There was nowhere to sit, and there were layers beneath the top of the console, shelves and nooks filled with more tablets and other bits of equipment Coop didn't recognize. There were also towers flanking the opening of the console, but those towers were obviously holographic. Even though they were black, Coop could see through them.

Xilvii looked at Coop as Coop came deeper into the command center, and for a brief second, a flash of irritation crossed Xilvii's face.

Finally, Coop understood why Xilvii hadn't appreciated the offer to return to the *Ivoire* on the mission to Sector Base E-2, even though Coop had wanted Xilvii to be part of the bridge crew. Xilvii had his own fiefdom here, and clearly liked it.

He was doing the job that Coop had assigned him.

That Coop had abandoned.

"I came for a report," Coop said, still feeling off balance. He hadn't come for a report. He had come to set up the defenses, rally the bored attendants working here, and see if he could find someone to operate whatever had been cobbled together.

He wasn't going to say that now, though, because Xilvii had it clearly in hand.

Xilvii nodded at the people he was talking to—three women Coop didn't recognize—and then walked over to Coop. Xilvii somehow moved Coop away from the doors, toward an alcove that Coop hadn't seen before, and did it without saying a word.

Coop had been disappointed in Xilvii a week ago, on that mission to E-2. Now, Coop realized that Xilvii had been out of his element there, and was fully in control here, in a way that Coop had never expected.

"Ilona contacted me," Xilvii said, "and told me to up our defenses. I'd done that when we returned from the last mission, figuring we'd be hearing from the Empire any day now, so I took the opportunity to place us on full alert."

He didn't sound defensive, and that was clearly intentional. He probably wasn't feeling defensive. He was most likely annoyed.

Coop remembered that emotion from his earlier years; he would feel like he had something under control, and then one of his superiors would enter and muck everything up.

Only technically, Coop was no longer one of Xilvii's superiors. Coop hadn't been given that status here. Irritation flashed through him—like it usually did—at the lack of hierarchy.

"Good," Coop said, then wished he hadn't. He didn't want to sound condescending. "I was just coming to make sure that you were aware of the possible threats."

Xilvii shook his head ever so slightly. "She said something about ships coming out of foldspace, and that was it."

Then he gave Coop a measuring look.

"I take it the ships coming out of foldspace aren't ours," Xilvii said. "Did those ships from E-2 find us?"

Coop suddenly realized that Lost Souls had more to deal with than the Empire or the five ships that Boss interacted with. The Not-Fleet was out there as well.

"I'm pretty sure we lost them," he said. And he was pretty sure that his maneuver into Empire territory went undetected. But he didn't know.

He moved his hand to the right, deeper in the alcove. But as they moved in that direction, he realized that this area had been repurposed. There were people inside it as well, and judging from the controls on their holographic screens, they were working on the weapons' systems for Lost Souls.

Weapons. Coop hadn't authorized more weapons, but he had told Blake that she needed better defenses. Now there was an entire area, with staff, who seemed to be dealing with weapons and other modes of attack.

He let out a breath, then glanced around in frustration.

"Is there somewhere we can talk in private?" he asked.

Xilvii smiled just a little. He seemed to understand that Coop had finally seen the changes that Xilvii made to the all-important defensive capabilities of Lost Souls.

"Um," Xilvii said, looking around. "Actually, no, there's no privacy here. It's one of the flaws in design. When I get a chance, I'll redo the layout, but it sounds like I won't have that opportunity for a while."

Coop nodded. He would have to talk quietly, then.

"All right," he said. "Let's move to the corridor, and I'll catch you up on what's been happening."

He led the way. Xilvii gave a few orders, then followed.

They stepped into the coolness of the corridor. It was calmer and quieter here.

Coop took a deep breath, then told Xilvii what had happened at the Boneyard—all of it, from the warships to the explosions to the destruction of the buoys. Xilvii frowned as he listened, standing straighter with each growing crisis.

When Coop got to the part about the ships in the Boneyard activating, Xilvii let out a small involuntary sound. It was either an acknowledgement or it was surprise.

"We don't know if she was followed through foldspace," he said. "We have to plan as if she was."

"By five ships or more?" Xilvii asked.

"More, I'd say." Coop glanced at the closed door. He was at a loss. It was clear they didn't have the personnel to mount a proper defense against a large contingent of ships.

The only reason Lost Souls had survived its encounter with the Empire a year ago was due to surprise. Lost Souls had bucked up its defenses since, but they were not on par with the ships Coop and Xilvii had seen with the Not-Fleet, and they certainly couldn't handle the Empire, if the Empire came into Nine Planets Territory with a wide array of ships.

If ships arrived from the Boneyard as well, then Lost Souls was in deep trouble.

And Xilvii knew it. His mouth was a thin line, his skin slightly gray, as the blood leached out of it.

"We can beef up the border," he said. "Maybe bring in more ships from the Nine Planets."

Coop nodded. He already planned to do that.

"But," Xilvii said, "if anyone comes here…"

His voice trailed off. He looked at Coop.

"We have enough crew to handle five DV-Class ships," Coop said. "We have not done enough training on weaponry or combat. We have more than five DV-Class ships, but most aren't in the best shape yet."

Then he squared his shoulders and spoke softly.

"But," he said, "it looks like you've stayed on top of Lost Souls' defenses. This is better than I expected."

To his credit, Xilvii didn't chide Coop for failing to visit. Maybe Xilvii realized that no one really was in charge of this part of Lost Souls.

"We have a lot of holes," Xilvii said. "The second space station has defenses, but no one to run them continuously, so I automated them. Our communications system is adequate, but it could easily be dismantled with the right kind of attack. We don't have fighters, really. Not just the ships, but the pilots. Half of the pilots for our smaller ships have left the *Ivoire*. I know because I went to find them, thinking maybe they could supply some training for the small ships. Maybe we could even come up with a plan for the border, in case the Empire decided to discard our agreement. And I didn't find anyone suitable. We need training from the ground up."

Coop nodded. "That's on me."

"No," Xilvii said. "That's on Boss. That's on Ilona. I've talked with her a dozen times about getting more personnel for defense, and she has said no. She's focused on making money. More people to engineer and manufacture equipment, to help sell the things that we've invented. But she doesn't seem to realize that we're a target, too. She thinks the defenses we have are enough."

Coop let out a small laugh. Maybe they would be enough, if he weren't here.

Although he wasn't the one who antagonized the Empire in the first place. That was Boss. But he had exacerbated it with his initial encounter at the Room of Lost Souls.

And it was Boss who attracted the attention of whoever owned those five ships, in the Boneyard.

Coop probably shook off the Not-Fleet, although they would be looking for him.

But Boss's explorations, her endless curiosity, was putting the business she built and the lives she was responsible for in danger.

"Do you really think those five ships she saw were Fleet?" Xilvii asked.

His words pulled Coop from his thoughts.

"Yash is checking that now," Coop said. "Or what she can check, anyway."

Xilvii shook his head. He seemed as off-balance from the news as Yash had been, as Coop still was.

"What does that mean for us?" Xilvii asked.

"I don't know," Coop said. But, for the first time since Ahidjo brought news of the Fleet, Coop felt grounded.

There might actually be a way out of this, and it wouldn't require weapons—at least at first.

"You got an idea," Xilvii said.

Coop did, but he wasn't going to share it with Xilvii. He needed Xilvii here.

"Shore up our defenses as best you can," Coop said. "Be ready to use weapons, if necessary. Get someone to power up the defensive systems on the various DV- and SC-Class ships, even if we don't have enough personnel to use those ships. We'll put them around the space stations, and run them remotely, if we have to."

"I've never done that," Xilvii said.

Coop hadn't either, but he did know it was possible. It had been part of his training, long ago.

"I have a hunch we're going to do a lot of things we've never done before," he said.

"What are you going to do?" Xilvii asked, and there was something in his voice. A neediness, maybe. A half-hearted request to keep Coop down here, to help if need be.

Coop grinned. "Were you on the leadership track? I don't recall off the top of my head."

"No," Xilvii said. "Systems. I preferred systems."

Coop nodded. Systems were easier and harder. But they made sense to someone with an organized mind. He didn't have one, at least, not like Yash or the engineers.

"In leadership training, they were pretty clear," he said. "If you didn't have the ability to fight an enemy, you had two choices."

"Two?" Xilvii asked. "I take it stay and fight was not one of them."

"Yeah." Coop was actually relaxing. He was beginning to feel like himself again. "Retreat is a good solution, particularly in a tough situation."

"But they're coming to us," Xilvii said.

"That's right," Coop said. "So we figure out what they want."

"So we can give it to them?" Xilvii asked.

Coop shrugged. "If it's easy and costs nothing, sure."

"And if it's neither of those things?" Xilvii asked.

"We talk some more."

Xilvii's brow furrowed. "Diplomacy?"

"Yep," Coop said.

"Do we even have diplomats?" Xilvii asked.

"We had a shipload of them," Coop said. "We were on a diplomatic mission five years ago, or had you forgotten?"

Plus, anyone on the leadership track, from Lynda Rooney to Coop himself had more diplomatic training than they ever thought they would use.

Xilvii shook his head slightly, as if the words just registered. "Yes," he said. "I had forgotten."

"You take care of Lost Souls defenses. I'm going to put a team together."

Xilvii nodded, then started to leave. He stopped just outside the door.

"You think something's going to happen," he said quietly.

"We've been stealing from that Boneyard," Coop said. "It has active ships. Something will happen. We just don't know when."

Xilvii let out a long breath. "Let's just hope they give us time. I might be able to add more defenses."

Coop almost said, *We will never have enough firepower to take on all those active ships in the Boneyard*, but he stopped himself just in time. He wanted Xilvii motivated.

He wanted everyone to be motivated.

Including himself.

They might not have enough firepower to take on those ships, but they had enough skill to talk their way out of any circumstance.

Provided they did everything right.

19

Captain Kayla Cohn walked around the floating screens inside her office, hands clasped behind her back. It had been a long day, and an even longer night, but she wasn't really tired. She had a wellspring of nervous energy that only being in a battle could give her.

Less than thirty-six hours ago, she had attacked two ships that had raided the Scrapheap. She had used the resources in her ship, the *Geesi*, to coordinate with the Scrapheap itself. The control towers actually responded to her commands, something she hadn't believed possible when she had first heard of this Scrapheap.

She paused in front of one of the holographic representations of the Scrapheap as it was now. She brought that holo higher, so that it was just below eye level. Through it, she could see the walls of the office, and through those, she could see the walls of the ready room.

She had one of the first offices in any Dignity Vessel that could be reduced to a small cube and stored anywhere on the vessel. In fact, she could use the office anywhere on the vessel if she so chose. The office was keyed to her DNA, and could be summoned for use anywhere on the ship.

She usually used it inside her ready room, another anachronism that future ship designs should jettison. She had told the Fleet that, but they had humored her. The Fleet liked its traditions, and was still uncertain about the mobile office.

She loved it.

She also loved the way it gave her extra privacy inside her ready room. No one on her crew, not even her first officer, could enter the office without her permission—unless Cohn herself was having some kind of medical emergency. That feature of the office allowed her a level of privacy she had nowhere else on the ship, except her quarters—and she truly hated working inside her quarters.

One of the secrets to her success—or so she believed—was that she used her quarters for rest.

Not that she had done so in the past forty-eight hours. She'd managed to get four hours of sleep before she brought the full force of the Fleet to those thieves in the Scrapheap, and another five hours of scattered sleep—a bit here and a bit there—in the past thirty-six.

She didn't feel like she needed any more sleep though. Besides the increased adrenaline from the attack, her brain was working overtime on the information her team had presented her about the thieves.

Those thieves had worked the Scrapheap for months.

And "worked" was the operative word. They had fought to get inside, finally using codes that had breached the Scrapheap. They had used ancient Fleet equipment to establish themselves, and then they had scouted some ships stored there.

At first, Cohn believed they were searching for a particular ship. Then she watched the meticulousness with which they entered a DV-Class vessel, stored near their entry point, and realized that they weren't searching for a ship or anything on it. They were exploring it, figuring out what it was, and if they could use it.

On the screens floating around her, she had frozen images of different moments in the thieves' exploration of ships and the Scrapheap.

The thieves hadn't really touched much of the Scrapheap at all. It was one of the largest Scrapheaps that Cohn had ever seen or even heard about. It seemed to go on forever—larger than most planets, almost as if a planet and its defenses had expanded to cover most of the area around that planet, encroaching on several other planets.

Only this Scrapheap used old and outdated Fleet technology, designed to hide secrets in plain sight by creating a sensor blackout. Most maps of the area showed the Scrapheap as a black emptiness, a void that seemed vaguely unnatural, in the middle of space.

The problem with that design, as the Fleet had learned long ago, was that not all maps read the sensor blackout the same way. Several could identify the Scrapheap on the map, and some could even get the details that the Fleet was trying to hide using this method.

That was why they had abandoned the method for stronger force-fields, better protection, and an opaqueness in the later design that made it impossible for a ship near the Scrapheap to see ships floating inside one.

This Scrapheap was visible to naked eye in any ship that got close enough to view the Scrapheap. So, someone looking out a porthole, would see the Scrapheap, even while the sensors showed nothing but blackness.

That design had, over the years, attracted pirate vessels and others who wanted to steal from the Scrapheap, but the Scrapheap's natural defenses destroyed any vessel that got too close.

The thieves had managed to avoid that defensive reaction. They had gotten shot at early on, but either the shots had caused little damage or the thieves had been expecting it.

Still, they came back with Fleet equipment, and a new way of entering the Scrapheap. They seemed dogged, which she quietly admired, and they seemed determined, although—early on in this work—she hadn't been able to see why.

The thieves were organized and dedicated. They had removed several ships, mostly DV-Class vessels from the Scrapheap, and used those vessels—now repaired and modernized (somewhat, anyway) to return to the Scrapheap.

That tactic was the most brilliant thing they did. Because it confused the Scrapheap, which saw the ships as being used but not stolen. The Scrapheap's contacts with the Fleet, initiated when the thieves first arrived, were detailed examinations of the thieves' initial entry into the Scrapheap, and then the theft of their very first vessel.

Even though the Scrapheap's records showed the thieves taking more and more ships (and returning in several of them, using the ship's own *anacapa* drive), the Scrapheap's interior defensive system did not activate again.

Cohn knew that the thieves had been unable to access the control towers. The thieves hadn't even tried, which she found odd. If she were stealing from something this vast, she would have wanted to shut down its defenses.

A lot of behavior from the thieves made little sense. Most thieves would have taken what they could and never returned. But these thieves seemed to believe that the Scrapheap was abandoned, and they could loot it for as long as they liked.

To be fair, though, the Scrapheap had been abandoned—for all intents and purposes. The thieves clearly didn't want to engage, and they had fled the moment the ships powered up around them.

Fled using *anacapa* drives.

The use of *anacapa* drives—more than once—concerned her. The fact that the thieves had been sending probes behind the forcefield protecting the Ready Vessels concerned her more. Those vessels were most likely intact and ready to go—even after centuries. They looked like they were part of a squadron, which they were. Had the Scrapheap not contacted the Fleet, these thieves would have had hundreds of intact and working vessels, more up-to-date than the DV-Class ships that the thieves had been repairing.

Cohn had no idea what the thieves planned to do with the ships they took out of the Scrapheap, but she figured this: If those thieves were willing to risk their lives for long-term mining of the Scrapheap, then they would have been happy to find the Ready Vessels.

Her communications module chimed, and then First Officer Sigrid Vinters' voice echoed in the office.

"Captain, I need a moment of your time."

Vinters knew better than to ask to enter the office. Cohn had denied Vinters access every single time. That galled her, so Vinters always asked sideways to enter the office.

And Cohn always ignored the request.

"In my Ready Room in five," Cohn said.

She stared at the open screens, floating around her. If she shrank the office, she didn't need to close the screens. They would come back up, exactly as they were.

But she was loath to leave them.

She sighed, powered down a few of them, then slipped out the office door into the ready room. She then compressed the office down to a small cube and attached it to the far wall.

She raised two chairs from the floor, away from the office, added a table between them in case Vinters brought something that needed to be set down, and straightened her uniform. Cohn had showered that morning, but the shower felt like a very long time ago, and she had been working hard.

She wondered if she had a moment to at least get some coffee, but the door opened. Vinters entered the Ready Room.

Vinters was the most competent first officer that Cohn ever had. Vinters was tall, thin, and so pale that people often did a doubletake when they saw her. Her winter white hair accented the paleness, so she usually kept it pulled back or piled on top of her head.

Today, it was slipping out of its pile, which it did when she stopped paying attention to anything except the task before her.

"I have the information you wanted on this Lost Souls Corporation," she said.

Cohn had asked Vinters to investigate the corporation when they learned that these ships had fled through foldspace to an area near Sector Base V. The ships had been going to and fro from the Lost Souls Corporation, which Cohn had never heard of.

The Scrapheap had pulled information from all of the ships, down-loading and storing their data from the moment the group was flagged

as thieves. Later incursions into the Scrapheap weren't considered crimi-
nal, so information was not taken from any ships after the first few, but
apparently, that had been enough.

The information that Cohn had asked for about Lost Souls was basic:
What were they? Where were they located? How were they tied to the
ships working inside the Scrapheap?

Cohn had thought the answers to those questions would be straightforward enough that Vinters could simply have sent them to Cohn's office.

Instead, Vinters felt she needed to brief Cohn in person.

Cohn felt a shiver run through her, and wasn't exactly sure why.
Maybe it was because Vinters looked slightly disheveled and very serious.

Cohn had no idea what there would be about some corporation in
a sector that the Fleet had been nowhere near that would upset Vinters.

Vinters hadn't moved away from the door, so Cohn swept her hand
toward the chairs. Vinters shook her head.

"This will only take a minute," she said.

"All right." Cohn frowned. "What did you find?"

"Lost Souls is a very new corporation," Vinters said. "They've only
been around five years or so. They're also exceptionally wealthy."

Cohn had no idea why that mattered, but she trusted Vinters. Vinters
liked to present a case, so each fact mattered.

"I take it they didn't start with money," Cohn said.

"From what I can tell, they started from a wreck diving business
for tourists, run by one woman, who barely eked out a living for years."
Vinters tilted her head slightly as if simply saying that information made
her feel uncomfortable.

"Wreck diving," Cohn said. That made sense, now, seeing how
the thieves had worked the Scrapheap. They had done so with the
meticulousness of people who ventured into dangerous spaces and
came out alive. "What are they doing, selling these ships or breaking
them into parts?"

"Neither, as far as I can tell," Vinters said. "They're doing several
things. They're affiliated with a DV-Class ship that has helped a group

called the Nine Planets defend their border with something called the Enterran Empire."

So, they needed ships for defense. On a basic level, Cohn couldn't argue with that.

"They seem to know how to exploit all parts of a DV-Class ship, so that when they're faced with a larger force, they still survive," Vinters said.

Cohn's frown deepened. That skill was usually trained. But, she supposed, if it could be trained, it could be learned by using training manuals or simply running the vessel for a long period of time.

Still, she mentally flagged that bit of information.

"So, a handful of ships will help them," Cohn said.

"I'm not sure the defense is being run by Lost Souls," Vinters said, "although they were under attack a year or so ago, because of that defense."

"All right," Cohn waited for the important piece of information. It was easier than quizzing Vinters.

"What's disturbing," Vinters said, "*deeply* disturbing is the way they've made their money."

Cohn remained very still. They were talking about thieves. Thieves who raided the Scrapheap and took valuable equipment, equipment that had information built into some of the ships.

But the information was thousands of years old. It couldn't be of value to anyone.

"They're taking the tech they've discovered in the Scrapheap, modifying it, and selling it throughout their sector," Vinters said. "I've looked at their sales information, and even took a look at the samples they've teased with."

She looked directly at Cohn. Something swam in Vinters' eyes. Anger? Concern? Maybe a bit of panic?

It couldn't be panic. Vinters didn't panic.

"Whoever is designing this tech," Vinters said, "they're very, very, very good. They've taken complicated things and made them so simple that anyone can use them."

"*Anacapa* drives?" Cohn asked.

"Not that I can tell," Vinters said, "and I doubt it, given the descriptions I've found of the items they're selling. They do have a pay-extra-and-we'll-upgrade-what-you-have section, but there's no mention of weaponry or any kind of shipboard engines."

"Well, that's something," Cohn said. She was answering more or less by rote. She wasn't sure how she felt about any of this. She would examine her feelings later.

"They're selling medical tech," Vinters said, "which, weirdly, irritates me, because I have this feeling that they should give the medical stuff away, even though we don't do it."

"Sure we do," Cohn said, "when we want diplomatic advantage."

But that was the only time. The Fleet was very proprietary about its tech. That paranoia was built in. They were afraid that someone would reverse engineer what they'd already done, and take over their tech somehow.

The paranoia partly existed because the Fleet had done that with a lot of tech it discovered. Although it never entirely could reverse engineer an *anacapa* drive, no matter how hard and how many centuries they'd been trying to do so.

"Maybe that's why it irritates." Vinters' tone said otherwise. Her face was closed off. She didn't want to discuss the medical tech. She wanted to discuss the rest of it.

Cohn nodded, encouraging her to continue.

"They're selling a lot of low-level stuff," Vinters said. "Environmental suits, communications systems—without *anacapa* drives, as far as I can tell—some truly basic tech that makes any work in space easier."

"And that's making them rich?" Cohn asked.

"No," Vinters said. "They're also taking orders for ships."

Cohn felt a thread of irritation. She had already asked about that. "So, someone orders a ship, these Lost Souls people come to the Scrapheap to get it, and then deliver it to whomever?"

"No," Vinters said. "They're only taking orders for small ships. What we call orbiters. Anything that can travel short distances and go in and out of atmosphere."

Cohn waited.

"They're building them from scratch," Vinters said. "And they're selling a lot of them, from what I can tell. No weapons system, but a lot of defensive tech built in. I suspect that if I were to query about the higher-level items, I would be able to order shields or forcefields. Or maybe some of the rescue tech, because I did see something about recovery vehicles."

Cohn let out a small breath. Defensive tech. That was a problem. Even if the tech was as old as the Scrapheap, a lot of it was similar to the tech that the Fleet used now.

In fact, the tech the Fleet used now was based on that tech. If someone had that tech and used it regularly, they would know how to defeat it.

They might not know the modifications the Fleet had made over the centuries but they might be able to figure out those modifications.

Cohn cursed.

She walked over to the chairs and put a hand on the back of the nearest one, to brace herself, not because her legs had given out, but because she would have felt the urge to pace otherwise.

"Are you sure they're not just taking orders, hoping to deliver something in the future?" Cohn asked.

"Yes, I'm sure of what I found," Vinters said. "They have time-lapsed recordings of ship-building. I went through those bit by bit. They're not faked. They're real."

Cohn set her other hand on the chair back, gripping the warm smooth surface.

"Our tech isn't that easy to replicate," she said.

"Not now, it's not," Vinters said, "and looking at what's in this Scrapheap, not with the older items either. Whoever is doing the designing is either some kind of genius or it's someone who has worked with Fleet tech before."

Cohn let out a quiet sigh. Now she would have to make some decisions. She had thought going after these people would be easy—and maybe it would be.

But she didn't know that for certain.

"What's their defensive tech look like?" she asked.

Vinters didn't realize that Cohn had mentally moved to a different subject. Vinters frowned at Cohn. "On the small ships?"

"At this Lost Souls," Cohn said.

"It seems pretty minimal, but most places don't advertise their defensive systems." Vinters could be forgiven for overexplaining that to Cohn. Cohn had caught Vinters off guard with the question.

"How many ships do they have that credibly do battle with ours?" Cohn asked.

Vinters raised her pale eyebrows, giving her an almost comical look of surprise. "Large ships? DV-Class? A few, although it's hard to say exactly, because they have some ships on that border. I'm not sure which ones on that border belong to a member state of the Nine Planets themselves."

"Do they have fighters?" Cohn asked.

"Not that I've found," Vinters said. "They certainly aren't selling any."

"Interesting." Cohn leaned harder on the back of that chair, putting a lot of weight into her palms. "They're not profiteering then. They're selling useful items, but not items that can come back and harm them in the future."

"That we know of," Vinters said. "I haven't gone for a direct contact, to see what else they offered. You had to qualify in currencies I didn't recognize, and I wasn't even going to try."

"So they know their market," Cohn said. "They're targeting someone specific and leaving out others on purpose."

"I guess." Vinters wasn't fond of this kind of speculation.

Cohn tapped the top of the chair, then walked around it. Apparently, she was going to pace after all.

"How long have they been doing this?" she asked. "As long as they've been stealing?"

She was having trouble putting the timeline together. Because it sounded like they had a lot of product. They couldn't have been making all of it, without a full-blown factory of some kind. That seemed like a lot to develop after discovering the Scrapheap.

"Oh, no," Vinters said. "Some of these products have been for sale for years."

Cohn stopped pacing. She had expected *a year* or a little more than that. But *years*? That didn't make sense, at least not connected to the Scrapheap. Because the thieves didn't have time to reverse engineer anything, let alone develop all of these products—not if they were using this Scrapheap as their source.

She clenched a fist, then loosened it, thinking as she did so. Years. Did that mean the thieves had a second Scrapheap? Or had they found some abandoned ships outside of the Scrapheap and reverse engineered what they had done?

"Years," she repeated.

Vinters frowned at her, but knew better than to interrupt.

"That DV-Class vessel you mentioned," Cohn said, "the one that guarded their border with the Enterran Empire."

"Yes?" Vinters said.

"Did they get that ship from the Scrapheap?"

"No," Vinters said. "Scrapheap records show that the ship passed near the Scrapheap more than a year ago."

"They got the ship from somewhere else," Cohn said, more to herself than to Vinters.

"Apparently," Vinters said.

Cohn nodded, then walked back to the chair, gripping it by the sides. If she could lift it out of its spot on the floor, she would have. She needed something to do with her hands.

Vinters didn't say anymore. She knew Cohn's process, maybe better than Cohn did herself.

"So," Cohn said, "we have a ship that knows how to defend itself against a larger force, someone who knows how to turn Fleet tech into useful tech for outsiders, and someone who knows ancient codes that got them into the Scrapheap."

Vinters nodded, but still didn't add anything.

"Do we know anything else about that ship?" Cohn asked.

"It's named the *Ivoire*," Vinters said. "I looked for it in our records, but didn't find anything current. There is mention of its captain being court-martialed, but we don't have those records. The *Tudósok* might."

The *Tudósok* was an older DV-Class vessel they had brought on this journey, against Cohn's will. Vice Admiral Mbuyi wanted the *Tudósok* along to do research work inside the Scrapheap, just in case the five ships that Cohn was currently commanding didn't find the thieves.

Now that they had found the thieves, Cohn had decided to leave the *Tudósok* here at the Scrapheap, so that it could gather information.

She hadn't really thought that the *Tudósok* might contribute to the second part of her mission—at least until now.

"How long ago was the court-martial?" Cohn asked.

"From what I can tell," Vinters said, "four or five thousand years ago."

"Thousand?" Cohn said.

"Thousand," Vinters confirmed.

"Well, that's not what I expected to hear," Cohn said. "Is the ship's age consistent with that information?"

"The codes are," Vinters said, "but the readings we have off the ship from the Scrapheap aren't complete enough to let us know more than that."

"We don't know what happened to the ship after the court-martial?" Cohn asked.

"The court-martial itself was just a passing mention. Something to do with the Enterran Empire's history, which I didn't delve into. I can let Captain Jicha know we're interested, if you would like."

Balázs Jicha ran the *Tudósok*. Cohn smiled, thinking of Jicha's reaction if one of her officers gave him an order. Jicha was one of the most prickly members of the Fleet she had ever met.

"No," Cohn said. "I'll deal with Captain Jicha. I don't think it would hurt to have him investigate this ship. We might be able to see if it was in a previous Scrapheap. If so, we might be dealing with some group that raids Scrapheaps."

"I don't think our records are that complete," Vinters said. "We don't keep track of ships placed in Scrapheaps."

"We did," Cohn said. "We had records of what happens to a ship when it's retired. But no one keeps track after that. I guess we assumed the ships were stable, once they were placed in a Scrapheap."

"Interesting assumption," Vinters said. She tilted her head, as she so often did when she was considering something. "If they stole the ship long ago and from a different Scrapheap, then they might have had time to learn how to use the ship."

"True," Cohn said. She was less worried about how someone learned how to use that ship than she was about what they were doing now. "And we don't know. They might have taken this *Ivoire* from the Scrapheap here."

"Wouldn't the Scrapheap have notified us?" Vinters asked.

"It might have tried," Cohn said. "We were lucky to get this last notification."

"That's true," Vinters said.

"But the speculation doesn't matter right now," Cohn said. "We have a larger problem on our hands."

Vinters lips thinned. She was clearly trying not to say anything. She had already come to that conclusion, or she wouldn't have come here in person.

"If I brought this information to the vice admiral," Cohn said, "she would tell us what we already know. This Lost Souls place is an active threat to the Fleet. They are selling our technology. They're stealing from us. And who knows what their end game is."

Vinters straightened. Apparently, that last part surprised her. "Active threat, captain?"

"Yes," Cohn said. "We don't know what they're after, but we do know that they know about us."

"Us?" Vinters asked.

"The Fleet," she said.

"Because we attacked them at the Scrapheap?" Vinters said. "Wouldn't they have known about us before that?"

"Not necessarily," Cohn said. "Before they saw us they might have assumed that the Fleet was long gone, just something that had existed in the very distant past."

Vinters' eyes narrowed.

"But," Cohn said, "we just confirmed that we're active and paying attention to that Scrapheap."

Vinters breathed in slowly, then she nodded, just as slowly. "They know we guard our ships."

"And if they have more of our technology," Cohn said, "they might be able to find us by searching foldspace."

"Foldspace tracking is an art form," Vinters said, clearly disagreeing.

"So is defending yourself against a larger foe, using only one DV-Class vessel," Cohn said. "And so is redesigning one kind of tech to be useful for other cultures. We don't dare underestimate these people."

Vinters nodded. "What are you suggesting, captain?"

Cohn patted the back of the chair, then stepped away from it. She clasped her hands behind her back, and paced. She had no suggestions at all. She had simply been thinking out loud.

"If we go back to the Fleet, get more ships, and go after this Lost Souls, we're definitely declaring ourselves." And, she thought but didn't say, they would also be going backwards, something she wasn't sure she would get approval for.

She tapped her thumb against her teeth, not looking at Vinters at all.

"But if we go after them on our own," Cohn said, "we have to make certain they have no backup. We don't want to attack and miss somehow. This is a fight we would have to win."

"Would you like me to set up a communication with the vice admiral?" Vinters asked.

That was the logical response, but the moment Vinters spoke it out loud, something inside Cohn rejected it.

"No," she said. "We get as much research done as we can, and then we go after them. They'll think we've forgotten them. We have to take out their defenses, and then get our ships back."

"Shouldn't we just destroy the ships?" Vinters asked.

"Probably," Cohn said. "That would be the safest. Although we need more information before we make any decisions. We need to find out what we can about their defensive capabilities. We need to know how much hardware they have, what kind of weaponry they're using, and, if we can figure it out, what their goals are."

"All right," Vinters said.

But Cohn wasn't done. "We also need to find out about this *Ivoire*. See how long it has been operational in that sector."

"Are you going to assign any of this to the *Tudósok*?" Vinters asked.

"Some of it, yes," Cohn said. "Including—perhaps—a history of this Empire that the *Ivoire* is battling. Something about all of this feels unfinished to me."

Vinters had bitten her lower lip. "It might not be connected at all."

"It might not," Cohn said. "The history might simply be us, connecting what few dots we have."

She tapped her right forefinger against the palm of her left hand. She had finally figured out what bothered her the most about all of this.

"The Ready Vessels," she said.

"Hmmm?" Vinters clearly hadn't followed Cohn's train of thought, perhaps because Cohn was just beginning to process the ideas now.

"They were trying to figure out how to get to the Ready Vessels," Cohn said.

"We're not sure these thieves knew the Ready Vessels were there," Vinters said.

"I know," Cohn said. "But if they've been stealing vessels from the Scrapheap, they might have stumbled across information about the vessels. And if the thieves are using their ships in a war against this Empire, what better way to win that war than steal hundreds of equipped warships?"

"I've looked at this company," Vinters said. "They don't have the personnel to run hundreds of warships."

"I heard you on that," Cohn said. "But the Nine Planets might have more than enough personnel to handle the warships."

"I don't think just anyone could handle those ships," Vinters said. She looked almost forbidding, as if she couldn't believe that Cohn was even suggesting this. "It takes special training to run DV-Class vessels. It was my understanding that the warship track made our work on DV-Class ships seem like child's play."

Cohn smiled. She'd heard that before as well, but she'd been with the Fleet long enough to know that sometimes, the Fleet discouraged people from trying something new by simply saying that it was hard.

"These people learned how to use a DV-Class vessel to its fullest capacity," Cohn said. "They are repurposing Fleet tech. I would wager they can handle Ready Vessels."

"But quickly...?" Vinters said, skeptically.

"I never said anything about quickly," Cohn said. "They were clearly taking their time here. They might have a long-term plan."

Ready Vessels would have changed the balance of power in that sector, and it would have done so quickly.

She had the Scrapheap under wraps for now, but she wasn't sure how durable the solution she found was. She couldn't leave these Lost Souls people to their own devices, so she didn't dare risk going back to the Fleet to get more ships.

She also didn't want to discuss this anymore with the vice admiral. Cohn wanted to finish off the Lost Souls problem, and then return to her normal duties.

She had a hunch the *Tudósok* would remain at the Scrapheap long after the other four ships in the Task Unit left. If there were further problems, the *Tudósok* would notify the Fleet.

Of course, she needed to discuss all of this with Jicha, but she had no problem doing that. And he would probably be happy to have both his research and what he would consider to be an important assignment.

Cohn hadn't expected this mission to become so complicated. She had initially thought this was simple theft. Now, it looked like something more. Something that might affect millions of lives.

She had already stopped the ongoing theft. Now she had to make sure it would never happen again.

She also had to make sure that there would be nothing left of the Lost Souls Corporation—and maybe the Nine Planets—that could threaten the Fleet.

20

I HAVE RIDICULOUSLY HUGE QUARTERS here at the Lost Souls Corporation. No single human being should need a space this large. Three bedrooms plus a master suite, two work areas, a "den" with games and holos and other amenities that could cocoon me for months on end, a living area, a personal kitchen which is bigger than some ships, and a catering kitchen in case—oh, I don't know—someone wants to cook dinner for an army.

The master suite is larger than any apartment I had before I met all of these people. It's larger than any captain's suite I've seen in any ship I have ever traveled on or any ship I've ever dived. There are four bathrooms, in case—I guess—I don't want to use the same bathroom twice in a row.

I had not seen or approved this place. Ilona calls it "the owner's suite," and she's very proud of it. She had informed me of it while I was so sick after that ill-fated dive in the Boneyard, the dive that nearly killed me and Elaine Seager.

You can come home, Ilona said to me then. *We will take care of you in style. We have finished more of the space station, and we finally have the proper quarters for you.*

The proper quarters for me would have been a closet barely big enough for a bed, a tiny bathroom, a galley kitchen, so I didn't have to see anyone when I was working, and a small area where I could research. All the rest of this is wasted space that makes me feel lost and embarrassed.

Ilona showed it to me herself after the meeting, and I made the appropriate *I'm-impressed* sounds—or I hope I did. She put a lot of thought into this. I'm on a center level with windows all around, so that I can see some of our ships and space beyond. The view is breathtaking, and it does change rapidly, since we're in orbit around Odite.

But I hate it here. I really, really hate it here. Ilona had someone move my stuff from the tiny apartment I had chosen for myself back when we founded Lost Souls into this cavernous space. I could spend the rest of my life searching for what few possessions I had left behind.

My civilian clothes are in the monster master bedroom, along with regular shoes, but I have no idea where my backup gear is. I can't find the trinkets I've saved from some of my earliest dives, although I did see a few things on a shelf.

And my dishes are just gone, replaced by something similar, fancy, and seemingly very fragile.

I sat at the long dining room table (oh, yeah, there's a dining room) and stared at the windows, watching bots or maybe my team (or at least, the people I pay) working on a DV-Class vessel in what Ilona called "the shipyard." The work was fascinating from a distance, or maybe I was just tired and shell-shocked and unsettled.

After decontamination and a moment alone with Coop, we headed into the meeting room. Mikk and Diaz joined us, although I left the rest of the team out of it—and Diaz was only there as a courtesy, really, since she wasn't deeply involved with our dives.

Mikk and I ran the videos like we used to do back on our dives, to make sure everyone was up to speed, and I studiously did not watch faces for reactions. I wasn't sure I wanted to see them.

When we were done, everyone scattered. Coop is terrified that these people—the Fleet, he hopes—will come through foldspace and destroy us. He wants our defenses to be as strong as they can. Ilona couldn't answer questions to his satisfaction, which actually made him angry (something I hadn't expected) and off he went to shore all of that up.

Yash wants to know what, exactly, we found, and what, exactly, had happened when the ships came alive inside the Scrapheap. She isn't looking so much at Lost Soul's defenses as she is to see if that activation means we actually found the Fleet.

I had expected that reaction from both her and from Coop. (I was surprised—am surprised—that he's a bit more interested in defense at the moment.) I am almost disappointed in Yash at how intent she is on learning whether or not these people who attacked us are Fleet. I don't like the fact that she's so very predictable. I always like Yash better when I can't predict what she's going to do.

Ilona has promised to help Coop with the defenses, plus she's doing some diplomatic work with the Nine Planets, warning them that some kind of space force might enter their territory. She did take the time to bring me here, though, and proudly show me around.

She doesn't understand the urgency, which is part of what enflamed Coop, I'm sure. She's great at running a business, but she has no idea how to handle external threats. Which is why, I think, the Lost Soul's defensive systems aren't as strong as Coop would like them to be.

I—oddly enough—found myself at loose ends when Ilona left. I explored this stupid suite, and realized how long it was going to take me to find my things. Not that they really matter to me, because if they did, they would have traveled with me.

But it's unsettling, to leave your possessions in one place, and have them end up in another, in a way that you would never have placed them yourself.

I can help Coop with defense, which is out of my depth, or I can help Yash search the materials she has downloaded off of the *Veilig*. I don't really want to figure out if we've found the Fleet. I'm much more interested in what set them off, whoever they are. The information that we managed to get just before everything went to hell is much more precious to me than figuring out who or what attacked us.

With that in mind, I contacted Mikk and asked him to meet me here.

The one thing I like about this suite—the only thing, really—is that I can isolate it from all of Lost Soul's systems. Whatever we work on here can remain completely private.

With Yash and Diaz hogging the *Veilig* and her systems, I don't feel like I have my own space to work, which is why I've moved everything here.

By the time Mikk arrives, I have everything set up in the smaller office area. The smaller office has permanent furniture—well, the entire suite does, really. None of the furniture is bolted down, and none of it recesses into the floor. As Ilona showed me the place, she reminded me that I owned everything, and I could request any furniture I wanted. She would make sure I got it.

I thanked her, and wondered how offended she would be if I simply had someone remove most of the furniture. I think I could handle the empty rooms much better than all of this stuff, set aside just for me.

I am sliding the furniture in the small office around, wondering who needs extra chairs, some upholstered, a large rug, and actual tables—not tables with tech built in, when Mikk knocks. I almost shout, "C'mon in," and then I realize he won't be able to hear me.

Ilona made a point of letting me know this entire place is well sound-proofed. I guess she thinks that makes me feel better about being here. I wipe my hands on my forest green pants—a pair I had found in my civilian wardrobe, then tug down a bronze shirt that had once been a favorite. It's actually a bit too big now. Apparently, I've lost weight since the injury and during all the dives.

I turn the wrong way as I leave the office, then realize what I've done. Mikk knocks again, and I mentally tell him I'm on the way. The door is farther from the office than I thought. Maybe I should shut off the gravity in here and dive the damn thing, just so I can keep track of the size of the spaces.

The though amuses me, so I'm smiling when I open the door.

Mikk's eyebrows go up and he takes a step back. Then he frowns and looks at me suspiciously. "You seem cheerful."

"I'm overwhelmed," I say. "Do you have everything?"

He lifts an extra-large canvas bag that seems overstuffed. He hands me a smaller bag as he walks through the door, then he stops as if he has no idea where he is.

He probably doesn't.

"They gave me a palace," I say.

"I see that," he says. "I bet you hate it."

"With a screaming passion," I say.

And finally, I get a smile. He shakes his head. "No matter how often you tell people who you are, sometimes they just refuse to listen."

"You need some furniture in your place?"

"Hell, no," he says. "I've got too much crap as it is. Only I have four rooms, not a thousand."

"I think I have fewer than that," I say. "But not by much." I heft the small bag. "Tablets?"

"From the *Veilig*," he says. "A lot of them are the non-Fleet tech. We can see what we find."

While we were in the Boneyard, we discovered that Fleet tech gave us different readings than tech that had no taint of Fleet technology at all. We were trying to understand all of the different readings just before we had to flee.

"I've also downloaded everything from the past two months off the *Veilig*," he says. "I only wanted our probes and the information we got off the ship just before it blew."

"Did you grab the images from the buoys too?" I ask, as we skirt some badly placed ottomans.

"And from the ships around us," he says. "We were taking readings as they powered up. Maybe you and I can figure out what triggered them."

We carry the bags into the small office, which seems even smaller with the furniture against the wall.

"Mind if I move some of this to a different room?" Mikk asks.

"I had just started when you got here," I say. "So let's finish that up."

He and I remove some of the chairs and two of the tables and leave them in the larger office which, effectively, makes it unusable. Not that I would have used it.

We keep two chairs in the smaller office, and three regular tables. We set the bags on the floor, and together, Mikk and I remove tablets from inside the bags, spreading them on the ugly brown carpet. I have no idea why there is carpet in here, probably as part of the soundproofing, but I don't like it.

"Now," Mikk says, "if only we had some way to process all of this."

"We do." I slap a hand on the wall closest to me. The front flips and on the other side are screens and keyboards, as well as more tablets and hand-touch boards that create instant holographic images. "This is the only part of the suite that I like."

I suspect the equipment in the larger office is more extensive, but it's just me and Mikk here, and this will do for now.

I tap in my new identification codes, which Ilona gave me and made me memorize, as well as press my entire hand against the access panel, just like she taught me to.

For a moment, I think it's not going to work, and then a female voice greets me with "It is a pleasure to finally meet you, my boss."

"My boss," sends a bit of an unpleasant shudder through me, but it makes Mikk bark out a laugh.

"Wow," he says, "another thing to love about this place."

I shut off the voice commands, which are never my favorite things anyway, and then isolate the system so no one can see what we're doing. We still don't upload anything, though, in an excess of caution. Mikk has to go through the system first to make sure that the isolation works.

He grabs one of the chairs, sits on it with his legs spread, so that he's pressed as close to the wall as he can be, and then he starts working his magic on the systems.

I don't watch. Instead, I call up the buoy imagery. When we were in the Boneyard, watching our automated runabout get reprogrammed and then sent on a path away from us, I had the buoy cameras already running, so that I could see the runabout when it exited the Boneyard.

Instead, I noticed five large ships—DV-Class vessels (I'm guessing) of a type I don't recognize, and an SC-Class vessel—silently approach the buoys. As we were in the middle of our experiment with our run-about, none of us—including me—paid much attention to the buoys, and by the time those ships registered with me, they had destroyed the first buoy.

They had known about us, and they had known we set up the buoys. From that moment on, those ships didn't want us to know where they were.

And indeed, I have no idea where they were when the ships around us in the Boneyard activated. I don't know if those five ships had entered the Boneyard or if they had done work from outside.

I'm not even sure if they were alone. For all I know, they might have had other ships inside the Boneyard.

In theory, Mikk brought all of our information on the Boneyard, from our dives and from the monitors we'd set up around the section of the Boneyard that we were going to dive. Maybe some of those monitors would give us additional insight into what exactly had been going on.

"We're isolated, and isolated well," he says, which relieves me even though I had done a thorough check before he arrived.

Because this suite has me so freaked out, though, I want to make sure my judgement is correct. Then I inwardly smile at myself. For a woman who likes being alone in space and isn't afraid of dying while exploring, I can be sensitive to the weirdest things.

Mikk pushes the chair back slightly. "Where do you want to start?"

"Yash will be focused on those five ships and whatever they activated in the Boneyard," I say. "I want to take a closer look at those warships."

Mikk smiles. "I figured," he says. "You want to know if it's worth going back."

"No," I say, as I heft one of the tablets. "I already know it's worth going back. We have a lot of information to gather."

Mikk blinks and leans back. I've surprised him after all.

He's waiting for me to clarify, so I do.

"I want to know how *soon* we need to go back," I say.

"Boss," he says, with just a bit of caution in his voice, "those ships attacked us."

"Technically, Mikk," I say, "they didn't attack us at all. Ships inside the Boneyard activated and shot at us as we were leaving."

We barely made it out as those shots went wild. And, as Diaz quietly told me, we were very lucky that nothing hit us while we went into foldspace.

I already knew that. The *Ivoire* crew is skittish about any shots fired near a foldspace window. That's how they got trapped in foldspace in the beginning.

"You and your technicalities," he says.

"They're important," I say. "We don't know what, exactly, happened. Did those five ships activate the ships in the Boneyard to attack us? Or did those five ships wake up the Boneyard and it defended itself? Or did it shoot at us, thinking we were part of a squadron from those five ships, worth attacking because the five ships shot at something close to the exterior shields of the Boneyard?"

He's frowning again. He folds his hands over his flat stomach, waiting for me.

"You don't believe any of that, do you?" he asks.

"I don't know what to believe," I say. "We're in Fleet vessels and you and I aren't Fleet. So why should we assume that the five ships are Fleet as well?"

"Because the Boneyard activated," he says. "And they activated it."

"We don't know that," I say. "For all I know, we hit some threshold of danger for the Boneyard itself, and it activated its defenses."

"You're reaching for an explanation that has nothing to do with the Fleet," he says.

"I'm keeping an open mind," I say.

"Because you want to dive those warships," he says.

I shake my head. "I'm not sure I want to *dive* the warships. I want to know if they're really warships or an illusion of warships. I want to know if they're an actual defense or a storage yard. I want to know what they're there for."

He lets out a small laugh. "You and mysteries," he says. "Wave something inexplicable to do with old ships at you and you immediately have to investigate."

"Not immediately," I say. "If I immediately had to investigate, I would have done so already. I want to *safely* investigate."

"I think safely investigating is no longer an option," he says.

"Why not?" I ask. "The Boneyard only had automated defenses when we found it."

"And the automated defenses are what attacked us," he says.

"Exactly," I say. "Let's figure out what they are and how they were activated and how to shut them off."

He stares at me for a long moment. "Why do you want to go back *really*, Boss? To see what's inside those warships? Because it's a mystery? I love a good mystery almost as much as you do, but it seems foolhardy to keep investigating this one."

I pull out the second chair and sit in it. I rest my elbows on my thighs, and let the tablet clutched in my right hand dangle between my knees.

"Automated defenses are designed to repel," I say. "They are designed to discourage."

His lips thin. He's trying not to say he knows that. But he hasn't thought it through.

"Most automated defensive systems are pretty dumb," I say.

"We thought there was a chance there was an overall intelligence in the Boneyard," he says, clearly unable to keep silent any longer.

"Exactly," I say. "We might've been right. But an *automated* intelligence is one that doesn't think all that well. It might assume that we're gone now. If we go back with different ships, it might not realize we're the same crew."

"You think if we're small enough, the Boneyard will ignore us?" he asks.

"If the Boneyard reacted the way it did because it saw us and those five ships as a united threat, then yes, I think if we go back with a ship or two, it will ignore us, particularly if we don't shoot any weapons near it." I swing the tablet just a little. I'd love to get to work, not have a discussion.

If I wanted a discussion, I would have prolonged that meeting with Coop and Yash and Ilona.

"And if you're wrong?" Mikk asks. "If those five ships did something to 'turn on' the Boneyard?"

"Well, then," I say quietly, "maybe we can reverse engineer that maneuver."

He stares at me for a moment, then shakes his head "Yash will figure that out," he says.

"Why would she?" I ask. "She's trying to figure out if those five ships are Fleet. And if they are, then she's going to figure out how to contact them or talk to them or convince them to take the *Ivoire* back."

My voice sounds a little shaky on that last part, and I clear my throat.

Mikk's gaze darts away, as if that little hint of emotion embarrasses him as much as it mortifies me.

"Wouldn't Coop want to know that?" Mikk asks, still not looking at me.

"That they're Fleet?" I ask. "Of course—"

"No," Mikk says. "How to activate the Boneyard."

"I doubt it," I say. "If he goes back, it'll be to meet up with those ships, not to explore the warships."

"Then I'm a little unclear about this," Mikk says. "You want to go back and dive the Boneyard, maybe even dive the ships?"

I smile. "Mikk," I say, "if we can activate the ships in the Boneyard, then we can defend ourselves against whatever comes our way."

"Inside the Boneyard, yeah, maybe," he says.

I nod. I'll give him that, because that was the thought that brought me to the one I'm about to express.

"There's more, isn't there?" he asks.

I let my smile widen. "Mikk," I say, "if we control the Boneyard, then we control the forcefields."

His eyes widen. He clearly hasn't thought of that.

"We can shut down the starfield-barrier," he says.

"Yeah," I say.

"Those warships—"

"If they are actually warships," I say.

"Can become ours," he says.

"I'm pretty sure Ilona would like that for a variety of reasons," I say. "I'm sure there's tech in those ships we can repurpose."

"I wasn't thinking of Ilona," Mikk says.

I sit up straight. "Really? What were you thinking?"

He smiles. "The Empire," he says. "We can finally take them on, in a way that would have made Squishy proud."

He's right. And I hadn't thought of that.

"We'd need trained crew," I say. "A lot of trained crew. So that's a long way in our future."

"But we'll have a future," Mikk says. "One we could agree on."

I let out a breath. I had brought Mikk here so we could see if there was a reason to return to the Boneyard. I thought we'd have to comb through all our data—and we do.

But we have a reason to do so now, and not just because I love a good mystery.

"You're not going to tell Coop yet, are you?" Mikk says. He clearly has seen something in my expression.

"Not until you and I figure out what exactly we saw those last few minutes in the Boneyard," I say.

And maybe not ever, I mentally add. Because if we can figure out a way to control the Boneyard, we have an advantage, not just over the Empire, but over those five ships.

If they're not Fleet, they're probably not friendly.

If they are Fleet, they might not be friendly either.

We have to take care of ourselves here at Lost Souls. And we have a lot of pressures on us. Not just that search for the Fleet that the *Ivoire* indulges in. But that looming presence of the Empire, lurking on the border between the Empire and the Nine Planets.

At some point, the Empire will come barreling through. We need to be ready.

And maybe, just maybe, the discovery we just made in the Boneyard will help us defeat the Empire, once and for all.

21

YVES BELTRAIRE LEANED AGAINST THE WALL near the entrance to the bridge on the *Roja*. He had his arms crossed, and one heel braced against the wall as he observed the beehive of activity around him.

The *Roja* was one of the Enterran Empire's premiere science ships. It had a small but exceptionally capable crew who were able to handle the demands of the scientists belowdecks.

Still, no one on this ship had ever encountered anyone like Beltraire. The *Roja's* captain, Mildred Krag, kept giving him sideways looks, as if she expected him to walk down the aisle past the well-placed rows of control panels, and take over the ship.

He could, and probably would, if this mission was being misman-aged. But he hadn't taken over any ship he'd ever been on. He always found it better to speak to the captain privately. Captains tended to stay in line when they realized they were being observed by Imperial Intelligence, particularly when the Imperial Intelligence officer was as high ranking as he was.

It was unusual for Beltraire to be on any ship at all. He hadn't been assigned here. When the call came out from the *Ewing Trekov* to send ships to the Room of Lost Souls, Beltraire essentially commandeered the *Roja*. It had just finished bringing materials to the largest stealth tech research facility in the Empire, and he just happened to be at that facility.

Beltraire was in charge of all of the stealth tech facilities in the Empire, which also placed him in the center of stealth tech research, even though he wasn't a scientist. But he'd been working with and around stealth tech for decades now, and he knew more about it than half the scientists who specialized in it.

Beltraire firmly believed that stealth tech would be the secret to taking over the entire sector, a goal he was quietly moving the government toward.

No one else on the bridge crew looked at him. If he was doing his job right, all ten people should forget he was there. The only person who hadn't was Krag, and that was because she was terrified of him.

They had worked together before, years ago, and he had had to dress her down more than once. He had thought then, and was seeing nothing different now, that she was not command material. It was his black mark in her file—a black mark she had never been able to access, although he knew she had tried three separate times—that kept her from helming any vessel that had the slightest chance of heading into battle.

Which was probably why she was giving him sideways glances now. She had probably thought when the call came up from Trekov that the *Roja* was heading into a battle. Then Krag received an order to wait for Beltraire, and she had probably thought he was going to take over the ship.

When he arrived, he hadn't said a word to her about the upcoming battle. He had doubted it would be a battle, and he had suspected that even if it was, no science ship would have been involved in it.

He had come on this trip because of the information buried in the request for more ships. The ships were to respond to an incident at the Room of Lost Souls, a place which had always intrigued him. It had had some kind of dangerous field around it for a very long time, something that killed rapidly or made people disappear altogether.

Then, mysteriously, that field had gone away, shortly after Elissa Trekov had encountered a mysterious man with a powerful ship at the Room itself.

Trekov believed that the man—who called himself Captain Cooper—had taken something from the Room, a weapon, maybe, or something else.

Beltraire had examined the information recorded by various entities about the entire incident—from the buoys nearby to the cameras the Empire had placed on the Room decades ago to the video and audio from Trekov's team, as well as from her ship—or, at least, what the Empire could recover from her ship.

There were some things about that incident that greatly bothered Beltraire.

Cooper hadn't fired on Trekov's ship, the *Discovery*. He had fired on his own man, clutching some kind of box on a landing platform at the Room. The box caused the massive energy release that had destroyed all of the ships around it—except for Cooper's ship.

From the images that Beltraire could find, Cooper's ship vanished without a trace. It looked like the ship ducked behind a shield of some kind, almost like a stealth field that an Empire vessel would use.

But, Beltraire postulated, if Cooper's ship had simply gone into stealth mode, then it too would have been damaged, and it clearly hadn't been. It had shown up years later in a skirmish at the border between the Empire and the Nine Planets, involving—fortunately—Trekov again. She recognized the signature of the weapon that Cooper planned to use, and retreated—against orders—saving hundreds of lives.

Beltraire had examined the after-incident reports for that event as well, and once again noted that there were command issues. Only they were not issues with Trekov. She had acted wisely. The problem in that incident was Flag Commander Janik hadn't believed her, and he had given the exact wrong order, costing lives. It should have cost him his career, but it hadn't.

Beltraire had sent the after-incident reports to the High Command, with a recommendation to examine all of the actions closely. He was convinced that note of his had guaranteed that Trekov kept her position as Commander, but it hadn't resulted—as he had hoped—in Janik's demotion.

That would come over time, and wasn't something Beltraire was going to worry about.

Instead, he kept his eye on Trekov. She had figured out how to identify Cooper's weapon, using an energy signature. Beltraire had taken that signature to the scientists at the various stealth tech sites and requested that they figure out what they were dealing with.

All of them thought it was a variation on stealth tech, but they had no idea how to recreate it or what, exactly, it did.

So, when Beltraire saw Trekov's name once again connected to an incident at the Room of Lost Souls, an incident that peripherally, anyway, involved the *Ivoire*, he knew he had to be there.

He brought some of his own people onto this ship, scientists who'd been studying the two incidents, and who were trying to figure out what the *Ivoire* was and where it came from.

It looked like a classic Dignity Vessel. There were dozens of abandoned Dignity Vessels scattered all over Empire space. The Empire itself had confiscated several of them, and had found some interesting materials on board a few of them. Nothing that the Empire found was as powerful as the weaponry that this Cooper had used, but it was all similar.

If Beltraire got his way, though, he would find the *Ivoire*, and confiscate it for the Empire. If he could capture Cooper or convince Cooper to cooperate, then Beltraire might learn what that weapon was.

The *Roja* was one of the last ships to arrive at the Room of Lost Souls, which irritated him. Trekov was already gone, the incident over. Beltraire could contact her, he supposed, but he didn't. Instead, he made certain that Krag had volunteered to do the research that Trekov had requested.

Krag's crew was receiving information from the battle that had occurred here at the Room. What intrigued him about that battle was the various energy signatures, all of them resembling the ones he had seen around Trekov's encounters with the *Ivoire*—and the *Ivoire* herself.

Krag looked over her shoulder again, and he couldn't take it anymore. Beltraire needed to deal with whatever was going on, so that he could speak to his scientists below.

He uncrossed his arms and beckoned her with one finger. An expression of annoyance that she didn't even try to hide crossed her small face. Her first officer, Floyd Walker, glanced over his shoulder as well, saw Beltraire leaning against the wall, and raised his head ever so slightly. Walker was a slim reed of a man with a long angular face. Everything about him screamed precision.

But Beltraire could never get a read off Walker, unable to tell if the man knew who and what Beltraire was or if the man was just incredibly political, trying to play both sides against each other.

Krag's lips settled into a thin line, accenting the frown marks on her face. She tucked her steel gray curls behind her ears. Then she walked slowly up the aisle toward him, stopping every few feet to talk to different members of her bridge crew. They were all studiously avoiding him. He even believed that some of them had no idea he was here.

She finally reached his side, and he was surprised, as usual, that she was as tall as he was. Her long torso and stubby legs made her seem shorter from a distance.

He opened the doors and swept his hand toward the corridor. "Let's talk here," he said.

She stepped out, and he followed. The doors closed behind them. The corridor was empty. It was narrow, to make more room for the bridge, and it was darker than he liked.

These old science ships had put most of their money in the labs on the lower levels not in the crew quarters or in the common areas, including things like corridors and mess halls.

The result was claustrophobic on the working crew levels, even though the science labs were bright and well stocked.

"Now what do you want me to do?" she asked.

"Lose the attitude," he said.

Her lips thinned even more. "Look," she said, "we both know you want to command this vessel, so why the hell don't you just do that, instead of playing this game?"

At least she was blunt.

"I don't want to command your vessel," he said. "I will do so, though, if you think that will make things easier."

"I can use the rest," she said. "You can have access to my team and I'll just put my feet up until this silly little mission is over."

He went cold. This *silly little mission* might make or break the Empire in its quest to expand across the sector.

He stared at her for a moment. Commanding a vessel, even one on a research mission, was time-consuming. He had other concerns.

But fighting with her would be time-consuming as well.

"All right," Beltraire said. "Retire to your quarters. I don't want to see you again until this mission is over."

Her eyes widened ever so slightly. Had she thought he was going to turn her down? Or was she surprised at how quickly she had won the argument?

"You'll need me to let the crew know that I've been relieved," she said tersely.

And he finally understood what was going on. She was going to do her best to get revenge on him for that black mark. She probably had a way of informing her crew that someone was not to be trusted.

Many captains did.

"No need," Beltraire said. "Head to your quarters, and I'll deal with all of this."

She frowned at him. "I'd prefer—"

"I don't care what you prefer," he said. "You're going to your quarters. You will not leave until this mission ends."

"You can't—"

"You know I can, captain, and so do I." He gave her a cold smile. "Go."

She glared at him, then pivoted and headed down the corridor. As she did, he went back to the bridge and stopped at the nearest control panel.

He used his personal codes to override all of the command codes. First, he shut down all of her comm systems, so she couldn't contact anyone. As he did that, he watched the bridge crew out of the corner of his eye.

Most of the crew kept working, including Walker. But the second officer, crammed against a wall on a control panel that was smaller than most, looked up in surprise. Then he hit several buttons, as if he were trying to restore some kind of service.

So the captain was contacting him and not Walker. That was good to know.

Beltraire made a mental note of all of that, then made certain that the captain's command codes only worked on the entrance to her quarters. The moment she went inside, those codes would deactivate as well. He left her emergency protocols in place—so if she had some kind of personal crisis, she could ask for help, just like any passenger on the ship could—but nothing else. She could access food and entertainment, and that was all.

He sent a coded message to the High Command and a second to Imperial Intelligence, letting them know what he had done. His actions wouldn't be seen as a black mark against him, but they might end her career entirely. If she had been good at her job and had only one person filing complaints against her, High Command would look at that as a personnel issue.

She wasn't good at her job, and the High Command knew it. They just didn't feel it was worthwhile to replace her. Commanding a science vessel wasn't a lot of work. It mostly meant ferrying the scientists from one location to the next, or doing strange nontraditional things because the scientists needed it done.

Very few captains would want an assignment like this, one that gave them mostly superficial control and easy-to-complete tasks. The High Command believed in keeping troublesome captains in roles like this, where the damage they could do was minimal.

They wouldn't replace Krag unless they were forced to.

Still, Beltraire felt no satisfaction in effectively confining her to quarters. It was simply something he had to do so that he could work unimpeded.

He shifted all of the captain's command codes to him, so that he didn't have the extra step of entering his Imperial Intelligence identification every single time he wanted to do something.

Then he shut down that command panel and strode down the main aisle to the captain's corner.

Walker tilted his head as Beltraire reached his side.

"First Officer Walker," Beltraire said, quite softly.

"Sir," Walker said.

"You will be commanding this vessel from now on," Beltraire said. "However, you will be taking many of your orders from me."

Walker's eyes narrowed just a bit as he processed the information. His longer-than-usual silence indicated that he had thought of—and discarded—several questions about Captain Krag.

Then Walker opened his mouth, and Beltraire subtly braced himself for a difficult question or two.

Instead, Walker said, "I have information on the *Ivoire*. I overheard you discussing the ship with the captain, and I thought perhaps you would want to know what the *Ivoire* did while it was near the Room of Lost Souls."

Beltraire smiled. "That is indeed what I want."

"We don't have many visuals," Walker said, "and that seems to be by design. If you let me show you…"

He didn't wait for Beltraire's answer. Instead, Walker flipped a screen up on his console, tapped a few buttons, and stepped to one side.

The image on the screen—a bit dark, a bit blurry—showed the space around the Room of Lost Souls. Beltraire recognized the edge of the Room. He'd seen it more times than he wanted to think about—those edges, softened by time, the strange tilt to the structure itself.

He'd had a team studying it, mostly from a distance, trying to figure out why it was shrinking. Its measurements had changed over the years.

But it still loomed in these visuals, dark and cold, and ultimately terrifying. A lot of people had died at the Room of Lost Souls, not just the six hundred who had died at the hands of this Captain Cooper of the *Ivoire*, but countless others, who had stopped here thinking it was an abandoned space station, and instead discovering that one of the interior areas actively killed most people who entered it.

Or that area had, until Cooper came along.

Walker was watching Beltraire, as if waiting for Beltraire's full attention. Beltraire met Walker's gaze.

"Watch this closely," Walker said, and his words almost sounded like a reprimand.

Then he hit another button. Beltraire watched the image, but it seemed frozen. The edge of the Room, toward the right side of the image, seemed small, which meant that they were looking at one of the buoys farther out.

Then the *Ivoire* appeared, blocking any view of the Room. The *Ivoire* seemed coated in an orangish-yellow light, making its hull glisten. For a moment, the ship seemed frozen in place, then the light vanished, and the *Ivoire* sped out of the frame, away from the Room.

A tiny emergency beacon remained next to the spot where the *Ivoire* had arrived. The beacon flared red, then blue, then white, then gold, and repeated the colors.

Beltraire had not seen a beacon like that before.

But he would worry about the signal later.

He wanted to follow the *Ivoire*, but just as he was about to ask where it went, another ship appeared in the same place. It looked similar to the *Ivoire*—some kind of Dignity Vessel—but it had a different coating on its exterior, and there were more open portals on the side. That new ship also glowed slightly, more whitish gold than orangish-yellow.

He knew what happened next. Empire ships arrived to help with the emergency beacon, only to discover a non-injured ship, and the battle for that area began.

"That's all we have?" Beltraire asked Walker. "I wanted to know what happened to the *Ivoire*."

"I know," Walker said. "I'll show you in a moment. But I find it fascinating that both ships appeared at *the exact same coordinates*."

He put a harsh emphasis on that last phrase. He also used the word "appeared."

Beltraire made a mental note about the word "appeared" and those coordinates. But he wasn't going to lose focus.

"The *Ivoire*," he said firmly.

Walker sighed, then his fingers danced across the buttons. The image on the screen of the new ship and the beacon vanished, replaced by a different view coming from a different buoy. That buoy didn't show the Room at all, but did show a few of the other buoys nearby.

Beltraire had ordered some of those buoys put into place, especially after the incident with Trekov and Cooper at the Room. Those buoys belonged to Imperial Intelligence; regular ships weren't supposed to be able to access them.

He glanced sideways at Walker, who seemed very intent on the screen.

Walker said nothing, but his lips hardened, as if he were holding back words.

Beltraire looked back at the screen in time to see the *Ivoire* zoom past the buoy, so fast that the ship looked like a dark blur. There was no orangish-yellow light, not even any kind of emissions trail from energy use. The ship was efficient and almost invisible against the blue-black of space.

Beltraire's eyes could track it, though, mostly because of its movement, and the angle of the buoy camera. If the buoy had been tilted even slightly, the *Ivoire* would have been impossible to see.

The *Ivoire* continued forward, getting so small that Beltraire wasn't sure he could see it anymore. Then it flared. That orangish-yellow looked like a small dot that appeared and disappeared very far away.

Beltraire frowned. He wasn't sure what he was seeing, and nearly said so, when Walker tapped a few more keys.

"I expanded the image," Walker said. "This is what we have. I'll go back just a bit."

The *Ivoire* dominated the screen for a moment, utter blackness that faded as the ship got farther away and bits of space became visible around it. Then that light flared, only this time, it looked like a door had opened on a dark night, emitting a square of orange-yellow light.

The *Ivoire* was outlined around it, only this time, the light seemed to envelop the *Ivoire*.

Then the *Ivoire* vanished. And unlike the arrival, after the *Ivoire* disappeared, no orange-yellow light lingered.

Beltraire did not express surprise. He'd seen something similar on the buoys when the *Ivoire* first arrived at the Room of Lost Souls years ago. The buoy cameras then weren't as sophisticated. He had upgraded them, and shielded them, because the buoys had gotten destroyed in that blast (or whatever it had been) that the *Ivoire* had unleashed the first time it was at the Room.

"The *Ivoire* does not appear on any of the buoys further out," Walker said.

Beltraire already knew that. He had checked for the path of the *Ivoire* after Trekov had sent her message. He had looked at Imperial Intelligence's buoys first, the ones he had placed on the various routes to the Room of Lost Souls.

He had seen nothing, no arrival of the *Ivoire* and no departure either. Beltraire had been unconcerned when he noted that. It was possible that the ship had taken a route not visible to the buoys.

But the way the ship had just disappeared and there was no way to track it, well, he didn't find that disturbing so much as intriguing.

He was trying not to get ahead of himself here. He had learned, working with scientists, that the worst thing he could do was look for things that supported his own conclusions, while ignoring everything else.

But it sure looked to him—and it had looked this way for some time—that the *Ivoire* could open portals and travel through them.

"Here's the other thing I want you to see." Walker tapped the console next to the one he'd been using, raising yet another screen.

On that screen, numbers scrolled and then they resolved themselves into bright blue and white lines.

"These are energy readings taken for the last few days at the buoy sites," he said. "I'll scroll fast."

Fast or slow, it didn't matter, because the changes were small, almost invisible. The lines' infinitesimal movement was visible only because he was scrolling quickly.

Then a bright orange spike occurred and Walker froze the image.

"I'm going to run that with the images of the *Ivoire*," he said.

"No need," Beltraire said. "That's the *Ivoire*'s arrival."

"Yes," Walker said.

"And, I'll wager, something similar happens when that new ship arrives."

Walker gave him a slight smile. "Yes."

"I suppose there's another one from the area where the *Ivoire* disappears," Beltraire said.

"Yes," Walker said. "But nothing in between. That energy spike vanishes when the *Ivoire* travels away from the Room."

Two different means of propulsion.

"This is good," Beltraire said. "We need to go to the site where the *Ivoire* vanished. We need to get energy readings from there."

He was hoping those readings would be clear. The readings he had from the *Ivoire*'s first appearance at the Room of Lost Souls years ago got contaminated in the attack. The new readings here at the Room of Lost Souls were contaminated by the arrival of the second ship.

But out there, where the *Ivoire* disappeared, those readings would be pristine. He would be able to trust them.

Beltraire's scientists probably had the same information. They were probably digging into the numbers right now, comparing and contrasting the energy signatures, but here, on the bridge, these numbers meant something else.

Beltraire smiled at Walker.

"Good work," Beltraire said.

Walker nodded, and bowed ever so slightly.

"Now," Beltraire said, "take us to the coordinates where the *Ivoire* disappeared." Beltraire used the word "disappeared" on purpose. "Do not take the same path to get to those coordinates. Stop us nearby, but not on the coordinates themselves."

"Yes, sir," Walker said.

Beltraire nodded at him. "I'll leave you to it," Beltraire said, and walked away from the command center on the bridge.

He resisted the urge to look over his shoulder at Walker. But if Walker's expression was anything like the expressions on the faces of the rest of the bridge crew, Walker was surprised at being left in charge with minimal instructions.

Walker would learn—they would all learn—that Beltraire had no interest in their ship. He was interested in the *Ivoire*. Or, more specifically, what the *Ivoire* had done and how it had left the vicinity.

He had other information to gather from Imperial Intelligence buoys farther out. But he knew that information would be incomplete. They weren't set up to cover the entire area.

If, somehow, the *Ivoire* had cloaked, and then traveled directly to another region of space, then those buoys might pick it up.

But that begged the question: Why hadn't the *Ivoire* cloaked the moment it arrived at the Room of Lost Souls.

Beltraire exited the bridge and headed toward the elevators that would take him to his scientists. He had a lot of questions, a handful of assumptions, and a lot to learn.

If they hadn't already split into different groups, he would have to split them up—one team would work on the disappearance, another team on these energy signatures, and still another team on the similarities between those signatures and stealth tech.

He would need one more research group. They would have to find the *Ivoire* now. He didn't need scientists for that.

He needed trackers of some kind. He wasn't even sure if there were any on this ship, but if there were, he would find them.

He needed to know where the *Ivoire* was. It couldn't just vanish. After its visits to the Room, the *Ivoire* had gone somewhere. It had turned up at the Nine Planets. He needed to know if that's where it fled again.

If it had fled again to the Nine Planets, Beltraire was probably going to have to talk to the High Command. There was a truce with the Nine Planets right now, negotiated, ironically, by Cooper.

But if Cooper violated that truce, then all bets were off. The Empire could go after the Nine Planets.

However, that wasn't a call Beltraire could make. It was not only something that wasn't part of his job, it was also something that didn't interest him.

He was much more interested in this technology that the *Ivoire* was using. He wanted to know what it was, how it worked, and—most important of all—could the Empire make it themselves? Could they use that same tech to their own advantage? Because if they could, they would be able to expand the Empire.

They would become the strongest force in the sector—and he would do everything in his power to make that force even stronger.

BATTLESTATIONS

22

NYGUTA PACED THE BRIDGE OF THE *BILATZAILEA*, hands clasped behind her back as she tried not to micromanage her bridge crew. They were—as she always reminded herself—the best in the Armada, but that didn't calm her.

They were on a mission she hadn't designed, taking action she didn't approve of. They were using new equipment that wasn't battle-tested, and they were traveling with two other ships, whose captains she had never met before this mission.

Never before had she led a mission planned by a member of the Jefatura and, if she survived this one, she never wanted to do so again.

The bridge crew were at their stations. She could see them out of the corner of her eye as she paced. Their workstations were behind what had been the captain's area, with the most annoying captain's chair ever built.

At least she had gotten the damn chair removed as the team of specialists chosen by the Jefatura upgraded everything from her shields to her weaponry to her foldspace tracking system.

The only thing they hadn't upgraded was the *anacapa* drive, and a goodly part of her worried that maybe, with all the stress she was putting on it, that was the part that *should* have been replaced.

As she paced, she caught Habibi's gaze. He raised a single eyebrow, then rolled his eyes. He had come to her quarters the night before the *BilatZailea* embarked on this mission, and expressed his qualms.

Two ships is not enough backup, he had said. *We have no idea what we're heading into. Maybe we should wait until our own incursion into Enterran Empire space is a distant memory.*

She agreed and had given the same arguments to Atwater, who was the mastermind behind this mission. Atwater had actually wanted to come along on it, but Nyguta had managed to squelch that idea.

The last thing Nyguta needed was a member of the Honored Families on board this ship. There was too much reverence for the Honored Families, and even more for Honored Family members who had actually made a name for themselves in their own right.

Atwater was an impressive woman who did not allow her privileged upbringing to get in the way of her work on *anacapa* drives and foldspace tracking. She saw this entire mission as an experiment.

She had convinced her Level One colleagues to back this experiment, and to approve a fast-tracking of the upgrades for the *BilatZailea*. Nyguta hated fast-tracking of anything. She preferred slow and cautious work, followed by testing, followed by more slow and cautious work, particularly when that work was dealing with *anacapa* drives, foldspace mapping, and foldspace tracking.

So much could go wrong.

And that didn't even count the tactical error that was going to start this little adventure. She had no idea how to get around it, though, and neither did her counterparts on the other two foldspace tracking vessels that would be traveling with her.

She had met with both Ifa Odeh, the captain of the *DetekTibe*, and Mekit Tua, the captain of the *MuhaQiq*, trying to see if there was another way to execute Atwater's plan without putting all three ships in danger.

None of the captains could come up with something better—or rather, something that Atwater would approve of.

Atwater wanted all three ships to arrive at the space station where the previous battle had taken place. Then they needed to track the *Ivoire* in regular space, which was more difficult than it sounded, given how many extra ship signatures there would be in the area.

Once all three ships found where the *Ivoire* went back into foldspace, the *BilatZailea* would track the *Ivoire*, with the other ships tagging along just in case. They would all end up wherever it was that the *Ivoire* had retreated to, and then proceed to deal with the vehicle.

Best case, the *Ivoire* would return to Base 20 with the three foldspace tracking vessels, but considering how hard the *Ivoire* had fought to get away from there, Nyguta doubted that would happen.

She expected that if she did encounter the *Ivoire*, she would need to be on her game. She would either need her battle skills or her long-rusty diplomatic skills. Neither of the other two captains had major diplomatic training, a fault of the plan, Nyguta thought. Atwater seemed to believe that because Nyguta had served as a diplomat before continuing with her leadership training, she would be the best captain for this entire mission.

But Nyguta hadn't handled a diplomatic mission of her own ever, and although she had been with others who had been more skilled, she had been dealing with cultures that had never heard of the Fleet or seen ships like the Armada's.

She had no idea how to approach someone who ran a ship like the *Ivoire*, and really felt out of her depth if she had to deal with someone like a Captain Cooper, who might have come from the Fleet thousands of years before through a foldspace malfunction.

But those were problems for the future. The current problem was bad enough.

All three ships had to leave foldspace cloaked, heading toward the space station, before picking up the *Ivoire's* trail.

Fortunately, Nyguta had been at the space station before, so she knew the coordinates intimately. She also knew of buoys near the station, so she hoped to avoid those.

The problem that worried her—one that she couldn't convince Atwater of—was that the battle that had taken place less than a week before might have made the Enterran Empire more cautious, not less.

If she were in charge of guarding that space station, she would have added a lot more surveillance equipment, and maybe even stationed some ships nearby to guard the place.

Atwater had smiled at Nyguta when she made that objection. *Well,* Atwater had said blithely, *you're not in charge, are you?*

Just thinking of that response made Nyguta's fists clench. Rather than hear the caution, Atwater had found a way to dismiss it all.

Now, the three ships were heading into a situation filled with unknowns, placing themselves in danger to find—what, exactly? Some kind of pirate who stole old ships and materials from seemingly abandoned bases? An old captain of an old ship? Or the Fleet itself?

All three captains were nervous: if they did find the Fleet, they weren't prepared for what would happen next. If the Fleet was as big and powerful as the Armada assumed it was, then the arrival of three foldspace tracking vessels was just plain suicidal.

Captain Odeh pointed out that if the Armada truly thought the *Ivoire* would lead the ships to the Fleet, then the Armada would not be sending three small ships on this mission.

That sounded good and logical and was probably right. But Nyguta liked to be prepared for everything, and that was one of the many scenarios that could happen on this mission that actually scared the crap out of her.

"We're nearly there, Captain," Rockowitz said.

She stopped pacing and let her arms drop to her sides. She almost missed the damn captain's chair because, in the past, it had given her a focal point, something else to concentrate on while she was dealing with some kind of crisis.

"Make sure the other two ships have the correct coordinates," she said.

The ships weren't going to come out of foldspace at the same time or even in the exact same spot. It was just too dangerous.

But they all needed to know where they were going.

The other thing the three captains had decided was that they would not arrive cloaked. They would arrive, and seconds later, raise those cloaks.

The technology was just too new and untried. All three captains were terrified that the cloak would interfere with the exit from foldspace.

Atwater, the foldspace expert, believed that it would not.

But believing something and watching it hold up through test after test after test was another thing indeed. Nyguta and the other two captains did not want to be the ones who discovered that Atwater's assumptions were incorrect.

Nyguta had picked a spot near the place where she had first arrived less than a week ago. But she would appear on the other side of the space station, about as far from the direction the *Ivoire* flew as she could get. She figured if the Enterran Empire put out new surveillance equipment, they would do so on the "front" of the space station, near landing bays and entry points, not on the back, which seemed to be sinking into foldspace all by itself.

She also made sure the coordinates were far enough away from the space station that the *BilatZailea's* foldspace bubble would not interact with the space station's foldspace bubble. There was simply too much happening for her to protect her ship against every contingency—unless she stayed as far from the space station as possible.

"They have the coordinates," Rockowitz said, "and they are as ready as they'll ever be."

Nyguta smiled. "Captain Tua's words, right?" she asked.

Rockowitz looked up from his console, surprised. "How did you know?"

Tua had a singular sense of humor. Dry, warm, so subtle that many people missed it.

Nyguta did not elaborate, though. "Remind them that we're going first," she said.

Rockowitz nodded, executing the command probably before she finished telling him to do so.

Nyguta stopped pacing. She called up a holoscreen, expanded it so that it surrounded her, and then stared at the new command screen.

Technically, she should let someone like Pereira handle this, but she wasn't going to. As good a tactician as Pereira was, he wasn't as well versed in this new system as she was.

No one was.

Not that she knew it well either. She had only had a day or so more practice on it than they had.

Besides, she wanted Pereira to monitor the area around them.

"You know your orders," she said to the bridge crew. They had actually run three different simulations of this moment in the last twenty-four hours. If she had to give them more instructions now, then they weren't as good a crew as she believed they were.

She waited just a few extra seconds to make sure everyone was in place. She would handle the quick commands. Intxausti would immediately search the area for any kind of surveillance. Pereira had his eye out for Enterran Empire ships.

The other two foldspace tracking vessels would arrive about five minutes after the *BilatZailea*—if they emerged from foldspace as planned. Her crew would notify them immediately if there was any danger in the area.

She glanced at the equipment in front of her. The command sequence wasn't engrained yet. She would have to think about each movement, which would add seconds to her response.

"We're emerging from foldspace now," said Rockowitz. He wasn't speaking for her benefit, but for the others, those who had jobs that had nothing to do with foldspace.

It also served as a warning for everyone belowdecks, just in case the transition out of foldspace was difficult.

She threaded her fingers together—she didn't want to accidentally touch any of the command screens—and then the *BilatZailea* started vibrating.

The vibration was subtle, not at all like the usual emergence out of foldspace. She had no idea if that was because of some of the new equipment Atwater had installed in the ship or if it was just because of the area near which the *BilatZailea* was emerging.

Nyguta didn't have time to think about that either. The vibration continued, light and almost imperceptible. She monitored the screens.

The telemetry showed the shift best, although the visuals in front of her also showed that weird glittery light display she often saw in a fold-space transition.

The vibration stopped and she immediately hit the cloak command. The *BilatZailea* vibrated again as the cloak slammed into place. She knew that there had been a vibration all three times she had activated the cloak before, but this time, it made her really uncomfortable.

She double-checked the coordinates, saw that indeed, they were out of foldspace, but still, she felt odd.

"Looks like a smooth transition," Rockowitz said.

He guided the *BilatZailea* away from the foldspace window. Nyguta looked at the images from the exterior of the ship. They were far enough from the space station that it didn't register on any visuals. If she called up long-distance telemetry, she would get a reading from the space station, but she didn't do that.

She was too busy monitoring the shields.

"No ships here," Rockowitz said.

"There are half a dozen near the space station." That voice belonged to Telli. She sounded tense. "I don't think they've noticed us, though."

"Be prepared to notify the other two ships the moment they arrive," Nyguta said. She was still wrestling with the cloak. The vibration continued, and that hadn't happened before. Maybe she had activated the cloak too soon.

She wasn't certain of that. If the vibration continued much longer, she would need to deactivate and reactivate, which worried her.

"There's surveillance all along this corridor," Intxausti said. "Dozens and dozens of tiny little…I don't know what they are. Buoys, I guess. But they're nothing like the big ones around the space station, although I think they're the same make."

"Confirm that," Nyguta said as she continued to work the cloak. She hated the words "I think" in the middle of an operation.

Intxausti knew that. She was letting everyone know the assumptions she was working off of, not the actual factual information.

213

Then Nyguta saw the *MuhaQiq* appear just a short distance from the *BilatZailea*'s window. The *MuhaQiq* vanished almost instantly. Her equipment, which had paired with the equipment for the other two ships before they had even left the Armada, showed that the *MuhaQiq* had moved slightly away from the *BilatZailea*.

They would wait for the *DetekTibe*, and then they would decide what the next step was. They needed to search for the *Ivoire*'s signature in regular space, and follow that to its last known coordinates, but that would be harder than expected, especially with actual ships operating in the area.

At least Enterran Empire ships did not use *anacapa* drives. That would make the search easier.

The *DetekTibe* appeared. It showed up for a moment on her exterior cameras, glowing slightly, with the light from foldspace still illuminating the *DetekTibe*'s exterior.

Then the ship vanished under its cloak.

Later, when they all debriefed, she would ask if they had an unexpected vibration as they cloaked. She wondered if they should have waited longer than a few seconds, maybe until the light from the foldspace transition left the ships entirely.

That light wasn't *anacapa* energy. The engineers thought it was the equivalent of a temperature variation, the way that ships carried the cold of space with them as they docked inside space stations.

But no one knew for certain—still—which irritated her. Sometimes the unknown could be ignored, and sometimes it caused problems that they never would have expected otherwise.

But all three ships were here, and all three ships were ready.

"All right, team," Nyguta said to her people. "Let's figure out where these ships are, and see if we can isolate their signatures before we search for the *Ivoire*."

"Already underway," said Kibbuku. She should have known he would have the work done before she finished her planning.

She made her screens smaller, and moved them to one side, so she could monitor everything. For a moment, she thought of turning on the wall screens so that she could see what was happening outside of the ship, but then decided that would be too distracting.

They all needed to concentrate.

All three ships had arrived safely, and hadn't somehow landed on each other or been delayed in foldspace. The cloaks seemed to have worked.

Now, all they had to do was find a trace of the *Ivoire*. Then they could move to the next part of the mission.

Nyguta wasn't certain if she was worried about those ships near the space station or not. She had planned on them being there, after all.

But she didn't like it. She almost wished she could talk to Atwater right now. It would have been an I-told-you-so discussion, though, which was never a good thing to have with a superior.

Still, if the rest of the mission went well, Nyguta would find a way to make her opinion about top-down delegation known.

Then she took a deep breath and focused.

They were only to the second stage of this mission.

There was a lot more to go, before she ever got a chance to communicate with the Armada.

Her I-told-you-so would have to wait.

Just like everything else.

23

THE SCIENCE LABS ON THE *ROJA* took up four decks. When there was dangerous work, it was confined to the outer edges of each deck. There was even an auxiliary lab that pivoted outward from the entire ship for extremely dangerous work, done in very safe conditions.

It wasn't good to have a lab sitting outside the ship, like an unwieldy appendage—at least in situations where the *Roja* could be attacked.

Still, Beltraire had ensconced his stealth tech scientists near that unwieldy lab, just in case he could clear the entire area near the Room of Lost Souls of any danger whatsoever.

In addition, his scientists and researchers had an entire side of the ship on all four science decks, plus access to that lab—because he had a suspicion he would be needing the safety protocols here. He figured his people would find something, and when they did, he wanted them to experiment with it on-site. He didn't want them to take the information back to one of the main stealth tech labs and start the work, only to discover they needed more readings or another test or something else from the area near the Room of Lost Souls.

He thought he had planned for everything. But he hadn't expected to make a discovery himself.

He was sitting in the back of a side lab, monitoring equipment and sneaking a bit of lunch—if some pita dabbed in overly flavorful olive oil, some badly made hummus, and a handful of nearly turned grapes could be considered lunch. He had just taken a sip of some sweet tea when all the screens around him flared.

He blinked at them, startled. He had reset them when he sat down, just like he always did when he settled somewhere for more than five minutes. He had taken it upon himself to monitor the Imperial Intelligence buoys scattered around the Room.

If someone had asked him what he expected to see, he wouldn't have been able to answer them. But he wanted to behave with an excess of caution. Something strange had happened here, and his instincts, which had been honed over dozens of years, told him that the strangeness was endemic to the area, so he had decided to remain alert.

He was glad he had.

The flared screens caught his attention. He held a grape he had been about to eat between the forefingers and thumb of his right hand. He didn't even want to set the grape down. He felt his breath catch as the screens showed him imagery that startled him.

A light formed ever so faintly near one of the buoys. The other buoys didn't pick it up. But all of the buoys near that first one caught the image of a ship appearing in that lit area.

The ship was another Dignity Vessel—or maybe it was the one that had destroyed the seven ships near the Room of Lost Souls. He couldn't tell at a glance, and he didn't want to look away for fear he might miss something.

The ship moved laterally, and then it vanished as if it had never been. He was about to call in some of his scientists when another light formed, not quite in the same spot as the first, but damn near. He sat rigidly, his fingers rolling the grape back and forth against his thumb.

The second ship also looked like a Dignity Vessel—again, maybe the same one that had been here for the attack. His stomach clenched around the half-digested hummus.

With his free hand, he tapped the edge of one screen, trying to see how far out those buoys were. He knew they weren't close to the Room, because none of the Imperial Intelligence buoys were nearby. He had set that up by design.

The second ship moved downward slightly, just as small a movement as the first ship had made, and then the second ship disappeared.

His fingers compressed the grape, and it broke open, sending juice all over the small desk he sat at. He grabbed a napkin, without taking his gaze from the screens before him, and wiped off his fingers, then pushed aside the remains of his rather disgusting meal.

A third light formed, centered between, but slightly above the first two. A third ship appeared—yet another Dignity Vessel. It didn't move at all, although the light faded. When the light disappeared, so did the third ship.

Beltraire's heart pounded, and he slid a keyboard toward himself, searching for telemetry on those ships. He got some, just after the moment of arrival, and then the telemetry disappeared.

So he used some of the more sensitive buoys to conduct a wide sweep, not for matching telemetry, but for ship-sized blank spots in the usual noise of space.

He found ship-sized blankness in the data. He altered what he found to be ultra-sensitive to stealth tech, and actually saw a grayish silver outline of all three ships, sitting in formation.

He had no idea what they were doing, but if he had to guess, he would guess that they were searching for something. Maybe evidence of that ship they'd been chasing. Or maybe something to do with the Room.

He sent the feeds he was getting to Gerty Meitner, his chief stealth tech scientist, but did so without commentary.

Beltraire had something else to do first.

Using an encoded command channel, he contacted all of the science and research vessels near the Room of Lost Souls.

"Enemy vessels are approaching," he said, trying not to sound too dramatic. "We need to evacuate the area immediately."

He got the response he had expected from the captain of the science vessel *Qian*.

"Our orders came from Commander Trekov. We need to stay."

Beltraire sent his identification. He didn't have an official rank, but he didn't need one. He outranked Trekov and more than half the upper-level command structure, simply by virtue of his post in Imperial Intelligence.

"I am issuing the order," he said, not in the mood to play pissing games or to ask anyone—especially Trekov—for permission. "You will leave immediately. If you have problems with this, report this incident after you have left the Room of Lost Souls."

The captain of the *Qian* did not respond, but the ship moved out, as all of the others were doing.

Beltraire then got the second message he had expected, this time from Walker.

"Are we leaving the area as well?" he asked.

"No," Beltraire said. "Do your best to shield this vessel. We're going to observe."

He grabbed his dishes and dumped them in the recycler near the front of the lab. He half-walked half-ran to the bridge, using his comm to give instructions to the crew there. He needed his own console, in the back, so that no one could see the information from the buoys. He had no idea if anything would become classified, but he didn't want to risk it.

He also didn't want to risk problems with those three vessels—whatever they were. They had made quick work of seven Empire ships. Yes, the battle had been a surprise to the Empire, but still. These three ships seemed to have technology he could only dream of.

Then, as he took the elevator up to the bridge, he smiled. He was dreaming of it. He was dreaming of stealing it—or at least, learning from it.

He had an opportunity here.

He didn't intend to waste it.

24

NYGUTA STOOD IN THE CENTER of her bridge on the *BilatZailea*, hands clasped. She was watching actual visuals of the area around the abandoned starbase in real time.

She had decisions to make, and she didn't believe any of them were major. She had to decide if she was going to destroy the surveillance equipment that surrounded her ships. She had to decide if she was going to threaten the smaller Empire vessels that surrounded the starbase.

And she had to decide how close she wanted to get to the starbase to look for what remained of the *Ivoire's* signature.

If she had her way, she wouldn't get close to the starbase at all. The *BilatZailea* didn't need to get near that thing again.

Her crew was already searching for the *Ivoire's* signature. The captains of the other two vessels that had come with her were waiting for her to give them some kind of direction.

They had already expressed a bit of impatience. No one really wanted to be on this mission, and it was starting to show.

Then, the small Empire vessels near the starbase stopped moving slowly around the starbase. All of the vessels changed direction, and zoomed away as if they had been called to another mission.

Or had been asked to retreat.

She touched her own screen, frowning at the vessels. They had moved away quickly, which suggested they had received some kind of command.

"Can you hack the communications between the Empire vessels?" she asked Kibbuku. He was good with other systems, and he was her best choice on the bridge at the moment to handle any change in his orders.

He gave her a reluctant look. He was actually interested in how to track the *Ivoire*, and she had just pulled him off that.

"On it," he said, as if he hadn't given her a sideways look at all.

She did feel slightly relieved, though, that the small ships were leaving. She really didn't want to get into another fight at this starbase.

Then something caught her eye on the edge of the visuals she was running. A ship, long and rectangular, with decks piled on decks that seemed almost unwieldy, had dropped back from the other ships.

And then, it shimmered, and didn't quite vanish.

An ineffectual shield, apparently. Or perhaps the shield was ineffectual for her equipment. Less sophisticated equipment might show a gap where the ship had been, or might not have registered the ship at all.

She turned to Telli. Telli stood slightly behind her, and seemed absorbed in three different holoscreens floating around her. The images from the screens reflected on her face, turning its unusual paleness blue, purple and a very faint gold.

"Anastasia," Nyguta said. "Did you notice that large rectangular ship?"

"You mean the one that thinks it's cloaked?" Telli asked. She smiled as she looked at Nyguta over the holoscreens.

"That's the one," Nyguta said. "Can you monitor it for me, please?"

"That's only fair," Telli said, "since it's monitoring us."

Nyguta raised her head in surprise. "Is there something wrong with our cloak?"

"Not like theirs," Telli said. "It probably works for their equipment, which is backwards as hell, but it kinda calls attention to itself in ours."

Nyguta didn't respond to that directly. She was still focused on the *not like theirs*. "What's wrong with our cloak?"

"Nothing," Telli said, "except that we had to wait about ten seconds before activating it. That drew their attention, and they've been trying to figure out where we are ever since."

"You know that how?" Nyguta said.

"They're sending all kinds of signals our way, from lights on different wavelengths to some actual scans. I'm pretty sure they can't see us or even register us, but if they're familiar with this part of space, their equipment might show that something is amiss."

Nyguta let out a small sigh. These Empire people would be the bane of her entire existence.

"What kind of weaponry do they have?" she asked.

"Not much," Telli said. "What they have seems to be designed more to startle us than hurt us. They might have some missiles, but nothing that will fire on us continuously."

"They're not a battleship?" Nyguta asked.

"They don't seem to be. If I had to guess, I'd say they're a research vessel of some kind." Telli glanced down as she said that, as if the answers were spread out before her.

Nyguta let out a small breath. That made sense. The small ships might have been investigative as well. Either they were trying to reconstruct the battle or they were trying to learn something about their enemies—which would be the Armada.

"Got it," Kibbuku said. "They were sent a message telling them that enemy ships were approaching and they needed to leave."

So much for arriving without being seen.

Nyguta scanned the telemetry in front of her, but she didn't see anything out of the ordinary. "Were messages sent to their command about us?"

Kibbuku shook his head. "Not that I can find. They don't seem to want to defend this place."

She frowned. Given what had happened a few days ago, she was surprised. Hundreds of ships had been on the way, ready to attack her.

And then she paused. Or maybe not. Maybe they had been going after the mysterious *Ivoire*.

She let out a small sigh. "Let's go about our business. Send an encrypted message to the *DetekTibe* and the *MuhaQiq*," she said. "Let them know we're being observed, but have them continue on the mission."

"Will do, Captain," said Kibbuku.

"I need more information on the ship that's monitoring us," she said. "Anastasia, I want you to find its classification and anything else you can discover about it."

"What about the surveillance devices around us?" Intxausti asked. She tugged at her ponytail, as if it bothered her.

"We leave them. Although let's see if we can pull information from them," Nyguta said. "The more we know about these things, the better off we'll be."

She didn't plan on being in this region of space long, but she wanted to be prepared. And if the *BilatZailea* could piggyback off of the surveillance devices, she might have warning before any Empire warships arrived in the area.

She didn't want to get into another fight with those ships. She wanted to find the *Ivoire's* trail, and then she wanted to track it, as she had been assigned to do.

The Empire was a distraction. Let them watch her. Let them try to figure out what she was doing.

From everything she had seen, their technology was no match for hers—unless their ships arrived in large numbers as they had before.

She needed to finish her mission here in Empire space and leave as quickly as possible.

She needed to find the *Ivoire's* trail...and fast.

25

ELISSA HAD CARVED A WORKSPACE for herself in the command center of the *Ewing Trekov*. For the decades that this ancient ship had been in commission, it rarely had a commander in the command center long enough to need some kind of workspace.

Technically, she was supposed to give her orders from the commander's deck, where she and a large team would make the proper plans for whatever action was about to happen. She would then be the one to consult with Flag Commander Janik, and then he would approve the plan, whatever it was.

She was working in the command center because too much information was flowing in. She could have the information sent to her in her own office or on the commander's deck, of course, but she didn't want that. Because that might mean she'd have to contact someone else to interpret some of the data that she didn't understand or she might need someone to bounce ideas off of.

There were no other commanders of her rank on the ship, and few people with the science skills to understand what would be coming at them. She had pared the *Ewing Trekov* of underlings who did not believe in her or understand her "obsession," as Janik called it, with the *Ivoire*.

The people who served on this ship now understood the importance of the *Ivoire* to stealth technology, and—more subtly—they understood that Janik couldn't always be trusted.

The command center was filled with officers and many members of the science and engineering teams. They were scattered along the consoles, a few even bringing in handheld tablets so that they could keep up with the information they'd gotten.

Other members of the various science and engineering teams were coming and going through the main doors of the command center, everyone filtering the new information as best they could.

Elissa had told them she wanted to find Cooper and the *Ivoire*, and most of the crew had served with her long enough to know that meant they might have to go after Cooper the moment he was found.

They wanted to be prepared.

And, she liked to think, many of them were as interested in finding Cooper as she was. Some were even more interested in the possibilities of stealth tech. A handful of the members of the engineering team here on the *Ewing Trekov* thought that stealth tech might be something much much much more than the Empire thought it was.

It helped that those engineers agreed with her.

Some of those engineers were in the command center now, mostly working toward the back, since they usually did not serve in the center. The center was large enough that Elissa could only see them if she slid her chair back and then leaned to one side.

She was on the right side of the command center, also in the back. The consoles she had taken over were pressed against the wall which meant that she only needed to put up one privacy barrier.

She was filtering through the information they had gotten so far. The more she looked, the more it seemed that the new ships—the ones that had destroyed the seven Empire vessels—also had a variation of the energy weapon that the *Ivoire* had.

There was no way, from what she had seen, that the *Ivoire* could have left so many strong energy readings near the Room of Lost Souls. The ship simply wasn't that big, nor had it been near the Room long enough.

Even when the *Ivoire* had discharged that weapon at her the first time, the energy residue hadn't been this strong.

Of course, it had taken longer for the Empire to send ships to investigate the area. First, they had been dealing with the dead on all the nearby ships.

She shuddered and forced herself to focus.

The *Ivoire* had left a specific trail in its haste to get away from the Room of Lost Souls. This time, that trail had been solid. It was one direct line—and then it ended, just as it had the time before.

This time, however, she wasn't blaming the energy weapon for the lack of a trail, or the inadequacy of the systems here on the *Ewing Trekov*. She had boosted them long ago, and she knew what she was looking for. So did the rest of her team, and they confirmed what she had found—at least so far.

"Commander Trekov?" The voice sounded tentative, which meant it belonged to Bahe.

Elissa sighed. She usually had time for Bahe's *timid-little-person* games, but not today.

"What do you have, Sub-Lieutenant?" Elissa asked—almost snapped—without looking up from her own work.

"The science and research vessels have left the Room of Lost Souls."

Elissa raised her head so quickly that she made herself dizzy. Bahe was standing just outside of the privacy screen, arms wrapped around a tablet as if it was a shield.

Elissa had given those ships explicit orders to remain at the Room until she ordered them away. They were just beginning to discover things. It was their work that had isolated and confirmed the path of the *Ivoire*. They had also found the intriguing energy signatures of those two ships that were chasing the *Ivoire*.

"I didn't tell them they could leave," she said.

"I know, ma'am," Bahe said meekly.

Elissa sighed inwardly. Bahe's eyes were never meek. They were always steely, just like right now. "Did you tell them—?"

"Yes, ma'am," Bahe said, and this time her response was not quite as meek. "They received orders from a higher-up."

"Flag Commander Janik," Elissa said, almost to herself.

"No, ma'am," Bahe said. "Someone from Imperial Intelligence."

Elissa frowned. "On *those* ships?"

"On the *Roja*, ma'am. It had arrived in that last group of ships. I checked. It had been serving at one of the stealth tech research facilities."

All of Elissa's annoyance at Bahe vanished. Elissa kept Bahe around because she was one of the most competent officers Elissa had worked ever worked with.

"That's fascinating," Elissa said, and meant it. It was fascinating. It meant she wasn't the only one investigating the *Ivoire's* ties to stealth tech.

"Indeed, ma'am," Bahe said, almost dismissively.

"Did they leave because the *Roja* took over the investigation?" Elissa asked. If that was the reason, then she would have words with this Imperial Intelligence officer.

He had to be pretty high ranking to overrule her. There weren't that many known members of Imperial Intelligence who outranked her. She probably knew him.

"No, ma'am." Bahe clutched the tablet even tighter. "They left because three enemy ships arrived. At least, that was what the captains of the science vessels were told."

"Enemy ships." Elissa frowned. She spun her chair so that she faced Bahe directly. "What, exactly, did that intelligence officer think were enemy ships?"

"We don't know, ma'am," Bahe said. "We've asked for proof, and have yet to receive anything."

Bastard. Imperial Intelligence officials were slippery types. He could have lied about the enemy vessels so that he could investigate everything himself, without any interference from her or the science vessels.

And if he did indeed outrank her, then he would be able to keep his discoveries secret from her.

"Contact the *Roja* for me," she said. "I want to know who ordered this change and why."

"Yes, ma'am. Where would you like to take the discussion, ma'am?" Bahe turned her head ever so slightly, indicating the very full command center.

Normally, contact like that would go through the center, but Bahe's subtle little movement was correct. It would be better to talk elsewhere.

Elissa repressed a sigh. Bastard. Ruining her day and probably stealing her work.

"In my office," she said. "I'll be up there in a moment."

She had to shut down her research here. She didn't want someone accessing what she was doing. Not that she was doing much that was top secret, but she was using information that was classified.

If she ended up making some kind of report on all of this, she wanted the report to be aboveboard. She didn't want someone else to dismiss it all because she had accidentally revealed a tiny bit of information to the wrong person.

Bahe had already left. Elissa shut down her research, feeling annoyed at it all.

Essentially, the bastard from Imperial Intelligence had already shut down her research. Now she had the pain-in-the-ass task of trying to figure out why.

She also needed answers to her questions. What kind of enemy vessels? Why hadn't Imperial Intelligence contacted her before countermanding her orders?

Was something else going on?

She would shelve her paranoia until she had a sense of what happened.

Which meant she had to move quickly. Because the longer her people were away from the Room, the more the information she needed would degrade or get co-mingled with information from other ships.

Just as she was making a breakthrough.

Just as she had finally caught a break.

She stood, not wanting to leave this spot, but knowing she had to.

Damn you, Cooper, she mouthed. If he had stayed away, she wouldn't be here.

But if he had stayed away, she wouldn't be gathering all of this new information.

She only hoped it wouldn't cost her a command. Because that was what always seemed to happen whenever he got close to her—she'd lose a command.

Not this time.

She would do everything she could to prevent it from ever happening again.

26

THEY FOUND THE *IVOIRE'S* SIGNATURE, but not where they expected it. The researchers on board the *BilatZailea*, the *DetekTibe* and the *MuhaQiq* found different traces in different areas, all of them on the far side of the starbase the Empire apparently called "The Room of Lost Souls."

Nyguta looked at all of the reporting, spread out along her holo-screens on the bridge of the *BilatZailea*. She found the name of the abandoned starbase intriguing. If she had had time, she would have investigated the history of it all. But she didn't. She wanted to get her ships out of the area, and onto the next part of the mission.

Initially, her people had searched for the *Ivoire's* signature near the abandoned starbase itself, right where it had apparently appeared and dropped that emergency beacon. But the energy readings in the area were scattered.

Nyguta's people had separated the signatures of their ship, and the *EhizTari*, figuring that was all they needed to do. After all, the Empire did not have *anacapa* drives.

But it turned out that the information they had about the Empire was wrong. There were too many muddied signatures near that starbase, and not just from the battle. All seven ships that Nyguta had destroyed had given off some faint *anacapa* readings, even though the ships clearly did not have *anacapa* drives.

If they had, the explosions would have been even more catastrophic than they had been.

The arrival of many other ships also muddied the signatures. And then there was that rectangular ship that thought it was cloaked, the *Roja*. It gave off a mixed energy reading that disturbed both Nyguta and her researchers. It seemed to have too much *anacapa* energy, more than any ship of its size would ever need.

Nyguta had already warned the captains of the *DetekTibe* and the *MuhaQiq* not to engage directly with the *Roja*. If they hit that ship with the wrong kind of weapon, they might destroy ships throughout the region.

The *Roja*'s *anacapa* energy was wild, almost out of control, and that worried her. If Nyguta actually expected to go into battle against the *Roja* or even to deal directly with that ship, then she would have warned her people to double the *BilatZailea*'s shields and to make certain that anything that could reverberate with or reinforce that rogue *anacapa* energy was under some kind of control.

Even now, she had ordered her bridge team to keep an eye on that ship, just in case she had misunderstood the nature of its mission.

Nyguta didn't want to outrun that ship, per se, but she wanted to put as much distance between it and her ships as possible.

So she had suggested to the other captains that they use unusual maneuvers to get to the far side of that starbase, where they had tracked the *Ivoire*'s signature.

The *Roja*, she realized, was less of a threat than she had initially thought it was. It didn't have the weaponry to be a threat to the *BilatZailea*. The *Roja* hadn't contacted any other ships, either, not after it ordered the smaller ships to leave the area.

It just seemed content to stay back and observe.

She wasn't quite sure what the *Roja* was looking for, and she didn't entirely care. For all she knew, the *Roja* was some kind of guardian of the starbase, stationed there to make sure that nothing untoward happened in the area.

Although she did have her staff go over the data they had gathered when the *BilatZailea* had first arrived at the starbase, right on the heels of the *EhizTari*. She had hoped to find more information about the *Roja* from that first visit, but she hadn't.

Even when Telli recalibrated all of their equipment to account for that bad cloak that the *Roja* had, the data still didn't show that the *Roja* had been anywhere nearby.

Which more or less negated Nyguta's theory that the *Roja* was some kind of guardian vessel—unless, of course, the Empire deemed it necessary to guard the abandoned starbase after the battle that she had fought and won there.

Such a decision was always possible, but she suspected that the *Roja* wasn't a guardian in the traditional sense. Whoever commanded it—and Kibbuku hadn't heard anyone call the commander by a title—seemed to be much more interested in what she was doing, for reasons she couldn't entirely comprehend.

If the *Roja* thought the *BilatZailea* was some kind of threat, the *Roja* wouldn't have told the smaller ships to leave and—or—would have asked other ships to come to the starbase, much as someone had done after her destruction of those seven ships.

This *Roja* was something different and it bothered her just enough to distract her slightly from her mission chasing the *Ivoire*.

She stood in the center of her bridge, hands on her hips, missing that damn captain's chair more than she expected. She hadn't realized how regularly she had flopped into it, particularly when she was viewing something she wanted to think about—like now.

She had activated the screens around the entire front of the *BilatZailea*. On them, she had plotted what she believed to be the course of the *Ivoire*, from all of the information that the researchers on all three ships had gathered.

The trajectory of the *Ivoire* in this region of space had been a short one: the *Ivoire* had arrived near the starbase. Then the *Ivoire* had dropped that emergency beacon and sped out of the area.

It had taken some searching to find exactly where the *Ivoire*'s signature went. The researchers had to go away from the buoys to find a clear version of the *Ivoire*'s signature.

But when they did find it, it was the only signature in the area, and certainly the only one with pure *anacapa* energy. That energy was just a suggestion, as it should have been with any ship that wasn't using its drive to cross an area of space.

That little bit of energy was different than the readings she and her team had gotten off those smaller ships. There, the *anacapa* energy was diffuse, as if it had been diluted somehow.

It seemed that the *Ivoire* had not gone far to escape the Armada ships chasing it. The *Ivoire* had gone just out of range of any good sensor system, before disappearing into foldspace.

At least, that was Nyguta and the others believed happened. Because the faint signature that they found just stopped.

There was a massive amount of *anacapa* energy where that signature disappeared which was exactly what she would have expected to find for a ship going into foldspace.

She studied the path of the *Ivoire*, at least as the teams seemed to believe it had gone, then looked at her bridge crew. Half of them were mimicking her posture, studying the screens ahead of them.

"We just got confirmation from Captain Odeh on the *DetekTibe*," Intxausti said. "They have mapped the same path for the *Ivoire*, and they too believe that it ends with an entry into foldspace."

"And Captain Tua?" Nyguta asked, without taking her gaze from those lines on the various screens.

"They're a little less certain of the path that the *Ivoire* took to that spot, but they agree: that's where the *Ivoire* went into foldspace." Intxausti sounded eager, almost as if she was ready to jump into foldspace after the *Ivoire* right now.

Nyguta certainly was. But she knew better than to do it without a few plans.

Either she and the other two ships all entered foldspace at the same time or they had to find some kind of rendezvous spot, so that they would be able to compare information about where the *Ivoire* ended up.

She preferred the idea of the rendezvous spot. She would have chosen a return to this very sector of space if it weren't for the *Roja*.

"What's happening with our little observer?" she asked Telli.

"It has rounded the starbase," Telli said. "It's hanging back though. It does have all of its scanning equipment working double-time."

"They're talking on their bridge about a search for the three ships," Kibbuku said. "I don't think they know where we are."

Nyguta turned to one of the consoles near her. She tapped on it for a moment, calling up extra information from the *BilatZailea*'s own scans.

"There are a number of surveillance devices around this part of space," she said. "Some aren't as visible as the others."

Just like they had been near the spot the three ships entered.

She studied those devices, wondering if she should destroy them.

She had had her team surveil the previous devices, pulling information off them, and there hadn't been much information to pull. Mostly the surveillance devices were simply cameras and small scanning equipment. They were passive devices that continually sent information to established nodes, but didn't interpret that information at all.

The *BilatZailea* and the other two ships would briefly have to shut off their cloaks before entering foldspace. She didn't want to have the *anacapa* drive interact with the cloaks in even a minor way. It was too great a risk. If she were in a battle, she wouldn't do so, but she could afford a modicum of caution here.

Most likely, those surveillance devices would record the appearance—and then disappearance—of all three ships.

She let out a small breath, considering what, if anything, that meant.

It meant the *BilatZailea*, the *DetekTibe* and the *MuhaQiq* couldn't use this region as a gathering point. It meant that the *Roja* would probably observe them leaving.

If Nyguta saw the Empire as a true threat, then maybe watching them disappear through foldspace would be dangerous. But once the

BilatZailea and the other two ships left this small region of space, Nyguta doubted they would return.

The Armada had no use for the Empire. They also didn't need to worry about it—much, anyway. And even if the Empire figured out that they had entered foldspace, then what could the Empire do with that information?

As far as Nyguta could tell, the Empire had had some small interactions with vessels that had *anacapa* capabilities and as yet hadn't figured out how to make the drives work for them.

The Empire did not seem to be a threat to the Armada.

The *Ivoire*, on the other hand, was. Its captain was smart, knew where Base 20 was, and had already infiltrated their systems using codes the Armada hadn't even realized were still active.

The *Ivoire* was a mystery that needed to be solved.

The Empire was just a government that was in the way.

Decision made: Nyguta wasn't going to destroy the surveillance devices although, as before, she would pull as much information from them as she could.

Once they tracked the *Ivoire* to its lair, they would know if it was a single ship and less of a danger than they all thought or if it was part of some larger group of vessels that might indeed threaten the Armada. Or, if the *Ivoire* was a part of the Fleet.

Her heart pounded at the thought. If the *Ivoire* was part of the Fleet, then she would be forever known as the captain who found the Fleet. After millennia of searching, she would be the one who finally found the bastards who had abandoned and nearly destroyed the ancestors.

The Fleet needed to see what it had created. And, if it were as evil as it had been back then, then it needed to understand why it needed to be destroyed.

She couldn't teach it all of the lessons, of course. But she could begin the Fleet's education into its own bad behavior.

She smiled ever so slightly. She knew why she wanted to find the *Ivoire*. She knew why she wanted it defeated. And yes, of course, it had to do with the bad situation that it had left her in.

But it also had to do with the history. The Fleet had tried to murder the Armada's founders. The Fleet never paid for that.

And now, maybe, it finally would.

27

BELTRAIRE STOOD ON THE BRIDGE OF THE *ROJA*, studying the wall screens and wishing that the hologram floating before him had better resolution. He wanted to see the entire area in three dimensions, but the *Roja*'s equipment wasn't military grade. The telemetry and data retrieval capabilities were amazing, but the screens and the ability to convert real-time data into different formats for military purposes were generally lacking.

He had been on the bridge for hours now, and had gradually moved down from the back to the front beside Walker. The information flowing through all the systems intrigued Beltraire.

He was particularly intrigued by the methodical movement of the three ships. One of the engineers had confirmed that the lead vessel was the same ship that had destroyed all seven ships days before.

The vessel's name was the *BilatZailea*. The other two ships were the *DetekTibe* and the *MuhaQiq*. They had definitely *not* been in the battle around the Room of Lost Souls.

The ships seemed uninterested in the Room. They were following the trail left by the *Ivoire*, and, judging by the way they were behaving, they were heading toward that area of space where the *Ivoire* had vanished.

"Um...sir." A member of the bridge crew, a thin young man with a prominent chin, stopped beside Beltraire. The young man wore a standard uniform, black with white piping.

Beltraire didn't know the young man's name. He didn't know any of their names besides Walker, and Beltraire hadn't taken the time to learn, either. The young man obviously didn't know what to call Beltraire, either, which was what had caused the hesitant "sir."

Beltraire looked over at the young man. "Questions go to your acting captain," Beltraire said, annoyed that he had been interrupted.

"I know, sir, but, um, sir, we're being hailed by the *Ewing Trekov*."

Beltraire bit back irritation. Walker turned toward the young man, movements crisp and precise.

"I'll handle it," Walker said to the young man.

"Beg pardon, sir," the young man said, "but the Group Commander would like to speak with the…um…you, sir."

And as he said that last, he nodded at Beltraire.

Walker said, "I'm acting captain. She can—"

"No." Beltraire sighed. "She wanted to talk with the intelligence officer, didn't she?"

He would have added the young man's name there, had he known it. But both men knew who he was talking to.

"Yes, sir." The young man lowered his voice. "I hadn't been told, but I assume that's you, sir. If I'm incorrect…"

"Your powers of deduction are sound," Beltraire said, rather surprised that he managed to keep from sounding too sarcastic. He was amused, in a dark way, that Trekov had no idea which intelligence officer he was.

The young man waited, hands dangling at his sides as if he was unaccustomed to having them be idle.

"Tell her," Beltraire said, "that I am busy and I will contact her when I get the chance."

"I did, sir," the young man said. "She is demanding to speak with you immediately, or she will go over your head."

There was no over his head, not in any meaningful sense. But Trekov could make his life difficult without a lot of effort.

Beltraire glanced at the three ships. They were moving deliberately, as if they were gathering information as they moved.

He turned to Walker. "Come get me if anything changes or if they get close to that area where the *Ivoire* disappeared."

"Yes, sir," Walker said with such determination that Beltraire had no doubt Walker would tell him anything he needed.

"All right," Beltraire said to the young man. "Take me somewhere private."

"The captain usually used her ready room, sir," the young man said.

Of course she did. For a split second, Beltraire almost said no to the ready room. Then he realized that Captain Krag had had no opportunity to change any of the settings so she could monitor what he was doing.

She was probably seething inside her luxurious captain's quarters, wishing she hadn't decided to step aside for Beltraire, especially since she couldn't communicate with anyone.

The ready room wasn't off the bridge like it was in so many warships. In this vessel, the ready room was a secondary office, for emergency meeting purposes. This ready room was off the corridor, across from the bridge, tucked into an extra space near the elevators.

Beltraire hiked up the aisle on the bridge to the doors in the back, crossed the corridor, and let himself into the ready room. It had a musty, unused quality. He wasn't certain what caused that. Maybe just his expectations.

A small desk was pushed against the wall to the left of the door, and the room's only chair was in the far corner on the right wall. There was an unnecessary end table in the near corner on the right, and enough space in the middle of the room for Beltraire to stand uncomfortably, if he wanted to.

The walls were shiny, and it took him a minute to realize that they were covered with screens. Those definitely had just a tiny layer of dust over them, the kind that didn't get filtered through the environmental system as a matter of course, probably because there was no real air movement in this room.

He doubted that Captain Krag used the ready room much at all, despite what the young man said.

"I'll pipe in the *Ewing Trekov*," the young man said, and before Beltraire could forestall him, the young man disappeared out the door.

Beltraire walked over to the desk. It was made of some kind of warm plastic material, and was sturdy enough to lean against, which he promptly did. He would have preferred to contact Trekov himself, rather than have it outside of his control.

He also would have preferred to avoid any conversation with Trekov at all. If he had controlled it, he could have postponed it. But clearly, that wasn't going to happen.

"To whom am I speaking?" Group Commander Trekov's voice was strong and a little loud.

Apparently, they were having a voice-only discussion, which wouldn't surprise him, given what he had heard about Trekov. She had been badly injured in her first run-in with the *Ivoire* and she had never had all the scars removed.

She had said—or so he'd been told—that she wanted them as a reminder of what Cooper could do.

Which, had she been one of his employees, Beltraire would have seen as some kind of dangerous obsession. He would definitely have kept her off any case to do with Cooper, nor allowed her to monitor the Room or any other place in the Empire where Cooper might appear.

Then Beltraire had a bit of a surprise: they weren't doing voice-only. Trekov appeared on the screen in the center of the ready room, the screen's fine layer of dust adding a softness to her appearance.

Beltraire had expected her to have facial scars and some serious disfigurement, but he saw nothing out of the ordinary. She had a thin strong face, the Trekov nose, and dark eyes that didn't seem to miss anything.

Beltraire turned so that he could face her. He saw a small image of himself in the corner of the screen. He looked thinner than usual, and a bit tired, which surprised him.

He didn't like the setup in here, but he didn't have time to reconfigure it.

"You are speaking to Yves Beltraire, Group Commander," he said. He wasn't going to give her any leeway. If she wanted to have a conversation, she had to initiate it.

"You should have contacted me before ordering my vessels out of the area," she said, looking down that imperious nose at him.

"I don't answer to you," he said.

"No," she said. "But those ships all do."

"We can argue this if you would like, Group Commander, but both tradition and regulation state that in the proper circumstance, Imperial Intelligence has sway over any vessels."

She smiled at him, but the smile did not reach her eyes. He had the odd sense, at that moment, that she was dangerous, and it surprised him just like the meeting had. Just like the fact that her famous scars apparently were not on her face.

"Tradition and regulation state that in the proper circumstances, Imperial Intelligence holds sway over any *military* vessels, Yves Beltraire."

She leaned on his name, making it clear that she knew who he was, and where he stood in the intelligence hierarchy. Which meant that she knew that in most circumstances, he outranked her.

"Those were not military vessels," she was saying. "They are science and research vessels and they are under my command."

She caught him, then. He thought for a moment, not sure how he wanted to play this.

He consciously modified his tone to something less forceful, something that seemed more collegial. "The ships were in danger," he said, making sure his expression was softer too. "I made a decision. I also believed we did not have the luxury of a discussion like this one."

"Yet you remain at the Room of Lost Souls while the other ships have left," she said, not arguing with him about the danger. Which meant that someone had told her about the three enemy vessels.

"I do," he said. "The *Roja* is monitoring three enemy vessels that have arrived here unexpectedly."

"Enemy," she repeated. "What makes you believe they deserve that designation?"

The tone of her voice led him to believe that this was the real reason she had contacted him, not to reprimand him from taking command of her ships, but to find out about the vessels.

"One of the ships is the ship that participated in the battle here at the Room," he said.

Her gaze was hooded. "And you didn't think to ask for reinforcements?"

"I was gathering information," he said.

"Allowing them to do the same." Her tone hadn't moderated. She was clearly unhappy with his decision and wanted him to know it. "Where are they now?"

"They're still here, Group Commander," he said.

"And they haven't attacked you?" she asked.

"They don't know I'm here," he said.

She barked out a laugh. "You underestimate them. You're not a threat to them."

"We're cloaked."

"Their technology is greater than ours," she said. "They have tools we're just beginning to understand."

He almost snapped, *I understand that, Group Commander. I'm studying stealth tech as well,* but he caught himself just in time. He was startled at himself. Somehow, she had gotten under his skin, and he had no idea how she had managed to do that so quickly.

Usually, he was aware of any kind of manipulation.

"I will send ships," she said.

"No, you will not, Group Commander," he said.

"We have been invaded by—your word—enemy vessels. I'm to let *enemy* vessels roam freely in our space, as if they're welcome here?" Her voice got even harsher.

"We're observing them," he said.

"The last time they were here—just days ago—one of them, just one, destroyed everything in its path. You didn't think that perhaps a confrontation is what they want?"

"I'm not interested in—"

"I don't care what you're interested in, Yves Beltraire of Imperial Intelligence. They killed hundreds of our people, destroyed seven ships, and you're just letting them travel through Empire space as if what they've done means nothing."

Her expression hadn't changed. It was imperious and forceful. He was beginning to realize that he had underestimated her. He had paid attention to the rumors about her and accepted them as true, something he always cautioned new intelligence officers against.

He would have to examine why he had done that...later. When he wasn't talking with her.

"They have a technological advantage," he said before he caught himself. Damn. That defensiveness was strong and real—and mostly unconscious.

"Military decisions are clearly not your strong suit," Trekov said. "We have no idea who these people are nor do we know whether or not they actually do have a technological advantage. We just assume they do. They caught us by surprise. We don't know if, in a fair fight, we would defeat them."

He knew. The enemy vessels clearly had an advantage.

"They have two forms of propulsion," he said.

Her expression didn't change, and yet something about her did. He had her full attention now, yet he had the sense he hadn't surprised her.

She had known about—or guessed at—the two forms of propulsion.

"The three vessels arrived from elsewhere," he said, not quite sure how to convey what he had seen. The vessels hadn't been in this part of Enterran space, and then they were. But he wasn't sure how to say that.

She waited, a technique he usually used. Let the person on the defensive do the talking.

He wasn't quite sure when this conversation had gotten away from him.

"Once they arrived," he said, "they cloaked."

Her lips twisted in contempt. "So you don't even know where they are," she said.

"I didn't say that," he said.

"No," she said. "But we both know we lack the technology to track cloaked vessels. How do you know they arrived from 'elsewhere'? How do you know they weren't just cloaked?"

He had done this to himself. He should have thought about the conversation before letting that young man contact her. He should have stopped the young man.

"Hmmm, Yves Beltraire?" The contempt in her voice matched the contempt in her expression. "How do you know?"

He wasn't going to tell her about the Imperial Intelligence buoys. She probably had clearance for them, but this conversation had become a battle, and he did not feel like confiding in her.

"I saw them enter," he said. "It was as if a door opened, revealing a well-lit room, and the ships came through it. The door then closed behind them."

"They came in together?" She sounded surprised—not at the door, but at them traveling together. She had seen this before, he was sure of it.

"One by one, each by their own door," he said.

"And you just happened to be nearby." That contempt again.

He was out of practice with being treated like an underling. He couldn't remember the last time that had happened.

It didn't matter that he wasn't her subordinate. The treatment felt exactly the same.

He wasn't going to let her continue to interrogate him.

"They arrived, one by one," he said. "The arriving ship moved away from their door just a little, hovered for a moment, and then cloaked. The next ship did the same, as did the third."

Her eyes narrowed. He could almost feel her weighing how he had this information. She was clearly savvy enough to understand that he had just dodged one of her questions.

If she was that savvy, she probably also just realized that Imperial Intelligence had buoys near the Room that they had told no one about, buoys he wasn't going to admit to.

"So," she said crisply. "That's when you lost them."

He was getting very irritated with her. "I never said we lost them, Group Commander. You made that assumption."

"You know where they are, then?" she asked, her tone so neutral he knew she was hiding surprise.

"I believe they are heading toward that point in space where your Captain Cooper vanished."

"He's not *my* captain," she said, managing not to sound irritated. She spoke as if she were correcting an underling. She was a lot better at this than he had expected. "How do you know where they are headed? Are you tracking their communications?"

It's the only logical thing, he nearly said, and stopped himself. She was asking for evidence, which he didn't have. At least not the kind of evidence she expected.

"They tracked Cooper here," Beltraire said, "and would have pursued him if he hadn't deflected them. It only makes—"

"It only makes sense, I know," she said with that sarcasm again. "Assuming we are dealing with Captain Cooper."

"He is in charge of the *Ivoire*," Beltraire said.

"He *was* in charge of the *Ivoire*," Trekov said. "We have no idea if he still is."

Beltraire felt the rebuke. Had this been a normal conversation, he would have asked her what she thought, although he knew it was rather clear: Cooper was cunning. They had already established that. And because he was cunning—and because the person who had come to the Room was also cunning, they assumed it was Cooper.

"You haven't told me how you know where they're going," she said. "Do you have communications from them? Do you know where they are right now?"

"We don't have any communications between them," he said.

"And you're guessing about where they're going and what they're doing." Trekov's mouth thinned.

He suddenly realized what was going on. She was furious at him. Apparently, she didn't like having her orders countermanded.

"They came for Cooper—"

"We don't know that," she snapped. "We know nothing about them. And now, you're losing track of them. Three very powerful ships that have very powerful cloaks. Ships that can destroy seven of our vessels quickly and without remorse."

Her anger ignited his own. He said, "Group Commander—"

"No," she said. "You don't get to speak. You probably thought you were doing the right thing, didn't you? You would spy on them, which is what you intelligence people do, and you'd save the information you gathered for something to be determined later."

"I—"

"No," she said again. "You need to listen to me. *This* is why you do not have a military command. You have allowed enemies—your word—into the heart of the Empire. You assume they're going after Captain Cooper, but you don't know that. You have no idea why he was running from them. You assume—we all assume—that he brought them here, but for all we know, the Room of Lost Souls is something that they're fighting over. Maybe this was part of a larger battle."

"Group Commander—"

"Or maybe," she said, leaning closer to the screen she was using, "this is some kind of attack on the Empire. We don't know if that maneuver, with Cooper and the *Ivoire*, was calculated. We have no idea if they meant to take out any vessel that arrived to respond to their emergency beacon."

He blinked, careful not to let his surprise show on his face. He hadn't thought of that.

"Then I was right to send the ships away," he said.

"Were you?" she asked. "Because we did have some military vessels as security. You sent them away as well, leaving yourself vulnerable. And how do you know they're not listening in on our conversation now?"

It's encoded, he almost said. Defensive again.

"They don't know we're here," he said.

"If you believe that, you're a fool," she said.

His cheeks warmed. He hadn't been dressed down like this in years. Maybe even a decade or more.

"You probably destroyed our last chance to figure out what is going on with those ships, all with the idea that you would spy on them." She shook her head. "I will be sending more ships to the Room. With luck, those three enemy vessels are still nearby."

"I'm sure they—"

"Based on what, Yves Beltraire of Imperial Intelligence? A hunch? Maybe some kind of half-assed system in your data tracking?"

"That's enough," he snapped. "I outrank you, Group Commander. You have no right to talk to me like this."

She smiled, but the smile did not reach her eyes. "I have every right. Imperial Intelligence thinks that, because it has the word 'intelligence' in its name, it is smarter than every other branch of government. It is not, and you are not. You stepped outside of your area of expertise, and for what?"

"They use a form of stealth tech," he said quietly. "It allows them to travel quickly from one part of the sector to another."

"You think I'm unaware of the link between their ships and stealth tech? Why do you think I ordered science and research vessels to the Room, Beltraire? It is because Cooper's vessel and the other two used a variation of stealth tech in their ships, and Cooper also used another variation as a weapon, which I have faced twice. Your enemy vessels did *not* use that weapon, which makes me wonder if the use of the weapon is common or if it is a last-resort weapon."

She folded her hands together, the smile long gone from her face.

"You have interfered with all of our intelligence-gathering efforts, and worse, you have let three ships loose in the Empire. I will be reporting you to Central Command."

"Do so," he said. "I'll let them know you put science and research ships in jeopardy."

"Except that I didn't, Beltraire. I had the ships monitored and protected."

He had no idea how she could say something like that without sounding defensive, and yet she managed. Maybe it came from her anger, which, he had to admit, was righteous.

He hadn't thought of the military implications, and, because he was not on a military vessel, no one on the bridge mentioned them to him. He *had* made a tactical mistake.

"You will send me the information you have on those ships," Trekov said.

"I will not, Group Commander. You don't—"

"You have no choice, Beltraire. I need that information so that I can properly defend the Room of Lost Souls and the Empire itself." She crossed her arms and glared at him. "You will also send me whatever you've rigged up to track those vessels. I want to know where they are and what they're doing in real time."

"Aren't you afraid they'll track that?" Beltraire asked.

Her smile returned—cold and vicious. "The only Empire ship that would get harmed if they were tracking these communications is yours, Beltraire. Thanks to you, we have nothing else close."

And then she signed off.

He frowned, disconcerted by the abruptness of her action. He hadn't expected any of that.

She had been right: he hadn't thought of the military implications. But he didn't believe the ships were a threat to the Empire. If he had to do this again, he would. He wanted to know how they were using stealth tech and how he could steal it.

He pushed away from the table, and glanced around the ready room. It was extremely spare, an uncomfortable place for an uncomfortable conversation.

She could bully him all she wanted, but he wasn't going to send her any of the information she requested. She did not outrank him, and she had no need of that information.

He wished she wouldn't send ships, but he wasn't going to argue the point on the off chance that she might be right. He didn't want to be the person who refused to properly defend the Empire.

But he couldn't believe that this was some kind of attack either. It didn't make sense.

Unless…these were some kind of advance troops.

But to what purpose? Because if they were advance troops, they had just revealed themselves. They let the Empire know that they could arrive in a stealth manner, and then destroy any ships that were nearby, easily and quickly.

If they were planning to attack the Empire, they should have done so with a similar strategy near the seat of government, not near the abandoned Room of Lost Souls. They should have arrived with a large squadron of ships, and they should have destroyed almost everything before the Empire could even mount a defense.

He shook off the unease he felt after the talk with Trekov. She had blustered at him, but she was wrong. This was a science issue, and nothing more.

He was right to spy on those three ships, and he would return to it.

He wanted to see what they did when they found where the *Ivoire* had disappeared from Empire space. He wanted to know how they would investigate.

He wanted to know, so that he could do the same.

28

IT WAS OFFICIAL: Nyguta regretted getting rid of her captain's chair. She had hated the thing. It had been the bane of her existence from the moment she took over the *BilatZailea*, but for some reason, she hadn't registered how much she used that stupid chair.

She would have used it while monitoring the conversation between the *Roja* and a ship called the *Ewing Trekov*. Quick research into the Enterran Empire suggested that the name Trekov was important in the Empire.

She would need Telli to investigate the Trekov name, particularly since the person who had contacted the *Roja* was called Group Commander Trekov.

Before the contact, Nyguta had decided that the three ships under her command would go around the starbase using different routes. They would also travel as close to the starbase as they could because of the mass of confusing *anacapa* energy in the region.

That would hurt the *Roja's* searches. Nyguta had found it both fortuitous and amusing that the *Roja* believed it was cloaked. The ship almost glowed white on her data streams. The cloak was that bad, and their continual searches hurt it as well.

In some ways, the cloak made the *Roja* easier to monitor.

Because she had gotten rid of her captain's chair, she had to pace as she listened to the conversation between a man named Yves Beltraire, and this Group Commander Trekov.

As Nyguta paced, she made certain that one of her screens followed her everywhere. She made note of the names and the rankings. The fact that Beltraire was with the intelligence service intrigued her. And she appreciated Trekov's exasperation.

Until Nyguta overheard this conversation, she had assumed that Beltraire was a military leader with a military leader's tactical abilities.

She had been wrong—gloriously so. Beltraire wasn't going to attack the three ships. He was going to observe them.

He would learn nothing more than he already had.

Initially, she hadn't planned to listen to the conversation, but Kibbuku, who had been monitoring the communications, flagged it for her.

She had listened to part of it, before waving her hand at the entire bridge.

"You need to hear this," she had said to them.

Occasionally, as the discussions went on, she would pause it, and order someone to investigate a name or a bit of history. She wanted to know more about the Enterran Empire. She wanted to know who this Trekov was, and who or what *Ewing Trekov* had been.

She wanted to know the hierarchy, so that she knew what she was dealing with.

She wished she had enough time to figure out why the *anacapa* energy was so out of control. She had a hunch the Empire called it stealth tech, but that was based on something this Beltraire had said, not on any research.

She wasn't sure she needed the research on that detail, but she wanted it. The more she knew about this Empire, the better off she would be.

She also wanted to know about the research vessels. What exactly had they been trying to figure out? How far away was their protection?

It didn't sound like the protection was returning to help out the *Roja*, which was good.

But what intrigued her the most was this Captain Cooper. The little bit of research her team had done earlier had connected a Jonathon Cooper to the *Ivoire*. He had had an ignominious career, but the one thing all of the research had established was that he had a creative mind.

If he was the same Cooper—a man who had traveled five thousand years into his future—he would have needed that creative mind.

She didn't want this Cooper to be the man from the past.

What she hoped was this Cooper was a distant relative of Jonathon Cooper's. Maybe the ship, the *Ivoire*, was the *Ivoire 25* or something, and it was a tradition that a Cooper had the helm.

After all, the Armada worked that way. The Honored Families all had inherited positions, whether they were suited for those positions or not. Most members of the Honored Families recognized their inability to fill the positions and either resigned or took a figurehead role.

This Cooper, though, he wouldn't be a figurehead, not the way that Trekov and Beltraire discussed him. He clearly had the talents of his ancestor...if, indeed, he was not the original Cooper.

She ran a hand over her face and suppressed a sigh of exasperation. The conversation droned on, seemingly longer than it should have been simply because she kept pausing it.

She put her hands on her hips and leaned backwards, listening to her spine pop. Her crew watched her surreptitiously. They had worked with her long enough to know that she was working on something mentally, and they shouldn't really interrupt.

She wasn't working so much as hoping. The other reason she did not want this man to be the original Cooper was the very one that Atwater had mentioned in the meeting of the Jefatura.

If this was the original Cooper, then he would have no Fleet backup. Nyguta wouldn't be discovering the Fleet after all.

In fact, all of Cooper's behavior made sense if he was the original Cooper, a man who had a single ship and no backup. He broke into Base 20, searching for information on the Fleet, not expecting to find the Armada. He had fled the Armada, using stealth and trickery, and barely got away.

Atwater wanted this Cooper to be the original Cooper. She wanted Nyguta to capture him, use his powerful mind and the codes he had to see if he could somehow help the Armada find the Fleet.

Nyguta would have to lie to him—at least according to Atwater's plan—and tell him that the Armada was the Fleet.

Nyguta didn't like that plan. She also didn't like how Trekov and Beltraire were talking about this Cooper. He sounded like as strong a tactical mind as Nyguta had worried about.

They reached the end of their conversation—or, rather, Nyguta reached the end of the conversation's playback. She felt a quiet empathy for Trekov. The woman was dealing with a military idiot. Beltraire should have left the ships, especially those guarding the research vessels.

The fact that Beltraire was the only commander of the only ship remaining was an absolute gift for Nyguta. She could do whatever she liked here and, most importantly, the *BilatZailea*, the *DetekTibe* and the *MuhaQiq* could enter foldspace one at a time, as they had when they arrived here.

Yes, it was a risk, but less of a risk than trying to enter foldspace together.

With a typical commander in charge of an enemy vessel (and apparently, the Empire now considered the Armada the enemy), Nyguta would never have let her ships leave one at a time. That risked exposing the one or two ships remaining to attack.

But Beltraire wouldn't know how to attack these vessels properly and, humorously, he thought he was cloaked. Any of the three Armada vessels could destroy his ship without much thought whatsoever.

She didn't want to do that. She didn't want to be at war with the Enterran Empire. They were an annoyance and nothing more.

Cooper and the *Ivoire* were her objective.

Now, she was intrigued about this weapon that Trekov had mentioned. Had Cooper found a weapon that no one had heard of before—or, perhaps, that Nyguta and the Armada hadn't heard of—or was he simply using the *anacapa* drive in creative ways?

She would need a history to know what Trekov was discussing, and at the moment, they had nothing like that.

"Were you able to get that packet the *Roja* sent to the *Ewing Trekov?*" she asked Kibbuku. "It would be nice to know how they're tracking us."

"Got it and examined it." Intxausti was the one who responded. "They're tracking us by an emptiness in space. The outlines of where we are. That's why they're pinging so much."

Nyguta smiled. She had hoped they were doing that. It was easy to defeat. It simply took the same kind of trickery that Cooper had used at Base 20.

"Let's set up some ghost ships," she said. "Let the other two vessels know what we're doing. We'll send the *Roja* on a merry little chase."

Intxausti lifted her head. Her smile was impish. Then she brought her head down again.

Pereira smiled as well. He kept his head down, but his fingers moved across his control board.

"You want me to let the other ships know we've got it handled?" Rockowitz asked.

"Yes," Nyguta said. "Tell them to meet us at the foldspace entry point in half an hour."

It wasn't really enough time for her to siphon all of the information from the buoys like she had wanted to do, but it would do. That information, plus everything they had been lifting from the *Roja*, would help with all of their research.

"Anastasia," Nyguta said to Telli. "I want you to search the records we're pulling from the Empire. Look for mentions of the *Ivoire* and Cooper. I want to see what kinds of tricks he's pulled on them—if, indeed, those are tricks."

"Will do," Telli said, hands moving quickly.

"And I want to know what this Nine Planets is. And why there are two mentions of Lost Souls. Are they related in some way?" Nyguta's orders were crisp, but she didn't have to explain much.

Her team—the entire Armada, really—preferred too much knowledge to too little. There were times when what seemed like excess knowledge would come in handy.

So the more she knew, the better prepared she would be.

"What do you want us to do about the *Roja*?" Habibi asked. "Should we threaten it in some way?"

"I think the ghost ships will seem like threat enough," Nyguta said. "He's alone here, because he sent his military backup away. He knows what we did to seven of their ships, and he doesn't have a tactician's mind. Whether he admits it or not, he'll be scared."

And that pleased her. Mentally, she tipped her hat to Group Command Trekov, whoever she was, who had to deal with an idiot who headed a ship in a situation where he should not have been in charge at all.

"Is there any way we can piggyback off the communications of the *Roja* and slide into the systems of the *Ewing Trekov?*" she asked.

Kibbuku answered. "Already tried. They're well shielded, as if they were expecting some kind of information barrage. They're also too far from us to use other methods of entering their control systems. We would have to know the specs of that particular ship, and we don't. Which is too bad."

That last bit caught Nyguta's attention. "Too bad?"

"Yeah," Kibbuku said. "The Group Commander is on some kind of Command vessel. She's in charge of a lot of ships."

"Do we know anything else about her?" Nyguta asked.

"Nothing that we can use, yet. I'll brief you once we enter foldspace."

Nyguta nodded. They weren't far from entering foldspace.

She needed to turn her attention to what was coming. Cooper, Nine Planets, some kind of corporation. And, of course, foldspace itself.

The thought of losing five thousand years sent a shiver through her. She thought about it for a moment, thought about relying only on this ship because there was no one else, and then she smiled.

She had the training for that.

They all did. And they had the constitution for it as well. The Armada had been formed out of a group of engineers, abandoned by the Fleet, and left on their own. The Fleet had thought they would give up.

But giving up was not in the Armada's nature. Not at its founding, and not now.

Nyguta straightened, the smile remaining. That little bit of joy she always felt when she thought about the original Honored Families not only made her feel better, it also gave her strength.

She could do this.

She had to put on her wiliest hat. She had to make decisions that would benefit her people. If she could find the Fleet, so be it. If she could capture Cooper, even better.

But if she had to destroy him and his friends at this Nine Planets, she would do so.

Unlike Beltraire, she knew how to command a mission.

She knew exactly what to do.

29

ELISSA TREKOV FLATTENED HER PALMS against her lower back, and leaned backwards ever so slightly. Her spine creaked, which she privately called the sounds of stress.

She was surrounded by self-important idiots. Yves Beltraire was just one of several, beginning with and ending with Flag Commander Janik. If these people—these *men*—would just listen to her, the Empire would be better off.

She straightened her spine and let her hands drop to her sides, thankful that she was the only person in her office. The room was small and comfortable, although she kept it as impersonal as possible. She used the office for enough private conversations with self-important idiots like Beltraire that she didn't want them to get the wrong impression from the personal details around her.

She moved her high-backed chair aside, and looked at the flat desk, which doubled as a console.

Beltraire had ruined her best chance at figuring out not just who this Cooper really was but at understanding the ships chasing him. She understood Beltraire's interest in stealth tech, but those ships were clearly dangerous, and she had no idea why they had decided to bring their fight to the Empire.

For all she knew, the scenario she presented to Beltraire was an accurate one: the little drama between the *Ivoire* and those three ships had been some kind of act, designed to see how big a military presence the Empire could summon to a remote spot on short notice.

Someone knocked on her office door, which surprised her. Normally, she received communications in here. No one came here directly.

The knock was solid, forceful when it came the second time.

"What?" she snapped.

"I have news, Group Commander." Paek's deep voice, modulated to sound as gentle as possible. He expected her to be angry. At him? Or had he sensed her mood when she had left the command center?

He had probably more than sensed her mood. She had probably radiated anger.

She leaned over her desk, touched the screen built into the surface, and the door slid open soundlessly. Paek stood outside, hands clasped behind his back, which had the effect of showing off his muscular biceps.

"You could have contacted me directly," she said. "You didn't have to come up here."

"I wanted to," he said, almost ominously. His gaze moved from her to the office behind her, signaling that he wanted inside, rather than hold the discussion in the hallway.

He was too professional to ask. She liked that about him.

She beckoned him with her right hand, then reached down to close the door, but he had gotten there first, touching the controls on the side.

"We've located the *Ivoire*," he said, as soon as the door closed all the way.

She straightened. This should have been good news, easily relayed, but the way he spoke made her brace herself against something difficult.

"It is deep inside Nine Planets' territory, at the Lost Souls Corporation," he said.

She nodded, letting out a breath. She expected no less.

"This is not a surprise," she said to him, "yet you came all the way here to tell me this in person."

"Because there are oddities, ma'am," he said.

She couldn't help herself. She tensed.

His brown eyes noted that, but his expression didn't change.

"And those oddities are?" she asked.

"There is no record of the *Ivoire* crossing the border between the Empire and the Nine Planets," he said.

"There are ways around that border," she said. "You know it. We would use those methods if we needed to."

"Yes, but any ship that crosses would eventually show up on our buoys or in the data stream of some other ship. I've had some of our best people check this: there is no record of the *Ivoire* crossing that border or even heading to the border."

He was using that tone again. Clearly, he found this information disturbing.

"Likewise," he said, "we have no actual record of the *Ivoire* entering Empire space from anyplace logical."

"Meaning?" she asked.

"Meaning what we see in our records might actually be what happened. The *Ivoire* appeared near the Room and disappeared not far from the Room."

She thought of the light she had seen against the ship, the light that had engulfed her and her ships when Cooper attacked the first time, the light that rippled outward when he attacked the second time.

Beltraire had mentioned the three ships entering through what appeared to be a door opening out from a well-lit room.

More light.

Beltraire clearly thought of it all as some kind of entrance. He seemed to believe that stealth tech could be used to transport ships somehow.

Did she actually have evidence of it with the *Ivoire*?

She wasn't certain.

"And then there's the timing," Paek was saying.

Elissa made herself focus on his words.

"The *Ivoire* arrived at Lost Souls within an hour of leaving here. Our stardrive—"

"Makes it to the border in half a day," she said, "and Lost Souls is some distance from there."

Some distance that she didn't know, not off the top of her head.

"So," she said, "they most likely have a better and faster stardrive than we do."

"Or they can teleport," Paek said.

She nodded, not really thinking about that. Their stardrive—or whatever they were using—did something with stealth tech that she didn't understand.

Damn Beltraire. If he hadn't gotten rid of her ships, she might have had a chance of surrounding or capturing one of them. Maybe she would have learned something about that stardrive.

Now, she wasn't sure what she could learn. A single ship, observing and studying trails and energy levels would tell her nothing.

Paek was watching her intently. Had he continued the discussion? She didn't know. She had gotten lost in her own thoughts.

Because she was going to do something she had considered earlier, but had mostly ruled out.

She was going to talk with Cooper, see why he had invaded her space.

"How many ships do we have at the border?" she asked.

Paek raised his eyebrows. She understood the expression. She had caught him off-guard.

"The usual contingent," he said. "I'd have to check for the actual numbers."

She didn't have to check. She was the one who had ordered the "usual contingent" to be at the border in the first place.

"Let's beef up our presence there," she said. "We need a good fifty vessels with more on the way."

Paek frowned, then glanced over his shoulder as if he were afraid someone was going to hear. Or maybe he was double-checking to make sure the door was closed.

"Shouldn't we speak to Flag Commander Janik about this?"

"Why?" Elissa said with a little more heat than she intended. "I have the authority to move ships throughout the Empire. I'm moving a few squadrons to the border because of a known threat. Let him deal with me on this. I'll…"

She stopped. She wasn't going to articulate the threat, not yet. But she would make sure that Janik was placed into the same category as Beltraire should they all be called before general command. These two men were mismanaging the threat.

She would make sure to record all of her reasoning, and blame them for the silence on this. Cooper and the *Ivoire* had been a threat for years. The three ships were another threat (or the same threat) and both things had been mismanaged by Janik and Beltraire.

She would make sure the situation with Cooper was handled correctly.

She shoved the chair toward Paek.

"Sit down, Tawhiri," she said. "This is going to take a while."

"What is?" he asked.

She smiled at him. "We're going to do a bit of diplomacy. And you're going to listen and learn."

"Ma'am?" he asked.

Her smile widened. "Just watch," she said, and leaned over her desk.

She needed a witness, one who knew her well and could attest to her mood and state of mind. There would be a recording of any conversation she had with Cooper (or anyone else for that matter), but recordings didn't deal with subtleties well.

She often relied on witnesses when she was delving into whatever a captain did that might have gone wrong.

She didn't expect this situation to go wrong, but she was dealing with Cooper of the *Ivoire*. He had surprised her every single time.

Paek sat in the chair reluctantly, his big hands on his knees. He watched her every movement. He knew she didn't give orders for unimportant things.

She didn't want him or any other member of her staff to track down Cooper. She was going to do it herself.

The *Ewing Trekov* had communicated with the *Ivoire* a number of times, most recently around their skirmish at the border a year ago. She could hail Cooper. It might take a moment for a response, but she thought it necessary.

She encoded her work, using a command code that the regular staff didn't have easy access to. They would see that she was sending a communique but they wouldn't see who that communique was going to.

The only thing she hesitated over was whether or not she would use a visual to communicate with Cooper. The hesitation didn't last long. She wanted to see him. She didn't know him well enough to know if he was lying, but she could watch anyway.

She sent the hail, then stood up, and met Paek's gaze.

"What are we doing now, ma'am?" he asked.

"We're waiting," she said. "And the only question before us is for how long."

30

IT HAD BEEN A LONG TIME since he'd held a meeting of his diplomats.

Coop thought of holding the meeting in a conference area of the Lost Souls Corporation, but that seemed impersonal. So he decided to hold the meeting in his favorite bar on the *Ivoire*.

He had been in the bar with Yash after they had returned from their strange trip to Sector Base E-2. After they had managed to escape from Nindowne, and shake off those Not-Fleet ships that had been chasing them.

They drank too much and made some vows he was no longer sure Yash could keep.

He wasn't sure he could keep them either, now that he knew the Fleet was still around, although he really didn't want to admit that to himself.

Not yet.

The bar was off the main commissary, and wasn't as big as some of the other bars on the *Ivoire*. The bar had twenty-five tables, which he hadn't seen full since he'd released the crew. He could have kept the crew on the ship to the end of their days, but that wasn't fair.

He believed—and they believed—that they would never return to their timeline, or to the Fleet for that matter, so he decided that each crew member and their family could choose how they wanted to live in this new future.

Which meant that a lot had left. Some had left altogether, finding homes planetside in the Nine Planets. Others had moved from shipboard work to more interesting work with Lost Souls.

About two-thirds remained, and served with him only when he called them up, as he had done with the trip to Sector Base E-2. Even then, he hadn't had a full complement of the new crew. Some, like Zaria Diaz, had been at the Boneyards with Boss.

And then there were the true lost souls. Like Dix, whom Coop wished he could stop thinking about. Dix, whom Coop had told the crew had committed suicide—and that was true, as far as it went, but Dix hadn't just killed himself. He had tried to take a lot of people with him. Only Coop and Yash knew that.

The last almost-normal evening Coop had with Dix had taken place in this bar.

The detritus from that drinking session with Yash remained until he arrived. Apparently, he and Yash had been too drunk to clear their glasses from the tabletop. Some empty bottles sat on top of the long bar. He'd removed those and polished the fake wood surface.

The brass touches around the entire bar still gleamed. He and Yash hadn't really cluttered the place up much except for the bar and the table where they had toasted the past and the future, not knowing what the future would actually be—or how quickly it would arrive.

He went to the wall controls. He reconfigured one corner of the entire bar. Three of the small tables receded into the floor, the planters with some greenery (which someone was still tending, although he wasn't sure who) slid sideways so they were against one of the walls, and a large round table rose out of the part of the floor where the small tables had receded.

He ordered up new chairs, making sure that they all had views of the windows, which were his favorite part of this bar. When the *Ivoire* was traveling, the windows here showed whatever the *Ivoire* was traveling near. Or they showed that particular region of space—ever changing and always lovely.

Right now, all he could see were parts of the Lost Souls space station, which excited him a lot less.

Not that he was here for the view.

He hadn't realized, until he'd summoned the diplomatic team, that half of the ship's diplomatic corps had left to go planetside. He supposed it made sense: they weren't as committed to shipboard life as everyone else on the ship. But it put him in a bit of a bind now. Some of his best people were gone.

It showed just how disengaged he had been as a captain over the past several years that he hadn't really registered who had left the ship, even as the names and the reasons for leaving had passed before him for review.

Sadly, he hadn't even met with them to urge them to reconsider what they were doing. He hadn't seen a point. He wanted everyone to live the life they wanted in this brand-new future.

Also, deep down, he hadn't thought of himself as their captain anymore. Not the man who could control what they were doing with their lives and careers by promoting or demoting them or moving them laterally or suggesting they would leave the ship altogether.

After calling up the round table, he went behind the bar, and set up an automatic service. Small floating trays would take orders and serve them. He needed to set it up to make certain that the trays had time to download the beverage list, after doing a quick inventory.

He, and many of the others, had partaken from the bar itself but he hadn't replenished like he used to when the *Ivoire* traveled across the stars. Back then, he had collected liquor from cities and starbases he had visited, liquor he knew he would never find again.

He had gone through a lot of that; more than he had realized before that drinking session with Yash. He'd spent his first year here, nursing his own sense of loss. Not that he had gotten drunk—that had been a rarity—but he had had a drink or two a night for that year, often to help himself sleep.

And he'd have the drink here, not in his quarters. He would stare out the window at the space he didn't recognize, at the new time he didn't recognize, and try to figure out just how he would cope with it all.

Eventually, that nightly drink disappeared as he found more and more challenges. He didn't stop doing it consciously. He just got busier and busier and more often than not, he forgot.

He ran a hand down his shirt, smoothing it. He wasn't even wearing a uniform anymore. His casual clothes were more Lost Souls than Fleet. His light tan shirt and brown pants were looser than regulation.

For a moment, he wondered if he should change, and make his clothing closer to regulation. Then he realized it didn't matter.

What mattered was how he would talk to the remaining diplomats, and see what they had to say about talking to the Fleet.

He smiled. In the past few years, he had faced a lot of strange things, but nothing was stranger to his mind than approaching an organization he'd served all of his life as if he had never met them before.

That both things were true sometimes made his brain hurt.

The first diplomat to arrive was Marissa Cumex. For as long as Coop had known her, Cumex was always early and always prepared. He had been pleased when he saw her name on the *Ivoire* service list. She had moved to Lost Souls to train new diplomats for new ships, but she had updated her service file herself, and flagged it with a comment that said she considered herself a member of the *Ivoire's* crew first and foremost.

She was a small woman with a dramatic shock of white hair along one side of her head. The rest of her hair was a dark brown that matched her eyes and set off her light brown skin.

She didn't wear regulation clothes either. Her outfit was similar to Coop's—loose tan pants and a slightly darker shirt. She had dressed that way on Ukhanda, when they had had that disastrous last diplomatic adventure, just before getting shot at and finding themselves becalmed in foldspace.

She smiled at him, and crossed to the bar.

"We get to drink in this meeting?" she asked.

"If you think you can do so and keep a clear head," he said. He had never known his staff to drink to excess except when they were off duty, so he wasn't worried that she would do something untoward.

She found a bottle of red wine underneath one of the cabinets which led him to believe she had stashed it there. She uncorked it, and poured herself a glass, then waved the bottle at him in an unspoken question.

He shook his head. He'd had more than enough alcohol this week. He probably wouldn't have more for at least a month or two, depending.

She recorked the bottle, then looked at him, glass in hand. "Where do you want us?"

He nodded to the round table near the windows, and she smiled, as if she had expected that. She walked around him, heading toward the table, as another diplomat, Rory Habnal, came through the door.

He wasn't wearing regulation clothes either, not that he would fit in them. Habnal had gotten heavier. His stomach had settled over his belt, and his face was fleshy.

The diplomats had a different charge than others on the *Ivoire*. They never had to stay in physical shape, although it was recommended. Habnal had always fought that stricture, but as a younger man, he had managed to remain relatively thin.

Now, he was not, and unlike the loose clothing that Coop and Cumex wore, Habnal's clothing was too tight. He was tugging on his black high-collar shirt as he came farther into the bar, his pants riding just a little high, revealing comfortable shoes.

He smiled when he saw Coop, who couldn't help himself; he smiled back.

That infectious smile was one of the great features of Habnal the diplomat. No person anywhere in the system had ever been able to resist his charm.

He stopped behind the bar as well, waving at Cumex. Unlike Cumex, Habnal didn't ask if they were allowed to drink. He found the automated system, grabbed a mug, and activated the (rather awful) coffee dispenser.

Coop seemed to remember that Habnal had some kind of problem with alcohol while living here at Lost Souls. He'd worked through it, and was being cautious about drink.

In the past, Coop would have been leery of anyone who had a history of substance abuse, but that was long in the past. Five thousand years in the past. Now, Coop understood that the situation had forced everyone on the ship to deal with their own demons, and some of the crew had found some very dark demons indeed.

Coop stared at that coffee for a moment, thinking of Dix. Dark, dark demons.

"How many of us did you bring in, Captain?" Habnal asked.

"All of the diplomats remaining," Coop said. "We're going to need all hands on this."

To his surprise, Habnal smiled. "Sounds intriguing."

He pressed the dispenser for dark chocolate and added a squirt of that into his coffee as well. Then he carried the large mug over to Cumex, leaving Coop behind the bar alone.

He looked at the automated system, thought about the awful coffee, and decided he'd stick with water for now. He picked up a mug that fit perfectly in his hand, and looked up to see his ex-wife Mae standing hesitantly in the doorway.

She looked frailer than he remembered. Her red hair was piled on top of her head, and her beautiful face had frown lines etched around her eyes and mouth. She smiled slowly when she saw him looking at her, and he smiled back. He hadn't been sure she would come.

She crossed to the bar, glancing at the others, who hadn't noticed her yet.

"Thank you for considering this," he said.

"How could I not?" she asked, her voice soft and rich. It sent a thrill through him, just like it had done the first time he heard it.

Sometimes he had thought he had fallen in love with her for her voice.

"I'm not sure what we're facing," he said quietly.

"You said that we might have an intriguing linguistic situation," she said, "mixed with a communications nightmare. That's got me written all over it."

Which was why he asked her. They had worked together well even after their divorce, which had been amicable—back before the *Ivoire* got lost in foldspace. Then she had gone on the mission that was supposed to bring two separate groups together on Ukhanda, and instead, the linguists and diplomats got slaughtered.

Mae was one of three survivors. She had emerged with her memory in tatters, and her emotions shredded. Everything had come to a head when the *Ivoire* had been becalmed in foldspace, and she had finally found a chance to move on.

Only there had been nowhere to move to.

Still, she had settled in, and created a life for herself here. It included a husband who was not Fleet, and two daughters under the age of five. Fortunately, the daughters looked like her and not her husband, who was a kind but doughy man who always receded quietly into the background whenever Coop was around.

"It does," Coop said, "but I wasn't kidding when I said this might be dangerous."

"We talked about it," she said, and the "we" must have meant her and her husband, "and decided I would hear you out before I made any decisions."

"You know the rule." Coop didn't want to insult her by reminding her that anyone who deliberately stepped into a dangerous situation had to be willing to accept the risks.

She put her hand on his arm. Her palms were calloused, which surprised him. He wasn't sure what kind of work she had been doing that would cause that.

"Captain," she said, putting the slightly sarcastic spin she had always used when she hauled out his title, "I'm still Fleet."

He smiled at her. He had missed her, but he had felt that, with her new life, he needed to keep as much distance as possible.

"Well," he said, "grab something to drink. I've asked for the entire team to show up, and right now, only a third of the people who said they'd show have."

"Discipline is getting lax, Captain," Mae said, in her warmly sarcastic tone. She grabbed a mug slightly smaller than his and filled it with water as well.

Then she graced him with a real smile, which still punched him in the gut whenever he saw it, and headed over to the table.

He wondered how many of the others would show. He wondered how long he needed to wait for them. He wondered if he could do the work with two full diplomats and a linguist who had moved to communications before spending her time in Lost Souls.

He was about to head to the table when the comm system chirruped.

The sound was startlingly loud, but no one at the round table even seemed to notice.

Then he realized that the ship had tapped his old personal comm system. He had embedded a comm chip in his collarbone when it became clear that he would spend as much time away from the *Ivoire* as he was going to spend in it. Back then—five years ago or so now—he had thought the ship would need him more than it had, that he would need to communicate with it more than he did, and that instant communication might be necessary.

The chirrup came again, much too loud. Was this the first time the ship had pinged him when he wasn't in uniform? It probably was, which would explain why the chirrup sounded so loud. He hadn't realized that he needed to modify the settings.

He moved to the edge of the bar, and pressed the regular comm, rather than his own internal ones.

A notification from the Ewing Trekov, the system said, just as loudly as it had in his ear. *Will you accept?*

That question, loud and insistent, in a flat machine-created tone caught the attention of the three at the table. They raised their heads, and Mae turned slightly in her chair.

They all looked as startled as Coop felt.

He touched the screen prompt that would allow him to accept the contact, but delay it while he went somewhere private.

The *Ewing Trekov*. The Empire ship that he had fought at the border, which, at the time, had been helmed by Elissa Trekov.

Or he thought she ran the ship. He didn't, even now, entirely understand the rankings on the Empire side.

He hadn't expected the contact, but it didn't surprise him. After all, the *Ivoire* had been in the Empire's territory.

He had just hoped that no one connected to the Empire had noticed.

"Do you need someone with you?" Mae asked. She must have seen the concern on his face.

"No," he said. He would make sure the conversation was recorded. "Let the others know when they arrive that we'll hold the meeting as soon as I'm done."

Then he pivoted and headed to the tiny auxiliary bridge hidden between the commissary and the regular mess.

He would talk with Elissa Trekov, or whoever needed to speak with him. The conversation wasn't going to be an easy one. No one had contacted him since he had negotiated the truce between the Empire and the Nine Planets.

Since he had won a battle against the Empire.

This time, though, this time he had invaded their space without permission. He had hoped he hadn't gotten caught, but given the timing of this contact, he had.

Now he had to figure out how to finesse the entire situation, since he really had been the one at fault.

31

Captain Cohn sat in the tiny study room in her quarters. She had her sock-clad feet on the table across from her, the thick comfortable chair tilted back so that her body bent in a V, her head resting in the divot built especially for her at the top of the chair itself.

Her right hand was wrapped around a warm mug of green tea, and with her left, she was rooting in a bowl of almonds, eating too many of them, especially since she had just finished dinner with her bridge crew.

She wanted them relaxed and ready when the *Geesi* left foldspace in just a couple of hours. So she had spent time laughing with them, and priming them for the hours ahead.

Not that she knew exactly what those hours would bring. None of them did.

She had been going through the files on this Lost Souls Corporation, the Enterran Empire, and this ship, the *Ivoire*, which seemed to be behind so much mystery.

Her team had consolidated all of the information for her, so that she didn't have to talk with Captain Jicha of the *Tudósok*. Jicha drove her crazy, although he seemed to have relaxed some when he learned that his vessel would remain at the Scrapheap, while the other four ships in this Task Unit headed to Lost Souls.

Cohn had briefed the other three captains, Gyda Fjeld of the *Mächteg*, Mihaita al-Aqel of the *Royk*, and Vilis Wihone of the *Sakhata*. They would be traveling with the *Geesi* to this Lost Souls.

The last time they had all traveled through foldspace, they had done so tethered to each other. Wihone had put the tether together—he had done a variety of things like that over his career, and he was good at it. The *Sakhata* was an SC-Class vessel that had rescued a number of ships out of foldspace, and Wihone knew how to prevent any foldspace tragedies—or at least, he seemed to.

She had talked with him a great deal before embarking on this journey to Lost Souls. He wasn't worried about this trip, since it was relatively short, both in time and in distance.

The trip they had made to the Scrapheap from the Fleet's location, though. That had been the longest foldspace trip she had ever taken. She was not looking forward to repeating it on the journey home.

Her chief engineer, Erasyl Iosua, also wasn't worried about this foldspace journey to Lost Souls. Iosua was renown through the Fleet as one of the few foldspace wizards. He seemed to understand foldspace better than most. He thought it might be better if the ships traveled separately.

Traveling tethered was always a danger. But arriving separately in an unknown situation was even more dangerous, which was why they all tethered the first time.

Here, it wasn't an issue. They had research on Lost Souls. They knew the firepower of the station, now, because of some battle they'd had with the Enterran Empire a year or so ago. There were records of that battle, as well as the border fights that Vinters had told Cohn about when Cohn first decided to head to Lost Souls.

Lost Souls' defenses looked minor. They worked well with surprise, but not against any major ships with the kind of firepower a DV-vessel had. She was going to travel into that region of space with three DV-Class vessels and one SC-Class vessel, all with weaponry that Lost Souls hadn't seen before.

She sipped the green tea. It wasn't relaxing her as much as she wanted. She was ready to take care of these thieves, and then get home.

This entire mission made her uncomfortable on many levels, the greatest of which was that she had no idea what she was facing.

The research from the *Tudósok* had clarified a lot, but it hadn't answered all of her questions. She was still uncertain about the woman who owned Lost Souls and the people who worked on the *Ivoire*.

At least she knew that Odite wasn't much of a threat. The *Tudósok* had found a lot about the various cultures spread across Odite's surface. None of them had the offensive capacity to take on Fleet ships in any kind of battle.

The ships that the various cultures of Odite had contributed to the boundary battles of the year before would have been almost laughable, if they hadn't seemed so determined.

Her ship could have destroyed all of them with a few well-placed shots, done in rapid succession. She was not worried about Odite.

She was worried about the *Ivoire*. Whoever commanded it seemed to know how to make the most of the ship's resources. In the border battle with the Enterran Empire, the ship had taken on powerful ships and defeated them with one single maneuver.

That it was a maneuver all Fleet captains learned in training bothered her, because the maneuver wasn't obvious to someone who had acquired a DV-Class vessel and researched its archives.

There was no record of how to make that maneuver work written down anywhere. The Fleet was careful about that, and always had been.

That maneuver was the mark of a desperate captain or one who viewed themself as completely alone. She was banking on the completely alone.

In her discussion with the other three captains in her Task Unit, she had pressed upon them the need to destroy the *Ivoire* upon arrival. Whoever captained the vehicle was creative and innovative. They had learned that particular maneuver, and they might have other, unexpected maneuvers up their sleeves.

She did not want to be a victim to surprise. She wanted to surprise all three entities—Lost Souls, Odite, and that pesky ship, the *Ivoire*.

Which was why she was in her comfy clothes right now, eating almonds and drinking green tea as she reviewed all the materials the *Tudósok* and her team had presented her.

She wanted to make sure she missed nothing. The *Tudósok* could find little about the *Ivoire*. A DV-Class vessel of similar vintage disappeared five thousand years ago, and sometime after that, its captain was court-martialed. The records of the court-martial were incomplete, but had something to do with a crisis on a planet called Ukhanda, which was deep inside what is now the Enterran Empire.

The ancient history did her no good. She set that aside early. Curiosities didn't matter to her.

What mattered was what would happen next. And the *Tudósok* was able to find out some information from what Jicha's scholars had gleaned from Enterran Empire records.

Apparently, the *Ivoire* had twice defeated a group of ships several times its size. The Enterran Empire's commanders believed that the first time was sheer luck, although the commander that faced the *Ivoire* thought they had deployed some kind of special weapon.

From the description, Cohn knew they had used *anacapa* energy to destroy the systems in nearby ships.

And, apparently, the *Ivoire* had done the exact same thing in its border skirmish. At some point, she would have thought that commanders from the Enterran Empire would learn to defend themselves against that kind of attack.

But, considering the attacks had only happened in the past few years, perhaps the Enterran Empire could not. Their technology seemed more advanced than the technology of the Nine Planets, but not sufficiently advanced to take on the Fleet.

Cohn was counting on that. She knew that the commander of the *Ivoire*, and by extension, she assumed, the commanders of the other DV-Class vessels, knew how to use their resources to the fullest.

Their technology was ancient, however. They didn't have defenses against many of the weapons developed after the *Ivoire* vanished from the records.

Her ship had those defenses and many, many, many more. Most of them were automated; she didn't even have to think about deploying them.

But she didn't want to go into the area around Lost Souls expecting to overpower the *Ivoire* and Lost Souls easily. She anticipated some kind of struggle. She told the other captains that as well.

Wihone was the one who thought they should go in as close as they could get to Lost Souls, and just destroy the space station with some well-placed blasts.

It was a good argument, but those defenses near the station seemed particularly attuned to nearby attacks. Cohn's four ships were technologically superior to the ships around Lost Souls, but four wasn't as big an advantage as she would like—especially for a mission that centered on destroying an important business in an area.

Besides, there was *anacapa* technology in and around Lost Souls. She didn't want to inadvertently set something off, some kind of chain reaction. If the *anacapa* drives were not being properly handled—always a risk with a technologically inferior culture—then the drives could destroy everything around them.

Better to go in cloaked and figure out what she was facing before she attacked.

She wasn't sure if she needed to destroy the DV-Class ships and leave the others alone or destroy the entire space station, and issue a warning to Odite and the rest of the Nine Planets to leave the Scrapheap alone.

She wasn't a big fan of warnings, especially over something like the Scrapheap. She felt that a warning might be seen as an invitation rather than a discouragement.

But she didn't tell the others that. She would go to that region of space, entering at the same point that the thieves had entered, and then she would make her decision.

She had several decisions on the table; she would make the right one for the moment when she was *in* the moment.

She sighed, grabbed another handful of almonds and ate them one by one as she shut down everything in her small study. Then she sipped the last of the tea, wandered into the main room, and placed the mug in her sink.

Now, she had to change clothes. As she donned her uniform, she would put on her captain's persona as well. She needed to be strong and forward-thinking. And judging by what she had learned in her research, she would also need to be creative.

She smiled to herself. She could do that.

She could make the best decisions possible, for her crew, her ship, and the Fleet.

And she would be able to do so soon.

32

Coop's mind raced as he headed to the tiny auxiliary bridge. There were two other command centers outside of the actual bridge—the one in the captain's mess, and the one in his quarters. The one in his quarters was much more complete.

These two command centers were really small control panels tied to engineering that allowed him to use command functions in an emergency. They also had good privacy measures. No one else could access these auxiliary bridges unless they already had high-level command privileges. None of the diplomats waiting for him in the bar had that kind of privilege.

He dodged the commissary, which had been shut down ever since the *Ivoire* arrived in this time period and glanced at the darkened regular mess hall. It used to be filled with dozens of people at any given moment of every given day.

The mess used to smell of whatever special the chefs had whipped up, partly—he always thought—to entice the crew to try something new. Beneath it, there was always the faint scent of baking bread and coffee. Now, there was nothing.

The crew had eaten here not five days ago when the ship had gone to Sector Base E-2, but apparently that hadn't made enough of an impact for the scents to linger.

He opened the door to the closet-sized command center and stepped inside. The lights came on automatically, and air from the environmental system tickled his skin. The environmental system refreshed everything the moment anyone came in here, just to make certain that whoever was here—and it would generally be the captain—would be comfortable.

As if sitting in a narrow room with control panels all along one wall, and a navigation system jutting out along that same side would ever be comfortable.

He hit the configuration for captain's command, bringing up one chair in the center, and making sure that the back wall was obscured.

Then he sat down and officially accepted the contact.

It was, as he suspected, holographic. Elissa Trekov's disembodied face floated above the console, her lips thin, her eyes surprisingly bright.

"Captain Cooper," Trekov said, her voice a bit wavery. That was the connection. He tweaked his systems, but they read fine.

The problem was clearly on her end. Empire technology was not as good as Fleet technology. Or rather, not as good as *ancient* Fleet technology.

"To what do I owe this honor, Commander?" Coop asked. At least, he hoped he had her title right. He hadn't had time to refresh his memory on her rank at the moment.

"Don't play coy with me, Cooper," she said, her tone harsher than it had been a moment ago. "You know why I'm contacting you. You violated our agreement."

So someone had seen him. He could lie, but he didn't think it would do any good.

"Technically, yes, I was in Empire space," he said. "But we weren't there long. We got out as quickly as we could."

"It was an accident, then?" she asked. "Your arrival?"

"It was…unavoidable," he said, even though that wasn't entirely the truth.

"No harm done, right?" she asked, and from her tone, or maybe the brightness in her eyes, he realized that the statement was a trap.

So he said nothing. He just waited for her to continue.

He didn't have to wait long.

"It was not a part of our agreement that you or any ship from the Nine Planets could casually visit the Empire, even for a short time," she said.

"I'm aware," he said, resisting the urge to say that the visit hadn't been casual. Like his team in the bar, he had had diplomatic training and he had used it often, but it had been a long time since he'd used it in a situation this tricky.

And he had never done so alone. Someone was always near him, to whisper through the comms or put a restraining hand on his arm. He wished now that he had allowed Mae to join him. Or maybe Cumex, since she was one of the best diplomats he had ever known.

He felt like he was walking into a trap of his own making, and yet he couldn't quite see what the trap was.

"Your entrance into the Empire," Trekov said with quiet force, "is an act of war."

A shiver ran down his spine. Served him right for always underestimating the Enterran Empire. Militaristic to a fault, rigid.

He should have seen this coming. She viewed this as more than a violation. It was an invitation to attack the Nine Planets.

But that begged the question: If it was an excuse to attack, she should have simply done so.

Maybe she didn't want to attack. Maybe she was giving Coop a heads-up so that he could remove the vulnerable vessels. Or, perhaps, get more ships in place.

Then he mentally shook his head: she would have no reason to do that. They were adversaries after all, and he had beaten her twice. Badly.

"We did not mean to provoke you," he said, "and we certainly didn't see our short time in the Empire as an invitation to fight."

"Oh, really?" That wavery quality to her voice had grown. Maybe it wasn't the technology. Maybe it was an underlying fury. He had cost lives in the Empire before, and Trekov had witnessed it. "Your actions caused the destruction of seven ships and the loss of hundreds of lives."

He carefully guarded his expression. Seven ships? Hundreds of lives? What had happened after he left?

"My actions?" He made certain his voice was as calm and impassive as possible. He didn't want her to know that she had startled him.

She was watching him closely.

Apparently, it was her turn to be silent. And it worked. He couldn't remain silent.

He concentrated on speaking slowly, so that he didn't sound as defensive as he felt.

"We took no action," he said. "We arrived briefly near what you call the Room of Lost Souls, traveled a short distance, and left. We did not engage with anyone."

"Yet you deliberately dropped an emergency beacon," she said.

He felt cold, and he knew that wasn't the air blowing on him from the environmental system. So the Not-Fleet ships pursuing him had arrived at Starbase Kappa. The gamble he had taken had delayed the Non-Fleet ships from following him here to Lost Souls, just like he had hoped.

But there had been a price, a greater one than he had expected. He had thought that the Empire would surround the ships chasing him— if the ships even arrived. He hadn't expected that the *Empire* would lose ships.

He didn't dare confess to releasing that emergency beacon, not until he knew what was going on.

"What exactly are you accusing me of?" he asked.

"You deliberately caused the destruction of seven of our ships. It went poorly for your people," she said.

His people? What was she talking about? She knew the *Ivoire* had left before the other ship arrived.

Then his chill got deeper. She thought the Not-Fleet ships were *his* ships? If that was the case, he could understand how she thought that was an act of war.

Although to what end? He had no idea and no time to figure it out.

"You lost a ship as well," she was saying.

He blinked. They defeated the Not-Fleet? Had they caught the Not-Fleet ships by surprise?

He didn't get a chance to ask, because she was still talking. Not quite yelling at him, but close enough.

"What was the point, Cooper? To measure our response time inside the Empire? Or to see how many ships we could muster on short notice?"

So that was her logic. She believed he was testing the Empire as he readied for a larger attack.

Hadn't she done her research? Didn't she know that the Nine Planets still did not have enough ships to defeat a large mass of Empire ships?

Although he had bluffed well enough. She probably knew he lacked the ships, but believed he had the weapons.

So, on some level, her reasoning made sense. She believed he had come in to measure how long it took the Empire to stage a large response, inside its own borders.

The idea was audacious, and maybe even something that a different kind of tactician might do. But Coop would never do that. Such an action would require a follow-up attack almost immediately, otherwise it would provoke a counterattack.

Of course, that counterattack would look like an act of war in and of itself, especially if there was no real record of the first incursion.

The imaginary tactics, and what they revealed about Trekov, intrigued him. But he set them aside for the moment.

Because the truth of it all was he would never have done a maneuver like that, for any reason. He had no interest in fighting the Empire. He just wanted them to stay away from Lost Souls so that he could build his own fleet in peace.

He was going to have to go with his gut. Trekov was smart. She had negotiated with him well in the past, despite her loss at Starbase Kappa. He had respected that in a commander.

He respected her right now, for coming to him, rather than sending ships across the border.

He only hoped that he was up to this conversation. The irony of it didn't escape him: he had the *Ivoire's* best diplomats in a bar yards away while he was having a tricky conversation on his own.

He could ping someone, he supposed, but they didn't have the background to understand what was happening.

Not that he completely understood what was going on, and he had the background to understand it.

"We were being pursued," he said in the same soft, reasonable tone he had used earlier. "We were in a situation that I doubted we would survive if we used standard measures. So I thought of your Room of Lost Souls. It was the most remote place I could think of. I wanted to escape, and I figured that area would give me the opportunity to do so."

"That sounds lovely and logical," Trekov said. "I would think that you were telling me the truth, if it weren't for that emergency beacon."

He waited, because he still wasn't going to admit to dropping it.

She was smart; she would know why he had done so.

"You dropped the emergency beacon," Trekov said, "so that my people would fight your battle."

Essentially, he thought but did not say.

"The *Ivoire* spent as little time in Empire space as possible," he said. "I would have contacted you and asked permission if I had the chance, but we were running for our lives."

"Why should I believe that?" she asked. It was a logical question. She believed he had great weaponry. She would want to know why he hadn't used it on the pursuing ships.

She had no idea how large a force he had faced back at Nindowne.

He wasn't sure if he should tell her, either.

Her eyes glittered. "The ships that attacked my people look just like your ship," she said, her voice wavery again.

Ships. She said *ships*. And earlier she had said that he had lost one of his *ships* as well. At first, he had thought she was talking about the *Ivoire* and another ship that followed him through foldspace.

But there was more than one ship. One had gotten destroyed. He had no idea how many others had come with it.

"I assume this was some kind of end-run, maybe a war game?" she said. "Only you lost a ship, and lives as well."

Lives, a ship. His head was spinning. They were both ill-informed. She was trying to figure out why he had brought enemy vessels into Empire space, and he was trying to figure out what kind of mess he had actually made.

"Why don't we stop playing, Commander," he said. She hadn't objected to the title, so he apparently remembered it correctly. "Tell me what happened."

Her chin lifted and her eyes narrowed. She was assessing the question. If—as she had accused—the other ships belonged to him, then he would know what happened. He wouldn't need to ask.

She was probably thinking this was some kind of test.

"Your second ship arrived as our rescue vessels did," she said. "There was a skirmish, and your second ship was damaged. Then your third ship arrived, and completely destroyed our rescue vessels. We came to help a ship in distress, and for that, we lost seven ships, Cooper. Did you think you would get away with that?"

She didn't believe it was him, or she wouldn't have contacted him. She would have immediately invaded the Nine Planets.

He still didn't know if she was under instruction to invade, but she had reason to hesitate. He wasn't quite sure yet what that reason was, but he respected her more than he had in the past.

She was making sure the Empire wasn't going to make a big mistake before coming after him.

He wondered how many ships she thought he had at his command. And what he planned to use them for.

"They weren't my ships," he said. "They were following me."

They must have been close in foldspace, probably entering foldspace through the bubble he had opened. He should have seen them, but he hadn't.

The Fleet tech he was used to would have made it impossible for them to hide, but they were Not-Fleet. And he had no idea where their tech differed from the Fleet's tech—or at least, the Fleet's tech from his era.

"So you brought them to us," she said.

"I thought your Room of Lost Souls was unguarded," he said. "I thought they would arrive, see nothing, and return to their base."

"Their base," she said. "How far away is that?"

"It's no threat to you," he said, wishing now he hadn't mentioned it.

"Because you have some kind of system that allows you to teleport?" she asked.

This was why she had come to him. She wanted to know more about their technology.

He didn't dare answer those questions.

"Let me see if I understand this," he said. "They brought two ships and one was destroyed by your people. The other attacked and destroyed seven of your ships? They only had two ships, is that right?"

She paused, staring at him, measuring him as he had measured her earlier.

"Who are they, Cooper?" she asked.

"I wish I knew," he said.

"They use your ships," she said.

"*My* ships?" he repeated. "What makes you think those ships are mine?"

"They're Dignity Vessels, just like the *Ivoire*," she said. "They have the ability to travel long distances quickly, and they use weapons like the one you used on us."

This time she didn't say *me*. Their conversations had gotten more impersonal over time.

"Abandoned Dignity Vessels—" God, how he hated that term "—are all over this sector. For all we know, those two ships could have been found abandoned and repurposed."

"I don't believe you did that, Cooper. The *Ivoire* seems too pristine for that," she said.

Pristine? That was an interesting analysis. Did she have some way of measuring the age of a ship?

He was going to ignore that, at least for the moment.

"The Empire repurposes Dignity Vessels all the time," he said. He had never faced any, but he knew they did, because Boss had had at least one ship confiscated by the Empire. "I'm sure others have found abandoned Dignity Vessels and rebuilt them, just like you have."

She paused, eyes narrowing. She apparently got the message that he would not dignify her question about his ship with a specific answer.

"So," she said, tone a little less strained, "what did you do to get these ships to chase you, Cooper?"

It was Trekov's turn to change the subject. But it was a question he didn't mind answering.

"We were exploring what we thought was an abandoned base," he said. "We triggered some kind of alarm and suddenly we were surrounded by hundreds of ships. I got us out of there, barely, by using a maneuver they didn't expect. But surprise only works for a few minutes, and I needed more than that. Which was why I essentially ran to the Room of Lost Souls to throw them off our trail."

Her eyebrows rose. "You're afraid of them, Cooper? I thought you weren't afraid of anything."

That was an interesting assumption.

"I'd be a fool not to be concerned about a group of ships that large," he said. "I had apparently—unknowingly—entered their base of operations. They had cause to go after me."

Her head tilted. Apparently his admission surprised her.

"Hmph," she said. "The abandoned Room of Lost Souls. Abandoned Dignity Vessels. An abandoned base, somewhere far away. What are you searching for, Cooper?"

That question cut a little too close to home. He would answer the question if he had any idea how to do so.

"What are you?" she asked. "Some sort of mercenary? Or are you part of the Nine Planets?"

He couldn't answer any of those questions, not in the way she wanted him to.

"What do you really want from me, Commander?" he asked. "An apology? Because I owe you one. I did not expect you to lose any ships due to my maneuver. I'm very sorry. I know that doesn't help when lives are lost, but killing your people, even inadvertently, was not my intention."

Her expression settled into something somber. Part of her face didn't quite move the way faces normally did. Probably more of that injury she refused to fix from his first encounter with her.

"I didn't come to you for an apology," she said.

"You didn't come to tell me that we had violated the agreement either," he said. "You could have swooped across the border and taken us by surprise."

She raised her chin ever so slightly. "I want you to call off those ships, Cooper."

"What ships?" he asked, thinking he already knew. But he didn't dare assume. He would make too many mistakes if he assumed.

"Those three ships that have returned to the Room of Lost Souls," she said. "Call them off."

The chill that ran down his back grew. "They're not my ships," he said again. "They're looking for me."

And that statement, he realized, counted as a blurt. He hadn't meant to reveal that information to her.

But the ships were looking for him. They had some kind of tracking system that was familiar. Because when he had been doing foldspace search and rescue, he would go in with at least three ships and map foldspace. If those ships knew where the *Ivoire* had entered foldspace, they would search inside of foldspace.

They wouldn't find the *Ivoire*, and tracking where a ship left foldspace, especially after this much time, was impossible.

Or, at least, it was for him.

"Because you entered their secret base," she said.

He wasn't sure secret was the correct word. Protected, maybe. Guarded, probably. But not secret. The locals on Nindowne probably knew about the base, maybe even worked in some of its recesses.

"Yes," he said, not knowing what else to do. "Because I entered an area I did not realize was off-limits."

"Strange thing to make them travel long distances to find you," she said. "Did you steal from them?"

"No," he said.

"Because you took something from the Room of Lost Souls when you were here," she said.

The *anacapa* drive. He had taken it, and he hadn't realized she knew what he had done.

"I didn't steal from them," he repeated. "But it is becoming very clear to me that some people don't like it when I enter their space."

He was being deliberate there, maybe even provoking.

"They dislike you enough to travel long distances to destroy you?" she asked.

"I don't know," he said, and he let the truth and frustration leak into his voice. "I don't know who they are. I don't know their culture."

And then he realized what she had said.

"They've returned?" he asked.

"Yes," she said.

He let out a breath. "Because you destroyed one of their ships?" he asked.

"Or they're after you," she said. "They're using technology we don't recognize."

Maybe Trekov's assumption about him—that he was in league with the Not-Fleet—was the very assumption they had made about him and the Empire.

Trekov might've been right; he might have provoked a war, but not one concerning him or the Nine Planets. One that centered around the Not-Fleet and the Empire.

"Have they contacted you?" he asked.

"Not yet," she said.

"Had other interactions with your ships?" he asked.

Her lips thinned. "Not yet."

Then he realized she hadn't told him everything. He didn't know how the first encounter resolved.

"What happened after their second ship destroyed your ships?" he asked.

Her gaze narrowed.

"You said three ships have entered Empire space," he said. "To rescue the two ships left behind?"

She shook her head ever so slightly. "One was damaged. The other ship rescued personnel, and then destroyed the damaged ship."

He let out a tiny breath. That was a Fleet maneuver. The Fleet often did that when one of their ships was disabled, so that no other ship could get information, not just on how the ship was built, but on the Fleet itself.

"And after that?" he asked.

"The ship left," she said.

She was leaving out something, but he didn't know what.

"Left," he said. "Did you chase it away?"

"Our ships had sent for reinforcements but they hadn't arrived yet," she said.

"Did the remaining ship know that you were bringing in reinforcements?" he asked.

"How should I know that, Cooper?" Trekov snapped. "We didn't communicate with them."

So it all depended on the remaining ship's scanning ability. They might have known. But they also had injured. And they hadn't come into the Empire to take down the Empire.

They had come after the *Ivoire*.

"And now, three ships have returned," he said. "How long have they been in Empire space?"

Her expression became impassive, but her eyes moved just enough so that he realized she was trying to think of a good way to answer him.

Apparently she was as alone on the diplomatic side as he was.

"We don't know," she finally said.

He frowned. "What do you mean...?" And then he realized: she had talked about teleporting.

She didn't know if they were traveling into the Empire via a method that brought them through the Empire itself or teleported them in.

Neither was accurate, of course. No one had ever come up with a working teleport—at least that he knew of—and the Not-Fleet were using *anacapa* drives.

He needed to reframe the question.

"When did these three ships arrive at the Room of Lost Souls?" he asked.

"Just a few hours ago," she said.

Which still didn't entirely jibe. Why would she contact him now about his violation of the agreement if the ships had just arrived?

"Did they attack again?" he asked.

"No," she said.

"Then what are they doing?" he asked.

That hesitation, that strange expression, the slight movement of her eyes. Then she sighed.

"They cloaked, Cooper."

"Cloaked," he repeated, trying to figure out what she was saying. And then he did. "You lost track of them. You were hoping I knew where they were."

Something relaxed in her face. That was exactly what she had hoped.

He thought about it, thought about the maneuvers, thought about what the Fleet would do in similar circumstances.

They were tracking him, but days later. They had missed the opportunity to do so when the Empire ships responded to the emergency beacon he had dropped.

He had thrown them off the trail, but they returned. To deal with the Empire? Did they think he was part of the Empire?

Or to track him down?

And if they were trying to track him down, then did that mean they had the capability to track him accurately in foldspace? Or did they think he was stuck in foldspace?

There was no reason to think he was stuck in foldspace.

He resisted the urge to run a hand through his hair. They were looking for him. He had made no friends in the Empire. They had found him; the Not-Fleet might figure out where he was as well.

If they brought a full contingent of ships to Lost Souls, he could not deal with it.

And that didn't even count the real Fleet. He had no way to defend against them either.

And now, the Empire threatened him with enforcement of the agreement over the borders.

He probably neutralized that. He hoped. Maybe. But there was nothing to prevent them from handing him over to the Not-Fleet.

After all, Coop had dropped that beacon. He had brought the Not-Fleet into the Empire. That might not be worthy of a full-scale attack, but it did mean they had no reason to hide his location from the Not-Fleet.

He had brought this on all of them.

"I don't know where they are," Coop said. "I don't know how they operate. You had ships in the area when they arrived, right?"

"Yes," she said reluctantly—or so it seemed.

"And those ships, they're unharmed, right?" Coop asked.

"They left," she said. "All except one, which is cloaked."

She sounded begrudging, as if she hadn't wanted to reveal that.

He nodded, not willing to tell her that Not-Fleet's tech matched his. The Not-Fleet could see through any cloak the Empire had.

The Not-Fleet knew where that ship was, and chose not to attack it.

Which meant they were searching for the *Ivoire*.

If they had wanted to continue fighting the Empire, the Not-Fleet had more than enough ships, just based on what Coop had seen less than a week ago. They wouldn't have arrived with three, cloaked them, and moved into the Empire.

At least, he wouldn't have.

He would have done some research, then figured out a plan.

Plus, the Empire was far from that base. Unless the Not-Fleet was some kind of warrior culture, which he wasn't ruling out, they had no reason to go to war against the Empire.

But they had a reason to find and destroy the *Ivoire*, particularly if they thought the *Ivoire* had gained information from that incursion he made into what had been Sector Base E-2.

The Not-Fleet. The Enterran Empire. The Fleet.

All bearing down on Lost Souls in one way or another.

He needed to break this off with Trekov. He needed to talk to Ilona Blake. Only Blake knew nothing about fighting or diplomacy. Boss didn't either. Boss was not politic. She had no idea how to finesse conversations with adversaries.

"So," he said, mostly to give himself a few more minutes to think, "you have one ship monitoring the three ships. And they're near the Room of Lost Souls."

"They're moving slowly," she said. "They seem to be gathering information."

The way that ships did as they were searching for another ship. Like his.

The question was, if they found him, if they could track the *Ivoire* to Lost Souls, would those three ships bring in reinforcements? Or would they go after him themselves?

Particularly when they saw just how meager Lost Souls' defenses were.

He didn't dare wait to find out. He had only a few choices.

He could take the *Ivoire* back to the Room, try to talk with the Not-Fleet. For all he knew, they'd try to destroy the *Ivoire*. He couldn't fight three DV-Class ships—if indeed that's what those were—all by himself.

These ships probably thought that the *Ivoire* was part of the Empire, if they understood the Empire at all. He couldn't bet on that. He couldn't bet on any of it.

If Not-Fleet could track ships through foldspace, and it seemed from their actions that they might be able to, then even if he left Lost Souls, they would be able to find him.

He supposed he could lead them to the Boneyard, and the real Fleet. He had no idea what would happen then.

He needed to think. He had no idea how much time he had, but the one thing he had to do—the one thing that was essential—was that the Not-Fleet couldn't find Lost Souls.

The Not-Fleet was the most dangerous group he had found since he had come to this time period.

They had only come with three ships. Three ships wouldn't be easy to defeat, but with help, he could do it.

The question was, were those ships communicating with the Not-Fleet and if so, what did that mean?

"Why did you contact me?" he asked Trekov. "You could have just responded to my action. You would have been within your rights."

Her eyes were hooded. She knew he was contemplating something.

"We had that discussion," she said.

Although she hadn't really answered that question, not really.

"You asked me if I was afraid of those ships chasing me," he said. "And I answered that. Now, you tell me, are you afraid of the three ships near the Room of Lost Souls?"

"I'm not afraid of anything," she said. "Not even you, Cooper."

He half-smiled. That was revealing, and she knew it. It was probably deliberate.

"But I am concerned, particularly now that you tell me they have hundreds of ships behind them," she said. "We don't need a conflict with an unknown entity."

He nodded. He didn't want it either.

"You'd be content to let them leave, right?" he asked. "After they found what they wanted? You'd let them leave."

She didn't answer that, and with that silence, he realized, she hadn't consulted with her superiors at all. They probably didn't know about the three ships.

And her superiors would probably want her to destroy those ships. After all, those ships were part of an organization that had destroyed seven of her ships.

That organization was invading again. She was within her rights to obliterate them.

And yet she wasn't. What kind of game was she playing?

He realized he hadn't asked one question directly, and he needed to. "Have you been in direct contact with those ships?"

"No," she said.

She didn't say *not yet*; she didn't hesitate the way that some people did when they lied. Just a firm *no*.

He believed her. He also believed that she would contact those ships if she thought it in her best interest. She could send them here, and have them destroy Lost Souls.

But she wasn't risking that. Instead, she had come to him.

What are you? she had asked him early in this conversation. *Some sort of mercenary?*

He hadn't answered her. Deliberately. Because he wasn't part of the Nine Planets, and he really wasn't part of Lost Souls either, although he had adopted them, and they had adopted him.

He originally hadn't answered because he hadn't wanted to tell her about the Fleet. He had thought of that question only from his own point of view.

Not from hers.

That might have been the question she wanted answered the most: *What are you? Some sort of mercenary?*

If he was a mercenary, she could hire him. She knew he had the technology to defeat them. Or at least fight them. And she was worried about the Empire's ability to do the same.

Given what her commanding officer had done during the last fight she'd been in with Coop, Coop definitely understood why she hadn't wanted to talk with her superiors first.

"How many ships do you have near here?" he asked, and then amended it. "Not the ones defending the border."

Her eyes narrowed just a bit. He was beginning to understand her. She did that when she was intrigued.

"I could bring in many ships quickly," she said. "Because of the border."

Of course. He noted that she hadn't given him an exact number.

"And how many are near the Room of Lost Souls?" he asked.

"Fewer," she said. "And it would take longer to get there. Why?"

"Because," he said, "as you have already divined, these ships—and the organization they represent—are a threat to us both."

"Are you suggesting we stop them together?" she asked.

"Isn't that why you came to me before you consulted your superiors?" he asked.

She smiled at him—a real smile, that hinted at a warmth in her he hadn't suspected.

"Well, then, Cooper," she said, "let me hear it. What, exactly, do you propose?"

33

THIS CAPTAIN COOPER OF THE *IVOIRE* was good. It had taken longer than Elissa liked to maneuver him into making *her* a proposal. For the sake of her own career, she hadn't wanted to make that proposal first.

Although she didn't believe she had maneuvered him at all. Cooper was too smart for that. He had known she had something in mind. He had tried to suss it out of her and failed, but in a way that they both could use.

Subtle techniques for both of them, something only experienced negotiators could do. He had known she had come to him for a reason, although she had been hoping he would have more information.

She suspected he was holding many things back, but she believed him when he said he had no idea who these ships represented.

It was taking all of her strength not to look at Paek. Paek sat stiffly in the office's only chair, his large hands resting on his knees, as if he was planning to spring up at any moment and flee.

He hadn't moved at all, which helped, because she didn't want Cooper to know someone else was in her office. Cooper probably assumed it, just like she had initially assumed that he was not alone either.

But something in Cooper's demeanor convinced her that indeed he was alone or, at least, his conversation wouldn't be reviewed by superiors. He seemed to have a lot more freedom than she did.

He hadn't answered her question about who he worked for.

The small office seemed even smaller with Cooper's face on the screen before her. Her attempts at using the holographic communications system hadn't worked, although she doubted Cooper had seen that.

"What do *I* propose?" Cooper said with some amusement.

He was a large man, with broad shoulders, and a worry-weathered face. She had noted his size when they met in person at the Room of Lost Souls, even though they were both wearing environmental suits at the time.

His eyes twinkled as he said that. He did know she had maneuvered him into making the proposal. Although, truth be told, she wasn't sure exactly what she could have proposed. Hiring him to help the Empire wouldn't have worked, but she needed his expertise. He knew how these ships worked; she did not.

"I propose," he said slowly, deliberately, "that we stop these three ships now. It's a gamble. At least one ship has left your Empire to get reinforcements. There will be some information on the Room of Lost Souls and what happened there. And, of course, there's the interaction with the *Ivoire*."

Of course, she thought, but didn't say. Better to let him talk.

"But if they haven't returned to the main part of their...I'm not sure what to call it. Organization? Government? Military unit?...if the reinforcements were nearby, the larger organization might not know what happened here."

She liked how he thought. And she hated that she felt a tiny bit of admiration for it. Although, if she were honest with herself, she admired him a great deal.

"You're gambling that they'll consider the three ships an acceptable loss?" she asked.

He nodded, just once.

"It depends on their culture," he said. "If they're a militaristic culture, then they might not. If they're explorers, they might. If they are wedded to their section of space, then they might judge the three ships an acceptable loss."

"If they don't have a lot of ships," she said, "then it is possible they'll defend the ships' loss."

"It's just as likely that they won't be able to risk any more losses," he said. "I believe that destroying those ships—quickly and without mercy—would be our best bet. The ships won't have the opportunity to send information back to base. It makes reinforcements less likely."

In spite of herself, Elissa smiled again. And she shook her head.

"I think gamble is the correct word, Captain," she said. "You like taking risks."

A shadow passed over his face—ever so quickly, but it was there. He didn't think of himself as a risk-taker, but he seemed to know he was.

Sometimes people became risk-takers when they had nothing left to lose. But he had something to lose, or he wouldn't be having this conversation with her.

"I propose," he said, clearly wishing to ignore that last sentence of hers, "that we let those ships arrive here. We destroy them—together— far from the Room of Lost Souls."

"I'm not sure that protects us," she said. "If they are being tracked, their people will come to the Room looking for them."

"Which is," Cooper said, "for all intents and purposes, abandoned, right?"

There was no reason not to confirm that.

"Right," she said. "It is abandoned. But here's the thing: if we fight the ships in Nine Planets' territory and defeat them, that benefits you. The backup won't arrive in the Nine Planets. It'll arrive in the Empire. Which means if things go awry, we have to deal with it."

His expression didn't change. He revealed nothing. Cooper had a marvelous ability to keep his emotions and his thoughts off his face.

"So the question, for me at least, is what do we get out of fighting these ships on your turf?" she asked. "Territory?"

"From what you're telling me," he said, "we may not have a choice of where to fight them."

He had a point, and the longer this conversation took, the more valid his point became, especially if those ships had a way to travel quickly.

She wasn't going to hurry, though. Hurrying led to mistakes.

"Assuming we do have a choice," she said, "what does the Enterran Empire get out of this temporary truce?"

"The remains of the destroyed enemy ships," he said. "You get the wreckage."

She almost took a step backwards. The offer surprised her. She hadn't expected Cooper to offer up potential information like that.

Of course, she hadn't expected him to offer up territory either—she wasn't sure he could—but the ships might be even more valuable.

Paek shifted in the chair, the first time he had moved since this conversation began. It took a lot of strength for her to ignore him. She wanted to consult. She wanted his thoughts on this.

Maybe the movement was a signal, but in what direction, she had no idea. He probably didn't want her to trust Cooper.

"And if the ships are just disabled, but filled with crew?" she asked.

"They're yours," Cooper said. "I have no interest in taking prisoners."

Somehow that sentence sounded chilling. It shouldn't have. It should have been very straightforward.

He had a different agenda, one she didn't entirely understand. She wasn't sure it should bother her.

Clearly Cooper needed her to defeat those three ships, which said something about their capabilities, or maybe about his.

But he was right: they didn't have a lot of time to make this decision.

"What do you want us to do, in exchange for these ships?" she asked.

He looked directly at the camera on his end. It felt like he was in the room, looking at her. "I want ships, as many as you can get to the area around the Lost Souls Corporation. I'd like a full show of force. I'd like to fire on those three ships the moment they appear."

"Appear," she repeated. "They're not going to traverse the distance of the Empire to get to the border, are they?"

"It will seem like they have appeared magically," he said. "One moment, they won't be visible and the next they will."

He didn't answer her. She hesitated for a moment—should she ask about the travel method? She had asked before, but he hadn't really answered, and he was being vague now.

"When they arrive," he said again, "I want as many ships as possible to fire on them. We will only get one chance at this."

He wasn't going to tell her what they could do, but he was willing to give her the three ships. She found that fascinating. Did that mean her engineers wouldn't be able to reverse engineer the travel method? Or did he just not care about that part of the equation?

She thought for a moment.

"If we succeed," she said, "I'd like to revisit the border treaty."

"No," he said. "The border is off-limits. But we could discuss an arrangement that will protect both of us against outsiders, like these ships. We could arrange a joint defense."

"Which will mostly benefit you," she said. "You don't have the ships."

"I don't have the ships *right now*," he said.

The wording caught her. Paek too, apparently, since he shifted again.

"Which means what, Cooper? You have reinforcements coming in?" Then she waved a hand. She knew he wasn't going to answer that. "So, all we are is an army for you, then, right?"

"There's a good chance I could defeat them on my own," he said. "Using the very technique I mentioned to you."

She let out a sharp laugh. "But you don't believe it."

"You should," he said. "You know what I can do."

His eyes were flat, and something about his face had become menacing. Or maybe it was just the memory of that first attack, and how she had barely survived.

Clearly, he wanted her to remember that. He was good, this man. He knew how to negotiate and get what he wanted.

"So," she said, "you're taking our help out of the kindness of your heart."

"No," he said. "I'm trying to be a good partner. You came to me with information. And you also came to me before taking action against me for my trespass. I owe you a favor."

"And you repay that favor by making me work for it." She smiled and shook her head. "That's not a favor, Cooper."

"No," he said. "The favor is sharing tactics. The favor is showing you how to defend yourself against these ships. And the favor is giving you their technology should we be as successful as I hope we will be."

"You don't see their tech as a threat then," she said. "It must be similar to yours."

"I don't know what their tech is," he said. "I know that we have access to similar ships. So do you, as we discussed."

"And if we destroy the ships utterly? Or they do? They blew up their own ship at Room to prevent us from getting our hands on it."

He let out a slight breath. She hadn't told him that, deliberately, and now she had. She wondered if it would change his calculation.

"We will do our best to make sure that doesn't happen," he said.

"Not good enough," she said.

"How about this, then," he said. "I promise that we will renegotiate if their ships are obliterated."

She would have to trust him; that was the implication. She wasn't sure she did.

She didn't have to agree to fight alongside him. She could wait until those three ships did whatever they were going to do, then swoop in and take more territory at the Nine Planets.

But one of his points bothered her greatly. He said that the organization running those ships probably believed the *Ivoire* belonged to the Enterran Empire.

The evidence was there for that argument. The *Ivoire* had fled to the Enterran Empire, and then moved on, as seven ships showed up to defend the Room and, perhaps, the *Ivoire*. When those enemy ships destroyed the Empire ships, more Empire ships headed toward the Room.

Elissa had no idea if those enemy vessels had known about the other ships. She would wager they did. And all of that was circumstantial evidence that the *Ivoire* was part of the Empire.

"You will teach us your tactics for fighting ships like these," she said.

"I'm hoping this battle won't involve a lot of tactics," he said. "I'm hoping that we will destroy them immediately."

"Hope has no place in war," Elissa said.

He started, his first emotional reaction since their conversations began.

"We differ on that," he said. "My people survive on hope."

Interesting thought.

"It allows us to plan," he said, but that sounded like a later addition, something he was saying to cover up what he really meant.

"You will teach us tactics for fighting ships like that," she said again.

He stared at the camera again, probably staring at her.

"Yes, I will," he said. "As long as I command this joint venture. I'm the one who knows how to defeat them."

"You will do so from the *Ewing Trekov*," she said.

"No," he said. "I will not. Your ship does not have the maneuverability or the technology to handle a sudden shift in fortunes. I will command from the *Ivoire*."

"I will send a team there, then, to observe," she said.

He opened his mouth, as if to disagree. Then nodded his head. "Three," he said. "You will send three people. That's all my bridge can handle during a crisis."

"All right," she said. "Three."

"We have an agreement?" he asked.

"Yes," she said.

"Recordings of this conversation will have to serve as the legitimate record," he said. "Because we need your vessels here as quickly as you can send them."

"I will have ships at your location within the hour," she said, knowing that once again, she was giving up tactics to him. If he really was trying to figure out response times, he was learning a lot.

But she didn't believe that. And she didn't believe one thing he had said to her.

He was scared.

302

And it didn't seem to be the three ships. He seemed to believe he could handle those three ships.

He was terrified of something else—and he didn't trust her enough to tell her exactly what that something was.

34

NYGUTA BROUGHT THE *BILATZAILEA* to a full stop near the spot where the *Ivoire's* real space trail ended. The ship remained cloaked, although she would break the cloak before the *BilatZailea* entered foldspace.

She stood near the dark screens on the walls of the bridge, hands clasped, staring at her own holographic screen. The Empire ship, the *Roja*, had been chasing one of the fake ships she'd ghosted. The *Roja*, with its own very bad cloak, seemed to believe the fake ship held some secrets for it. The communications coming out of the *Roja's* bridge were just plain embarrassing.

The man in charge, Yves Beltraire, wasn't communicating with other ships, even though he had received the instruction to do so from Group Commander Trekov earlier in the day. He was communicating with the bridge.

The bridge crew, including the first officer, would try to steer him differently, but he either didn't hear their polite nudges or he didn't care what any of them thought.

He was just blathering on about stealth tech, and learning how it worked, and figuring out what the connection was to this mysterious energy signature the three ships were giving off.

Nyguta actually enjoyed listening to him. His ignorance amused her. If she had more time, she would have dropped fake clues and bad energy readings throughout the sector. That would have put his precious research back years.

But she didn't. And she knew she would be giving him a tiny gift when all three vessels went into foldspace. He would be able to observe that again.

Except that she had had Habibi shut down most of the functions of the nearby buoys, particularly those that had an Imperial Intelligence identifier. Habibi had kept the visuals and the ability to transmit those to various ships, but everything else—from telemetry to in-depth energy readings and even to the system that identified ships—was completely disabled.

That would drive Beltraire crazy once he realized he couldn't get the kind of information he believed he needed.

She smiled just a little, and checked her screen. The *DetekTibe* arrived, stopping just above the *BilatZailea* and to the *BilatZailea's* left. She was about to send a hail when Captain Odeh sent her a private communication.

That idiot on the Roja *made our jobs a lot easier.*

He did, Nyguta sent back. She had been worried about this part of the trip for a variety of reasons, most importantly because she was worried that she might find herself in a battle again.

The *MuhaQiq* arrived as well, remaining a slight distance behind the *BilatZailea.* Nyguta checked in with the *MuhaQiq's* captain as well.

All three were ready to head into foldspace. She had decided that they would enter separately, using the coordinates they had taken from the *Ivoire's* entry, and assuming that Cooper was taking the *Ivoire* to this Lost Souls at the Nine Planets.

Nyguta could have gone directly to the Lost Souls or at least the area around it, but she didn't trust all of the information she was getting from Trekov and Beltraire. They had been guessing almost as much as Nyguta had originally.

Besides, she wanted to see if the *Ivoire* had made some kind of side trip.

She was going to have to travel through foldspace either way. It was best that she do so along the route that the *Ivoire* used.

She opened a public channel to the other two ships, making sure that the captains knew they were no longer communicating with her privately.

"All right," she said. "We will head into foldspace, using the same rapid method we used on our way here. This time, I want the *DetekTibe* to go first, followed by the *MuhaQiq*. The *BilatZailea* will arrive last."

She double-checked her readings, then sent the entry coordinates to the other two captains.

"These coordinates are the ones we will use," she said. "Clear a path for the next ship, just like you did the last time."

She took a deep breath and surveyed her own bridge crew. They were working on their separate assignments, heads down, fingers moving. Some, like Intxausti, were coordinating research with other team members not on the bridge. The rest were monitoring for any problems.

Even though Nyguta had ruled out the Empire as a threat on this trip, she wasn't careless enough to think that the Empire might not suddenly turn dangerous once again.

But she was about to make one of those foldspace speeches, the kind she always hated. The speech made her feel even more uncomfortable now that she suspected that Cooper and his crew had disappeared for thousands of years because of some kind of foldspace malfunction.

Nothing could please her more than learning that the five-thousand-year assumption was wrong.

"If," she said, "we end up at different times or locations, because, after all, this is foldspace, do your best to communicate with me."

She had already had the long conversation with the captains about what happened in the event one of the ships got separated from the others. That conversation had happened before the ships even arrived in the Empire.

The decision had been that they would return to the Armada rather than going forward to find the *Ivoire*. If finding the *Ivoire* proved too difficult, then all three ships would eventually return to the Armada, and Nyguta would let the Jefatura make the decision about what to do next.

Still, she was going to remind them all—not just the other captains—that they had choices.

"We have—no pun intended—all the time we need. So, if you find yourself alone for longer than an hour when you arrive in foldspace, wait for at least two days before returning to the Armada."

Two days was arbitrary, but it was also a marker. If the other ships hadn't arrived in two days, they might not arrive for weeks or even months. Or the first ship might have ended up at a different foldspace location. Rather than trying to figure out what small thing had gone wrong, and rather than having that small thing turn into a large thing, all three captains had agreed that returning to base was the most sensible maneuver.

"All right," she said and made herself smile. She wasn't using anything visual, but she knew they could hear the smile in her voice. "I will see you on the other side."

That last was a saying an old captain of hers used, back when Nyguta had first started working on foldspace runs. Her attachment to the phrase had become almost a superstition with her, one she wasn't afraid to admit.

The other two captains wished her well also, and then they all signed off. The *DetekTibe* pulled ahead of her, just outside the coordinates.

Nyguta watched her holographic screen, seeing all three ships together. Hers and the *MuhaQiq* were outlined and faint, which was how their telemetry registered matching cloaks.

If she looked somewhere in the distance, on the far side of the starbase, she would see the *Roja* glowing like a well-lit house.

She watched as the *DetekTibe* uncloaked, then slid into the coordinates. A faint window etched itself around the *DetekTibe*, the foldspace bubble as so many of the engineers called it, before the *DetekTibe* disappeared altogether.

For three seconds, the window lingered. And then it too faded.

Tua of the *MuhaQiq* was too good a captain to ever let her ship cross into a foldspace bubble at that moment of transition. Unlike the captain of the *EhizTari,* Tua knew that too much could go awry following that closely.

Instead, she clearly waited until the *DetekTibe* and the bubble were gone before she opened her own foldspace window. Unlike Odeh of the *DetekTibe,* Tua waited until the window was open before uncloaking her ship. The window opened, the *MuhaQiq* appeared ever so briefly, and then it went through the window, the light from the other side—whatever that was—illuminating the smooth edges of the gigantic ship.

The ship vanished, the window closed, the bubble faded.

Nyguta let out a breath, then nodded at Rockowitz. "Let's do it," she said.

He smiled at her—his acknowledgement of her extremely casual command.

Foldspace windows felt different from the inside. It was impossible to feel a cloak vanishing, but the entry into foldspace was always distinctive.

The *BilatZailea* started to move, and then it vibrated ever so slightly. Unlike some of the other foldspace journeys she'd taken to get to this Empire, this one was starting off better.

The vibrations were small and comfortable, the kind of vibration she associated with short easy trips that had nothing to do with rescues.

She knew better than to let down her guard, however. Too much could go wrong.

She waited as the *BilatZailea* continued vibrating. She did not look at the holographic screen. It would show a weird gray blankness, something that no amount of tinkering by any of the engineers could fix. She didn't shut down the holographic screen, however, because she felt there was no point in doing so. She would just call it up again, on the other side.

Then the vibrations ceased. She glanced at Rockowitz who nodded at her.

They were through.

Without waiting for her team to tell her anything, she looked at her holographic screen. The *DetekTibe* and the *MuhaQiq* waited for her.

She let out a breath she hadn't even realized she had been holding.

"Do we know where we are?" she asked Rockowitz.

"As much as we ever do in foldspace," he said. "This is exactly where we should have ended up."

"And," Habibi sounded triumphant, "we are almost on top of a trail left by the *Ivoire*."

Not only triumphant but relieved. Nyguta was relieved as well. She didn't like tracking in real space. She was much more comfortable here, in foldspace, than she would ever be in real space.

Because her equipment was calibrated for foldspace, her tracking data worked better here. She opened a second screen, one with scrolling tracking telemetry, and watched as the numbers and dots appeared.

Habibi was right: the *Ivoire*'s trail here was firm and bright, unlike the trail the *Ivoire* had left in regular space.

Two important hurdles crossed. Her ships were all here, and they would be able to trace the *Ivoire* in real time.

The next hurdle wasn't as easily solved.

Once they arrived at the *Ivoire*'s destination, at least from this fold-space journey, she would have to decide if they were going in cloaked, so that they could observe, or if they were going in visible and hot, as a threat.

The *Ivoire* had seen them as a threat from the start. Maybe she should continue taking a page of the *Ivoire*'s playbook and ghost some ships, so that it looked like she was coming in with a large force.

She would make that decision once they reached the edge of this foldspace trail.

Once she knew more about the *Ivoire* and Cooper. She hoped she would have that kind of information before she encountered the ship again.

35

ELISSA LET OUT A SMALL BREATH, and made sure that everything in her office was shut down. Any communications she'd had with Captain Cooper were done now. Normally, she would have made certain that Cooper had not placed any kind of tracking or listening device into the feed that had come from his ship, but she had to trust this time that this communication had been handled well.

Normally, when she double-checked something like that with her staff, they gave her a sideways why-don't-you-trust-us look. So, for the first time in a while, she would trust them more completely than she ever had.

As she gathered her things, already quietly planning what she had to do next, a movement caught her eye.

Paek unfolded himself from the chair. He stood slowly, his gaze on her. When he reached his full height, he tilted his chin back just a little so that he looked like he was the one in charge.

"What makes you think you can trust him?" Paek asked.

"We can't trust him, not entirely," she said, almost dismissively. She wanted to get to work. "He can't trust us entirely either. That's what will make this alliance work, at least in the short term."

Paek studied her for a moment. She'd never seen him look so serious—at least at her.

"He's bested us—you—before," he said.

"He's a good tactician," she said.

"He could be lying right now," Paek said.

"He could," she said, "but I don't think he is."

"I don't understand why," Paek said.

His response startled her. He had listened to the entire conversation. He knew what Cooper had said.

"We have only his word that he has nothing to do with those ships," Paek said. "And they're similar vessels. I still believe the idea of an attack from him and his compatriots is likely."

"I already sent information to Command Central to monitor the border," she said. "If he's building up some kind of force, we'll know it before our ships even get close."

"But you don't think that's likely," Paek said.

"That's right," she said. "I think he needs help. I think he will owe us a favor."

"Again." Paek's voice remained steady, his posture stiff. "I do not understand why you believe him."

"I've been studying him and the *Ivoire* for quite a while," she said. "Even in the worst of the skirmishes with us at the border, he has never brought more than three Dignity Vessels including his. Lost Souls has found more Dignity Vessels, and seems to be rebuilding them, but I know for a fact they do not have enough personnel to rebuild the ships quickly or to completely staff those ships. He needs us, Tawhiri."

"If these three ships are his enemy," Paek said.

"That's the gamble." She wasn't going to discuss that further. It was her risk, and her career, and she was staking everything on it. "We need to get moving. We have ships to send across that border, and quickly."

Paek took one step toward her, then he reached out, as if he were going to stop her, but he let his hand drop.

"Let's assume the battle this Cooper expects does happen," Paek said. "Let's assume that we win. Let's assume we get those damaged ships—if there are damaged ships to get."

"All right," she said.

"What's to stop us from taking over that corporation right then and there?" he asked. "Or going deeper into the Nine Planets, taking territory for ourselves?"

She felt a jolt, and it took her a moment to realize that the jolt was anger.

"What's to stop us?" she asked. "My word, that's what."

"But what does your word mean when you give it to a man like Cooper? He's already cost us hundreds, maybe thousands of lives."

She couldn't tell if Paek was angry at her for coming up with this, or if he was just asking because he needed to learn.

She had never seen him so emotionally distant before. She suspected he was appalled at her.

"My word," she said, trying to keep her own anger in check, "is *my* word. If we decide to fight Cooper and the Nine Planets, we will do it on another day."

"Wouldn't it be better to let them fight their own battles?" Paek asked. "If he loses, we could go in and pick up the pieces, quite easily. It will benefit us a great deal."

Even though she had the anger under control, she didn't stop the irritation from flashing across her face.

"You don't believe that these people who command those three ships will come after us?" she asked, allowing the edge in her voice. "Even though we've already fought with them?"

"We don't know who they are," Paek said. "If we ally with Cooper, then they really will think that we are all one big happy family."

She paused. She hadn't thought of that, not quite in those terms anyway. She rolled the idea around in her head, then set it aside. She had a lot of deaths to avenge. Seven ships full, at the hands of this new enemy.

If she believed Cooper—and she did—then he had no way of knowing those ships would destroy Empire vessels. There might have been a skirmish, but that was all. At least, that was what she would have expected.

But that wasn't how it turned out.

Paek clearly saw her hesitation, and decided to press his point. "We don't know who they are."

That decided her. "We don't have the time to find out," she said. "They are dangerous."

"You believe that because Cooper said it," Paek said.

And that was it, that was when she'd had enough. Paek was supposed to be behind her, supposed to understand what she was doing, and even if he didn't understand it, supposed to back whatever she planned.

"I believe that they are dangerous because they destroyed our ships," she said. "I believe it because we can't track these three ships, even though they arrived deep in our territory. I see them as a major threat, Sub-Lieutenant. Why don't you?"

His mouth opened ever so slightly. She usually didn't reprimand her staff, at least not like that.

He nodded, then tilted his head, as if he had made an internal decision. "Forgive me, ma'am, but there are other ways we can fight them."

"Cooper knows how to track them," she said.

"We think," Paek said.

"No," she said. "He admitted it. The ships are similar, and unlike us, Cooper and this mysterious organization know how to make the ships work for them."

Paek took a deep breath, nodded as if that argument made sense to him, and then said, "All right. But, Commander, I'm still not sure what exactly we get out of this. I understand the damaged ships, but reverse engineering them might take us years."

Her anger was dissipating. Finally, he had asked a good question.

"What do we get, Sub-Lieutenant?" she asked. "We get something I've wanted for a long, long time. We get Cooper's weapon."

"It might not be part of the ships, though," Paek said. "It might be something else."

"It might," she said. "But I'll have staff on his bridge. We'll watch him deploy it. We'll finally know what it is, and with luck, we'll be able to manufacture one for ourselves."

"That's a hell of a risk, ma'am, for something that might not work out the way we think it will." Paek's eyes seemed to brighten, as if he was thinking something he didn't dare say, something he wanted his entire expression to communicate.

"I'm aware of that, Sub-lieutenant," she said. "I trust that when you contact Flag Commander Janik, you'll let him know that I chose the best of all of the bad options."

Paek's eyes widened. "I'm not contacting the Flag Commander, ma'am. This conversation was just between you and me."

She studied Paek for a moment, startled at how one conversation could shake her like this. She usually relied on Paek's support. That he wasn't giving it automatically disturbed her.

But she was relieved that he wasn't going to Janik with this.

"For now," she said. "If the circumstances arise that I will be unable to communicate with the Flag Commander, and he disapproves of what I've done, I trust that you will tell him you objected."

"Commander, I—"

"Promise me, Tawhiri," she said.

He shifted, his perfect posture failing him for the first time. "Ma'am, you know I support you."

"I do know that," she said. "But if I'm not here, you might have to save your own career. I would like you to do so."

He frowned, then nodded, just once.

"I hope that it won't come to that," he said.

"Oh, me too, Tawhiri," she said with feeling. "Me too."

36

COOP SPRINTED OUT OF THE TINY COMMAND CENTER near the officers' mess. He needed to do a lot in the next hour. He needed to contact Yash and Xilvii. Coop needed to see what they could do to beef up the deep-space scans around Lost Souls. He needed to brace Boss for what was coming, and he needed to get Ilona to talk with the Nine Planets.

He rounded the corner into the bar, and skidded to a stop. All of the diplomats he had invited for his meeting had arrived. They had been sitting at the round table, talking and laughing, all of them with a drink in hand. But the moment he arrived, they stopped, and turned toward him, looking startled to a person.

He didn't run. Not usually, and not on the *Ivoire*. He probably looked panicked. He wasn't, but he was damn close.

He'd seen what the Not-Fleet could do. He needed to cage those three ships somehow. He needed to prevent them from communicating with their compatriots—the last thing he needed, the last thing they *all* needed, was the Not-Fleet showing up outside of Lost Souls.

"Jonathon, what is it?" Mae asked. Of course, Mae was the one to question him. She could read his moods better than anyone, maybe even better than Boss.

Coop swore softly under his breath. He had to handle the diplomats first, because he needed them, and they were right here.

Only he didn't have the time to explain things in depth. Too much was happening at once.

"We have an emergency that I need to deal with," he said, as he walked toward the table. The area around it smelled faintly of beer, as if someone had spilled. But from the look of the various glasses scattered around the table, the smell wasn't coming from a spill. It was coming from the fact that damn near all of his diplomats were drinking beer of one kind or another.

He stopped at the table, behind the only empty chair at the table's head. Clearly everyone had been waiting for him.

Eight faces turned toward him. Three men, five women, all looking at him intently.

Mae turned her chair so that she could view him better.

His fingers tightened around the seatback, as he scrambled to settle his mind down. He had had a long speech planned, then time for discussion, then a bit of back-and-forth on what, exactly, the diplomats needed to do and could do, in discussions with the Fleet.

First, though, he had to prepare them all for the fact that the Fleet still existed. It had been something he had hoped for, but with his hands-off way of handling his crew, he hadn't known if all of them felt that way.

He'd planned to be sensitive and diplomatic with his diplomats and he didn't have time.

"What can we do?" Marissa Cumex asked.

He knew what she was doing; she was putting him at ease, which was a diplomat's first job.

He smiled gratefully at her.

"You can let me apologize," he said. "I had planned a bit of a long discussion with you all, and circumstances are not going to allow it. I might have to pull you from one task to another, which I had not planned."

He was thinking aloud, again, something he rarely did.

A little frown had appeared between Mae's eyebrows, a sign that she was deeply worried. She could probably tell just how unsettled he really was.

"I'm going to blurt something at you all," he said. "I had planned to do more to prepare you, but there simply isn't time."

Everyone stiffened, except Cumex and Mae. They hadn't moved at all. They were already in diplomatic mode, apparently.

"It looks like Boss ran into the Fleet," he said. "The modern Fleet. We don't know that for certain, but it seems likely."

"Son of a bitch," Rory Habnal muttered.

Two of the diplomats both turned gray. A third leaned back in his chair, the surprise on his face impossible to miss.

Mae's look of concern deepened. Only Cumex seemed unaffected, which made Coop worry about her the most. This was news that they all had been waiting for in one way or another. They should have some kind of reaction.

"The diving we've been doing at the Boneyard provoked them," Coop said.

Habnal closed his eyes ever so briefly, then steeled his shoulders.

"We got our people out the moment we sensed a threat." Coop really should have been more careful with his language; he had nothing to do with the escape, and they would eventually learn that. But he didn't have time for that kind of caution at the moment. "However, we don't know if the Fleet will track us here."

"The Fleet," Cumex said. "You think they can do that kind of tracking?"

"They might have followed the *Sove* and the others into foldspace," Mae said, not taking her gaze off Coop. "Not every ship emerges from foldspace at the same time."

"Exactly," Coop said. "If they come at us thinking we're pirates or thieves, they might attack shortly after they arrive. We don't have the defenses."

Five ships, that was what Boss had seen. Five. And three coming from the Not-Fleet. And he had his deal with the Empire. That would be hundreds of ships.

He really needed to get out of here and prepare Xilvii and Blake and Boss.

"The only way we can deal with the Fleet," Coop said, "is diplomatically. We need to somehow get their attention, let them know that the *Ivoire* is an active Fleet vessel that got lost in foldspace, and convince them that Lost Souls is a Fleet operation."

"But it's not," Habnal said.

"It's what we've got," Coop said. "You'll have to work with that."

"Yes, but, the *Ivoire* was not at the Boneyards," Cumex said. "Why would the Fleet believe that?"

"Well, if I had the time, I'd work with you on that," Coop said. "I'm not even sure they're going to be speaking a form of Standard we recognize. I'm not sure of anything."

"Surely, you have some kind of plan," Habnal said.

"My plan was to talk with you all, figure out the best way to handle the Fleet—if indeed the ships that Boss saw were Fleet—and then somehow get them to assist us."

"What has made that impossible?" Cumex asked. Her voice was measured. She was working him, now, as if he were the one she had to treat carefully.

Maybe he was.

"The Not-Fleet," he said to Cumex. She had been on the *Ivoire* at Sector Base E-2. "I didn't shake them off like I thought I had."

Finally, her diplomatic poise crumbled. "Oh, my," she said. "Where are they?"

"At the moment, I don't know. I need to deal with that, though, right now. We can only speculate about whether or not the Fleet is going to arrive. I know that the Not-Fleet is looking for us. So I have to deal with the Not-Fleet, and leave you all to deal with the actual Fleet."

He let out a small rush of air, resisted the urge to grab the nearest stein and down the beer.

"I'm not sure there is a Fleet to deal with," he said. "This might be all noise. It might be me worrying about something that's not going to come to pass."

"Are we free to tell our families about the Fleet?" Habnal asked.

"Not at the moment," Coop said. "Let's get through the next day or two, shall we?"

He tapped his hand on the back of the chair, feeling his own internal clock ramping up. He had to get out of here, and do so quickly.

"I know you have a million questions," he said to them. "I hope to get time to answer them. But in the meantime, figure out what would convince you that some ship invading a storage area and taking things actually has the right to do so."

"Can we send them our information?" Cumex asked. "Can we use the Fleet identifications?"

"Sure," Coop said. "Anything that might work. But you know the Fleet—or at least our Fleet. Five thousand years was an eon ago, and they dumped a lot of the history. If this is the Fleet, I figure that part hasn't changed."

"Five thousand years is a long time." Mae spoke softly. "Everything might have changed."

"Yes," Coop said. "We won't know until we face them, if we face them, if they're Fleet. But your goal is to keep them from prosecuting some case against us for theft, however they'll do it. We have to convince them we're not the enemy."

"They should have records of us," Habnal said, and stopped the conversation. Everyone looked at him as if he had lost his mind.

"We don't have records of every ship," Coop said, keeping his voice level. He'd already been too open with these diplomats. He'd lost a lot of his training, at least when it came to his emotions.

He should have been calmer, although it was hard right now. He needed to get out of here.

"What did they do, at the Boneyard?" Habnal asked. He seemed to have his feet under him now.

That was a good question, worthy of an answer. This group had to know the risks.

"They blew up one of our small ships," Coop said. "They tried to destroy the *Veilig*, but Boss got it out of there just in time."

"Destroy how?" Habnal asked.

"That I don't have time to answer," Coop said, "and it's not relevant. They used the Boneyard, an option they don't have here."

"Used the Boneyard?" Habnal asked as if Coop hadn't tried to deflect it.

"What kind of ships are we talking about?" Cumex asked.

"DV-Class, mostly," Coop said. "Five, if they don't bring reinforcements."

"Can we take on five ships if we have to?" Cumex asked.

Another good question, although it presupposed failure.

"I don't know," Coop said. Even if they didn't have the Not-Fleet coming, even if the Empire wasn't on its way, Coop doubted they had enough firepower—hell, enough personnel—to take on these five Fleet ships.

Habnal looked at Cumex, and said, "If they're standard DV-Class—"

"We don't know if they are," Coop snapped. He had enough. It was time to leave. "They have obviously kept the exterior design, but we have no idea what kind of upgrades they've made."

Mae put her hand on his arm. The touch sent a shiver through him that he tried to ignore.

He looked down at her fingers. He had already moved away from the chair, and he hadn't even realized it.

"What's the chance this isn't the Fleet?" she asked.

Another good question.

"I don't know that either," he said. "And I don't have time—we don't have time—to debate it. Assume the chance that they're not part of the Fleet fifty percent and plan arguments for both scenarios."

"If they let us talk," Habnal said.

"There's that," Cumex said. She looked up at Coop. "Who is handling the mission?"

Meaning, who would make the decision to break off talks and step into a fight—if a fight was needed.

He had no idea who that would be. Normally, it would be him, but he might have too much on his plate.

Still, he would need to know.

"I hope it doesn't come to that," he said, knowing that was not an answer.

But diplomats often went into difficult situations without a lot of military backup. Sometimes military backup made things worse.

Not, however, in a situation like this.

"I'll handle it," Mae said. Her voice was very small. "I'll contact you if we need you."

He looked at her. He had no idea if she could stand up to the pressure. She'd been one of three diplomats to survive one of the worst massacres Fleet diplomats had ever faced—at least, until that point—and she had had her own form of PTSD for a while.

"I can't do that to you, Mae," he said quietly.

"This is where you cease being my friend," she said, "and be my captain. You need me to do this. I am the one with the most experience in things going awry."

Good argument, but not necessarily the one he wanted to hear from her.

Her hand tightened on his arm. "It'll take me fewer words than it'll take anyone else to communicate with you, Jonathon."

There was that. She could get through to him, even when he was distracted. He would believe her, too, whereas he might not believe someone like Habnal.

"All right," Coop said. He patted Mae's hand, and she removed it. He stood up tall.

They all watched him as if they had no idea what he was going to do next.

"You will need to set up an area to work near the Lost Souls' defensive array. Make sure that Jason Xilvii knows you're watching for Fleet vessels that were chasing the *Veilig*. You'll need to deal with them the moment they arrive, so have a plan. Know who will communicate with them, be ready to pivot."

Coop had no idea what else to tell them. He was going to have to trust them more than he wanted to.

He made sure he met the gaze of every single diplomat. He began with Habnal, then worked his way around the table before ending with Mae.

"I'm sorry to throw this on you," Coop said. "But I have no other choice. With luck, this discussion will be a theoretical one."

He didn't think luck was going to play in his favor though. He was going to have to trust them, and he really didn't want to.

He hesitated for a half second, wondering if he should give them even more information about the Not-Fleet, about the three ships coming, about the Empire ships heading toward Lost Souls.

He decided not to. He couldn't handle the questions. If only he had more than an hour to deal with all of this.

"I'm trusting you," he said. "We've been searching for the Fleet for years now. And it looks like they might arrive here."

"So don't blow it, right?" Habnal asked with a smile.

Coop didn't have a smile in him, not even a polite one in response. "Oh, we might have already blown it," he said. "I'm just trusting you all not to make things worse."

37

BELTRAIRE STOOD BEHIND THE CAPTAIN'S CHAIR on the bridge of the *Roja*, his fingers digging into the chair's soft sides. His gaze kept shifting from one screen to another, trying to keep track of the ships that had continued to arrive at the Room of Lost Souls.

The ships were all of the same type as the enemy vessels that had arrived earlier. They were moving slowly throughout this sector of space, apparently investigating the battle that had occurred here days ago.

He hadn't expected this. He had expected the ships to continue their search for the *Ivoire*, but he hadn't expected them to stay and more ships to arrive.

Captain Krag's crew was extremely efficient. They were monitoring the ships, making certain that the *Roja* was well back, even though it was shielded and hidden from the enemy vessels.

The enemy vessels didn't seem to care about anything in the area. In fact, the telemetry he was getting from them was bland and repetitive. He'd asked one of the crew members about that, and the young woman—a redhead whose dark skin made her green eyes even more vibrant—had frowned when she looked at him.

"It looks to me, sir," she had said, "as if they are using the telemetry almost like a shield."

He wasn't quite sure what that meant. He was very well versed in stealth tech and in other forms of military grade experimental science developed throughout the Empire. But when it came to actual military technology, he simply didn't understand it. Not at the level of this crew.

He had to rely on them.

His head was spinning. He couldn't keep track of everything, not on the poorly designed holoscreen before him, not on the big wall screens, not on the captain's screen that he had open near the chair.

He usually prided himself on his ability to multitask, but he was trying to multitask in an area where he had minimal training, and that training had been decades ago.

He felt the lack, and he also felt the consequences of his own pride. He could go back to Trekov and let her know that even more ships had arrived near the Room, but he was waiting to do so.

And, to their credit, the *Roja's* crew did not question that decision.

Yet.

Something about those ships bothered him. He wished he was in his own single ship or that he was in one of the large labs at one of the research stations where he usually worked. He would be able to increase the telemetry, change systems or even change the visuals.

The ships looked indistinct to him on the screens. The telemetry was repetitive. The movements seemed almost wooden as if the ships themselves had no crew.

But he personally had run a scan of each ship, and they had the exact same number of crew members, almost as if that number was a hard-and-fast requirement on these enemy vessels.

"Um, sir?" Another of the crew was looking at him. This one was a young man with a sharp chin and narrow dark eyes. His entire face looked like it was pointing whenever he turned it, probably not assisted by the fact that his nose was as sharp as that chin.

"Yes," Beltraire said curtly, not just because he didn't like having his thoughts interrupted, but because he was annoyed at himself.

He could have taken fifteen minutes to memorize everyone's name and position after he had wrested command from Captain Krag. Then, at least, Beltraire would know what type of crew member was speaking to him and could probably guess as to why.

He had not been thinking as clearly as he would have liked on this entire trip. Or rather, his focus had been wrong. He had been thinking only of gaining more knowledge into the origins of stealth tech, and he wanted to understand that weapon that the *Ivoire* had used, which also seemed to be made of stealth tech energy.

He made himself focus on the pointy-faced young man who was staring at him with something like irritation.

"Yes?" Beltraire repeated.

"The original enemy vessels?" the young man said, clearly not done relaying information, but ending the phrase in a question anyway.

It was a manner of speaking that Beltraire had trained his own staff out of. It was annoying, particularly in someone who had a bit of authority.

"What about them?" Beltraire snapped. He knew he sounded cranky. He no longer cared.

He was going to have to make the hard decision soon, and contact Trekov, and that irritated him much more than anything this crew could do.

"One of them…um…reappeared, sir," the young man said.

The original three vessels were the only ones that remained cloaked, something that bothered Beltraire as well. He worried that they were doing secret things, things his equipment couldn't pick up.

The *Roja's* crew was scanning for the three ships constantly, but the new ships kept getting in the way.

And even though Beltraire had asked repeatedly and had been told repeatedly that the scans wouldn't alert the new ships as to where the *Roja* was, he doubted that was true.

Or perhaps it was fair to say he *worried* that it wasn't true. Because if they could see him, and they eventually attacked, and he survived, the conversation with Trekov would not be pretty.

And yes, he knew that on one level he was very ridiculous. He would have to survive an attack to be embarrassed to talk with Trekov.

But she had unsettled him more than he wanted to admit—almost more than these ships had.

"The ship reappeared where?" he asked.

He cleared a screen in front of him, seeing nothing about the original enemy vessels near the Room.

"You know where the *Ivoire* vanished? At those coordinates, sir." The pointy-faced young man seemed to believe that this information would anger Beltraire, but it didn't.

Instead, it vindicated him. He'd kept the Imperial Intelligence buoys working at full capacity near there, because he had a hunch those vessels would reappear nearby.

"The others will show up there as well," he said.

He brought up the images from the nearby buoys, but couldn't seem to download anything else.

"I need telemetry from the area," he said. He looked at Walker. "*Now.*"

"We're trying to get that, sir," Walker said. He nodded at the pointy-faced young man who moved to a different console. The young man started working the controls.

None of the crew was working with the Imperial Intelligence buoys, though. Beltraire was the only one who knew how to make them function properly, and he was having trouble.

The ship simply sat in place, as if it were waiting for the other two.

They would all disappear there, he knew it. They would behave just like the *Ivoire* had—whatever that was.

Maybe there were doorways in certain sectors of space, things set up long in the past, maybe back when the Room of Lost Souls was a viable space station and the Dignity Vessels actually controlled the area now called the Enterran Empire.

That theory made as much sense as any, but Beltraire was aware it was just a theory.

Still, he might have to tell his people to explore it, because that might be why stealth tech worked so well in some parts of the Empire and seemed to explode of its own accord in others.

Besides, if there were actual doorways scattered throughout the Enterran Empire, he might be able to find them and make use of them. If he could identify them, and figure out how the enemy vessels opened those doorways up.

He made a mental note of all of that while he was trying to get more telemetry from the buoys.

"I can't get any kind of reading on the ship except the visual," Walker said. "None of us can."

Beltraire nodded. He should have expected this. The buoys weren't hidden. They were just scattered. And the enemy ships had been combing the area, so they would have found the buoys and probably disabled them.

Strange that they would have left the visuals though. Maybe to slow the Empire's response down?

Or were they taunting him?

He felt a shiver run down his spine. Something had been bothering him all along, and that something just pinged at him.

They were taunting him, he knew it. He just didn't know how.

But he boosted the *Roja's* scanners—or tried to.

"If you want to scan at that level, sir," Walker said somewhat softly. "We'll need to drop the cloak."

The scans were the reason he had stayed here alone, that he hadn't contacted Trekov, that he hadn't called for military vessels to intrude on this region of space.

He wanted to read the energy fluctuations. He wanted to learn from these ships, and if he ended up losing the *Roja*, so be it. He was trying.

"Drop the cloak," he said.

"Sir," Walker said. "The other vessels—"

"Don't really care about us. We're one small ship, and they have dozens. At worst, they'll surround us and threaten us." He thought about that for a moment. He could prepare for that. "So, make sure that you're ready to send all of our data and an emergency request to Group Commander Trekov, should that happen."

"They might block our requests for help," the pointy-faced young man said.

"We'll see them moving toward us," Beltraire said. "We will have a few minutes before they even think of blocking our transmissions."

He spoke with a confidence he didn't feel. But at least he had a plan.

"Now," he said, "drop the damn cloak. And start the scans immediately."

Something flared on his command screen, telling him the cloak was down. Then a little notification went by, letting him know that the scans had started.

He double-checked them. He wanted a more intense scan.

He had just placed his fingers on the controls, when the original enemy vessel shot forward. A window opened up, and the vessel was encircled in light.

It did look like a doorway. It looked like the doorway into a bright room, one he wanted to go through.

He glanced just briefly at the scans, not to see what they told him, but to make sure they were actually working.

They were.

"Sir," Walker said.

"If it's not a problem that I need to handle, then give it a rest," Beltraire said. These people needed a different kind of commander, a top-down person, which he was not.

As the doorway disappeared, another enemy vessel appeared. It moved forward.

That same doorway opened again, or rather, it engulfed the ship. From the visuals that Beltraire had, he didn't see an opening at all.

"Sir!" Walker sounded insistent.

Beltraire did not look up. The same light, the same shape, the same encasing around the ship, as if it were moving into some kind of light.

And finally, as he expected, a third ship appeared.

"Sir!" Walker said again.

"What?" Beltraire asked.

"The ships are vanishing," Walker said.

"I know that," Beltraire said, sarcasm dripping from his voice.

"No, sir," Walker said. "The *other* ships. The ones around the Room."

That caught Beltraire's attention. If he could get the buoys to relay readings from the Room, then he would have a wealth of information to sort through.

He was torn between looking at the other enemy vessels and watching the original ones disappear through that door.

"Are there doors everywhere, then?" he asked, almost to himself. He wasn't sure if Walker would understand him, and he dreaded explaining.

"No, sir," Walker said. "I mean the ships are literally disappearing."

"What? Is there something wrong with our scanners?"

"Not that I can tell, sir." Walker sounded perplexed.

Beltraire glanced over at the images coming from the Room. There were visibly fewer ships around the room. Maybe a third of the ships remained.

That pinging feeling returned. He had a hunch he knew what he was missing. The sameness of the ships, the way that they seemed to move in unison, the fact that the readings were so damn precise.

He swore quietly, and glanced at the remaining original enemy vessel. Unless he missed his guess, that was the original vessel, the one that had destroyed seven Empire ships.

It paused on the coordinates where the *Ivoire* had first disappeared. Then the original enemy vessel was engulfed in light. It hovered there, in that doorway, as if it were taunting him.

It probably was, because he finally understood what would happen when it disappeared.

The light faded, the ship vanished—and sure enough, so did the remaining ships around the Room.

"They were scanner echoes?" Walker muttered, clearly in disbelief.

"No." This was something Beltraire was certain about. "Those extra ships were created just for us. They weren't echoes. They were some kind of scanner spoof, which meant that these vessels knew how to trick our sensors from the very start."

That shudder he had felt earlier had become a full-blown chill. They knew how to trick the sensors, which meant that they had known he was here, observing them. They hadn't attacked him—at least not with weapons. They had attacked his information systems, which now meant that he couldn't trust the readings.

It also meant that they had deliberately kept the visuals working. They wanted him to see their ships as they went through that doorway. They wanted him to know that, the moment the original three ships left, all the other ships vanished.

He clenched his fists, feeling anger course through him. He slowly released them, finger by finger. It had been decades since he'd been played like this. He should have trusted his gut sense. He should have looked harder.

He opened his right hand wide, letting the muscles relax, making himself think. Would Trekov have been fooled by the other ships? He liked to think so. This bridge crew of Captain Krag's had been fooled, and she probably would have been too.

Who prepared—who even thought—that an opponent would clone the sensor data, to make it seem like there were so many ships?

He let out a sigh. He had no idea what the answer to that was. Maybe the military leaders learned about this maneuver. Maybe not. Maybe it was unique to these vessels. They certainly made the imagery cloning seem easy.

Beltraire didn't meet Walker's eye. They had all been fooled, but Beltraire had been in charge. He had let the three enemy vessels get away. Not that he had worked on holding them.

And, unlike what Trekov had feared, the enemy vessels hadn't been here to attack the Empire. They had clearly been tracking the *Ivoire*.

Beltraire let out a relieved sigh. His mistake seemed like less of a mistake now. He would let the rest of the Empire know about this maneuver—in a way that played down his ignorance of it, in case some of the Empire's commanders used it—and then he would declare a victory.

Because it had been a victory. He got the energy readings he needed. He had six of them—from the first buoys when the enemy vessels arrived, and now, as the vessels left.

He might even have the information he needed about this cloning practice. He had no idea how much information that process left behind.

He was going to have to have someone scrub the *Roja's* systems, though. If he had been the mastermind behind that cloning technique, he would have done it from *inside* the *Roja's* systems, not outside of the systems.

And, he would have thought, once he was in the systems, he would have made certain that he pulled information out of the systems, and left more little presents so that he could spy on the ship whose systems he had invaded.

He had a lot of work to do. Everyone on the *Roja* had a lot of work to do.

But first, he had to contact Trekov. He had promised her that he would let her know the moment those ships left this system.

He needed to inform her.

Only he would tell her that the enemy vessels "retreated" from the area around the Room.

Retreat. That was a good word. It had a nice spin, even if it wasn't entirely accurate.

The lack of accuracy didn't bother him. If Trekov caught it, Beltraire could claim the problem was in his communication with an underling. If Trekov didn't catch, then it would fade into irrelevance.

What he needed to do, though, was get these energy readings back to the stealth tech researchers. He might send some ships of his own out here, to investigate the coordinates, and see if they could figure out a way to open those doorways.

The answers he wanted were bigger than a momentary battle. They were bigger than a fight with some enemy vessels that might or might not be a real threat to the Empire.

If he figured out how these enemy vessels (and the *Ivoire*) had repurposed stealth tech into something more powerful—and if he figured out how to open doorways like the ones he had seen—then these small mistakes he had made wouldn't matter.

If he actually succeeded in augmenting stealth tech, he would become the father of the Empire's scientific resurgence, a resurgence that would end up making the Empire the strongest force in this sector.

The Empire would finally gain territory again. It would grow and become stronger.

It would become the dominant force in an ever-larger region of space. A force he had created, through sheer will.

38

Nyguta sat at her favorite table in the regular mess. The table was in a corner, ringed by plants on three sides. On the fourth side were windows that, in the right circumstances, remained unshuttered. Should the *BilatZailea* come under attack, a strong shield would slam down around all of the windows, portholes, and vulnerable spots on the ship's exterior.

Right now, though, she felt relatively safe, as the ship made its way along the *Ivoire's* trail in foldspace. If the *BilatZailea* was going to be attacked, it would be from an entity she hadn't even heard of.

Then she smiled at herself. An entity she hadn't heard of…like the Enterran Empire.

She had gone through the line rather than order from her tabletop. She had taken comfort foods—a cold noodle salad with sesame dressing and fresh greens from the hydroponics bay, some whole wheat bread layered with a sweet almond and garlic paste, and a mushroom soup heavy on the pepper, just to keep her awake.

Of course, she was washing it all down with a coffee that had more almond milk in it than actual coffee. Her regular, which she didn't indulge in enough.

The last week had had more stress than any other week this year, and she knew the stress wasn't about to end. She welcomed this breather, though, and she would probably prolong it, just so that her crew—and the crews of the other two ships—could get rest before they headed into whatever they would find when they found the *Ivoire*.

She finished dipping another piece of bread—this one without the paste—into the soup, chewing as daintily as she could while trying to keep the broth from dripping down her chin. The last thing she wanted to do was change her uniform before heading back to the bridge. The bread was supposed to be her dessert, but it wasn't working that way. She craved something sweet.

She was just about to stand up when Telli slipped around the greenery and sat down at the table uninvited.

Telli had never been good at following the minor rules of rank, particularly when she was tired—and she was usually tired. She had twisted her hair into two buns on the top of her head. The buns were held in place with clips that were too small, so strands of hair were slipping out. The entire hairstyle looked like a disaster unfolding in slow-motion, and it took a lot of Nyguta's own concentration not to stare.

"So," Telli said, without so much as a hello.

She had brought a tray covered in food, so this meeting wasn't as off the cuff as it initially seemed. She had what Nyguta privately called "glop." Some kind of casserole, made out of brown ingredients, and another casserole, with a yellow sauce. One of the casseroles had a lot of garlic. The other had a lot of curry. It was impossible to tell which was which.

Telli also had two slices of the whole wheat bread which was, Nyguta had to admit, one of the mess's specialties.

"So?" Nyguta said.

"So," Telli said, pulling the plates off the tray, and setting the tray on a nearby chair, "this Captain Cooper, he seems like the real deal."

Nyguta suppressed a sigh. Sometimes getting Telli to focus on what she was saying was a chore.

"What do you mean?" Nyguta asked.

"I mean, I've been researching Cooper, the *Ivoire*, and the Fleet." Telli leaned sideways and grabbed a handful of napkins off the tray. Then she frowned, as if she hadn't thought much about what she was doing, and leaned over again, grabbing silverware.

Nyguta was aware that Telli had been researching Cooper. Nyguta had put a number of the research team on Cooper, thinking if she could figure out who he was, she might be able to figure out how he would respond to a threat from her.

"As far as I can tell, looking at all the Fleet records we've acquired over the generations, and looking at our own records, there is no other ship in the entire Fleet *ever* called the *Ivoire*." Telli stuck a spoon in the brown glop, and pulled some chopsticks off the tray to put into the yellow glop.

Nyguta grabbed her own napkin, held it tightly, and dipped the bread again. She was almost out. She wished Telli had come sooner, so that Nyguta could excuse herself and head back to the line without seeming rude.

"And that makes sense, really," Telli said, almost as much to herself as to Nyguta.

"What makes sense, really?" Nyguta asked. She swallowed some irritation. This was going to be one of *those* conversations with Telli. A conversation that would require Nyguta to play catch-up half the time.

"Well, you know, if a captain of a particular ship gets that ship lost and then it's revealed that he did something so heinous that he's court-martialed in absentia, it's not exactly a ship that you'd want to honor, now would you?"

Telli finally looked up. The circles remained under her eyes, but they were very bright. She clearly had enjoyed this particular assignment.

"Okay." Nyguta agreed with Telli's premise, but refrained from pointing out that a premise was not evidence. "Any other Coopers?"

"None," Telli said. "That's the other thing. Apparently this guy never procreated. He's the end of the Cooper line, at least in the Fleet itself. Now, granted, he vanished in what we would call the middle of his life, so there was plenty of time to father little Coopers. But he didn't do it when he was with the Fleet—that I know of."

"What do you mean, that you know of?" Nyguta asked.

"We have Fleet ship records, mostly, and records from the sector bases we took over. Not all of them include family histories." Telli picked up her loaded spoon and shoved some brown glop into her mouth. She barely chewed it before swallowing.

Then she waved the spoon at Nyguta, who leaned back, in case bits of food were still on it.

"And, you know, there's that tendency, especially in the Fleet, for people who leave the actual moving ships to change their names, particularly if they come from some suspect family."

"Like the children of someone who was court-martialed," Nyguta said.

"Exactly," Telli said, snapping the spoon for emphasis. "Which means that the Cooper that we encountered is not related to the earlier Cooper, unless he's the same Cooper, which makes him not a relative, right? But the real deal. Because, I guess you're related to yourself, but not in the way that we're discussing—"

"You've been working for hours, haven't you?" Nyguta said. She'd had circular conversations like this with Telli before, and they always came when Telli had thought herself into little circles. "I'm glad you found time to eat."

"I didn't, actually, but when I got here, everything smelled so good, I realized I couldn't remember when I last ate." She shoveled some more brown glop into her mouth. "Besides," she said, talking around it, "I really like some of this stuff."

Obviously, Nyguta almost said, but didn't because it might've been rude.

"You thought something important enough to find me," she said blandly.

"Yeah, Cooper," Telli said. "I'm ninety percent sure we have the original. Which means that when the *Ivoire* disappeared it went thousands of years into its future. Which sucks for them."

Nyguta let out an involuntary laugh. "Yes," she said. "It does."

"So, if we're planning to battle this Cooper-guy, we're probably safe in assuming he does not have Fleet backing." Telli grabbed a piece of bread and used it to sop up some of the brown glop. Then she shook the dripping bread at Nyguta. "I mean, that sucks too, right? We were all hoping to be the ship that finds the Fleet."

"We might still be that ship," Nyguta said. "You're making up these percentages, right?"

"Based on something like evidence," Telli said. "Our Fleet records are inadequate to say the least for the past two thousand years, but if there were no Coopers back then, then I can safely assume that there are no Coopers now."

"I can't," Nyguta said. "Someone might've taken on the name of an Honored Family."

"I'm pretty sure they don't do that," Telli said. "I never saw an Honored Family mentioned anywhere. I doubt the Fleet has that concept. I thought it was unique to us."

Nyguta let that pass. She had no idea if the Honored Family was unique to the Armada.

"Is there a chance that the *Ivoire* is the same ship and Cooper isn't the same man?" Nyguta asked. "Just someone using an alias."

"Sure." Telli wadded the bread into a soggy ball and shoved the whole thing in her mouth. "But this is something I'm pretty sure of. That ship is not five thousand years old. It's not five thousand years old with fixes or rebuilds. It's about a hundred years old. And its design is ancient. That type of DV-Class ship hasn't been made in the Fleet for at least four thousand years. So, yes, it's possible that the *Ivoire* is the same ship, but it's the ship that moved into the future. So maybe this Cooper is a baby Cooper from whenever they moved into the future. Hmmm. I hadn't thought of that."

She talked fast and around the food so half of what she said was garbled, but her point was made.

The odds were that the *Ivoire* was the same ship that had vanished in its battle against the Ukhandans. That made sense to Nyguta. Disappearing into foldspace was a common tactic in the middle of a heated battle.

But the *Ivoire* had been fired upon, which meant the *anacapa* drive could have been damaged. And if it was, then anything could have happened in foldspace.

If the ship arrived here or in the area—which was near where it was lost—a hundred years ago, then the captain of the *Ivoire* could be the son or grandson of the original Captain Cooper.

And if they were, then they would have learned tactics at their grandfather's knee. He—and the ship—would have survived for decades by being scrappy and quick-thinking.

"All right," Nyguta said, pushing her plate away. Her interest in dessert had faded as her mind got busy with thoughts of the *Ivoire* and Cooper. "I will accept your ninety percent odds."

Telli's eyes widened. "Well, you're the one who asked if the odds were based on anything, and ninety percent is one of those numbers that people throw out. I mean, I can't guarantee—"

Nyguta held up her hand and smiled. "I know that, Anastasia. But I am agreeing with you that the chances are that this Cooper is probably either the original captain of the *Ivoire* or a near descendant."

Telli nodded, then wiped a hand over her mouth, dislodging enough brown glop, apparently, to make her grab a napkin and scrub it off her skin.

"So," Nyguta said, "what I want you to do is coordinate efforts to find me all the information you can on the original Cooper's leadership skills and his tactics."

"From the records?" Telli asked.

"And from the Empire, too," Nyguta said. "We accessed the *Roja's* network, so there should be something in their history. We'll also use what little we have on the *Ivoire* as well."

"What do you want, exactly?" Telli said.

"I want you to gather the information, and before we leave foldspace, I need our engineers to develop an algorithm, predicting his behavior. I need to be able to anticipate what he's going to do, and I don't have the time to study him."

"We should be able to put something together." Telli's eyes had brightened. She loved this kind of challenge.

"We'll share it with the other ships as well," Nyguta said, "but we will have to stress that an algorithm is not the same as their judgement. If they believe we're doing something wrong, they will have to say so."

"Yes, Captain," Telli said in a tone that was much more prim than she usually used.

Nyguta realized at that moment that Telli didn't want to interrupt her by correcting her. Nyguta had been thinking out loud. *She* would have to stress that the algorithm was not the same as judgement, which would probably insult her compatriots. But she needed to do so, just to make sure they were all in agreement.

"I'll make sure the other captains get the algorithm when it's finished," Nyguta said.

Telli smiled, and in that smile was a bit of relief. So she had worried about correcting Nyguta. Sometimes Nyguta couldn't figure out Telli. She didn't worry enough about protocol, and at the same time, she observed protocol at the strangest moments.

"Are you worried about this Cooper?" Telli asked.

"Worried about fighting him?" Nyguta asked.

"I don't know," Telli said. "You seem very focused on him."

Nyguta was focused. Either Cooper and the *Ivoire* were part of the Fleet—which seemed increasingly unlikely—or, according to Atwater, they would lead the Armada to the Fleet.

That too seemed somewhat unlikely. But Nyguta knew what she had to do now.

She had to capture Cooper and his ship.

She needed him to tell her everything he knew.

ARRIVAL

39

COOP ARRIVED IN THE *IVOIRE'S* BRIDGE not ten minutes after leaving the diplomats. He was breathing hard. He had run almost the whole way, except for a short stint in the elevator between decks.

His heart pounded, and he was silently cursing himself. Trekov had said she and her ships would arrive "within the hour" and he had already used twenty-five minutes of that hour.

He wasn't ready, and neither was the Lost Souls Corporation or the Nine Planets or anyone else.

The bridge was empty, which always startled him. The *Ivoire* was not designed to have an empty bridge. It wasn't designed to be abandoned in any way.

The ship was a living, breathing home for hundreds of people—or it should have been. It had once been that, and now it was a tool, one that he wasn't using properly, one he needed to use more.

He hurried through the main aisle to his captain's chair, manually turning on systems as he went. He needed the entire ship to come back to life. Screens up, consoles on, defensive systems at the ready.

He reached the captain's chair and plopped into it. It was easier to run some systems from the chair than it was to stand and monitor them. His hands were shaking just a bit, which he hoped was adrenaline, not his subconscious telling him he had made the wrong decision.

The looks on the faces of the diplomats when he told them about the Fleet made him uncomfortable. He wasn't sure he could trust them to handle any delicate negotiations with the Fleet, not even with Mae in charge. She knew what to do, but she was rusty. Cumex wasn't as rusty, but he didn't know her as well as he knew Mae.

And he needed to be able to trust—on some deep level. He trusted Mae, just not enough.

He sent a systemwide hail to his best bridge crew, except for Lynda Rooney. He needed her to captain the *Shadow*. He needed other good captains as well, but he didn't have enough. He was half tempted to tell Yash to take the *Sove*. But that would require explaining.

All of this would require explaining, and he wasn't sure how to do it.

He needed his crew here, though, so that he could captain the *Ivoire*. He had promised Trekov that she could plant three of her own people on this ship, and he had to be here to monitor them, along with everything else.

He was hoping he would have the time to be cautious, but he was afraid he did not. Before he could even talk to Boss, he had to attend to some other matters. If he didn't, there would be a severe loss of life.

And that would be one of the laws of unintended consequences.

He made himself breathe, slowing his heart rate. He couldn't make decisions out of a sense of panic. He'd learned that a long time ago. Taking a moment to get himself under control would help a lot of people by making him think much more clearly.

He needed a plan to keep the Empire in check. He would have to make that plan with others.

But first, he needed to contact his ships at the border.

And he needed something to tell them.

He glanced around the bridge. It seemed so much smaller without the crew. Smaller and ineffective. It was slightly cold here, and smelled faintly perfumed. Someone had put the wrong chemical order in the cleaners again.

He used that scent, and the slight chill, to ground himself to this moment—not the moment he wanted it to be, not with the perfect crew or the perfect decisions. Not the perfect moment at all.

Then he opened a channel to the commanders of his vessels at the border. He was doing all of this without the permission of the Nine Planets. When they heard about his order, they would go to him or to Ilona Blake to figure out if something had gone wrong.

He hoped they would come to him.

He was going to need Blake, though, to talk to the Nine Planets. He was going to need a lot of things.

The channel opened. He made sure all of the ships were on this particular communication. He didn't want one rogue vessel to make all of his plans go awry.

He could send an individual greeting to each ship, but he did not.

Instead, he launched right into his speech.

"This is Captain Jonathon Cooper of the *Ivoire*," he said. "You can check my credentials, which I am sending as an encrypted part of this message, along with our agreed-upon command code."

He made sure at that moment he was sending the correct code. He was. He was using the code for extreme emergency.

"Within the hour, you will see Empire ships bearing down on your position. I have given them permission through Group Commander Elissa Trekov to cross the border. This is a one-time permission, due to an emergency we're having here at Lost Souls."

He wished he could explain but he didn't dare.

"If any Empire ship fires upon you, do not retaliate immediately. Withdraw and contact me. The ships are supposed to have free passage for this afternoon only. You will understand why after a later communication."

As he sent this, he received contact from the *Kuat*, one of the DV-Class ships that Lost Souls had mostly restored. The contact was encrypted and marked *emergency*. It came through his private communications link.

Captain Cooper, if you are operating under duress, please use the designated code words. We shall issue the appropriate warnings.

He mentally applauded them. That was exactly the kind of message he should have been receiving. He had no idea who was captaining the *Kuat* right now, but whoever it was knew their job.

He sent a second command code, one that included a built-in *all is well* communication.

"The Nine Planets' vessels need to remain at the border, and remain on alert. If you receive a second message from me or from Lost Souls declaring the Empire the enemy again, then destroy the ships here."

He let out a breath. He had no idea if that would happen or not. He doubted it.

"You will receive a second command code, the one for this week, along with that order. Do not act unless you receive it."

He was standing up. He didn't remember rising, but he half-smiled when he realized it. His training had kicked in.

A commander stood when he gave extremely important orders, as he was doing now.

"As for the *Kuat* and the *Xoog*, you need to return here as quickly as possible. I need you battle ready."

Or as battle ready as they could be. Neither ship was at its full compliment. The *Xoog* had received its final rebuild just a month or so ago. It had an even smaller crew contingent than the *Kuat* did.

"Our enemy this day is *not* the Empire," he said. "I repeat. Our enemy is *not* the Empire. We don't know the name of the group threatening us, but they have DV-Class ships as well, rebuilds, with different technology than I have ever seen. When you return to Lost Souls, you will take orders from me, unless I am not in a position to give those orders. I am and will remain onboard the *Ivoire*."

He paused, wondering if he should have said that. But he couldn't imagine fighting any kind of enemy from a static location, like Lost Souls.

"I need you to return immediately," he said. "I hope that I will not require your services, but this situation is fluid, and I need you at Lost Souls in an excess of caution."

He signed off. Then he ran a hand over his face. He had been rotating the young officers who had been on the leadership track on the *Ivoire* into positions of command on the three most active DV-Class vessels here at Lost Souls.

All of those captains had some combat experience, but none in command. He'd figured they could get that experience should there be skirmishes at the border, but there had been none since his truce with the Empire.

So all the would-be captains could do was wargames and simulations, which Coop had insisted on.

But he knew from personal experience that wargames and simulations were not the same as an actual in-person battle.

What a mess.

But he didn't have time to contemplate it. He had been overconfident, and he knew it. He had thought he could handle the Empire—because he had been.

He hadn't thought of the Fleet as a possible problem. He had thought *he* would be able to approach the Fleet, not the other way around.

And of course, he hadn't contemplated the Not-Fleet at all.

He hoped the two DV-Class ships would return fast. He also wished that he had focused more on training crew. He hadn't given it thought because, oddly, he had thought he would have time.

He didn't have a lot of time now. He remained standing, feeling very alone, and contacted Xilvii. Xilvii had known that Coop wanted the defenses shored up. Xilvii hadn't planned on actually fighting in the region near Lost Souls. He had expected Coop to work with the Fleet diplomatically, because Coop had planned to work diplomatically.

Xilvii appeared as a hologram before Coop, lines around his eyes and his mouth.

"I'm not seeing anything Fleet yet," Xilvii said.

"Good," Coop responded. "Because we have a larger problem."

He explained everything to Xilvii, as quickly as he could, about the three ships from the Not-Fleet. Xilvii had been on the mission to Sector Base E-2, so Xilvii knew that the Not-Fleet had pursued them. Coop didn't have to explain that.

But he did have to explain the Empire involvement, and that took more time than he wanted. He tried very hard not to look at the time, clicking away on one of the screens.

To his credit, Xilvii didn't ask if they could trust the Empire. He knew the answer. He also knew that Coop's decision was final.

"I also need you to recalibrate the long-range sensors," Coop said. "You'll need to set them up on the Not-Fleet's specs as well as the specs Boss gave you for the Fleet vessels. I want to know when those ships arrive. I don't want to trust the Empire for that."

"Consider it done," Xilvii said.

Coop trusted him to do that, and do it well. Although, because Coop was the man he was, he would also be using the *Ivoire's* long-range scanners for the exact same search.

Then Xilvii straightened. He made a small, almost involuntary wince. Apparently, he was going to ask a difficult question.

"Am I supposed to talk to Ilona Blake?" he asked.

"No," Coop said. "I've got that."

At least, he hoped he did. Because he was running out of time, quite literally. One thing that seemed to be uniform among every single military person he had ever encountered was their sense of time. They made estimates on the long end of what they could deliver, so that often, they delivered early.

Trekov had said *within the hour*. She hadn't said *in an hour* or *in seventy-five minutes*. She had said *within the hour*.

And they were within the hour right now.

"I only have one more question," Xilvii asked. "I've had some command training. Did you want me to take out the *Madxaf?* Would that be more useful than having me stay here?"

Coop was shaking his head before Xilvii had finished asking the question. "I need you to handle the station's defenses. You did an amazing job a year ago. You'll do the same now."

"If I use the same weapon," Xilvii said, "I'll shut down every ship near Lost Souls, including ours."

"We have other weapons," Coop said. He had made sure of that ear-lier. They weren't as effective, but they would have to do.

Xilvii looked skeptical. But he didn't question. He had his orders. Everyone did.

Except Blake and Boss.

And time was running out.

40

THE FIRST AND ONLY REAL TEST of this agreement that Elissa had made with Captain Cooper would come at the border.

Elissa stood in the command center, filled with her entire staff. She had made it clear she was running this mission. She did so partly because of the tricky nature of the mission, but also because she didn't want anyone else to take the blame with Flag Commander Janik should this mission go awry.

The command center was bustling, the kind of bustling that Elissa liked. Every single console was full, sometimes with several people huddling or conversing, keeping track of all one hundred ships that she had ordered to head into the Nine Planets. She was hoping to peel off one or two, so that they could investigate internal defenses inside the Nine Planets, after she and Cooper defeated the three ships.

If they defeated the three ships.

She paced across the back, so she could monitor screens and workspaces. She would pause occasionally to make sure that the ships she was bringing into the Nine Planets were on their way.

The *Ewing Trekov* had just joined the ships a few minutes ago. Having the ships at her back made her feel calmer. Despite the confidence she had expressed over the deal in her conversation with Paek, she had a nagging feeling that Cooper would best her in this moment as well.

"Commander?" Paek said, as if he heard her thoughts. "We have a message from Yves Beltraire. Did you want me to handle him?"

"No," she said. "I'll take it in the corridor."

She didn't feel like she had enough time to get to her office, especially if Beltraire had bad news for her—not that she knew, exactly, what the bad news would be. She could imagine it, but she had learned long ago to rein in that kind of imagination. Things could get worse on their own.

She didn't need to borrow trouble.

She eased her way past a small group of cadets who huddled near the doorway. They'd been assigned to the *Ewing Trekov* to learn command skills and just happened to find themselves in the middle of an adventure.

Her younger self envied them; her cadet posting hadn't been nearly as interesting.

But because she was the scary Group Commander, she made a point of not smiling at them to reassure them. Instead, she did her job and pretended that they weren't even in the command center.

She wished she had time to give them real work, but she didn't. She passed them, and stepped into the corridor.

It was narrow on this side, and oddly lit. The light was a brownish yellow, as if the coverings hadn't been cleaned for a long time. Even though she knew that wasn't true.

She spun around, made sure no one else was in the corridor—not that it really mattered. She doubted Beltraire could tell her much of anything confidential. But caution was an old friend, one she trusted.

When she was convinced she was alone, she opened the comm.

"I understand you have news," she said.

"Yes," he said. "They've left."

"The three enemy vessels," she said, not quite a question.

"Yes," he said.

"They've left the Room of Lost Souls," she said.

"As we expected," he said. "At the very coordinates where your Captain Cooper disappeared."

She hated that rhetorical trick of Beltraire's, and had called him on it before. She wasn't going to call him on it again because then he would know that he had gotten to her.

"I'm thinking they've installed some kind of doorway that they can trigger," Beltraire said. "That's what it looks like anyway."

Elissa wasn't going to speculate with him. She had more pressing matters on her mind at the moment.

"They arrived on one side of the Room, and have left on another, just like the *Ivoire?*" she asked.

"Technically, they arrived in a much different location than the *Ivoire* did on its last visit," he said.

"But they left in the exact same place," she said.

"Yes," he said. "I think—"

"It's a doorway, I know. You said that." Her tone was drier than she had planned.

She would actually ask Cooper when this battle was over. She had a hunch, though, that the opening only looked like a doorway. It was some other kind of travel portal, one she didn't have time to think about.

"What I would like to know," she said, "is if you know where the ships were heading."

"Probably the same place that the *Ivoire* has gone," he said.

The words sent a chill through her.

The *Ivoire* had gone back to the Nine Planets, which was where she was going.

"Thank you," she said. "I'll take it from here."

"I will be investigating—"

"Yes, I'm sure you will," she said. She didn't have time for this self-important creature. "Just make sure my science vessels return to the room, as well as the military guard."

"I figured you could assign that," he said.

She nearly snapped at him, telling him that she had more pressing concerns, and damn near revealing what those concerns were.

Which was precisely how people like him got information that they were not entitled to. They figured out how to anger someone and then that someone revealed too much in the heat of the moment.

"You figured incorrectly," she said. "You will order their return. If they're not back at the Room soon, I will report you. After you bring them back, you can move on to whatever you do, Yves."

She deliberately used his first name, and deliberately set him down. Once this possible battle in the Nine Planets ended, she would make sure that he had brought her ships back to the Room.

But not now.

Instead, she signed off without so much as a word. He wasn't worth a word.

She was about to head into the command center, when she realized her irritation was making her careless.

She needed to tell Cooper that the ships had left the Room, that they were on their way.

She had no idea how long it took ships to travel through that "doorway," if indeed that was what it was, but she had a hunch it didn't take all that long.

She would need to contact Cooper from her office. All the conversations she had with him needed to be recorded, just for safety's sake.

And she needed Paek with her.

She sent for him, on their link, then headed to the office, to contact Cooper one last time.

41

I'M SUPPOSED TO BE WITH MIKK, trying to figure out what exactly happened in those last fifteen minutes in the Boneyard, but instead, I'm in Ilona Blake's office, getting a dressing down.

Okay, it's really not a dressing down. First, she technically doesn't have the power to dress me down. She works for me. But I have given her a lot of latitude over the years.

That latitude is something I'm currently regretting.

I'm standing in the middle of her office, which is really more like an office suite, hell, more like an office floor. It seems every time I visit her in her office, her office suite/floor has gotten more expansive.

It curves around some poles in the center of Lost Souls, and if we go outward, we can look out a few windows. Ilona isn't about windows. She's about walls and screens and things. There are floating charts on one wall, and diagrams of the future Lost Souls station on another.

Then there are the diagrams of the various ships, along with a hierarchy of personnel, both the personnel that we have and the personnel needed.

I have no idea why she uses floating charts for all of this, nor do I understand why she uses it as decoration, but she does. She has also accumulated some weird knick-knacky things from various ships we've recovered. Odd shaped light fixtures and plates that she has put on little stands, and some jewelry hanging off pegs.

More inspiration, I suppose, but the one time I asked her about it, she told me that a lot of beautiful things got abandoned along with those ships, and she finally decided that someone had to give those things a home.

She sits behind a broad brown desk which is either made of mahogany or is the best fake wood I have ever seen. She keeps it polished to a sheen.

She has two consoles on top of the desk, not built into it, which looks uncomfortable to me, but hey, it's her office, not mine.

She's also taken to wearing less militaristic clothing, looking a lot more like the Blake I'd first hired years ago. Now she wears colors and flowing garments, which simply aren't practical in many circumstances.

Today's outfit is a pale teal with sleeves that drape like blankets hanging off the side of a bed. Her hair is pulled back and her expression is tired.

She's worried—we all are—about the impending arrival of the Fleet, but that's not why I'm here.

I'm here because I want a ship. I really don't want to wait until Mikk and I have finished the research. I want to head back to the Boneyard now.

I'm restless, and I hate waiting, and if the Fleet is going to come after anyone, then they should come after me.

Besides, there's a lot to explore out there, and nothing to explore here.

It'll take weeks to put a ship together—I know that—but if I get the process started now, it should bring down my restlessness, at least a little.

"Let's set common sense aside," Ilona said, as if she were my parent instead of my employee. Common sense being not antagonizing the Fleet or whomever those ships are, all over again.

Yeah, let's set that aside. Because I'd like to.

"The other issues," she is saying, "are personnel and money. Coop has already made it clear that we need to staff up our vessels and we need to do it now. We don't have a big enough defense, not our defense systems on the station, and not with the ships. We don't have enough trained people—"

355

"I was at the meeting," I say quietly. I hate it when anyone assumes that I haven't been paying attention. I have been paying attention. I'm just not that interested.

"Then you know that we can't willy-nilly send people to the Boneyard, even if we had a good reason to go."

The "even if" makes me bristle, as I suppose it's meant to. I'm pacing—of course I am—because I don't want to sit down in this vast office suite/floor and get smothered by all the stuff.

Besides, if I sit down, I acquiesce to her power, which is not something I'm willing to do.

"The other issue is?" I ask, not because I'm interested, but because I don't feel like arguing right now.

"The other issue is money. We have a lot, but money is finite." Ilona tucks her hands inside those massive sleeves as if she's cold. "We're going to have to move resources so that we can rebuild more ships. We're also going to have to recruit, which costs money, and pay the new recruits— also, money—and figure out how, exactly—"

I wave a hand. I don't want to hear it. I hired her to handle all of this, and I'll walk away as easily as I have in the past.

I don't care about money, which Ilona knows. I never have. Money is a means to an end for me, not an end in and of itself. I've only noticed money when I need some to get something done.

I suppose, technically, I need some right now. I will take my usual crew back to the Boneyard, with or without Ilona's approval, but I'd like some of the *Ivoire* personnel, Zaria Diaz and a medic or two, as well as someone to handle weapons and things I don't want to think about.

"You're just worried that we're going to be in danger," I say.

"Damn right," she says. "What you're suggesting is reckless and impractical and defies common—"

"Common sense, I know." I stop in front of her massive polished desk. It smells faintly of lemons, which I find weird. Must be some kind of cleaner. "But if I had what you folks call common sense, you wouldn't be here, Lost Souls wouldn't be here, Coop and the *Ivoire* would still be stuck in foldspace, and the universe as we know it would be very different."

"And we wouldn't be vigilantly watching for five Fleet vessels to bear down on us, and maybe blow us to smithereens," she says.

"Coop thinks he knows how to handle that," I say, which is probably denial rather than the truth, but I want him and Yash to handle it, not me and Ilona, which is another reason we're having this discussion right now instead of a few weeks from now. She needs the distraction too.

And she's looking distracted at the moment. She's frowning and staring at something on her console.

She pokes at the screen. I know that movement. It's a denial in and of itself. *Surely*, the movement says, *what I'm seeing is not real.*

"The five ships?" I ask, wincing as I do so. I really don't want to know the answer. I don't want the ships to be here, and I don't want to be the one who brought them, and I mostly certainly don't want them to muddy up my planned return trip to the Boneyard.

Ilona shakes her head once, very slowly. Then again, only it's a half shake, her gaze still down as if she can't believe what she's seeing.

Her skin has gone gray, her lips bloodless.

"The Empire has crossed the border," she says.

"What?" I cross the office, go around the desk and poke the damn screen myself. Finger hard, resetting everything, and still the data stream shows exactly what she's talking about.

Empire ships, one hundred of them, have crossed into the Nine Planets.

And what's worse is that our ships have gotten out of the way. They allowed it.

There was no defense at all.

Ilona looks at me, stunned, her mouth open, eyes wide. I feel a surge of anger. I didn't hire her so that she could freeze in an emergency. Not that she usually does.

But this isn't her kind of emergency at all.

It's not really mine either.

My stomach clenches, and I slap my hand on another part of Ilona's console, summoning Coop from wherever he is.

He doesn't respond, and I hope to hell that means he's busy guarding us from these damn Empire ships, and not because he's taken to ignoring my hails. Or that he's gone out of communications range while he's working on something to do with the Fleet.

I slam my hand down again, and mutter, "Dammit, Coop, where the hell are you?"

And then he answers, not an audio chirrup, but a full hologram. He waivers into place. He's on the bridge of the *Ivoire*—I recognize the chair behind him, as well as some of the consoles.

"One-hundred Empire ships have crossed the border," I say. "I hope to hell you already know that and are doing something about it."

His expression is odd, closed-off, and a little—soft? Apologetic? Something I have never seen on his face before.

"One-hundred-and-one," he says.

"Fine, one-hundred-and-one," I say. "I don't really care except that there's a lot of them, and not a lot of us, and what the hell happened on the border? Wait, don't tell me. Just tell me how we're going to handle this."

That expression hardens into something fiercer. His gaze flickers to one side, and I realize he can see Ilona beside me.

She seems to be a lot more focused now that he's before us.

"We're not going to 'handle' this," he says. "I asked them to come here."

"You *what*?" I reach for the console. Maybe this isn't Coop. Maybe he's been compromised somehow. Maybe this is a cruel prank. He's worked against the Empire almost from the moment he's been here— hell, if you count the battle at Vaycehn, he *has* fought against the Empire from the moment he arrived.

"I asked them to come," he says. I recognize his tone. It's strained and almost dismissive. He clearly doesn't want to have this conversation, and probably believes we don't have time for it, which I suspect we don't, given the speed at which the Empire ships are traveling.

"Why in God's name would you invite them here?" I ask.

"And open the border?" Ilona says. "We have an agreement with the Nine Planets."

"We do," Coop says. "I wouldn't be doing this if it weren't an emergency."

"One-hundred Empire ships is a goddamn emergency," I say.

"No," he says. "Three Not-Fleet ships is a damn emergency, along with five possible Fleet vessels, all converging on us."

"Three Not-Fleet...?" My brain isn't making the jump. "What are you talking about?"

He glances over his shoulder, nods at someone, and then turns back to us. "Remember I told you we went into the area around the Room of Lost Souls to escape the Not-Fleet?"

I nod. I'm in as much of a hurry as he seems to be.

"Apparently, we were being pursued. We shook them off, but the Not-Fleet had a run-in with the Empire and destroyed seven of their ships."

"And I'm supposed to be sorry about that?" I ask. My entire history with the Empire has been one of loss and imbalance, of fighting to keep them *out* of my life, not deeply in it.

"Those ships are coming here," he says. "And we're not set up for them. Plus, the ships you've led here—"

"We don't know they're coming," I say. "They should've been here by now."

"There's no should have with an *anacapa* drive and the Fleet," he says. "Besides, the Empire was going to invade anyway. We violated our truce with them."

"You violated it," Ilona says, her tone flat. "You made that decision unilaterally."

"It was the only way to save the *Ivoire*," he says. "We did that, and got here, but now, with three different much larger forces headed our way at the same time, I had to make some decisions."

"Without us," Ilona says, which is a good thing that she spoke first, because I would have been a lot more personal and a lot more petulant.

"I'm the one who handles our defenses," he says, "and we do not have the capability to fight the Empire, those Fleet ships we saw, and the Not-Fleet one at a time, let alone all at the same time."

I'm getting my feet under me in this conversation. Anger clarifies things for me; it always has, and probably always will.

"How did you know that the Not-Fleet is coming?" I ask.

"Group Commander Elissa Trekov contacted me," he says. "She should have just come through the border with an invasion force—"

"Like she did right now," Ilona says.

"It's not an invasion force," he says, and then waves a hand at us. "Let me, okay. We have almost no time here."

I glance at the console. He's not kidding. The Empire is moving much faster than I expect.

"But she didn't invade," he says. "She saw what those ships can do. She's afraid there's more of them, and she might be right. She wants to stop them from invading the Empire."

"So let her," I say.

"They're not after the Empire," he says. "They're after me."

There's nothing I can say to that. Ilona seems like she's struck into silence too. I'm all over the place emotionally; I feel betrayed. This is my business, my home, my universe, and he's messing with it, without permission.

And at the same time, he seems quite certain of himself.

"What exactly did you do?" Ilona asks in that same tight voice.

He looks annoyed. "I told you when I got back," he says. "I told you again when I told Boss."

He hates using my nickname. That he is doing so is a sign that he's very stressed. He looks over his other shoulder this time, and nods again.

I realize, as I watch that, that he is greeting the *Ivoire's* bridge crew. It seems he told a lot of people about the Empire's arrival, before he told me and Ilona.

"You're sure those three ships aren't tied to the forces Boss found?" Ilona asks.

"They come from vastly different places," he says.

"Still," Ilona says.

"From different sectors," he says. "Very far away from each other."

Ilona seems like she's about to say more, but I forestall it with a hand on her arm.

"Trekov told you about the ships?" I ask, feeling slightly queasy.

"Yes," he says.

"How do you know this wasn't some kind of ploy to get an invasion force into the Nine Planets without us putting up any kind of fight?"

Irritation crosses his face. If the bridge crew is arriving, then they can hear this discussion.

"I've thought of that," he says, "and we'll deal with it after the ships are gone."

"So you think this is an invading force," I say, maybe a little too belligerently.

"I think it could turn into one, under the right circumstances." He sounds like Captain Cooper now, a man I barely know. "But I've seen the footage of the ships, and I've verified the telemetry. There are three Not-Fleet ships. They just entered foldspace near the Room, and they're on their way here."

"I'm sure you believe that," Ilona says, "but—"

"But nothing," he snaps. "We don't have the time for this discussion. We are going to deal with these ships, with the help of the Empire. I will be in charge. You don't have to like it, but you should take a deep breath and think about it. I'm the only one with enough experience to deal with any kind of battle."

Implied are the words, *and you've thought so in the past.*

"What happens if those five Fleet ships arrive?" Ilona asks.

"I've got that handled," he says.

"Handled?" That unsettled feeling remains. "What do you mean, handled?"

He looks at me, a clear but silent order to stand down. If he's right, if those three ships are coming, then he's right about something else. We can fight later.

I make myself take a deep breath. He's fighting on at least three fronts. He has to keep the Empire under control. He needs to get rid of the Not-Fleet ships, and he's facing what might be a personal dream—hooking back up with the actual Fleet itself.

I have to step past myself or we're not going to make it through this.

"What do you need me to do?" I ask.

My tone is different because my attitude is different. Ilona glances over at me, almost in shock. Or maybe she is in shock. She hasn't expected that of me.

He looks at me as well, as if my shift startles him. Then he smiles, just a little smile, and it's just for me. It's a *thank-you*, maybe, or a *I-knew-I-could-count-on-you*.

"I need you and your team in the *Madxaf*," he says. "We don't have enough people to properly staff the DV-Class ships, but we can use the weaponry and the equipment. I need you to monitor the area. The moment those ships come out of foldspace—"

"You'll see it," I say.

"But I might be busy," he says. "I need you as backup."

I nod. "What about Yash?"

"I'll need her on the *Ivoire*," he says. "I haven't contacted her yet."

Which makes me even more uncomfortable. Usually he tells her everything.

"I take it Lynda's on the *Shadow?*" I say.

"Yes." He glances over his shoulder a third time, and this time, his greeting nod is curt. He's feeling the press of time, much more than the rest of us are.

"Who is on the *Sove?*" I ask.

"No one," he says. "We don't have enough personnel."

"We need someone there, even if it's junior crew members." I turn to Ilona. "You figure it out."

"What?" she says.

"You've been hiring personnel. Get the best you've got onto the *Sove*."

"Wait," Coop says. "I'll need someone to command the *Sove*. Someone who knows how to follow Fleet orders."

"Use Diaz," I say. "If you've got Yash, you don't need a second competent engineer."

His smile is weary this time. "You can be so naïve," he says, and I bristle. "Battle is complicated. I have no idea if I'll need—"

"It doesn't matter what battle is," I say. "We have limited capacity and we have to use it as best we can. I'm going to get my team to the *Madxaf*. What else do you want Ilona to do?"

"After she gets the *Sove's* crew?" he asks. "Stay out of the way."

Ilona looks at me, offended. He's right. That moment of anger following a freeze is the last thing Coop needs as he fights this.

"After you get crew members onto the *Sove*," I say to her, "make sure you contact the Nine Planets. I'm sure they're panicked right about now."

"And tell them what?" she snaps. "That we authorized an invasion?"

"If that's how you want to play it," I say. "But I'd rather you were a little more positive."

Coop barks out a surprised laugh, and then he becomes a lot more serious. "I'll be in touch with you and the rest of the team," he says to me. "I'm hoping that we'll get through this quickly."

Which means he doesn't think we will.

"Me, too," I say. I glance at the console before me. The Empire is almost here, and we don't really have a plan.

Well, Coop probably does, but he's not sharing it.

He's right about me not knowing anything about battles. I don't fight them. I leave before things get too difficult.

I wish we can do that here—all of us. I'd pick up Lost Souls and move it elsewhere.

This, *this*, is why I never stay in one place for very long, why I live on my ship when I can. When life throws challenges at me, I can leave the ones I don't want to face behind.

Ilona is watching me. I have no idea if she can see what I'm feeling on my face.

"We have to get organized real fast," I say to her. "Get Diaz."

Ilona nods and turns away from me.

I cross her office, then glance at it and its ridiculous size, wondering if I'll ever see it again.

This entire situation that Coop has set up could go very, very, very wrong.

In fact, with only a bit of time to contemplate it, I can't see any way in which it can go right.

I straighten my shoulders and let myself out of the office. To the *Madxaf* it is, then, much as I would prefer my own ship, the *Nobody's Business Two*. I'll follow Coop's instructions, only because I can't figure out anything else to do.

42

"MAKE-WORK." YASH'S VOICE ECHOED THROUGH THE BRIDGE.

Coop had his back to her, so he could safely close his eyes and hope for a lot of strength. Yash had entered the bridge of the *Ivoire* without so much as a hello. Instead, she went after him.

"You're giving them all make-work when it's pretty clear that we're all going to die?"

He didn't have time for the drama and yet, it seemed, he couldn't avoid it. He turned.

The bridge was mostly full, but the current bridge crew was not his best bridge crew. Lynda Rooney was helming the *Shadow*. Xilvii, who had acquitted himself well on the last trip, was manning Lost Soul's defenses.

At least Anita Tren was here, at her normal console which had been reconfigured for her small size. Kjersti Perkins stood next to him as an Acting First Officer should. He'd appointed her because he trusted her more than anyone else on the bridge except Tren.

Everyone else was a lower-level officer, not ready for promotion had they stayed with the Fleet, but promoted here from necessity. Coop barely registered their faces. If he looked too hard, he would get lost in regret.

He should have run battle simulations. He should have taken them out on training missions. Hell, he should have had everyone stay on board the ship, and do their best work as if they were still moving, rather than letting them run loose on Lost Souls.

"Since when did you become a pessimist?" he said to Yash, trying to shut her down.

"Since one hundred Empire ships barreled across the border, and all I got was a coded summons from the person who supposedly had my back." Yash's face was flushed. "You didn't ask me if we could handle three Not-Fleet vessels."

"It's not that simple," he said, "and I don't have time to argue. Besides, we also need to prepare for those five vessels that might be coming here from the Boneyard."

"I could do that from my lab." Yash was still standing near the doors to the bridge. "Oh, wait! I *was* doing that from my lab."

"This takes priority," Coop said. He needed to cut Yash off. She was taking liberties she never would have taken before they arrived in this timeline. "I need you in Engineering."

"Then why did you have me report to the bridge?" she asked. "To hear the end of your *mea culpa* with Boss?"

And Blake. If only he were that devious. He wasn't.

"I needed you here so that I could brief you, with the rest of the team," he said. "Only you're late, and I don't have time. Someone else can catch you up."

"I heard a lot of it," she said. "We have no good options."

He wasn't going to agree or disagree. He'd had this conversation with himself during the discussion with Trekov. If the Empire had come in at full complement on the other side, Lost Souls would not have survived.

At least right now, he had a fighting chance.

"We still have setup to do," He wasn't about to tell her that the moment the Empire arrived, he would have to take on three observers. If Yash was angry about all of this, she would be furious about the observers. "Get your best team to Engineering."

"My best team retired years ago," Yash said.

Yeah, I get that, he almost said, but bit it back. He didn't want to insult the crew members who had shown up.

"You can help us, Yash," he said tightly, "or you can get out of the way. Go back to your lab on Lost Souls and pretend none of this is happening."

Her face settled into something sharp and furious. "You're a son of a bitch, Coop."

Using his nickname was deliberate. So was the way she spun, heading back out the door. He had insulted her, so she insulted him back.

They were tense and they were out of practice with this kind of crisis. He needed military discipline back, and he needed it now.

Yash was gone; he couldn't yell at her.

"All right," he said to the assembled bridge crew. "We're running this operation, including all one-hundred-and-one vessels from the Empire. I want you, Teresa, to monitor everything the Empire does."

He had to turn slightly to see Teresa Bollinger. She was lanky, with questionable posture, but she had the ability to move from job to job with ease.

That was one reason why he had chosen her to join the bridge crew weeks ago. Of course he hadn't had time to train her the way he would have liked.

"If it seems like any of those ships are veering off, not following the plan, looking to move deeper into the Nine Planets, you need to let me know," he said.

"Yes, Captain," she said.

He glanced at the Empire ships. They had almost arrived.

"We have one other wrinkle," he said, suddenly glad that Yash was not on the bridge any longer. "We will have three Empire observers on the bridge during this entire battle."

Perkins frowned. Tren's mouth opened, as if she were going to object, and then closed. No one spoke, although most of the crew looked at him as if he had lost his mind.

"That was part of our agreement," he said. "We are not going to discuss anything *anacapa* while they are here, at least as a separate drive, nor do we mention foldspace if we can at all avoid it. I'm going to give my orders to you by command sequence numbers as well as defense sequence. I hope to hell you're up to date on those. If not, get up to speed quickly and if that's not possible, set up some kind of coded cheat sheet, because I don't want the Empire to know all of the things we can do. Is that clear?"

He got nods and yessirs. Three of the younger officers suddenly bent over their consoles, apparently to set up those cheat sheets.

"That seems like a hell of an agreement to make," Perkins said to him, rather quietly. "I assume there's a method behind it."

She did not ask a direct question, but she was asking a question. He suppressed a sigh. He hadn't realized just how lax discipline had become on his ship.

He said softly, "The Empire was about to retaliate for our intrusion at Starbase Kappa. I managed to turn that around."

Perkins's eyes widened. "Well done, sir," she said. "Three threats are now two."

"Two-point-five," he said. "I don't completely trust Trekov and I'm sure she doesn't entirely trust me."

Not that it mattered. They had to get through this.

He was as prepared as he was going to be. He was ready. His crew was ready.

He just wasn't sure exactly what he was ready for.

Now, he joined the rest of his bridge crew in studying his console. He was going to assume that the Fleet would lag. Or maybe not arrive at all. Or, if he was lucky, listen to his diplomats.

He needed to get the Empire in line before the Not-Fleet ships showed up.

He had gotten his teams lined up as best he could. He had an idea what to do.

He hoped to hell he would have enough time to execute it.

43

THE FIRST THING THAT ELISSA NOTICED as the *Ewing Trekov* arrived at the coordinates Captain Cooper had sent was that the Lost Souls Corporation was much bigger than she expected. Two space stations, not one, both in stationary orbit over Odite.

The stations were among the largest space stations she had ever seen. Ships similar to the *Ivoire*, in partial states of repair, huddled against the stations' sides, on an exterior docking ring, probably used for less valuable and strange ships.

They seemed small next to the stations, and Elissa had thought nothing could make those ships seem small.

The *Ivoire* itself floated just outside the coordinates that Cooper had sent her. He had also sent her a deployment packet, with battlestations and the loose outline of a battle plan. In it, he had mentioned that the observers on his ship might have to relay some of the commands to her.

Apparently he was worried that the enemy vessels would somehow get ahold of these plans. She didn't entirely understand the worry, but she didn't know the capabilities of these ships either.

She hoped that would change by day's end.

She had passed the deployment plan to her captains as if the plan were her own. They hadn't questioned her, but they might have been within their rights to do so.

The deployment plan was extremely unconventional. With one hundred ships, the Empire generally used a square or rectangular model—five ships wide, four ships tall, five rows long. If need be, a row could peel off, fight its own battle, make its own formation.

Sometimes the rows became a fence or a bridge, something long and secure.

Cooper's plan required the Empire vessels to form a loose ring around Odite, outside of Odite's gravity well. He left the position of the *Ewing Trekov* up to Elissa, telling her that she could either be far from the battle zone, between her ships and the planet itself, or out front, like the *Ivoire* would be.

In fact, Cooper appeared to have five active ships similar to the *Ivoire*. These ships were placed in front of the Empire vessels, facing away from the Lost Souls space stations and Odite itself.

Everything formed a circle, with points in front of the circle. There was nothing above or below the circle, no real solid geometric formation. Just ships, facing toward an attacker—if the attacker was going to appear outside of that ring.

Elissa's worry was that the attackers would appear *inside* the ring. Afterall, the enemy vessels had the same capability as the *Ivoire* for long distance travel. If that travel wasn't composed of doorways, if it was something else like a transporter, then the enemy vessels could appear as close to Odite as they wanted.

Surely, Cooper would have thought of that. Surely, he would be protecting against it.

As she thought about it, she realized he had not included two other lines of defense in his plans. She knew, from experience, that Lost Souls had its own defensive systems. Odite probably did as well.

Cooper had probably adjusted for them in his plan. He expected both Odite and Lost Souls to carry their own weight—something Empire commanders never did.

The difference here, of course, was that Cooper appeared to be in charge of all three layers of defense—the ships, the space stations, and the planet.

When she received the deployment packet, she wondered if he expected her to argue with him or consult on it. There was no invitation to do so, and he had stressed in their negotiation that he would be in charge of the fight against the three enemy vessels.

He probably did not want her to question, not that it mattered. Her strategy questions would come later, after the battle—if there was one—was over.

There was a lot missing here. The formation was intact. The actual plans were not.

The *Ewing Trekov* was a command vehicle, not a warship, although it could defend itself, perhaps better than most ships.

She decided the *Ewing Trekov* would place itself behind her ships, between the space stations and the circle itself. The *Ewing Trekov* would be on the *Ivoire* section of the battlefield. She wanted to observe Cooper in action one more time, even if being near the *Ivoire* might be one of the most dangerous positions in the entire battlefield.

The command center still bustled, only now, the screens that surrounded her on all sides alternated between telemetry, and views of the other ships, just the way that the Empire usually did things in battle.

She had ordered Paek to make sure an entire subgroup monitored the Nine Planets themselves, particularly the space beyond Odite.

She wanted to make certain that Cooper's strange battlefield configuration didn't make her ships too vulnerable to attack from behind while they were dealing with the enemy vessels in front.

Not that she knew exactly what "in front" and "behind" meant in these circumstances. For all she knew, the enemy vessels could suddenly appear above her, and attack from there.

She just wanted to make sure that the Nine Planets did not take advantage of her ships' vulnerability and attack from a completely different angle.

Although, she had studied both Cooper and the Nine Planets. Aside from their magical weapon (and that was a major aid, since the weapon could destroy a lot of ships with one blast), they did not seem to have a large force.

Taking that weapon into consideration, this deployment was logical. The *Ivoire*-type ships, the Dignity Vessels, would release the weapons *toward* the enemy vessels, and the power coming from those weapons would not hit other ships in the formation.

The comm link that she had sent to Cooper chirruped. She leaned forward and activated it. Paek moved closer to her, his expression flat. He leaned in, touched the console, and looped himself into the conversation without asking her permission.

Clearly, he remembered her admonition to monitor everything. He was going to make certain that she had the protection of his observations, if it came to that.

"Welcome to Lost Souls, Commander," Cooper said, sounding cheerful. She noted that he did not activate any kind of video link. "Do not get too comfortable here."

Banter. She hadn't expected banter.

"We don't have time for levity, Captain," she said, sounding prim, which she immediately regretted. "I have been notified that the enemy vessels have left the area around the Room of Lost Souls. They left the same way that you did, at the very same coordinates."

There was a half second of silence, before he said, "Well, then, we'd best get to it. If you want observers on my ship, you'll need to send them now. Use your smallest vessel. We'll be expecting it."

Then he signed off.

If. As if she didn't want observers, as if this plan would work without them.

She looked at Paek. His expression still remained unreadable. They had talked about the observers before, but had not made any final choices.

"I have given it a lot of thought," he said. "I would like to be on that ship."

She hadn't put Paek's name into contention. She needed him at her side. But he had a point: at her side in this instance might be in her place, observing Captain Cooper.

"Sub-Lieutenant Bahe will be able to assist you," Paek said, as if he needed to convince Elissa. "I have discussed it with her."

"Your suggestion is a good one," Elissa said, feeling a pang. She wanted him beside her during the upcoming battle. She had come to rely on him, probably in an unhealthy way.

She would worry about him over there. The three observers could become prisoners of Captain Cooper if something went truly awry.

Paek knew that. She had discussed it with him as they were trying to figure out who the observers would be.

"I worry, though," she said. "You have a lot of valuable information."

He smiled, just a little. They had already discussed how advanced Cooper's technology seemed to be. The information that could be compromised was more tactical than technological.

And truly, what tactics did they need to hide from Cooper? He had a different agenda than most other commanders she had encountered in her long career. He didn't seem to want to destroy the Empire. He just wanted it to leave the Nine Planets alone.

"I'm not the only one," Paek said. "Anyone you send—"

"I know." They'd had that discussion too. She already knew who the other two would be. Leticia Honoré, a weapons specialist, and Maliu Faifai, an engineer. It wouldn't hurt to have a pure soldier at their side.

Elissa let out a sigh. Of all the decisions she had to make today, this one felt the hardest. Maybe because it was the last one she actually had time to contemplate. Any future decisions she would make would be in the heat of battle—she assumed, anyway.

"All right," she said. "You can go. But I want to hear from you regularly."

Paek half-nodded and half-bowed. "I will be as communicative as possible."

Which might mean that he wouldn't be communicative at all. Sometimes Elissa wondered if she was outsmarting herself, by sending these folks over.

By being here at all.

But it was too late. The decision was made.

"Get the other two," she said. "And you heard Cooper. The smallest ship."

"The smallest military vessel," he said, almost like a clarification.

"Not any of the fighters," she said. "Something with good defensive capability."

She half expected her people to flee the *Ivoire*. She wanted them to have strong enough shielding to return to her.

Paek was already halfway to the door.

"Sub-Lieutenant," she said loudly enough to stop him. Then, softer, "Tawhiri."

He turned his head so that he could see her out of the corner of his eye. He still looked like he was in motion, even though he was not.

"Group Commander?" he said, apparently choosing to be formal.

"Be safe," she said.

They both knew that wasn't possible, but it was her way of trusting him. Her way of letting him know that she cared, not just as his commander, but as one person to another.

The side of his mouth turned up in a smile. "I will," he said, and then let himself out of the command center.

She stared at the door a minute too long, resisting the impulse to call him back.

This was one of those change moments. If things went awry—and maybe even if they didn't—everything would be different afterwards.

She held onto this moment, this last little bit of *now* before it became something else entirely.

Then she turned back to the screens of the command center, forcing herself to think of the battle ahead.

44

I STEP ONTO THE BRIDGE OF THE *MADXAF*, and realize immediately that I am making a mistake. The only reason I don't turn around is simple:

My team is here.

Orlando stands near the captain's chair, with Mikk beside him. Tamaz hovers near a console. Roderick is standing near one of the large screens, hands on his hips as he studies something I can't quite see.

Fahd Al-Nasir is consulting with someone I don't recognize, probably sent over by Ilona to help with the technical side of the *Madxaf*. Nyssa Quinte leans against another console, as if she doesn't want to be here either.

The surprise is Denby. I would have thought that he would have joined Coop on the *Ivoire*, or been required to be with Coop, instead of me.

Denby has a holoscreen open before him, with all of the Empire ships displayed in a wide circle around Odite. Each of Lost Soul's functional Dignity Vessels is supposed to be out front, ahead of some of those ships, which just plain makes me nervous.

Coop might trust Elissa Trekov, but I sure as hell don't. I've spent my entire life pushing back against the Empire.

I understand why he made this agreement. I even understand why he thinks it's a good one. But I can't help the way I'm feeling.

Mikk turns, almost as if he senses me standing there.

"Boss?" he asks.

There are two other people on the bridge that I don't know—a man and a woman. They look familiar. I've seen them around and maybe even been introduced to them. But I don't know them.

That's definitely Ilona's doing. She has probably salted the ship with trainees or whatever Coop would call them. People with some expertise on Dignity Vessels, more than my people have, and who are probably going to be useful in this upcoming battle.

Mikk is watching me, maybe because I haven't answered him. Nyssa has turned her attention to me as well.

I look past both of them, at the housing for the *anacapa* drive. This bridge is bigger than my single ship. The bridge has room for more crew members than I have worked with on any team in my entire career.

I know what we're supposed to do. I've even piloted the *Shadow* a few times, just to get the experience. I understand how Dignity Vessels work, and I know how very powerful they are.

But I don't belong here. I don't care how much experience I have or don't have.

My talents will be wasted here.

I let out a breath, then beckon Mikk. He walks up the aisle, and to my slight annoyance, Nyssa joins him. That makes me wonder if she's worried about my health.

Half the team still worries about my health after the near-death experience I had in the Boneyard. I suppose I would worry too, but I wouldn't coddle. I hate being coddled and they know that.

Nyssa knows that. Yet she does it anyway.

Just as Mikk reaches me, I say softly, "I'm not staying."

That disapproving look I'm becoming used to covers his face. He doesn't even try to hide the expression.

"Coop needs us," Mikk says. "He doesn't have enough—"

"I know," I say. "I want you all to stay here."

"Where are you going?" he asks.

I stare at him, not wanting to lie to him. He stares back. He's not going to back down.

"I'm going to my single ship," I say quietly. Nyssa turns her head slightly, as if she can't hear me clearly, which is what I hope. I don't want my entire team to argue with me.

"What the hell?" Mikk says, louder than I want him to.

Orlando looks over his shoulder. I recognize his expression. He's going to join us if this goes on much longer.

"These Not-Fleet ships that are coming are Dignity Vessels, right?" I ask.

Mikk shrugs one shoulder. "I know probably less than you do."

"And," I say, "we still have those ships that chased us out of the Boneyard."

He waits, thank heavens, because I don't want to hear the small objections. Rodrigo exchanges glances with Nyssa, who shrugs as well. I think she can only hear part of this conversation.

"My ship does not have any Fleet tech." I say that with an urgency. I want Mikk to make the leap. No Fleet tech means that I might see things on my telemetry that none of the other ships can see.

"Neither does the Empire," Mikk says.

"Yes, they do," I say. "They have stealth tech, and they don't realize that it's based on *anacapa* energy. They've woven stealth tech throughout all of their systems."

His eyes narrow. He glances at Nyssa whose mouth forms a thin line. I'm not sure if she's disapproving of my argument or of the fact that she can't hear my argument.

"Then we should be on the *Business*," Mikk says, meaning the *Nobody's Business Two,* my main ship. "All of us."

I shake my head. "Coop needs the *Madxaf*. His plan won't work right without it, and we don't have the personnel to handle it. I'm useless on a Dignity Vessel. I can do something out of my single ship."

Mikk opens his mouth to argue with me. I see the frustration building in his eyes. He closes his mouth, then shakes his head.

"Just get up here, Boss," Orlando says, sounding truly annoyed. "We don't have time to mess with these plans. For God's sake, we have Empire ships all around us."

We do and that makes me nervous. This whole thing does. But I'm afraid that we can't see what is actually coming at us.

The Empire reported that there were three ships. Not anyone else. And if those ships have the same kind of masking tech that the Boneyard has, then we won't see the enemy (if indeed they are) until they're right on top of us.

Mikk is weighing my arguments. Orlando looks over his shoulder, then looks down at his console. He gives Tamaz an exasperated look, as if Tamaz is somehow at fault. Rodrigo curses under his breath, but loudly enough for all of us to guess at the intent.

"Just…stay behind the Empire ships, okay?" Mikk says. "You don't want them to attack you by accident."

He's giving in. Which is easier than I thought.

"I doubt they'll even be able to see me," I say.

"Boss," Mikk says, chiding me.

"If you're going to leave the *Madxaf*," Orlando says, blowing all of my illusions that the team couldn't hear the conversation, "you want me to let Coop know?"

"No," I say a bit too quickly. "I don't want him to know. He will understand that I'm not the one in charge of the *Madxaf*. I don't have enough experience with these vessels."

"Not many of us do," Mikk mutters.

"That's what Gustav is for," I say. "He's the best we've got."

Denby looks up in surprise. The surprise is so deep and profound that it makes me wonder if I have ever given him a compliment.

I tilt my head slightly and smile at him, acknowledging him. He smiles in return.

"So," I say, waving a hand awkwardly at my team, "you've got this. Do what Coop says and you'll all be fine."

I hope. I'm not the give-speeches-and-rouse-the-troops type and we all know it. I wave my hand and leave the bridge, feeling the tension leave my shoulders.

But apparently, I'm not done. Nyssa joins me.

"I'm worried about you going out there alone," she says. "Maybe we should take one of the smaller ships together."

She's not much of a diver. She's the medic, and she did save my life at the Boneyard. She's kept a wary eye on me ever since.

"I'll be all right," I say.

"If something happens, you'll be alone." She sounds terribly distressed.

"Something?" I ask. "We're going to be in the middle of something happening. Technically, we already are in the middle of something happening."

Those Empire ships are evidence of that.

"You know what I mean," she says, her mouth tilted downward in concern. Her entire face reflects that concern. A frown forms between her eyes and she seems almost sad.

"I actually don't, Nyssa," I say, then wish I hadn't. I want to get out of here and get to my single ship.

"Your injury," she says. "It's healed, but I'm worried."

"I get that," I say. "There's no need."

"But there is," she says. "I think—we all wonder—if the adrenaline is too much, we worry—"

"We?" I ask.

"The medical community here," she says. "We think you might be at greater risk of stroke."

Someone told me that as I was healing. Then someone else mentioned it. They wanted me to curtail my life, do a lot of things differently, take the stress off my body. They really wanted me to stop diving, because the changes in air pressure might be deadly to me.

She's almost in tears, she's so worried.

"Nyssa, what's the difference if I have a stroke on board the *Madxaf* or in the single ship?"

"Besides the care?" she says.

"This isn't a fully functional ship," I say. "You're the medic here, but you don't have a staff."

"I have a full medical bay," she says. "I won't be near you if you stroke out in the single ship."

Her voice wobbles on that last bit. She's actually worried about it.

She doesn't understand—no matter how many times I've told her or the team—that diving is dangerous. That the risk of death is high. That each choice could lead to something deadly.

That's how I live. That's what I love. Apparently, I haven't communicated that to her properly. Maybe I haven't told anyone that.

I put my hand on her left shoulder and squeeze once. That's as close as I get to something touchy-feely.

"Nyssa," I say gently. "If I die in space doing what I love, I die happy."

"But you won't be diving," she says, then bites her lower lip. It almost sounds like she lets me dive because she knows how much I love it.

I'm grateful for that. At least she understands a small part of this.

"I'll be in my ship, working," I say, leaving out one of the crucial words for me. *Alone. I'll be in my ship, working, alone.* "That's enough for me."

"But you might—"

"We all might die today, Nyssa," I say gently. "It's up to you to keep the team going, no matter what."

Her eyes tear up, which surprises me. Then she nods, once.

"All right," she says. "I just wish we could do this differently, that's all."

"Yeah," I say, strugglingly not to make the word sound dismissive. I'm not one for regrets and wishes. I'm ready to move onto the next task. We have a challenge ahead, and I'll do my part, even if it's not the part that Coop imagined for me.

I pat Nyssa on the shoulder again, and walk away before she can delay me further.

I have a ship to get to, and a job to do. I smile to myself as I hurry, because I finally recognize the emotion that I'm feeling.

I have the gids. Of course I do.

45

Sub-Lieutenant Tawhiri Paek docked the small ship on the *Ivoire*. He had piloted the ship into the largest internal ship docking bay he had ever seen. It was mostly empty, which probably made it seem larger. But the doors alone intimidated him as they slid open.

They shouldn't have. He'd seen the interiors of Dignity Vessels before. He had just never seen a functional one. He had a hunch he was in for a lot of surprises.

He turned in the pilot's chair to look at his companions. Leticia Honoré was tiny, fierce, and wiry. She had shaved her head shortly after he met her in a weapons' class decades ago, because she didn't want her hair—which was unusually straight—to get tangled in any operating system she was working on.

She kept her nails short for the same reason, and anything that dangled on any of her uniforms, even if the dangling item was a signal of rank, privilege, or valor, got cut off.

She wore her most functional dress uniform, gray-black with white piping, and ostentatiously carried two laser pistols, one on each hip. She had told Paek, when he questioned her choice, that she expected the pistols to be removed, but she wanted the *Ivoire* to know that she meant business.

He had no idea how anyone looking at Honoré would think otherwise.

Her gaze met his, her prominent eyes—her most startling feature—calm and measured. He nodded once, and she nodded in return.

Maliu Faifai watched them both as if she didn't understand the gesture. She had been a risky choice, but Group Commander Trekov had picked Faifai because she was so incredibly smart about systems. Show Faifai a system, explain once what its job was, and she could not only understand how it functioned, she could—in many cases—reverse engineer it.

Of course, she had only been tested on Empire systems, but Trekov thought the ability would translate to other systems.

Paek hoped she was right.

Faifai removed the safety belt she wore on every trip in every small vessel, and looped the belt on the back of her seat. She too was small and wiry, but she lacked that essential toughness that Honoré had. Maybe it was the nimbus of coal-black hair that floated around Faifai's head or maybe it was the narrow set to her jaw or maybe it was the way that her eyes seemed to stare right through anyone she was conversing with.

Faifai seemed to occupy another plane of existence altogether, which made Paek nervous. He had never really been able to talk to her, perhaps because he really didn't understand her.

He stood and adjusted his own uniform. Like Honoré, he had worn a functional dress uniform—not just to convey authority to the crew of the *Ivoire*, but to feel authoritative himself.

He walked past the other two to the edge of the small area that served as cockpit and passenger seating. This little ship had almost nothing to recommend it. It was a ferry from one vehicle to another, and little more. It had a good communications system, but not much else on its navigational panel.

Someone—not Paek—had ensured that no one put any compromising information on the ship at all.

He walked to the only real exit off the ship. He had to manually release the ramp along one side before even opening the door. He did so, using his right fist, then tugged the sleeve of his uniform over his tattoos. He didn't want questions.

He didn't want to make conversation with these people, but he would have to make some. He knew that people would be waiting for him.

The airlock door silently slid upwards. Since the atmosphere inside this ship and the *Ivoire* was more or less the same, Paek didn't linger. He went into the airlock and released the exterior door.

It slid sideways, which always startled him about this design. He glanced over his shoulder to make certain his colleagues were following him.

They were.

Then he looked forward, careful to stand with military precision, every muscle in his body on alert. He was much bigger than his colleagues, so if this Cooper was going to try something here—like harming the three observers, or even grabbing and imprisoning them—Paek was ready to stop them.

A single person stood at the foot of the ramp. That person was not wearing a uniform, as far as he could tell. Just some tan pants and a brown shirt that looked vaguely like a sweater.

The person had short black hair, green eyes, and sharp, serious features. The person took a step forward, bowed slightly, and said, "I'm Ensign Emma Gataki. I'm to escort you to the bridge."

Until she spoke, Paek hadn't been certain that she was female. But her voice was musical and strong. She spoke with a slight accent that he couldn't place, as if Standard was not her native language. Her green eyes seemed to miss nothing.

He was surprised she had such a low rank, given her age. She had half-stumbled on the word "ensign" and he thought that odd as well.

"Sub-Lieutenant Tawhiri Paek," he said. "Sergeant Faifai, and Chief Honoré."

He did not list their true titles, because those included their jobs. He felt it important to keep the jobs quiet, although he had not been instructed to.

Gataki nodded at them. Then her gaze went down to Honoré's laser pistols. "All weaponry must remain on your ship," Gataki said.

Honoré's lips thinned, and for a moment, Paek thought she might refuse. If she did, he had no idea what to do with her. Send her back? Lock her in the ship?

He removed his own laser pistol from its case against his leg. Honoré took both of hers, and held them with one hand, a bit too loosely for his tastes.

"Take mine," he said to Honoré. She frowned at him, knowing that he was giving her a sideways command.

She took his laser pistol, then raised her eyebrows at Faifai, who said, "I never carry a weapon unless I'm instructed to."

Faifai sounded condescending, probably deliberately so. Paek felt a surge of irritation at these two. He needed this to go smoothly, especially since they were all pressed for time.

"I'll be right back," Honoré said, somewhat sullenly.

Honoré bounded up the ramp to the little ship, opened the main doors, and set the weapons just inside the airlock. She closed the doors, pivoted, and hurried back down.

Gataki watched it all with a closeness that Paek didn't like.

Once Honoré returned to the same position she'd been in a moment before, Gataki turned her attention back to Paek.

"I am not giving you a tour of the ship," she said. "We are to go directly to the bridge. We do not have time to answer questions. You will observe only. If that is not possible, then please leave now. We do not need the distraction."

This bluntness, coming from such a low-ranking officer, startled him. He resisted the urge to look at his colleagues.

"We understand," he said.

Gataki swept her hand toward the right. At the far end of the large docking bay, there were tall doors.

"This way, then," she said. "I will walk behind you. Once we're through those doors, I will give more instructions."

Behind, where she could observe them, and make sure nothing went wrong.

The tension Paek had felt from the moment Trekov had made this deal ratcheted up even more. He didn't like the situation, and he was beginning to doubt that they would get anything useful out of it.

They might have been better off leaving one of their best weapons specialists and a gifted engineer on the *Ewing Trekov*.

Gataki had given him an opening, and he could return right away, but he didn't hesitate. Trekov had given him an order. She had believed this partnership would serve them in the short term and it was up to him to execute it.

Paek led the way around the empty bay, heading toward the doors. The bay was cooler than he expected, although some of that might have come from the arrival of his ship. Still, the temperature was almost chilly.

The floor was smooth, as were the walls, and they all seemed to be made of the black material that lined the exterior of the ship. The lights were brighter than he expected, though. On Empire ships, areas like this dimmed lights for energy conservation.

That did not seem to be an issue on the *Ivoire*.

It didn't take as long as he expected to reach the exit doors. They opened as he approached, and they weren't silent. They made a slight groaning sound, as if they needed maintenance, and no one had done it yet. Or maybe the sound was by design, so that someone in the area outside knew that the doors were being opened.

He glanced over his shoulder. Faifai was looking at the systems around the door. Honoré walked near Gataki, almost as if they were partners in this entire project.

Honoré, apparently, felt she needed to keep her eye on Gataki at all times. Gataki didn't seem nervous about this small group at all. She seemed calm and in control, as if she escorted people through the *Ivoire* all the time.

Paek stepped through the doors, and into a wide, well-lit corridor. It too seemed to be made of the same black material. Every surface was smooth. There were clear controls on the walls with words that covered parts of the panels. He recognized a few of the words as a very

very very old version of Standard, something he'd seen in other old Dignity Vessels.

But this vessel wasn't old. Even with the creaky doors, it seemed new and contained, everything in its place. He felt out of his element, even down here. He didn't see anything he could just open up and figure out how to use.

He also expected to see more people, crew members going through the corridor, going about their business.

Just like he had been surprised to find very few ships in that large ship bay.

"To your left," Gataki said, "there are elevators."

Paek turned in the indicated direction and saw an endless corridor. He had to trust her that there were elevators, and it made him nervous. He was the one who had mentioned to Trekov that Cooper might want the three observers on board as hostages, guaranteed to keep Trekov and the others doing what Cooper wanted them to do.

Trekov had nodded, and said, *It's a risk, but a slight one.*

Paek's stomach tightened, but he kept going in the indicated direction. It seemed odd to him that there were no doors in this corridor, nothing but an endless hallway.

Then he stopped and turned, looking behind him for the entrance into the ship bay.

He saw nothing along the corridor itself, even though he had just come from that direction.

Gataki's gaze met his. He wasn't sure he liked those green eyes at all. They seemed to see too much, and right now, they seemed to notice that he was looking for the doorway he had just left.

But it wasn't visible. Somehow, they managed to shield even their doors from people in the corridor.

"We don't have a lot of time, Sub-Lieutenant," she said.

He nodded, then turned back around, feeling somewhat stupid. Like a rube who had never seen a starship before.

Paek finally reached the elevators. They, at least, were visible. The sliding doors were recessed, and the edges were slightly curved. If they were in the same position they were in on other Dignity Vessels, then they would be in the center of an important part of the ship—crew quarters, or maintenance quarters.

He didn't have the kind of brain that could extrapolate a map from the ship's exterior shape once he was inside. Maybe Faifai did. He hadn't asked, and he had no idea if Trekov knew whether or not Faifai's mind worked that way.

Faifai stopped beside him, her brow furrowed as she looked at everything. She was probably trying to figure out how it all worked.

Honoré seemed calm as she stopped at the elevators. The only time she had shown any emotion since the group had arrived was when she had been told to give up her weapons. And, weirdly, she should have expected that. Maybe she had thought she would put up a fight.

Gataki reached them, looked at them all as if she were assessing them, and then she ran a thumb along the right side of the nearest elevator door.

The door slid sideways, revealing a wide well-lit little room. The elevator was much bigger than Paek expected, as if it was designed to carrying more than human cargo. Maybe it was.

He stepped in, and glanced at the walls. Just as shiny as the walls in the corridor, but not black. Still, very smooth. He wondered if the black material came in different colors, and if so, why they had made the interior of the elevator white.

The three women boarded, and the door eased shut. Paek braced himself for the elevator to move, but it didn't.

Or, rather, it didn't seem to. It must have moved because the doors opened into another corridor, this one wide and almost circular. There seemed to be one fork off to the side that led who knew where.

Gataki got off the elevator first and the others followed. Gataki stood in the center of the corridor. The elevator door closed behind them, shutting off the bright light, and making the corridor seem darker than it had a moment before.

"You are here at the request of your commander," Gataki said. Her voice was flat, almost as if this speech was rehearsed. Maybe it was. "Her request was granted by our captain. He asked that you observe only. If you do not follow instructions, you will be sent back to your vessel immediately. Do you understand?"

This was a different speech than the one she had given in the ship bay, but the content was similar. Be an observer, or be asked to leave.

Paek would observe. He would stay as far in the background as he could, so that he could learn as much as possible.

He hadn't really given a command to Faifai and Honoré to do the same thing, but he thought—he hoped—they understood.

Gataki waited for them to respond to her question, which they all did with a mutter. Then she led them across the corridor, to two doors that opened wide, almost like the mouth of a gigantic creature.

Paek expected a large bridge. He'd been on ancient Dignity Vessels. They all had oversized bridges, at least to his mind.

But he'd never seen one peopled before. Each station was filled, and everyone looked busy. Wall screens were on, showing all of the Empire ships in their formation, as well as areas beyond.

Small screens rose above consoles, and some holographic images appeared on surfaces, glimmering with bits of light.

The people weren't wearing uniforms—at least as he recognized them. Paek would have called what they wore casual clothes, the kind that only belonged in their quarters or on their off-hours.

But everyone seemed to be working hard, and no one acknowledged him as he entered. He scanned the bridge for Cooper, the only person he would recognize, and then wondered how he had missed the man.

Cooper stood in the very center of the lower part of the bridge, near a big chair, surrounded by floating screens and some holographic maps. A tiny woman stood near him, waving her arms as she talked.

Paek was too far away to hear even the sound of her voice. He realized in that moment, he would have heard every word on an Empire vessel. But he heard nothing here.

This bridge was better designed than he had thought. Sound didn't travel here, like it did on Empire ships. That in and of itself was an improvement.

Honoré had come up beside him and was staring at the consoles as if they told her something. Faifai had moved to one side, leaning slightly so that she could actually see what was on some of the console screens.

Fresh air blew across his head, cooling him. The bridge didn't smell hot or sweaty. It didn't seem like a place where people worked for hours, often under great stress.

It smelled almost new, and unused, as if this ship had never been flown before. He had never been on a working bridge that actually seemed fresh and clean and bright.

Gataki pushed past him, and headed down the main aisle. She beckoned him and Faifai and Honoré to follow, at least that was what he assumed that gesture she made meant.

He walked down the aisle behind her, and stopped just near the large chair.

"Captain," Gataki said.

Cooper turned. He was a large man, with firmly etched features, piercing eyes and black hair that almost seemed unruly.

Paek had seen Cooper on visual before, several times before, and was surprised, actually, that Cooper looked in person exactly like Paek had thought he would.

Usually people he had first seen through some kind of projection looked smaller when he met them.

If anything, Cooper seemed larger.

Cooper turned toward Gataki's voice. His gaze took in Paek, Faifai, and Honoré, as if he were seeing if they measured up.

"Sub-Lieutenant," he said to Paek, who was surprised that Cooper knew who he was. "Welcome aboard the *Ivoire.*"

Cooper's tone didn't exactly sound welcoming. It sounded vaguely annoyed, as if Paek's presence was unwanted.

It probably was. Trekov had insisted, and no commander liked having conditions slapped upon them.

Paek murmured a thanks for the welcome, which Cooper acknowledge with a nod.

Then Cooper continued, "You, Sergeant Honoré and Chief Faifai will remain over there. You may leave the bridge for food or other necessities in the company of Ensign Gataki only. She will be here to keep an eye on you."

So much for becoming invisible. Paek had been hoping that Gataki would leave the moment she delivered them. Surely, she had other duties somewhere.

Cooper turned away from them, looking at something else another woman—taller and with an air of authority—was showing him on a floating screen.

Paek didn't just feel dismissed, he felt forgotten. Paek looked at the screen, saw the formations and the preparations for the arrival of three ships. It seemed like overkill to him, but this was the response that both Cooper and Trekov believed was needed.

So, yes, Cooper had other priorities.

Gataki stepped between Paek and Cooper, sweeping an arm toward the area in the very back that Cooper had indicated. It was one of the few areas without screens or consoles, a small pocket that probably had a door or some other function that Paek couldn't see.

He glanced over his shoulder one more time at the screens, the ships preparing for a battle that had everyone spooked.

He wished now that he hadn't volunteered for this assignment. He would have to stand and watch while everyone else worked.

He had to remember that he was standing on the bridge of an enemy ship, learning their methods and methodology. He would remember it all.

It was the least he could do.

46

I SIT IN THE PILOT'S CHAIR OF MY SINGLE SHIP, trying to remember the last time I took her out on any mission. I can't. It might've been years.

I know it was years ago when I instructed Ilona to keep my ships in top shape even though I wasn't using them. Top shape meant that they were to be flown regularly, not just run through some kind of systems check on a quarterly basis.

I glanced at the maintenance logs before I got on the ship. The last time she was out was only a week ago, and the pilot—whose name I don't recognize—had found nothing amiss.

Which relieves me, more or less. I would have been more relieved had I been the one who took the ship out or had I known the person who had. Then I would know if the notations about what good shape the ship was in were accurate.

I have to trust them, though. I loathe trusting other people in times of stress, but I put myself in this situation. I didn't have to take this ship out. I could have remained on the *Madxaf*.

Then I smile at myself. Who am I kidding? I could no more have stayed on the *Madxaf* in this emergency than Coop could have stayed off the *Ivoire*.

The single ship feels both familiar and tiny. I haven't been on a ship like this in years. The pilot's chair conforms to my body because I designed the chair that way—and fortunately, despite my absence, the chair is still comfortable.

It's not too comfortable, though, because I don't want to sleep in it. I can put this ship on autopilot if I want, and crawl over the seat, out of the cockpit into what looks like another chair in the back. It's actually a fold-down bed that is much more comfortable than the chair.

But nothing in this ship is too comfortable. It's designed for short trips of a few days or so, even though I've been in the ship longer than that, eating food out of the storage area. I initially wanted this ship to take me to starbases where I would spend the night, but I soon learned that I was more comfortable on my ship than I ever was in some ground-based or ground-aspiring station.

I have reconfigured all the controls. The worst part about letting someone else touch my ship is that the someone else—or all of the some-ones else messed with positions, controls, and settings.

I also toggle the telemetry feed, so that I have several. I smile at the toggles. The ship is not really old—it's younger than I am—but it has an Empire design that I modified so that I could find ships.

Back in the day, one way I found ships was to scan for stealth tech. As I ease the ship out of the bay Lost Souls had stored her in, I'm toggling a lot of things, because there's more stealth tech and *anacapa* energy here than in some parts of the Boneyard.

But this energy is regular—or as regular as stealth tech energy can be. Maybe the best way to describe what I'm seeing is that the Empire ships that have stealth tech (and it's not by all means all of them) have it somewhat under control. I recognize the signature, and barring any serious crisis, that energy is predictable.

The *anacapa* energy is different and much more under control. It's probably invisible to the Empire ships.

The only reason I can see the *anacapa* energy at all is because I have reconfigured all of my data streams to show me the slightest hint of *anacapa* energy.

Back when I was on my own, looking for historical wrecks to dive, I found a lot of Dignity Vessels by following a single thread of an unusual reading, something I didn't entirely understand.

I let out a breath. I can almost hear Mikk's voice in my head, mixed with Orlando's and Nyssa's. *You have the gids, Boss. You need to come back to the ship.*

I have the gids. I have known that as I ran for this ship, as I slid inside her cockpit, as I pulled the levers bringing down the airlocks and the protections, raising the small shields that I have, and activating the one warning laser weapon that I installed in a moment of panic decades ago.

I have to trust that the weapon works, because I didn't have time to run a prolonged systems check.

It took all of my willpower to run a minor systems check, one that any pilot would run on any ship before taking her out—for whatever reason.

The minor systems check showed everything was fine, but I designed that systems check so long ago, that I have no idea if it incorporates the weapons system or not.

I do know that it incorporates shields, because I learned the hard way that shields need to function well no matter what. I nearly died in this ship alone more than once, but it only took once with a shield malfunction that happened *before* I took off, for me to ever take my shields for granted again.

The little ship has great scanners, better than some of the scanners on the little ships that the Fleet designed. It has better than average shields. It has that weapon, which surprises larger ships and usually gives me time to escape.

But it doesn't have much more. Even if Mikk hadn't admonished me to stay between Lost Souls and the Empire ships, I would have done so anyway. If something tried to attack and I was out front, not only would I get shot at (and probably destroyed), I wouldn't be able to get out of the way fast enough.

Because I'm an emotional coward and I loathe confrontation, I head out on the opposite side of Lost Souls from the *Ivoire*. I'm hoping that my little ship will be so insignificant that no one will tell Coop about it.

I can't shut off communications. I need to talk to the *Madxaf* and my crew. If only I could block the *Ivoire*, but I don't dare. Coop is running this operation, and I will need to reach him fast, if I'm seeing something I think he can't see.

It's too hard to explain how the old screens work, how the old information can filter into this ship in ways it doesn't filter in anywhere else.

And, I have a hunch, it's not just about the old screens and data streams. It's also about who interprets them. I see things faster than my team sometimes, especially out here, alone.

I actually feel like myself in this ship. I'm relaxing. The gids are fading, because I'm in my world.

The top of the ship has a clear double hatch that I use most of the time. I can raise an actual metal shield over that part of ship when I feel threatened, but I don't think I need it here.

If this little ship gets hit with some kind of weapon, loose shots or whatever Coop is going to use against those ships (if they come), the little ship and I will disintegrate. It won't matter if that extra shield is on top of it or not.

I'm doomed out here in any kind of pitched battle, and honestly, I don't mind that. If I die here, then fine. I always figured I would die in space. Whenever that happens is fine with me. I've had a good life.

I shake off the thoughts of death. I always have them when I first sit in this ship (and I had forgotten that) because the harshness of space is only centimeters away from me. I'm protected by a razor-thin lining—at least compared to all of the walls and nanobits and shields and such that protect even the smallest of Fleet vessels.

I force myself to look away from the screens and controls, and look up, through that hatch. The edge of the nearest Lost Souls space station darkens my view. The lights from the station here are shielded, almost impossible to see.

Beyond it is Odite, which I can't see with the naked eye. Above me are distant planets and stars, some cosmic dust that seems faint and far away.

The view in a crowded, inhabited area always makes me long for the vastness of space. I want to take the single ship far away from here, head out to territory unknown, at least to me, and see what I can find.

Instead, just ahead of me, Empire ships loom. They're in a formation that Coop gave them, making them a tall wall that acts as some kind of barrier—if the Not-Fleet ships show up on the same plane as the Empire ships.

The ships' captains aren't as creative as Coop. Each ship faces the same way, instead of all of them pointing in different directions. They seem to anticipate an attack from outside of their formation, instead of one inside the barrier that they set up.

It's not that the Empire captains are stupid. It's that they don't understand how *anacapa* drives work. They have no real idea that a ship with an *anacapa* drive can program in any coordinates, and arrive there—and I'm sure Coop hasn't told them.

Although I'm not sure why Coop didn't advise them to face a variety of directions. Maybe he hasn't thought of it. Then I half-smile.

When it comes to tactics, Coop thinks of everything.

He probably doesn't want to take the time to explain the *anacapa* drives. In fact, I'm sure he doesn't want to explain the *anacapa* drives at all.

Our DV-Class vessels are behind the Empire barrier, and I know for a fact that Coop's people—our people—are thinking about attacks from all angles, not just from something in front.

I make myself study the view for a moment. I will never see anything like this again. I want it to soak it.

This is one of those turning point moments. Maybe the Not-Fleet never shows. Maybe the Empire betrays us. Maybe the battle is more destructive than we think it will be.

I have no idea, and neither does anyone else.

I return my attention to the controls and screens. The light across them from the hatch varies as I move. The light from the Empire ships is bright, an almost clear white, the kind that I find blinding.

I hadn't realized until this moment that the light given off by DV-Class vessels has a bit of gold in it, making it much easier on the eyes.

I ease the single ship forward. I've picked a position that is equidistant from two of our DV-Class vessels and far enough away from the barrier of Empire ships that they probably won't even notice me.

Then I anchor the ship into this area, like I used to do when I would sleep onboard her, and then I open up all of the data streams.

I'm going to monitor everything—from the tiniest change in all of the energy around me to the light coming off the ships and the station itself. I'm going to monitor visually through the hatch and on my various screens, and I'm going to use the telemetry coming in from the space around me, in the way I would have if I were entirely alone.

In fact, I'm going to play this as if I *am* entirely alone. I will get better information if I don't use anything that's been touched by Fleet tech, and I certainly don't want to listen to anything the Empire ships have to say to each other.

I reinforce my shields. I make sure I can reach my somewhat useless weapon if I need it to startle some late-arriving ship.

And then I wait.

47

COOP WAS BEGINNING TO THINK he had been at the Lost Souls Corporation too long. The Empire ships made him nervous, even though, essentially, he commanded them.

He stood near his captain's chair on the bridge of the *Ivoire*, studying the screens before him. He didn't like looking at all of those ships. There were too many of them, and they were too close.

They were also probably overkill. Even though the Not-Fleet vessels would outgun the five DV-Class ships here at Lost Souls, the Not-Fleet vessels would be no real match for twenty or thirty Empire ships—properly commanded that, is.

The biggest problems the commanders of those vessels had had back at the Room of Lost Souls was that they had no idea what they were facing. They didn't know the capabilities of Not-Fleet vessels, and certainly didn't know how to fight them.

He did know how to fight them, up to a point, unless they had weaponry he hadn't seen in that battle in orbit around Nindowne. He was just going to have to be smarter than those three Not-Fleet ships were.

He would have to deploy all of his resources, and keep an eye on Trekov as well.

He wished he hadn't acquiesced to her request to place three observers on his bridge. She had out-thought him here. Had she simply asked to send three observers to his ship, he could then have sent the three to some belowdecks area, maybe even have them sit with the diplomats in the bar.

But she had specified the bridge, and he was going to keep his word, even if a tiny part of his brain was now in that back corner of his bridge, wondering what those three were seeing.

He had insisted on meeting them after Ensign Gataki brought them on board. He wanted to see if the observers were pro forma, younger officers with no knowledge of anything, which was what he had hoped.

But as the three of them walked down the aisle toward him, he watched them on a small screen near his captain's chair. They weren't young, by any measure. The sub-lieutenant, whom Trekov had said was in charge of their little group, was a muscular man with eyes that missed nothing. He was probably a few years younger than Coop, and had risen to a higher rank—if the Empire system were being translated into the Fleet system.

Which meant that the sub-lieutenant was bright and engaged, with a career in mind. It also meant he was someone that Coop didn't dare underestimate.

The two women with him were as brilliant and engaged as the sub-lieutenant was. The engineer, a woman named Faifai, reminded Coop of Yash. Nothing seemed to go past her. She was looking at everything.

Faifai was the reason he had moved them to the back left corner of the bridge. If she were any closer, she would be able to see the *anacapa* casing and maybe even some of the commands on the screens. If she was anything like Yash, she might be able to compile information about the drives from what she had observed.

The weapons' specialist had an air of aggression that bothered Coop. If something bad happened between his ships and the Empire, she would be the one to isolate quickly. He would need her off the bridge.

Coop brought Perkins over after the three retired to the back of the bridge, and told her, in the language they had both grown up with, what he had seen and what he worried about.

She nodded, promised she'd make sure the rest of the bridge and the security detail (such as it was) would have the same information.

Perkins had reverted to her crisp, no-nonsense persona. Almost everyone had. They were ready to fight this battle, should the battle arrive.

Coop expected it would. He was monitoring all of his screens, even the large wall screens, and making certain that his team remained on top of the information as well.

That last message from Trekov bothered him more than he was willing to admit. The three Not-Fleet ships had left the space around the Room of Lost Souls at the same coordinates he had used. They found those coordinates days after he had left.

The ships also seemed to be in no hurry. Two ships had followed him in the heat of battle, which was the kind of quick and easy tracking he understood. It wasn't easy to track a ship through foldspace, but if you left at similar coordinates and within the same time period, tracking was possible.

But days later? Not as easy. And those ships were not moving with alacrity. They had taken their time.

He had no real evidence, but he suspected they knew how to track in foldspace. Not the kind of half-assed tracking the Fleet of his day had used, filled with grid searches and guesses. But actual tracking, the kind any ship of the Fleet could do in regular space.

If these ships could do that kind of foldspace tracking, then they would appear here at Lost Souls at the very same coordinates where he had arrived.

Even though he had the Empire ships all pointing their weapons outward, he expected the Not-Fleet ships to arrive on his side of the box-barrier he had built with all of those ships.

His other reason for facing the Empire ships away from Lost Souls was simple: he didn't want them to easily turn on Lost Souls or Odite. He wanted them focused outward.

He'd seen Empire ships in battle. Properly commanded, they did just fine. But some were commanded by careless captains whose weapons' fire went awry.

Out-of-control weapons' fire could damage the active shields around the space stations, and maybe even penetrate the shields guarding Odite. He would certainly lose some of his own small vessels, the ones docked outside of the stations, the ones the stations had no real room for.

He threaded his fingers together and reviewed his plan one last time.

If the Not-Fleet ships appeared inside the box created by the Empire ships, the initial fight would be up to Lost Souls itself. Coop had prepared Xilvii for that contingency. But it would be an ugly one, filled with a lot of losses.

Coop hoped that wouldn't happen.

As he reviewed everything, from the capabilities of the Empire vessels surrounding Lost Souls to the locations of the DV-Class ships, his eye caught an anomaly in the data.

A single ship floated not too far from one of the Lost Souls space stations. The ship was barely a blip in the data, so small that he might have missed it if he hadn't been scanning the entire area for anything unusual.

His heart rate—which had remained steady once he had come onto the bridge of the *Ivoire*—increased rapidly. He felt a half-second of anger, before he tamped it back.

He used one finger to show more data on that single ship. His own systems hadn't flagged it as a threat, which meant that it had probably come from Lost Souls or Odite. And if the ship had come from Lost Souls, he knew who was piloting it.

Sure enough, the data streamed toward him, showing him that the single ship was an older one, registered to the Lost Souls Corporation. A notation in the data made it clear that this ship was to be maintained should its original owner need it day or night.

The original owner wasn't listed, but she didn't have to be for him to recognize the instruction.

The instruction had come from Blake, which meant that the owner of the single ship was Boss.

Coop swore quietly under his breath. He needed her on the *Madxaf*.

He whirled, about to leave the bridge, then stopped himself. The woman drove him crazy. She had just made him lose focus.

He had no idea what she was thinking. That damn ship was too small to be of use in any battle. It had shields, sure, but in the kind of firefight he was worried about, her ship would be obliterated.

Besides, he had no idea what she would accomplish out there, by herself.

Instead of leaving the bridge, he brought up several screens, surrounding himself. Then he contacted the single ship.

The communication went through easily, which was a relief, because he wouldn't put it past her to shut down all communications.

He didn't get a visual, though. Just audio.

The visual was blocked.

"I need you on the *Madxaf*," he snapped.

"Well, hello to you too," Boss said, with a smile in her voice, almost as if she had expected him to find her and yell at her.

"No games," he said. "I have no time for them. Get out of there, and onto the *Madxaf*."

"This isn't a game, Coop," she said.

"Damn straight," he said.

"I went to the *Madxaf*," she said. "I spent some time looking around, and decided I'm of no use to you there."

"Well, I'm not going to worry about you in the middle of all of this," he said, and heard how furious he sounded. He knew she'd be able to see right through that. He would be worrying about her, and he didn't want to be.

"Good," she said. "Because you need to focus on whatever's coming."

"I need you on the *Madxaf*," he said again.

"One," she said, finally sounding irritated, "I am not under your command. In fact, there could be an argument that you work for me."

He opened his mouth to respond, then stopped himself. Damned woman was under his skin and distracting him. He couldn't be distracted right now. He didn't dare.

"Two," she was saying, "I am of no use on the *Madxaf*. I'd be in the way."

"So go back to Lost Souls," he said. "And—"

"*Three*," she said, the irritation in her voice growing, "you need me here, to monitor whatever is coming out of foldspace."

He was about to argue when he understood what she meant. There was information that had only showed up on her equipment when she was inside the Boneyard. The Fleet equipment showed none of it.

"This isn't about the Fleet," he said. "This is Not-Fleet—"

"In Dignity Vessels," she said. "You have no idea what their tech is like." She had a point. Dammit.

"So let me hover back here, out of range, and I'll monitor. It's better than me being in Denby's way on the *Madxaf*."

Coop didn't entirely agree. He didn't like where she was or what she was doing.

"Monitor their tech on Lost Souls, then," he said. "Get out of the battlefield."

"If I'm located in the battlefield, then Lost Souls is in trouble," Boss said, making another good point.

"Get out of there," he said. "That's an order."

"See point one, above," she said.

"You can monitor from Lost Souls," he said.

"No, I can't," she said. "There's too much Fleet tech mixed into their systems. I'm staying here, Coop. I know that irritates you. Get past it. We have more important problems."

And then she signed off.

He stared at the screen in front of him, where he still saw the data from her ship, floating in space.

Would he have let some other officer hang out in that single ship? He wanted to say no, he wouldn't have, but he wasn't sure. He didn't consider the value of lives in a battle. He considered the value of *knowledge*. He never put someone with specialized knowledge in harm's way.

Everyone else had signed up to be in harm's way, and as their leader, he couldn't ignore that. Over the years, he had developed a way not to think of his friends and colleagues as friends and colleagues when they were all in a dangerous situation.

He hadn't developed that with Boss. He didn't want her there. He didn't like it.

She was too vulnerable, and the position was too dangerous. He was right: if the fight came to that part of the battlefield, she would die.

But she was right too: if the fight had come there, then most of Lost Souls would be destroyed.

He clenched his fists, unclenched them, let himself feel the anger for a moment, and then, with as much effort as possible, worked to set it aside.

He was mad at her for a thousand reasons. He was mad at her because she never listened to him, mad at her because she was maddening, never doing what he wanted, mad at her because he cared about her way too much.

If he didn't care, she would be so much easier to deal with.

Then he let out a small chuckle. That was a lie. If he didn't care, he might've gotten even angrier at her. She might have been harder to deal with because he would have understood her less.

She was too much like him; she had to be in the middle of the battle, not on the sidelines.

And on the *Madxaf*—hell, anywhere else in this battlefield—she would be on the sidelines.

"Godspeed," he whispered to her, using an ancient seafarer blessing, one he hadn't used in years. He knew she couldn't hear him, but he hoped she could feel his mood shift.

He would be able to focus now. He had to.

They were heading into something difficult and he needed to be at the top of his game.

He brought the screens down, then turned to his team.

"You okay?" Tren asked quietly.

"Yeah," he said without adding the sarcastic *Never better.*

Waiting. It got to all of them. And right now, nothing was going to happen until those three Not-Fleet ships arrived.

If those three Not-Fleet ships arrived.

And—oddly—he had no idea what would happen if they didn't.

48

I SLAM THE HEEL OF MY RIGHT HAND against the side of my pilot's chair. If I hit anything else in the cockpit of this single ship, I will change something, damage something, activate something. I want to flail around in fury for a moment.

I want to open up a channel of communication and yell at Coop again. He has no right to order me around. He completely ignored me when I pointed out that *he* works for *me*.

He's not acting that way. Whenever I go on dives, I test my companions on an easy dive first. If that companion doesn't listen, then they don't accompany me on any more dives.

Then my thoughts register. I did not listen to him, either. He's the one with the plan. Hell, he's the one with the experience. He knows how to fight, even if I don't agree with his methods sometimes.

He has a right to be angry with me. Hell, *I* would be angry with me.

Of course, if he had bothered to tell me what he was going to do from the start, I could have helped him plan. I could have pointed out where my people would have helped the most. I could have given him suggestions that might have helped all of us, instead of causing us to lose time in a senseless argument that he was going to lose anyway.

He can't control me, no matter how hard he tries.

I make myself take a deep breath. The heel of my hand aches from the force of that blow, which is just ridiculous. *I'm* being ridiculous. We're all tense, and I don't like the Empire here. I would have argued against that maneuver, right from the start.

Which is probably why Coop didn't tell me.

The Empire ships loom in their formation, and they surround Odite and Lost Souls as far as the eye can see. I would normally say that I feel small in my single ship, but that's an understatement. I feel like a speck of dust in a nebula that spans lightyears.

I understand why Coop is worried about me. Maybe beneath my anger at him, I'm worried about him as well.

I've been staring out the hatch while we've been fighting, but I have also been monitoring the telemetry, and all the other data flowing on my regular screens.

I just have focused on that data. I've been too lost in my own head, which is a rookie mistake. I warn divers of that all the time. They need to be solid and present and conscious of everything they're doing.

I let that large breath out slowly, then take another one and repeat. I had the gids when I got into the single ship, and then I got angry. I'm not following my own guidelines, which is a serious, serious problem.

The data scrolls, so much data that I'm having trouble processing it. I stare at the area closest to the *Ivoire*, thinking that if Coop knew anything about where those three ships might arrive, he would place himself as close to all that as possible.

And as I look at the data from that area, it changes ever so slightly. The numbers form a spiral pattern that I've seen before.

My heart starts pounding, hard. I glance at the two-dimensional visuals, and see an actual spiral. On the two-dimensional black-and-white screen, that actual spiral looks like a whirl of water heading down a sink.

I've seen this pattern more times than I want to think about since I've met the crew of the *Ivoire*, since I founded Lost Souls, since we brought in ships with *anacapa* drives.

A foldspace window is opening.

I slam the palm of my left hand on the comm, probably too hard. But I want to reach Coop now.

"What?" he says, sounding so irritated that it takes me aback.

"They're coming," I say. "The coordinates aren't far from you. A foldspace window is opening there."

"I'm not getting any—." He stops himself, probably realizing why I'm contacting him. The very reason that I have come out here in the single ship has paid off.

"Got it," he says, and this time his tone is all business.

He disappears from the comm without signing off.

I sit at loose ends for a moment, in my vulnerable single ship, staring at the slow spiral which has grown into a larger whirl. If that image is correct, and if it is showing itself to me in real time (which I have no real reason to doubt), then that foldspace window will open completely in less than five minutes.

Coop wants me out of the area. He wants me either inside Lost Souls or the *Madxaf*. I toy with doing just that for a half second. And then, another swirl starts near those coordinates. And another.

I'm not sure Coop can read any of this.

I'm staying, whether he likes it or not.

49

COOP SPUN IN THE COCOON OF HIS SCREENS on the deck of the *Ivoire*, frustrated that he couldn't see the opening of a foldspace window, like Boss could. His equipment should have read any change in the area, any change at all.

Anacapa drives sent a tiny little burst of energy before opening a full window. The energy acted like a probe. It didn't always stop the ship from arriving on top of another ship, but it did stop the ship from arriving in the middle of—say—another planet.

If a Fleet vessel opened up a foldspace window near him, he would see that little probe. He had been counting on seeing that probe, but he didn't see anything.

Boss did.

And she just contacted him to let him know she saw two more.

Anyone else but Boss, he would have doubted one hundred percent. Anyone else.

But she turned out to be right: her equipment got different readings than his and she was seeing what he expected to see—what he hadn't told her he would see—the probing before the opening of a foldspace window.

He had to trust this.

Besides, those coordinates were right in the area he expected those Not-Fleet ships to show up.

He had to keep remembering: the Not-Fleet was different than his Fleet. Many of the Not-Fleet ships looked like Fleet vessels with weird parts grafted on. The nanobits on Nindowne had been brown, not black, and somewhat flaky.

The Not-Fleet's tech was different from the Fleet, from *his* Fleet anyway, and he had to account for the differences.

"They're almost here," he said to his bridge crew. "They're arriving right now."

"I'm not getting anything," Tren said. "Anywhere."

He gave her the coordinates, and then squared his shoulders. Time to take command of all the ships before him.

He used the comm code that Trekov had given him, which opened up the comms to all of the Empire vessels and the other Lost Souls vessels.

"We have readings showing that our mutual enemy will arrive within the next few minutes. On my verbal command, you will open fire at these coordinates."

He both rattled off the coordinates and sent them through the comm. Perkins gave him a sideways look over his screens. She wasn't sure about this, because she clearly didn't have readings either.

But this barrage of weapons' fire was going to have to be all about trust.

He understood, on a deep level, how ironic that was: he hadn't trusted Boss with a lot of information, nor had he trusted her to make the right decisions in a battle, and—if she was correct—she was just about to give him and the Empire vessels the big advantage that they needed.

Or she was going to destroy any credibility that he had with Trekov and with his own people.

And maybe with himself.

He stared at the streaming data, at the holoscreens with visuals, at those coordinates, feeling each second as if it were an hour, each minute as if it were a day.

And then, just when he was starting to feel despair, he saw the largest foldspace window he had ever seen flare open.

"Fire!" he shouted. "Fire now!"

50

Nyguta stood on the bridge of the *BilatZailea*, feet slightly apart, hands clasped behind her back. She still felt stupidly unmoored without her captain's chair. But she had decided, somewhere on this trip through foldspace, to reclaim her own position on the bridge.

She added one more holoscreen, so she was surrounded by six of them now. There was little to see because the *BilatZailea* had bumped its way into foldspace, but she was ready for whatever faced her on the other side.

Based on the research her team had done into this Captain Cooper and the *Ivoire*, she had a vague idea what to expect. From the partial transcripts of his court-martial, she gathered that the original Cooper had always been a bit of a maverick. He followed orders unless he thought them reckless. Then he would argue, and if that didn't work, he sometimes took matters into his own hands.

She hadn't understood all of the ins and outs of those transcripts—she wasn't entirely sure what he had done to cause the court-martial—but she did understand this: Cooper was an original thinker, which meant that he would be difficult to best in a pitched battle.

However, from what she could gather, he or his grandfather had been catapulted into a future with no support whatsoever. He had built some kind of base with the Lost Souls Corporation, which seemed to be supplying tech and materials to the Nine Planets Alliance.

That meant that the Enterran Empire was Cooper's enemy.

And from what Nyguta and her staff could glean from the current records, the Nine Planets Alliance was a half-assed alliance, each planet more concerned with its own problems than anything to do with the Alliance.

The Alliance was formed as protection against the Enterran Empire, and probably would have fallen to the Empire if it weren't for Cooper and his strange tactics.

So, she was guessing but not banking on the fact that he was alone in this new future of his. He might have a few ships he could conjure to save him in a battle, but not many.

And he wasn't expecting her to follow him to the Nine Planets. In his day, the Fleet did not have adequate foldspace tracking, so he did not know that Nyguta was on the way.

Her days-long wait probably convinced him he was safe.

So, the plan she formulated, with minimal assistance from the captains of the *DetekTibe* and the *MuhaQiq* was a pretty simple one. They would arrive at the coordinates that the *Ivoire* had gone to in the Nine Planets Alliance.

There would probably be a response, maybe even a nearly immediate response, but Nyguta was wagering that Cooper wouldn't be able to put up enough of a fight to stay ahead of all three Armada vessels. He would, eventually, surrender, maybe even try to make a deal to protect the Alliance or Lost Souls.

She would let him, as long as that deal included his knowledge of the Fleet, as well as his archives.

She wasn't planning on winning immediately. She wasn't even feeling overconfident. She did an internal check, knowing that overconfidence could get in the way of any response to a new situation.

She had discussed all of her assumptions with the other two captains, as well as her own tactical team, and everyone believed that Cooper—while creative—didn't have the resources to withstand a prolonged attack from ships as powerful as the ones she was bringing into the Alliance.

She just had to make it through his initial bout of creativity.

She looked over her screens at her team. Habibi was monitoring his own screens. Intxausti was bent over her console, making last minute adjustments. Pereira had moved to a console close to Nyguta, because he figured she would need him close, since he was the best tactician she had.

The only person who seemed at all tense was Telli, and that might have been because she hadn't slept much in days. Her hair had fallen out of her makeshift buns and she was chewing on one strand like a two-year-old, watching the wall screens as if their foldspace darkness could tell her something.

She had warned both Nyguta and the other captains that Cooper might have amazing defenses near Odite and Lost Souls. Cooper was aware that he didn't have outside backup, so he might have created it himself.

Telli believed—and she was probably right—that the moment of arrival would be the most difficult moment of the entire trip. All three vessels would arrive from foldspace, without shields and uncloaked. It would only take ten seconds or so for full shields to activate, and about a minute or so before the cloak took complete hold.

Nyguta was less worried about that than Telli, simply because Cooper wasn't expecting the three ships. He might see them when they arrived, but he wouldn't be able to track them well. Ancient Fleet equipment was no match for modern Armada technology.

The Jefatura made sure of that. They were always changing up their technology, whenever they discovered something new in the abandoned Fleet vessels they found inside the Scrapheaps and in the wild, as Rockowitz liked to say.

He was standing on her other side, arms crossed, a frown on his face. He agreed with Telli: the moment of arrival would be the ship's most vulnerable.

And they were nearly out of their foldspace window.

Nyguta clasped her hands even tighter. She wanted to be out of this, and to know exactly what they were facing. She had decided that the *BilatZailea* would arrive first this time, partly because she wanted to see what they were facing, and partly because she didn't really want to happen on a disaster that could have been avoided like she had at that space station inside the Enterran Empire.

"We're nearly out," Rockowitz said, and as if to confirm his statement, the *BilatZailea* started vibrating again.

Nyguta had no idea why the vibration was worse in this region of space, but it seemed to be. That would be something she would take to the engineers when she went back to the Armada.

The *BilatZailea* bumped out of foldspace, and the screens filled with information and telemetry in a way that she had never seen before. Dozens—hundreds?—of ships stood before her, a wall of ships.

"Holy shit!" someone said, and Nyguta concurred.

"Shields!" she shouted, but it was too late. Weapons fire slammed into them, more weapons fire than she had ever faced, more than she could comprehend.

As she slid into fight mode, trying to deal with everything before her, and figure out a new set of tactics, while saving her ship, her brain was trying to reorder everything she knew.

Cooper and the Enterran Empire? He had fled there, then, because he was part of the Empire, and expected them to save him?

She didn't have time to think that through. She needed to figure out how to contact the other two ships. They were still in foldspace, and she needed to protect them.

But the *BilatZailea* was taking heavy weapons fire, and the reports of damage were coming from all over the ship.

"Where are my damn shields?" she shouted.

"Damaged," Rockowitz said.

"Those ships knew what they were targeting," Pereira said, and Nyguta felt her heart sink.

"Retreat into foldspace?" Intxausti asked.

"And leave the *DetekTibe* and *MuhaQiq* to fight this alone?" Nyguta asked. "No. We're staying, at least until they arrive and we can warn them away."

That would take another five minutes.

She had no idea if the *BilatZailea* had five minutes. She wasn't even sure exactly how to respond.

She had no idea where the command vessel was, who was in charge, and how to decapitate this overwhelming force.

She had no idea how to fight this, and she had almost no time to figure out it.

51

COOP STARED, GAPE-MOUTHED, at the Not-Fleet ship being buffeted by overwhelming firepower. The ship had arrived out of foldspace with shields down and no cloaking.

He didn't dare look at his team here on the bridge of the *Ivoire*. They were not firing on the ship, but monitoring it.

The Empire vessels were using all of their considerable firepower on it.

So far, they hadn't hit the *anacapa* drive, but it would only be a matter of time.

He had been right that an ambush would work, but he had been wrong about the ship. It should have been shielded. Although, if their shields were like his, they sometimes distorted the foldspace window. So to travel safely, they'd need the shields off.

The damn ship had arrived alone. He hadn't expected that. He expected one large barrage of fire, and then a call for surrender. But he couldn't, not yet. If the other ships appeared in different places around Odite, then this battle would be bigger.

Maybe Trekov's intelligence was wrong.

Then a second ship appeared, and the weapons hit it squarely in the center. Someone in charge of the Empire's response had managed to coordinate the firepower.

The problem was that they would destroy these Not-Fleet vessels, and Coop needed at least one of them. At this rate, no one would survive. The *ships* wouldn't survive, and he wouldn't get the information from them that he needed.

He wasn't sure how to call this off, at least not without tipping his hand about the *anacapa* drives. If one of those got hit, ships all around that ship might be destroyed—depending on how the drive was protected.

If the drive was protected.

"You're going to destroy the damn ships!" The voice was tinny, but it belonged to Yash. She was sending him messages from Engineering, as she watched this whole thing too.

He shut off direct communication from Engineering, at least to him. Right now, the *Ivoire* was in no danger, so he didn't need to keep all channels of communication open. Besides, if Yash needed to contact him, she would either contact someone else on the bridge or turn the communication back on.

She had that power.

But he didn't need the nagging, not right now. He knew what was at stake.

Parts of the second ship were glowing, and he couldn't tell if that was from the Empire's weapons or if the hull had been breached in several places.

He bent over his own telemetry, searching for answers, and waiting on that third ship.

Once it arrived and was disabled, he would call an end to this.

He only hoped that Trekov would listen.

52

Trekov had her hands on the back of a chair inside the command center, watching everything unfold on the gigantic screens before her. Telemetry flowed around her—she had been doing her own monitoring before that ship arrived.

She hadn't heard from her team on the *Ivoire*, and she wished she had set up some kind of special communication with them. Because she needed to know several things, things her staff on board the *Ewing Trekov* had no idea about.

Such as how did Cooper know to target that point in space a minute or two before that first enemy vessel appeared? His order was very specific, the coordinates clear.

He even knew which ships should fire what. He asked for a specific level of firepower from all of the ships in the formation before that small area of space, and he had specified how much power to use.

The ship wasn't destroyed, but it was damaged. It had come through that lighted doorway, just like she had seen before, and it looked like it had been completely unprotected.

Someone in central command had said, in awe, that there were no shields, and she started, thinking she should check the telemetry, but that meant taking her eyes off the battle before her, and that battle was riveting.

Especially now that the second vessel had arrived.

Didn't they have a way to communicate with each other? Shouldn't the first vessel have warned the others that they were facing a veritable wall of ships?

And then, as she watched her ships punch holes in the hull of the second ship, she wondered if Cooper had known this would happen all along. Was this why he had told her she could get the ships when it was over? Because he had known the ships would be destroyed?

She wouldn't put it past him. He was a canny tactician, someone who knew what was going to happen long before it did.

Like that opening in space. She had no idea what that opening was, and why the second ship didn't come through it. It had come through its own opening.

The second ship was getting more damaged than the first. Someone in that block of ships had given the order to consolidate firepower. She hadn't.

She needed to put a stop to it before the consolidated firepower destroyed that second ship. The first was listing, and seemed darker than it had before, as if lights had gone out all over the side facing her.

Trekov wasn't sure of her position here. Should she just order her vessels to cease? She had promised Cooper, though, that he would be in charge of the attack, and the third ship was missing.

Besides, Cooper had known where the ships would be. He might know where that third ship was.

She needed to wait until the third ship appeared and was disabled before she made any movement to stop this thing. They could afford to lose both ship number one and ship number two if they captured the third ship.

She dug her fingers deeper into the back of the chair.

She hated not understanding exactly what she was seeing.

She hated not being in charge.

She hated not being the one to figure out what to do next.

53

THE *GEESI* BEGAN ITS TRANSITION OUT OF FOLDSPACE. Cohn stood beside her chief engineer, Erasyl Iosua, and watched as he manipulated the controls. The *anacapa* drive casing glowed ever so slightly, not something she ever liked seeing. But Iosua, wizard that he was, smiled at her and told her not to worry about it.

Too late, she wanted to say to him. *I worry about everything.*

Of course she didn't say that. A captain exuded confidence, even when she was heading into an area she had never seen before, on a mission that she sometimes felt was a foolish one and at other times she believed might be the most important of her career.

Her bridge crew behaved no differently than they had on any other mission. Whenever the *Geesi* used the *anacapa* drive, Iosua came to the bridge and worked alongside Aksel Priede, the navigator. On this mission, she was getting used to seeing both men working side by side.

Most chief engineers stayed in engineering, even on difficult missions, but Iosua needed to work hand in glove with the navigator in charge, and felt it more polite to do so on the bridge. Besides, then Iosua could see the *anacapa* drive and its casing in real time.

No matter how hard he worked, though, he never looked entirely serious. He was a short round man with chubby cheeks and an infectious smile. His eyes betrayed his extreme intelligence which, when Cohn met him, he had been doing everything he could to hide.

Priede was standing slightly back from the console, watching Iosua work. Priede was just as short as Iosua, but spacer thin. Every time Cohn watched the two of them work, she had the sense that Priede was studying Iosua's every move, so that Priede could one day be declared the wizard of foldspace within the Fleet, maybe after Iosua retired.

If Iosua retired.

The rest of her crew was spread out at their consoles, holographic representations of the Nine Planets floating in front of several of them. First Officer Vinters worked the console to Cohn's right. Vinters' white hair was pulled back in a tight bun, probably so that it wouldn't interfere with her work. Her face seemed even more lined than usual as she frowned at a holoscreen before her.

Cohn had already commanded her bridge crew to come out of foldspace cloaked and with shields up. It took more power to come out of foldspace that way, but it was the safest.

The other three captains had agreed to the same maneuver. It wasn't something done much outside of an actual battle, but for all Cohn knew, she might be arriving into an area with automated defenses. The last thing she wanted was the *Geesi* to arrive defenseless.

Still, the strain on the ship worried her, but not as much as arriving without every defense in place.

Fortunately, Jicha and the *Tudósok* remained in the Scrapheap. The *Tudósok* was too old to safely emerge from foldspace with both cloak and full shields on. That ship was in great condition, but it was so old that it would have been a liability should anything go wrong here.

The *Geesi* began to vibrate, as it made its way out of foldspace. The entry into foldspace had been relatively easy this time, but the exit felt a lot like the beginning of this very long journey, when all five ships left the Fleet, tethered to each other.

They weren't tethered this time; this time, they were going to arrive separately, which was another reason to cloak.

They had all thought that the tether, which reinforced the energy from the various *anacapa* drives, had caused the vibration as they left foldspace. But without a tether, and going through foldspace alone, she was no longer certain of that interpretation. Maybe this section of space—from the Scrapheap to the Nine Planets—had an element that made the ship vibrate more than normal.

She glanced at Iosua to see if he had something to say about that, but he seemed wrapped in his work—which she needed him to be. Vinters grabbed the edge of her console, even though this particular vibration did not rise to the level of seriousness of the earlier vibrations.

Cohn did catch Vinters' eye, and nodded. Vinters gave her a tiny, tense smile, which showed that the earlier trips into foldspace had rattled Vinters more than she had let on.

Cohn moved closer to her own screens, ready to see whatever was on the other side of this journey.

The *Geesi* bumped its way out of foldspace and then the screens flared red and orange and a brilliant blue. Bridge crew member Carmen Gray, who was just barely in Cohn's line of sight, raised her hands at the brightness rather than adjusting her own screens.

"What the—?" Vinters muttered, before catching her breath.

Cohn didn't react. Instead, she looked at the telemetry, feeling cold. The images around her resolved into a wall of ships, all firing at two DV-Class vessels. One of those vessels was listing, lights off, and it looked like it was filled with holes. The other was returning fire.

"Carmen," Cohn said to Gray, "when the other ships arrive, warn them to back far away from this battle. We don't want to get hit by wayward fire."

She wasn't sure that was possible. The battle looked terribly uneven. The wall of ships extended all around Odite and Lost Souls. Only one part of the wall was firing on the DV-Class vessels.

And, as she looked, she saw the *Ivoire* behind the wall of ships, almost like a command vessel.

But none of the ships in the wall of ships looked like a make or model she was familiar with, at least not visually.

"Anyone know who is attacking whom?" she asked.

"Looks like a defense of the Nine Planets," said Priede.

"Or maybe a defense of Lost Souls," Iosua said.

"The ships belong to the Enterran Empire," Vinters said.

Cohn swiveled her head and looked hard at Vinters. "What? Which ships?"

"The ones attacking," she said.

"And the *Ivoire?*" Cohn asked.

"If I didn't know better, I would say it's a command vessel," Vinters said.

"Are we leaving?" Iosua asked. "Because, Captain, this isn't our fight."

"It isn't, is it?" Cohn asked. "But it's curious. Let's see if we can figure this out."

"One of the ships that we nearly destroyed at the Scrapheap is near Lost Souls," Vinters said. "I don't understand what we're seeing."

"Neither do I," Cohn said. "So let's pull as much information as we can through scans and back off to observe."

"If you'll let me," Iosua said, "I'd like to go to Engineering. We might be able to tap into some of the computer systems of those ships, and see exactly what they are."

"Go," Cohn said. "We need to figure this out. Have we caught the attention of any of these ships?"

"No, Captain," Gray said. "At least, not in a way that's changing their behavior."

"Let's keep it that way," Cohn said.

Then she crossed her arms and leaned back, watching. She felt more alive than she had a few moments ago. She hadn't expected this.

Maybe the thieves had a reason for stealing from the Scrapheap besides profit. Maybe they needed the ships for defense.

Although that didn't make sense. They clearly had enough ships to fend off…whatever those DV-Class vessels were. And the two DV-Class vessels were getting the worst of it. She had no idea how they would survive the onslaught much longer.

A number of things here disturbed her, but she would let them play out. Then she would work at understanding them.

Because the DV-Class vessels, from the *Ivoire* to the ships being fired upon, were all ancient models, judging by the telemetry she was getting. Which meant they were all stolen, because no part of the Fleet was this far back.

She might have stumbled on something much bigger. And if she was right, then the Fleet needed to make some changes.

And maybe some important ones, starting right here.

54

THE AIR, FILTERED THROUGH THE ENVIRONMENTAL SYSTEM, smelled like burning metal. Or maybe the filters had shut down.

Nyguta didn't know and didn't care. She was doing her best to fight back against a force she hadn't anticipated.

The *BilatZailea*'s weapons worked, barely, but not the ones originally built into the ship. Those had been targeted immediately, along with the shields.

Whoever was firing at them knew exactly what they were doing.

"Where the hell is the *MuhaQiq*?" she asked, in general.

Her crew was doing its best to stave off the overwhelming weapons fire coming from wall of ships, but nothing she or the *BilatZailea* was doing seemed to penetrate their shields.

And it should have, because what she was doing had worked at that space station in Enterran space. These ships seemed to be altering their shields on a frequency in a pattern that she didn't have time to comprehend.

She needed to slide back into foldspace, but she wasn't going to do so until her third ship arrived. The *DetekTibe* was completely disabled, although not destroyed. She needed to get a rescue team over there, but not yet.

Saving the *BilatZailea* first took top priority. And warning the *MuhaQiq* the moment it arrived. Then she and her crew could escape.

That wall of ships was Empire-built, the very type of ships she had surprised and destroyed near the space station. She wanted to let loose like she had done there, but she didn't dare, not with the *MuhaQiq* on the way.

At some point, though, she was going to have to ignore the *MuhaQiq*, assume it was lost or delayed in foldspace, and hope to whatever gods were watching this that the *MuhaQiq* wouldn't arrive in the middle of this onslaught.

The stench coming through the environmental systems made her sinuses ache, and she knew that soon, she would end up with a headache. At some point she and the entire bridge crew might need to put on environmental suits.

And then her training kicked in. *At some point* meant now.

"Get your suits," she said. Better to have them on than to put them on too late.

Yes, her team would lose precious seconds grabbing the suits, but those seconds might be more than made up for in survival on the other end.

She sent the *suit* message throughout the entire ship, hoping it wasn't too late for crew members near the space where that stench was originating.

She sprinted across the bridge, realizing that it was not at the proper angle. Had they lost attitude control then? They still had gravity, which was something.

As she reached the closet, she almost collided with Intxausti, who had the door open. The fact that Nyguta hadn't seen her until that moment told Nyguta everything she needed to know about the air quality on this vessel. The air quality was decaying rapidly, and there was some kind of particulate that was not being filtered out.

She could barely see her colleagues. The bridge hadn't been hit, so she knew that this was filtering in through from another deck, and that wasn't good.

None of this was good.

Intxausti handed Nyguta her environmental suit. Intxausti's expression was strained, but she nodded, then turned around and grabbed another suit.

She was already wearing one, and Nyguta hadn't noted when she put it on.

Nyguta grabbed hers, pulled it open, and stepped in, feeling it seal around her.

She wasn't thinking as clearly as she liked, so she put the hood all the way up, and turned on the internal environmental systems.

Instantly, clean air cooled her and cleared the ache between her eyes. Her sinuses were clearing up, which told her right then just how compromised she had been.

"The *MuhaQiq* is here," Rockowitz said through the comms. "I've warned them to put up their shields."

Nyguta turned, looked at the nearest screen, just in time to see weapons fire hit the *MuhaQiq*. The entire ship lit up, as if it were outlined in light—and that was when she realized that it hadn't even completely emerged from foldspace yet.

"Oh, shit," she muttered to herself.

The light turned from a pale white to a silver blue to something along the greenish gold scale.

"Move us away, move us away, move us away," she said to her team, and then lost her balance as the *BilatZailea* lurched. Attitude was definitely compromised.

But the *BilatZailea* moved, and just in time, because those lights blended and the outline of foldspace wrapped itself into the entire area around the ships.

"Shields, as much as you can," Nyguta said, because it was clear that the *MuhaQiq* was going to blow, and when she did, the *anacapa* drive's power would probably mix with whatever energy was coming out of foldspace.

Her engines were too compromised to handle a quick retreat from the area, and she wasn't even sure where a retreat would take her. But maybe the explosion would damage that wall of ships, maybe *all* of the ships, and she could affect some kind of rescue and get the crew of the *Detek Tibe* out of here.

If they were still alive.

She wasn't going to check.

She needed to get her own crew to safety first—if that was even possible. And she wasn't entirely sure that it was.

55

THE EMPIRE SHIPS WERE DOING THEIR JOB TOO WELL. They hit the third Not-Fleet vessel with everything as it was emerging from foldspace.

Coop gripped the back of his captain's chair as he watched. His fingers dug into the material.

He had never seen a ship turn such a vast array of colors as fast as that ship did. He wondered if that was what the *Ivoire* looked like as it took fire just before jumping into foldspace.

He'd studied what happened to his ship enough to know that the mixture of foldspace energy and *anacapa* energy and weapons' fire had led to the *Ivoire's* becoming becalmed in foldspace, and ending up in its own future.

He had no idea what would happen to a ship *emerging* from foldspace, or to the other ships around it.

And then he got a clue.

"Son of a bitch," he muttered. The explosion of that Not-Fleet ship would be bigger and more destructive than the wave of energy he had sent at the Empire vessels on the border.

"Anita," he said to Tren, "make sure our ships have the proper shielding. This is going to be ugly."

"Already have," she said.

"And fucking let Boss know," he added, so that he wouldn't think about her.

The rest of his bridge crew was working as hard as they could, moving deliberately, so that they got as much done as they could.

"Has anyone contacted Xilvii?" Coop asked. "We need the Lost Souls defenses on high."

"Already done," Perkins said. "Contacted Odite too. Doesn't hurt to have their protective grid working."

He hoped. He had no idea how all of this equipment and different energy sources would interact. He was most worried about the *anacapa* drives, though, because they tended to harmonize and build on each other.

He didn't even have to ask his crew if they had contacted Trekov. They left the communications with the Empire up to him.

He hit the comm, and got her immediately, which was more of a relief than he realized. Audio only.

"You see what's happening to that third ship?" he asked, but didn't wait for a response. He couldn't. "That explosion will make all the others you've experienced seem like nothing. Make sure your ships are shielded, and your crews prepared. I'd tell you to change formation, but it will do no good. The wave from that explosion will hit everything here. Be as ready as you can."

"Thank you," Trekov said, although she didn't sound thankful. She sounded stressed.

He didn't care. He was stressed, and worried about that upcoming explosion. If the Not-Fleet had altered the *anacapa* drives in any way, like the Empire had with their so-called stealth technology, then the explosion would be even less predictable, and maybe even more violent.

He braced himself, and glanced at his crew.

They were ready.

He just hoped everyone else was.

56

EVERYONE IN THE COMMAND CENTER HEARD Captain Cooper's warnings. Elissa watched as her team sent messages to her ships, warning them to be prepared for an explosion the likes of which they'd never seen.

For a moment, she toyed with having them all move away, but she had no idea where they would go. There were so many of them, and they would need to activate their drives. They didn't have enough space between them for that, or enough time for that matter. It took a good thirty seconds to prepare the drives on most ships, unless their captains had the drives on standby.

Some ships might collide with others, just because of placement. This kind of super-explosion was something she hadn't even contemplated.

She had asked Cooper if he worried that the Not-Fleet would use that weapon he had used on her ships, and he had said it wouldn't happen if those ships were disabled as they arrived.

Now, one of those ships had been disabled, was changing colors so many times that it seemed like it was running an internal light show, and Cooper was now telling her that this explosion would be *worse* than what she had experienced.

"We're as shielded as we can be," Bahe said. "Commander Derrida says the *Ewing Trekov* is surrounded by a ring of shields."

Of course it was, since everyone on the force was trained to think of the command vessel as the most important.

"Tell the other ships to reinforce their own shields, not ours," Elissa said. If the third time was a charm in facing this kind of super-explosion, then so be it. She would die out here.

But she didn't want her team to, and she wanted all of her ships to survive. Otherwise Flag Commander Janik would claim he was right and she had been wrong.

Even in death, she wouldn't be able to abide that. She would haunt the entire Empire to defend herself.

She leaned over the screens, toggling them, so that she could see which ships were effectively shielded. Their shields grew stronger as they followed her orders, not to have them bleed any energy over to the *Ewing Trekov*.

Then the third enemy vessel glowed a weird purple-silver, a color she had never seen before. The light filtered into the command center from all the screens.

"Shut down the visuals," Elissa commanded. "We can't have that light in here."

It was nearly blinding, and she didn't want to see any more. They could watch the telemetry.

The screens shut off, but not before that light got even brighter. One screen hadn't entirely powered down when that light subsumed everything around it. The light flared across the entire sector—up, down, around, backwards, forwards, traveling as far as she could see—until the screen shut off.

That light still reflected across her vision, nearly blinding her, and probably doing the same to the rest of the team. No one complained. No one said anything.

She watched the telemetry, saw the energy field grow and grow, creating a knot in her stomach, and then the wave hit her ships, slamming the front ships in the formation first and going all the way back.

The formation nearest that explosion broke apart, ships disappearing from her data stream. Command Central was eerily silent, as the entire team waited.

Then the wave hit the *Ewing Trekov*.

She felt the wave in her teeth, in her bones, in her damned scars, and the energy felt familiar, almost like a violent and untrustworthy old friend. She clutched the console as tears formed in her eyes. Pain vibrated through her, shaking her internally, and then the vibrations stopped.

She let out a shaky breath, noted that the data stream was still flowing, the lights were still on, the air was still warm, and she was still breathing. Score one for her. This wasn't as bad—at least in the *Ewing Trekov*—as the wave Captain Cooper unleashed on her years ago.

But she hadn't been prepared for that, and her ship had been much closer.

She checked the readings, saw that the energy wave had passed through the *Ewing Trekov* and had moved on.

She turned on the visuals—small, ever so small—on the screen before her, but there was no light.

That enemy vessel—whatever it had been—was gone. The second enemy vessel, the one that had arrived and nearly been destroyed, looked like it was ancient, with parts floating around it in space. The original enemy vessel was farther back, but dark.

All of Elissa's ships were dark as well—at least in that first formation, the one that had been firing on the enemy vessels.

She studied the formation for a moment. Something was wrong with it.

And then the "something" registered. The formation was incomplete. A good twenty ships were gone out of the front of the formation, like a giant hand had come through and swept them away.

Her heart twisted. She combed through the data, saw explosion after explosion that had happened while she had been in pain.

Ship after ship destroyed.

And the ships in the back of that formation dark. She needed to mount a rescue effort.

Before she did, though, she looked. The ships in the other formations, facing the other directions, still had lights and power. All of Cooper's ships were intact, as well as the Lost Souls space station.

She wasn't sure how she felt about that. She wasn't sure how she felt about anything.

She frowned, then looked at the spot where the third enemy vessel had been. Light still burned in that area, in an almost square form, as if that door was still open. The light was that purple-silver, but it wasn't bright. It was fading.

As she watched, it faded in on itself, became a square, then a small circle, then a pinprick.

She flagged that area in her data stream for review later. Something had happened there. Something she didn't understand.

She let out a breath.

Cooper had sounded almost scared when he told her that the coming explosion would be bad. He clearly hadn't expected it.

Something had gone wrong.

She only hoped her team on Cooper's bridge would glean what that something was.

Because she wasn't going to trust him to tell her.

Just like she wasn't going to trust him to give her those remaining enemy ships. She was going to take them.

She was going to take them now.

57

I COWER IN MY SINGLE SHIP. The shields are on full, the shutters over all the vulnerable places on the ship in place, and all nonessential systems are shut down. It's damn dark in here, on purpose, because I deemed lights nonessential.

I pulled my environmental suit's hood up, and turned on the internal systems the second that I got the warning from the *Ivoire*. The warning didn't come from Coop. It came from Perkins—at least, I think it was Perkins. Whoever it was only identified themselves as part of the *Ivoire*, and they were sending the message on Coop's behalf.

It took me a second to realize it wasn't personalized, either. The message went out to a bunch of ships, not just mine.

Coop warned me that I wouldn't survive some kind of major attack, and I hadn't listened. Now, I'm in that moment, the moment when I'll probably die, and I'm stunningly calm.

In fact, I want this whole thing to end, because I'm not in control of it. I can't move my ship (Perkins or whomever warned against using any auxiliary energy), and I can't use my weapons, not that I had anything to shoot at, and I can't take on whoever or whatever it is that's coming my way.

I have left the telemetry on. I had a small screen going with visuals as well, but there was an odd purple-white light I'd only seen inside the Boneyard on our scans, far from where we were located.

Yash had looked at it back then, and looked away. Then she tapped the image in front of her.

We're never going there, she said, and I forgot about it. I forgot about all of it until now.

I shut down that small screen here in the single ship because the light became unbearable. It stabbed my eyes. The music started—faint and beautiful. Choral music that soothed my ears but punched a vulnerable point in my brain.

The music scares me. It's *anacapa* energy, rogue *anacapa* energy, someone said, out-of-control *anacapa* energy others have said, too much *anacapa* energy, and it can be unbearable. It's really not music, but that's how I experience it, how many of us experience it. The vibrations create a sound in our bones, and we translate it as music.

The vibrations must have started because the music is getting louder. I bend my head and put my arms over it—stupid, I know, but there's no point in watching telemetry or looking at bright lights on screens or doing anything else.

Either this energy wave that's vibrating out toward me will pass quickly or it'll settle, and if it settles I might go insane.

And I can't shake Nyssa Quinte's voice, calmly (or maybe not so calmly) telling me that I'm at greater risk of stroke when my adrenaline goes up.

Well, screw the gids. I'm way beyond those. My heart is pounding, my breath is short, and my face aches already. The music is so loud that it's piercing. I can't understand why I ever thought choral music beautiful.

It's assaulting me, attacking me from the ears in, slamming my face with chord after chord that reverberates all the way down my spine. My head aches, and I'm terrified. I wonder if I can actually *feel* a stroke hit or if everything just ceases to function like a ship.

Ship. I grasp onto the word, and make myself focus.

Before this all hit, before I got that message, I saw another spiral, near the other Empire formation, near the coordinates where the *Madxaf* returned from the Boneyard.

I saw it, I know I did. Not the Boneyard. A ship, looking ghostly, like it was cloaked, and I swear, I swear on everything I know that the ship was one of the five that had attacked us at the Boneyard.

I need to let Coop know. That's what I'd been thinking when I got the shelter-in-place message. I'd been thinking *Tell Coop the Fleet is here, Tell Coop the Fleet is here, Tell Coop…*

I recite it in my head like a mantra, trying to ignore the pain of that music as each note slices through me.

But the mantra isn't working, so I remind myself that pain proves I'm alive. Pain shows me that I can get through this.

I hope I can get through this, because my ears ache, my face aches, my brain aches, all of me aches and my environmental suit is yelling at me to *breathe! Breathe slowly and evenly. Breathe to calm yourself.*

I do. I take one large breath, and as I do, I realize that I *heard* my environmental suit. The music is gone. The ache remains, but the music that echoes in my ears is like an imprint of that bright purple-white light against my retinas. That music *is* an echo, a reaction, a memory already.

I am alive.

I made it through this.

I sit up, realizing I'm a mess of fluids. I think I've been crying because my face is wet, but is that crying or is it just leaking tears from all the pain. There's something wet on both sides of my neck that feels different than the sweat that's coating me everywhere.

I've heard of bleeding ears. I wonder if mine are doing that. I have no way to check, not without removing my gloves and my hood.

That's when I realize I'm not tracking well. Because I can just ask my suit.

I'm about to when I change my mind. I don't want to know if I'm bleeding. It's not relevant. I'll deal with it later.

Every muscle in my body aches, or maybe it's every bone. I have to heed that voice. I breathe, and the air tastes fine, fresh, reviving. Yash designed this environmental suit, and it has so many weird features that

I always forget about them. Then they please me, like this one. The fresh air is reviving.

I slowly move my arms away from my head. I sit up, and the movement comes with its own music. The clicks in my spine, the moans as I move. I wonder if I should have lived through this, and I'm not going to ask anyone, because then they'll *I-told-you-so* me.

I blink, still hearing that music, but it's fading away. Maybe it's not all an echo. Maybe I'm hearing that wave dissipate or slide away from me.

I run a diagnostic on the single ship, and am startled to see that the shields held. The ship itself is undamaged. It's only me that got hurt, and I'm not even sure if I am.

I certainly didn't have a stroke. I smile at my defiance. I hate warnings like the one Nyssa gave me. Because then I focus on it, instead of on what I need or want to do.

What I need to do now is see what's happening.

I reboot systems. The single ship beeps as everything starts back up. I open my control panel and scan, plus I put the screen back up—the one with the visual.

The area around me looks exactly the same, so none of the ships near me were damaged. I scan for the *Ivoire*, and see it, lights on, glistening behind an array of ships.

Only that array looks nothing like it had a moment ago. Instead of a wall of ships, there's a tangle. They're listing, at all different angles, and in different parts of space. It's like a gigantic ball went through them, knocking them aside.

Most of them have no power. They're black blobs against the dark blue of space.

I look at Lost Souls. Both space stations are fine. The warnings from the *Ivoire* were timely, and seem to have saved lives.

One of the Not-Fleet vessels has turned upside down from where it had been before the wave. There's bits of ship everywhere around it, suggesting it lost parts or the explosion destroyed something nearby. I can't tell of the bits of ship are Empire vessels.

That wall of ships which had been facing the Not-Fleet, that's the wall that's tumbled and destroyed, and I don't think I'm seeing enough ships.

My stomach clenches. If the Empire lost ships because of this, and it was Coop's idea, will the Empire retaliate against us?

I don't want to know the answer, not right now.

Another Not-Fleet ship is farther away than the one I was looking at, and that ship seems mostly intact. It has no power either. I do not scan it. Someone else—Coop most likely—is taking care of that.

I want to contact him, but I'm not going to. We're not out of this yet. He needs to focus on whatever's ahead.

And then I remember my mantra: *Tell Coop The Fleet Is Here.*

But is it? I move the scans to a different part of the space around Odite and Lost Souls, the area where I had seen that single Fleet vessel hovering like a ghost.

The vessel isn't there. I let out a small breath. But to be thorough, I scan nearby.

Farther back, away from the explosions, four Fleet vessels hover, in the same formation that I first saw them in. Two on top, two on the side. Only then there had been five vessels—and that had been at the Boneyard.

But three Dignity Vessels and an SC-Class ship, just like before. The Dignity Vessel that isn't here is the one that didn't match the others, the one that they seemed to be bringing along with them.

The hair rises on the back of my neck. They tracked us.

They found us.

And now they've seen this.

58

COHN STOOD IN THE CENTER OF THE BRIDGE of the *Geesi*, arms at her sides. Her team was coordinating with the other three ships, as well as pulling information from the two remaining ancient DV-Class vessels.

The explosion of the third ship just as it emerged from foldspace had created a disaster of a size and scale Cohn hadn't seen in years. That ship had been obliterated, as well as at least twenty Enterran Empire vessels. The Enterran Empire ships that had been hit most directly with the wild *anacapa* energy wave were without power, and listing.

The ancient DV-Class vessels behind them were fine. Apparently their shields could absorb that much energy or, like the *Geesi's* shields, constantly changed pattern and could fling the energy wave aside.

That wave had flowed over the *Geesi*, the *Sakhata*, the *Mächteg*, and the *Royk* as if they were rocks in a stream. Maybe that energy wave had done some microdamage. Cohn had assigned her engineers to check. But from a quick early diagnostic, the ships—all four of them—were just fine.

She had decisions to make now.

There were dozens of damaged ships out there, and they probably had injured and dying crew members. She could swoop in, along with the other three ships, and save as many people as possible.

But there were a lot of other ships nearby, and from what she could tell, they were mounting a rescue.

She knew absolutely nothing about the two groups at war with each other. She had no idea what she would be walking into.

Fleet captains were trained to help in emergency situations, but to be cautious. Sometimes emergencies with unknown groups could lead to disasters of epic proportions. She didn't know customs, she didn't know language, and she didn't know how to care for them.

She had her eye on the two ancient DV-Class vessels, though, the ones that were being attacked, not the ones taking part in the attacking. They were odd, and that explosion even more so.

That purple-white light meant that the *anacapa* energy had mixed with the foldspace energy, but the ship shouldn't have exploded. Not in that way. The explosion was too big. An *anacapa* drive mixing with foldspace energy should have caused a wave explosion, but not one that slammed across so much distance.

It was almost as if the *anacapa* drive was larger than any she had seen in use.

And there were other features of those ships, features she didn't entirely understand. Her crew had been pulling data from them since the *Geesi* arrived, but they hadn't come to any conclusions yet.

If she was going to rescue anyone, it would be from those ships.

Although the *Geesi,* the *Sakhata,* the *Mächteg,* and the *Royk* were very far away. Other ships would get to those ancient DV-Class vessels sooner.

She didn't want to fight anyone for anything.

She would observe a bit longer, see if any of the still-surviving ships headed toward the ancient DV-Class vessels. If not, she might move in and take them away.

She rocked back on her heels. The scene before her was fascinating, the possibilities surprising. She hadn't expected such a battle. She hadn't expected DV-Class vessels on both sides of that battle.

She needed more information. Some of it would come from the ships' data she had her team pull.

This was so much bigger than a theft. This was something that the Fleet was not involved in, but her vessels—her abandoned vessels—and her technology were deeply in the middle of.

Was it the Fleet's fault that hundreds of people were probably dead or injured because of an *anacapa* explosion? Did these DV-Class crews understand the technologies they were playing with?

And what, exactly, did it all mean for the Fleet?

This was all happening in an area the Fleet itself had abandoned a long time ago. Did they just continue moving forward?

The idea of that made her shift slightly, as she looked at the destruction before her.

If either of those sides had Ready Vessels, then this battle would have been worse.

Or it would have ended with little or no carnage at all.

She shook her head. These decisions were not for someone like her. There were people with higher rank who could make those decisions—after she made the one in front of her.

She kept her gaze on those two disabled and ancient DV-Class ships. If no one else moved toward them in the next fifteen minutes, she would.

She could save people on board those ships, and get answers at the same time.

Answers she desperately wanted.

She hadn't come across a situation that had intrigued her this much in a very, very long time.

59

NYGUTA CAME TO SLOWLY, wondering why she had volunteered to sleep in zero-g. She was floating and slightly dizzy. Her mouth tasted of metal and her eyes felt sticky. In fact, she felt sticky everywhere.

And sore. She was very sore. That was what woke her up. She wasn't strapped in place. She was floating, and she'd hit something, sending a shudder of pain through her.

She opened her eyes, although it took great effort. They were stuck shut, by tears or sweat or sleep or something. And there was something wrong with her environmental suit, because something had covered the clear part of the hood, making everything dark.

Then she realized nothing had covered the hood. She couldn't see because it was dark wherever she was. Not full dark. It was almost like she had something over her eyes in a brightly lit room. There was a grayish color to the dark that had to be coming from some kind of lighting.

She pushed off whatever it was that she had bumped into and then floated upwards. Her up, anyway. And as she did, she rotated a little, and saw the emergency lighting. It was only half on, and only underneath a section of flooring, near the *anacapa* drive.

Then it all came back to her. She was on the bridge of the *BilatZailea* in the middle of a battle. The *MuhaQiq* was coming out of foldspace when weapons' fire hit it, and the ship exploded.

She swallowed against her dry throat. She had tried to warn both the *MuhaQiq* and the *DetekTibe* about the attack. They should have gotten her message as they were leaving foldspace. It should have given them precious seconds to get their shields up, maybe shoot at the Empire vessels.

But neither of them had. She had no idea if her message had gone through or if the ships had come into this battle as startled by the opposing force as she was.

And then there was the explosion itself. The weapons' fire had concentrated on the very center of the *MuhaQiq*, where the bridge was located. Where the *anacapa* drive was located. Nyguta couldn't believe that the concentrated fire was a lucky shot.

Someone had told them how to completely destroy a DV-Class ship, and make it into a bomb that would take out all around it.

But whoever had given that order had either not cared about the ships that she'd seen in formation or about anything else in the vicinity. That weapons' fire guaranteed that those ships were going to be damaged or destroyed, unless they had some kind of special shielding to protect them.

Clearly, the *BilatZailea* had been damaged, worse than in the original firefight. She was floating on the side of the bridge, along with a great deal of debris. She didn't see the rest of her crew. Either they had gotten out and left her for dead, or they were somewhere that she couldn't quite see yet, even though her eyes were adjusting to the grayish dark.

She turned on the exterior lights on her environmental suit. The bridge looked worse in the beams of yellow extending from her shoulders and wrists. Once the ship lost its environmental controls and gravity, it must have rolled. Anything that wasn't attached had scattered across the bridge, causing some damage in the screens, and probably in other parts.

That glow underneath the *anacapa* drive was the only thing that made her feel better. The reinforcements that the Legion of Engineers made to the *anacapa* drives in all new DV-Class ships had worked.

Otherwise, her *anacapa* drive would have blown when the wave of *anacapa* energy went through.

Technically, the *MuhaQiq*'s *anacapa* drive shouldn't have blown either, but something must have hit it exactly. Or the *MuhaQiq* hadn't entirely left foldspace when the shots hit it. If that had happened, then the resulting explosion would have been a hundred times greater than anything that Nyguta had ever gone through before.

If that had happened, then she was lucky to be alive. The *BilatZailea* was lucky to still be here, and she was even luckier to have the *anacapa* drive intact.

A headache had lodged itself in the back of her skull. The soreness in her body had grown worse, not better, and she was dizzy. She had no idea how long she had been out.

But she had a duty first, before she could look for her crew members, before she could even check to see if she could right the *BilatZailea* and protect it again.

She had to check that *anacapa* drive. Because if it still worked, then maybe the communications *anacapa* did as well. And if they both worked, then she would get a reading that would tell her if the emergency beacon activated.

She had no idea how long it would take an emergency notification to go all the way back to the Armada, nor did she know what they would do if they received one, but she would be happy if they did. Because then they would know that the three vessels she had brought here had been attacked.

They would know, at least, what happened to her, and they would be able to decide what to do about these people, the *Ivoire* and the Empire. She might not be able to inform the Jefatura about what she had learned, but they would realize that something had gone very, very wrong.

Or maybe she could inform them, if she still had a communications *anacapa*.

She pulled herself across what had been the ceiling of the bridge, using handholds she had privately believed to be ridiculous. They weren't ridiculous now; now, they seemed prescient. Apparently, whoever had designed them had realized that sometimes people needed a handhold, no matter where they were.

As she traveled across the ceiling, the ship kept moving. The ceiling slowly became the left wall. The ship had lost all of its attitude controls and everything that made her feel as if she were in any kind of stable environment.

She had trained for this though, and she reached for that training, a combination of concentration and slow breathing, to keep herself calm.

The word "calm" made her realize that she was too calm. She was probably in shock, and moving only because of her training. She probably wasn't thinking as clearly as she needed to be.

She couldn't concentrate well, so she needed to take what came at her, one problem at a time.

First, the *anacapa* drive, then the communications *anacapa*, then the request for help. After that, reviving what surviving members of the crew she could find.

Or restarting life support, assessing damage, figuring out if the *BilatZailea* had been abandoned after it was hit. Was the battle still going on? She had no idea.

If it was, she was in trouble here.

Because someone would board the ship or take her prisoner or destroy the ship.

She pulled one hand over the other. This was taking entirely too much effort. Since there was no gravity, she shouldn't have been pulling so very hard.

That meant her muscles were compromised. *She* was compromised. She might not have a lot of energy left.

She had to reach the *anacapa* drive, and the closer she got, the farther away it seemed.

Time distortions. Feeling clammy despite the environmental suit. The effort it was taking just to cross an expanse of ceiling, something she should have been able to do in a matter of minutes.

Maybe it had been minutes. She had no idea. She let out a small snort of amusement, but the amusement died quickly. Her small snort had covered the clear hood before her with a smattering of blood.

Oh, no. She wasn't sure if she thought the words or spoke them, not that it mattered. She shouldn't have been injured, not in the environmental suit.

Then her brain cleared that up. The injury had nothing to do with the environment the suit created. She had been out, unconscious, compromised. Everything ached—no, everything was *sore*—and that was wrong.

She had been hit by things, things that had not compromised the suit. Maybe other people. Their suits wouldn't have hurt hers.

She made herself take a deep breath. That metallic taste grew, but now she knew what it was. She was bleeding somewhere—face, nose, cheeks, internally. She had no idea and this suit wasn't capable of that kind of diagnostic.

Even if it was, she wasn't sure if she would use it or not. If she thought she was fine—more or less—she would act fine. She didn't want the suit to tell her that she was seriously injured, so that she would have to quit whatever she was doing, and roll over and die.

The light above the *anacapa* container was brighter here. Not quite dark gray, more like a light gray. The gray had some brown, and she realized what she was seeing wasn't just darkness, but floating nanobits of two kinds. The black nanobits that the Fleet had initially put into this vessel and the brown, more sophisticated, nanobits that the Legion of Engineers had invented.

None of the nanobits were supposed to unbond, and yet they had. Probably because of the power of that energy wave.

She had some engineering, but not enough to tell her if the unbonding was done, or if the entire ship would come apart.

She couldn't focus on that. Instead, she needed to reach down, and look at that *anacapa* drive.

The casing, not the drive. She needed to look at the casing.

She dug the toe of her boot into one of the rungs she'd been clinging to, and bent at the waist so that she could reach the *anacapa* drive casing. The movement made fluid audibly slosh in her head. She didn't want to think about what that fluid could be, so she didn't.

Bending was hard, and it hurt like nothing had ever hurt in her life. She set the pain aside—she had no choice—and gripped the side of the casing. Inside the *anacapa* drive glowed golden, just like it was supposed to.

She took both hands and pulled herself down to the casing, unhooking her feet as she did so. Then she slid her feet into two other rungs, placed on either side of the drive.

When she got back to the Jefatura (*if* she got back), she would complement them on the new design. It worked really well in emergencies— so much better than using the gravity in her boots. The way she felt, turning on the gravity in her boots would have slowed her down.

And she had a hunch she shouldn't allow anything to slow her down.

She pulled open the secondary container, the one that had the emergency kit. The emergency lighting was faint, half compromised, then, or maybe that was all the energy the system could muster.

She checked the little band beside it, saw that yes, indeed, the emergency beacon had been activated. But it was a general beacon, one that went all over the sector.

She almost shut it off, then stopped herself. No. The *BilatZailea* was in need of assistance—any kind of assistance. And shutting off the beacon would let their enemies know that someone was still alive on the ship.

She wasn't sure why that mattered to her, but it did.

She moved ever so slightly to the right, and searched for the emergency notification system, the one that would send information back to the Armada itself.

The first notice had gone off shortly after the *BilatZailea* had been compromised. She was liking that word, "compromised." Because she couldn't face what was beneath the euphemism. "Damaged." "Destroyed."—She wrenched her brain away from wordplay and forced it to concentrate. Concentration and focus were getting harder and harder. Her nose was clogging—probably dried blood—and that metallic taste was getting worse.

She made herself mentally repeat what she had just learned. A message had gone to the Armada, saying that the *BilatZailea* had been attacked and was in distress. Maybe the same message had gone out from the *DetekTibe*. The *MuhaQiq* had been blown up too fast for anything to leave.

But if that foldspace window was still open when the messages went out, who knew where the messages went? That window could have altered everything. The messages might not get home.

Her fingers were locking up. It was getting harder to breathe, and even harder to think.

She had to do two things before she lost consciousness again.

She pressed a smaller pocket in the container, saw the readings coming from Engineering. It was down as well, but not gone, because—according to this—the communications *anacapa* was completely functional.

The communications *anacapa* was so tiny—a fingernail sized slice of a larger *anacapa*—that it could have even more reinforcement than the bigger *anacapa* drive on the bridge. That communications *anacapa* was designed to survive damn near anything.

And maybe it had.

She needed to send the last download of all of the information in the *BilatZailea's* system back to the Armada. The backups were made every night, unless she asked for an extra one in unusual circumstances.

She should have asked for one when they left the Enterran Empire and came here, but she hadn't. She hadn't expected all those ships, all of those weapons. She had thought she would have more than enough time…

She had been wrong, not that it mattered. Because she was in a completely different circumstance now. Completely different.

With her stiffening fingers, she managed to find the backup control, the one that would send the logs of everything except today back to the Armada. Maybe they could figure it all out.

Maybe they would come here, and rescue the ship. Rescue her.

She smiled at the thought. That wasn't going to happen.

She was in hostile territory. The *BilatZailea* was so badly damaged that it might not function again. She wasn't sure she could get it out of here.

She had to protect the information, the Armada, her people. But she wasn't sure how to do that.

Then clarity hit her brain—just enough—so that she could remember the proper procedure.

She needed to establish a safety perimeter around the *anacapa* drive. That way, if some outsider found their way on board, they wouldn't be able to steal—or even decipher—the means of propulsion.

She needed to type in a code, followed by three other system checks, then another code. It was purposely old-fashioned, and purposely complicated. That way, no one could just stumble upon it.

If her people were able to get the ship going again, they would know how to disable that code. No one else would know. It wasn't written down anywhere.

She needed to remember the code. And then, two things...

Two things, she had told herself. Two things. Send the backup home. Protect the drive.

Really, she needed to do three things.

She needed to figure out who else was alive, and if they needed help.

She closed her eyes. She couldn't breathe easily. Maybe if she let go of the drive, let her feet fly free, let herself roll, her body would take care of itself.

Sure, sure it would. Her body would take care of itself.

She felt herself shudder, her body jolt a bit. Her body itself seemed upset at the lack of oxygen, but she couldn't really bring herself to care. Shouldn't the inability to breath terrify her? That seemed logical.

Everything seemed logical. But she had set aside emotions. She had made herself concentrate on ... something...and now that she had completed...whatever...she just needed to...oh, she had no idea. She really had no idea.

She was slipping away. From herself. Slipping away from herself. She should panic about that, the way she should panic about the lack of oxygen, but she knew, everything would be fine.

She had no idea how she knew that and even as she had the thought, she knew it was wrong. Nothing was fine. The ship was damaged, she was dying, and she could no longer bring herself to care.

Maybe someone else would care soon. Maybe everyone else had survived. If so, she apologized to them mentally. She had done all she could.

She had done more than she could.

Her suit was beeping. She recognized the beep. It was to remind her to inhale. Well, consider herself reminded. She would inhale when she was ready.

And she wasn't ready.

She had fought enough for one afternoon.

She had fought more than enough.

60

"The last life sign just winked out." Perkins spoke softly. She meant the comment for Coop and the *Ivoire's* bridge crew, but she was clearly aware of the observers in the back.

Coop did not turn to look at them, even though he wondered what they thought of all of this destruction. A good twenty of their ships simply vanished. Did they know that?

If he had been assigned an observer role in a situation like this, he would have been clamoring to either help or return to his own ship. Instead, these observers had remained quiet, almost as if they wanted their presence forgotten.

"Which ship?" Coop asked. Perkins had been monitoring the Not-Fleet vessels, which was one reason that she had spoken so softly. She hadn't wanted the observers to know exactly what she was talking about.

Also, Coop knew Perkins well, and she would have thought it a tad rude to discuss a handful of life signs on enemy vessels when on their allies' ships, people were clearly struggling, maybe dying.

"The first ship," Perkins said. "The one that came through fol— appeared here first. On the other ship, no one survived at all."

Coop frowned and looked at the destruction on the holoscreen before him. There was a gaping hole in the center of the formation of the Empire ships.

The blast wave had gone through the middle so the destruction went deepest there, but it had taken out ships two deep on the top of the formation and the bottom. The remaining Empire ships were powerless, and listing.

His crew was monitoring the situation, but not like they were monitoring the Not-Fleet ships. He figured that Trekov would handle her own part of this. She certainly had enough vessels to initiate a rescue.

Besides, he really didn't want to talk with her yet. He had told her where to target the Not-Fleet vessels and her ships had done so. Would she blame him for that explosion? Because he hadn't expected the final ship to still be half in foldspace when the ship's *anacapa* drive exploded.

Even then, the explosion was different than any he had ever seen. The *anacapa* energy had clearly mixed with something coming out of foldspace, and destroyed the ship in the middle of all of that mess.

He expected that, and he had even expected the blast wave that had come from the explosion. He hadn't told Trekov how to tweak her shields, but he had warned her that there was the potential for a surge of energy like those she had experienced twice before. If her people hadn't figured out how to protect against a surge like that yet, then their engineers weren't doing their jobs.

Maybe he had been cruel, not giving her the proper shield harmonics to protect against a blast wave, but he hadn't wanted to give up too many secrets. He had figured that this alliance was temporary, and Lost Souls and the Nine Planets would still be at a disadvantage when the alliance ended.

He hadn't planned on the complete obliteration of at least twenty ships and the destruction of many more.

He made himself focus on what was before him. The foldspace window took forever to close, releasing who knew what kind of energy into the area around it.

The ship that had been coming through was also obliterated, after a spectacular purple-white light show. Coop was certain Yash and her team would be studying that when they got the chance.

He wasn't certain if that lightshow came from something unfamiliar in the *anacapa* drive or if it came from the mix of energy itself. He would leave that problem to Yash, in the after-action debrief.

That debrief would be ugly. He had wanted prisoners from those two ships. He wanted to know who had been coming after him, and what they actually wanted.

But there was no one left. The blast wave would have destroyed systems, but there should still be some information to pull from the ships.

Only he had promised the spoils to Trekov.

He turned ever so slightly so that he could see the reflection of the observers in the screens nearest him. They were not huddled together as he expected. The one in charge, Paek, stood near one of the consoles. He seemed to be watching someone work.

The engineer, Faifai, had moved to a different part of the bridge, still in the back, so that she had a good view of what half of his team had been doing. Fortunately, they hadn't been doing anything that would give her a lot of information about a DV-Class vessel.

The third person, Honoré, was standing too close to one of the consoles. Her gaze met Coop's in the reflection. Had she been trying to figure out what the blast wave was?

It hadn't been his ship that had caused the explosion. While these observers had been on the ship, he hadn't used a single weapon and had only warned his crew to strengthen their own shields. Nothing more.

Honoré couldn't get information from these consoles, not right now. But she seemed to think he knew more about the blast wave than he was letting on. Which he did.

He shifted slightly, so that he could speak to Tren. "I trust our shields held throughout. Lost Souls is okay?"

He already knew it was, but he wanted verbal confirmation, so that the observers thought he was working on that.

"It is," Tren said, sounding just a little confused. She knew that he didn't need her to explain that.

"All right," he said. He felt frustrated. The observers were hampering him. "I'll be in my ready room."

He almost added *for a moment* but he didn't. He slipped away from the captains' chair and headed to the room he almost never used. He pulled the door open. It smelled musty in here, although it couldn't be. It was just his reaction to not using the *Ivoire* much.

He opaqued the door and windows, then contacted Yash. He made sure she could see that he was in his ready room. She was near the secondary bridge controls in Engineering, which was the kind of good planning he needed from his Chief Engineer. She had been making certain that someone would be in charge of the ship had the bridge been destroyed.

"We need to get to those two Not-Fleet ships," Coop said, without preamble, "and quickly. I can't, because of the observers here on my bridge, but I need you to take a team and go. Do you think much survived that blast wave?"

"If it were one of our ships, sure," Yash said. "We're protected against something like that. But that explosion was odd, and I don't know if it's because of their equipment. So I'm not sure what we'll find."

Coop nodded. That was what he had thought as well. "All right," he said. "Go quickly. I promised these ships to Trekov, and I know she'll be preoccupied in the short term. Get the information we need and take the *anacapa* drives off of both ships—if the drives are still there."

There was the possibility that something had happened to the drives in that blast wave. Coop would have thought that any *anacapa* drive hit directly by a blast wave would explode, like the one had on the third ship, but these ships were different.

"How about I just set the ships to blow when I'm done?" Yash said. "We can travel over there cloaked, and then destroy the ships, and no one will be the wiser. We'll call it a delayed reaction to the blast wave."

Coop paused. He hadn't thought of that. His mind had been filled with too many other things.

Then he shook his head.

"No," he said. "I promised her. We're already going to have issues because of the loss of life on the Empire side. I want to make sure we keep our other promise to her."

"Except you promised her the ships, and I'm sure she wants the full ship, not something modified to hide things," Yash said.

"What she wants and what she gets are two different things," Coop said. "I wanted the crew of both ships alive. I want to know who they are. I'm not going to be able to talk to any of them."

"It's a little different, Coop," Yash said.

"Not really," he said. "We hadn't planned for this level of destruction."

Yash lowered her head just for a moment. The loss of life in that strange few minutes had been staggering. It just hadn't happened to their people.

"You need to go now," Coop said. "Bring a good team, be cloaked, and get this done fast. I'd tell you to send two teams, one for each ship, but you—"

"Wouldn't trust that," Yash said.

And Coop let out a short sharp laugh. That had been what he was about to say.

"Exactly," he said.

"Can I bring Boss?" Yash asked.

Coop raised his head, surprised. He hadn't thought of Boss since the explosions. He had asked for confirmation of everyone in Lost Souls, but he hadn't asked about her specifically.

He wasn't sure what that meant. Did it mean he had trusted her to make it through or that he didn't want the distraction if she had died?

He would have to examine those feelings later.

"She's nowhere near the ship," he said. "Won't that slow you down?"

"No," Yash said. "She's in her own ship. You knew that, right?"

He nodded, feeling that surge of anger again at the danger Boss had placed herself in. "As long as she can join you without being seen," he said.

"I doubt anyone will be checking on a tiny single ship," Yash said, "but I'll make sure."

"You can get to the ships without her," Coop said.

"But she's the expert," Yash said. "She'll make it all go faster."

Ships with no power, ships that were damaged, ships that were filled with hazards. Yes, indeed, Boss would make the trip go faster. Boss and Yash together would be able to find whatever they needed quickly. Boss could handle the other team members, and Yash could handle the information.

"Yeah," Coop said. "Bring her, and maybe her entire dive team."

Yash smiled. "Let's not go overboard," she said, and signed off.

Coop stood there for a moment, feeling a little disconcerted. Yash seemed to be on top of all of this, in a way that he wasn't. And he envied her. He wanted to go onto those Not-Fleet ships. He wanted to figure out what they were.

He would get the information though, and he supposed that would have to be enough.

He needed to focus on Trekov and see what he could do to help her. And to keep her attention away from those Not-Fleet vessels, until they were ready for her.

He had a lot to do, which was not something he would have minded in the past. Now, though, he wanted to join Yash.

He was different, and he kept realizing it, every single day.

61

MY HEART POUNDS. The interior of my environmental suit feels humid and sticky. The single ship seems fine, though, but I haven't run a diagnostic. I'm afraid of losing the images of those ghostly Fleet ships, afraid they might be some kind of data system error.

I let out a breath, straighten my sore spine, and reach toward the console with my right hand. I'm about to contact Coop when I stop.

If things are the way they were in the Boneyard, then he won't be able to see the Fleet vessels. And I don't want to worry him if what I'm seeing is a data error.

So, instead of contacting him, I hail Mikk.

He answers quickly. "You okay?" he asks.

I resist the urge to roll my eyes. I suppose I deserve this constant worry after that near-death experience, but the worry just gets in the way of living.

"Look on our old equipment," I say, deliberately not answering his barely concealed panicked question. "I have coordinates that I want you to look at."

"Here?" He gives me the coordinates I was about to give him. "We were about to run a diagnostic, to see if that was some kind of echo in our system after that blast wave."

"No echo if you have them too," I say. "Four Fleet vessels, right? Three DV and an SC, and unless I miss my guess, the same ones we saw at the Boneyard."

"Yeah." He sounds disappointed. And I finally follow his train of thought.

A data systems echo makes sense on the *Madxaf,* which had actually been in the Boneyard. A data systems echo makes less sense on my single ship because that ship hasn't been out of storage in nearly a year.

"Then we have another problem," I say. "A big one."

"They just watched massive destruction of a lot of vessels," he says. "They'll know how to destroy our vessels."

What an odd statement for Mikk to make. It takes me a moment to realize that the events of the past few hours have actually frightened him. It takes a lot to scare Mikk. I've only seen it a few times.

"I suspect they knew how to do that already," I say in my most gentle tone. "I'll let Coop know they're here. He might have to coordinate with you to be able to see them."

"All right," Mikk says. His tone hasn't shifted. He's still scared, and I've done nothing to alleviate it. Not that I really tried.

We sign off, and I'm about to contact Coop when I hear from Yash. She contacts me audio only, and the channel is scrambled.

"We're going to make a quick visit to the Not-Fleet vessels," she says. "I'm lead, and I need you. We have some things to accomplish."

She's clearly being purposefully vague. I more or less follow her. Coop wanted information from the Not-Fleet ships, some of which would be taken before he turned the ships over to the Empire. I suppose that the Empire is busy right now, dealing with their significant losses.

"Let me contact Coop first," I say. "I need—." And then I cut myself off. I can't tell her on an open channel about the Fleet. Exactly.

"You don't need to contact him. I've already done so," Yash is saying. She sounds annoyed. "The order's coming from me. And—"

"Yash," I say to shut her down. "The party we've been worried about has shown up. I can see them on my ship."

She pauses, as if she doesn't know what I'm referring to. Then she says, "If that's the case, it's even more important for us to get to those Not-Fleet ships."

"After I talk with Coop," I say.

"All right," she says, sounding strangely reluctant. "I need to plan with you. So contact me as soon as you're done."

"Will do." I let out a small breath, and do a self-check. I'm not light-headed. I don't have the gids. If anything, I'm a bit subdued, probably a result of that sudden adrenaline spike, which is now gone.

I make myself reach for the console, and contact Coop. It takes a moment to reach him, which does not surprise me. He's dealing with a lot.

I can only imagine what his Empire friends are saying to him at the moment.

"Quickly," he says, without so much as a hello.

I toy with telling him to go somewhere private, but we probably don't have time for that. So I settle on the same thing I had done with Yash. I settle on vague.

"Those ships we encountered in the Boneyard?" I say. "Four of them are here."

I tell him the coordinates, and I hear him breathe as he moves somewhere. He sounds as ragged as I feel. I haven't even asked if the *Ivoire* survived that blast wave well, or if he's all right.

Maybe he would tell me, or maybe not. But he would be able to get the information to someone else if need be.

"I don't see anything here." He sounds impatient and frustrated.

"Mikk does," I say, "but they're not showing up on Fleet equipment. Only my old stuff."

Coop curses. "Do you know how long they've been here?"

"At least one saw the entire battle." *If you want to call it that,* I add mentally. Because those Not-Fleet ships, which we'd been so afraid of, had been mostly obliterated.

Coop cursed again. "I can't fight something I can't see."

"I don't think you should fight them," I say, "but we need to keep an eye on them. I'll see if Ilona has anyone on the station who can send a ship out—"

"We don't have time for that right now," Coop says. "You can be my eyes."

I feel a flash of irritation. Hasn't Yash contacted him? Aren't they both on the plan to get equipment off those Not-Fleet ships?

And then I realize what Coop's doing. He doesn't want me to go with Yash. He's as damn worried about me as everyone else has been.

"I can't be your eyes," I say. "Hasn't Yash contacted you? I'm joining her at the—"

"I know," he says, cutting me off. He doesn't want me to label the ships, which means he's not alone. He probably has those observers near him. "I don't want you to go there."

"I'll be fine," I say. "Work with Mikk."

And then I sign off. That irritation has grown into a low-simmering anger. *I don't want you to…* Coop has no right to give me orders and he's been doing it since we got back, maybe longer.

Then I mentally shake myself. The last thing we all need right now is for Coop and I to fight.

I glance at my console. I need to focus on what Yash wants. I'm not even sure I can do it. That stickiness in my suit might be something, and I don't have time to get to the *Madxaf* to change suits and see what's going on.

I'll also have to weave my way through or around the damaged Empire ships to get to the Not-Fleet vessels. I can do that pretty easily. One of the best parts of the singleship is that it has speed. But I have to stay off their telemetry or someone has to notify them that I'm coming. I don't want to be seen as a threat.

First things first, though. I need to make sure I'm well enough to dive those damaged Not-Fleet ships with Yash. We're going to need to hit them fast and be surgical with what we remove.

She's right: she needs me. She's a good enough diver, and she knows where everything is (or should be) on a DV-Class ship. But she doesn't know how to instinctively watch out for the dangers of a damaged vessel.

I know, but I might have to talk her through it instead of diving with her. Or maybe figure out how to send Orlando or Tamaz or one of the others.

They're not me, but they'll do better than she will.

Now I feel the fluttery edges of the gids, and I smile at myself. I want to do this. I don't want to hand it over to someone on my team.

And if I'm going to do this, I need to treat myself the same way I would treat them.

I take a deep breath, and run the environmental suit's diagnostic.

It first gives me a report on itself. No holes, no tears, no wear. Which I knew, since I hadn't left the seat.

Then, in rapid fire information, it gives me a picture of my own condition. The stickiness I feel isn't blood; it's sweat. I sweated through my clothes. That off feeling I have is, in part, dehydration, which I can fix.

There is a miniscule amount of blood on the outside of my ears, but I can hear, which is all that matters. I'm not dizzy so my eardrums are intact.

But I should stand just to see if I can move, because if I can't move without getting dizzy, I certainly can't dive.

I place my hands on either side of me, and lever myself upward. I'm not really standing—it's almost impossible in this cockpit—but I'm close enough. The movement does not make me dizzy. It does make me breathe a bit more, which I also seem to need.

The suit's comparison of me when I entered the single ship and me now shows that the only differences are the sweat, the minor dehydration, and the miniscule amount of blood near my ears.

I have cleared myself to dive. And Mikk will be happy, because I did so sensibly.

I double-check the environment inside the single ship. I don't need my hood. So I open it, letting it fall against my back. Then I open the small emergency supplies case underneath the console, and remove a bottle of replacement fluids.

I attach the bottle to tiny holder in front of my left shoulder, and thread the drinking tube up the neck, using the system exactly as Yash had designed it.

I peel back the edge of the tube, put it in my mouth, and suck, wincing at the sour lemony taste. Next time I get in a bad situation, I'll make sure the replacement fluids taste like something I love.

I drink as I hit the console to contact Yash.

We need to plan, and we need to do so quickly.

I don't like the hovering presence of the Fleet, and I really hate traveling around that many Empire vessels, even if we did ask them to be here.

I want to get this mission done. Because the thing that's gone unsaid, the thing that Coop is clearly worried about, is that Yash and I will not have much time when we get to the Not-Fleet vessels.

We have to move fast, and we will be at great risk—and that's just from the dive.

Who knows what will happen with our two different enemies. What I do know is this: No one will be able to protect us.

Once Yash and I and whatever team we have get to those Not-Fleet vessels, we will be very much on our own.

62

ELISSA'S TEAM IMMEDIATELY LAUNCHED INTO ACTION. Central Command was filled with coordinated orders, low tense voices, and the occasional demand for silence.

The air had a sharp tang of fear and sweat. Elissa had no idea how many of her people had a reaction to that wave of energy, but no one was showing it. Her bones still ached and her scars felt like someone stomped on them. She couldn't open and close her right hand with anything approaching ease.

But she didn't have the time to care. She had two things to do: she had to supervise this rescue mission, and she needed a team to secure the two damaged enemy vessels.

Normally, she would have sent Paek, but he was on Cooper's ship, and apparently learning some things, although she wasn't exactly sure what. Cooper must have been conferring with his team on the enemy vessels as well, and they seemed to have some thoughts about those vessels, thoughts no one was sharing.

Elissa had no idea how, exactly, to secure those enemy vessels. She wasn't getting the kind of readings she liked—everything was fuzzy and almost impossible to read.

She wasn't sure if that data blockage came from the enemy ships themselves, from that big energy wave, or from some damage to her own systems. A large portion of the engineering staff was going over the *Ewing Trekov* bit by bit to make sure the ship was fine—just like she had ordered for every remaining Empire ship in the area.

All of them had assigned their engineering staff to repairs of the ships that seemed undamaged. It was the ships that had received the full brunt of that wave that had her the most worried.

No one here in Central Command had been able to find the missing twenty vessels. Elissa had held out a (tiny) hope that the ships had been displaced by that wave, sent to another part of the area, but they weren't visible at all.

Those ships had simply disappeared. She hadn't seen that with the previous two attacks, initiated by Cooper. When he had hit her ships with a wave, that wave had crippled the ships, but not made them vanish.

She wasn't sure if the vanishing was something that happened with a high dose of that energy wave—maybe sending the ships through one of those doorways—or if the vanishing meant the ships were completely destroyed.

Her heart told her that the ships were gone, that once again, hundreds of Empire military lost their lives because of a proximity to Captain Cooper.

Although she couldn't really blame him for this attack. He had tried to warn her. And he had seemed panicked.

The less damaged—or unaffected—ships were already sending rescue teams to the badly damaged vessels. The rescue effort could be considered coordinated only because it was following Empire protocol, but no one had to instruct the various captains on how to pull this off.

They knew what to do, and her people on the *Ewing Trekov* were providing information in real time. Which ships were the most badly damaged, which appeared to have the most injured, which appeared to have the most dying, and which ones had become ships of the dead.

She was letting that information flow over her. Her people could handle it. She would have to take responsibility for it at some point, certainly when she went before Flag Commander Janik yet again, letting him know that somehow, Cooper had managed to destroy a large number of important Empire vessels.

Her career was probably over, not that it mattered. The loss of life here was shocking, and she needed to prevent it from getting worse.

She also needed to justify her actions—truly justify them. If she left here empty-handed, then all of this loss would be in vain.

She studied the screens before her. They showed the destruction. She couldn't look at that.

She needed to make other decisions.

She made herself look at the two enemy vessels. They had no energy signature—that she could read. And they also didn't appear to have life signs. But she couldn't guarantee that.

So if she was going to secure those ships, without Cooper's help, then she needed a multi-tiered plan. She looked up, searching for Bahe. Bahe was consulting with the head of the medical rescue unit, and looking very serious.

Bahe was busy—and she wasn't Paek. If Elissa discussed a plan with Paek, he always understood where she was going with it. He had worked with her for a very long time.

Bahe wasn't that focused on what Elissa wanted or needed. Bahe was focused on the *Ewing Trekov* as well as the ships under their command. She might be a good consultant on which ships to send where, but only after she had done some research.

Elissa didn't have time for research. She kept expecting to see Cooper's ship approach those damaged enemy vessels. If there were injured people on board, then Cooper would pick them up and probably use humanitarian reasons for refusing to hand them over to Elissa.

She couldn't let him do that. She couldn't even give him the opportunity to do so.

She had to trust herself on this.

Then she allowed herself a bitter half-smile. She had trusted herself on this entire mission and it had destroyed twenty ships (at least) and killed hundreds.

This was one of those moments—at least according to the memoirs of her ancestor, Ewing Trekov—that made or broke a commander. Sometimes victories looked like defeats early on. Sometimes the heroics came in the reversal of fortune, not in the initial skirmish.

She squared her shoulders and moved to a different console, checking the status of the ships closest to the enemy vessels.

If those ships weren't obliterated, then they were damaged. So she needed the closest undamaged ships, and commanders she could trust.

Before she even did that, she needed to figure out exactly what she wanted them to do. They needed to capture those ships and take them back to the Empire. If she did that quickly, then Cooper couldn't mount a resistance. He simply did not have enough force.

She wasn't sure what kind of damage his ships had suffered from that energy wave, and she was certain he wouldn't tell her.

She wasn't going to count on his ships being disabled, but she was going to count on him being preoccupied.

So, if she tethered the two ships and dragged them back to the Empire, she would at least need ships to handle the tether and ships to guard them. The tethering would take four ships, and the guarding would take another six minimum.

Plus those ships needed to go to the enemy vessels in a force large enough to keep Cooper or his people away from those vessels.

She studied the ships before her, and their roster. She also needed some excellent medical personnel, just in case there were survivors on the enemy vessels.

Medical personnel and a solid brig.

She let out a small breath, then ran her aching right hand through her hair. She raised her head just a little. No one was watching her. They were all working exceptionally hard, sending rescue vehicles, coordinating, figuring out which ship needed what kind of aide first.

Then she brought her head back down. She looked at the crew manifests for the ships on the opposite side of Odite, farthest from those explosions.

She needed to divide that larger force into smaller military units, and send two units to the enemy vessels. She needed to make sure the ships she was sending were in good condition, and that they would be able to leave immediately, with the two enemy ships in tow.

Cooper wouldn't notice if a group of ships left that formation. He would assume they were going to help with the rescue efforts—which, she noted, he hadn't volunteered to help with at all.

Maybe that was a sign his people had suffered from the energy wave as well.

But she wouldn't count on it.

She made a copy of the roster lists, and then veered away from Central Command. She'd go down to her office to contact the captains of the vessels she needed to get those enemy ships out of here.

She felt more determined than she had for a long time. This battle, this *destruction*, would not be in vain. She would have those ships and their secrets back at the Empire before Cooper even realized they were missing.

63

WHEN COOP CAME OUT OF HIS READY ROOM, he was angry. Angry at all of the destruction, angry at Boss for cutting him off.

Angry that the Fleet was here (if that was the Fleet) and not only could he not see them, he didn't dare talk to them, not at the moment. He had to take care of the problems in front of him first.

The bridge crew was working tightly. Because of the observers, no one had holographic screens wide and open like usual. The screens were folded and darkened, so that it was impossible for someone to see exactly what was going on.

Coop had had enough. Which probably wasn't true, but it felt true. He strode up the aisle to Sub-Lieutenant Paek. Paek's expression looked exactly like it had looked when he and the other two observers had arrived: flat and calm, as if nothing had an impact on him.

"Have you checked with Commander Trekov?" Coop asked. "I'm sure that your crews are all-hands-on-deck."

"They can handle the emergency," Paek said in a flat voice. "Three more people won't make any difference at all."

That wasn't Coop's experience. The right three people made all the difference.

He almost said something lashing, like *I guess you three aren't that important then*, but he caught himself.

He wasn't angry at them. He was angry at the situation, and Boss, and the fact that he wasn't going to those Not-Fleet ships to see what they were about, nor was he going to talk with the Fleet, whom he had been waiting for for years.

"Well, should you be needed and have to leave," Coop said, "let one of the crew know."

Paek's gaze met his, and Coop couldn't read it. Coop usually had no trouble reading other people, but something about Paek was hidden. Honoré had walked over.

"You're not going to tell us what that weapon was that destroyed those ships?" she asked Coop. It was clear she thought he was hiding something—and he was.

"Your weapons destroyed those ships," he said.

"Because you told them to target a certain part of the ship," she said.

"I did," he said. "If your weapons hit the vessels I'm familiar with, you would have destroyed the bridge, not the entire ship. I have no idea what was on those ships that caused this to accelerate like that."

"Except that you let everyone know the explosions would be out-sized when that third ship arrived," Honoré said. "What was that?"

He could answer a thousand ways, none of them true or good. Or he could be truthful, to a point.

"The colors," he said. "The light around the ship turned a kind of purple that I'd seen before. It's devastating."

If he added *I don't know why* she wouldn't have believed him. Besides, people often did that when they were lying.

"Captain," Perkins said. "Mikk has sent me coordinates."

Coop raised his head, then pivoted, thankful to be pulled out of the conversation that he had started. Perkins was good; she hadn't said what the coordinates were for, and he was moving too far away for the observers to ask.

"See what you can figure out," he said, hoping that Honoré and the others would think he was talking about the explosion.

He reached the captain's chair and pulled up his own screens, keeping them slightly opaqued. Yash had sent him notice that she was leaving in a runabout with a single pilot, which was not following Coop's orders.

He had wanted her to take an entire team. The anger he'd thought he'd suppressed rose again. And then he swallowed it back.

Usually he wasn't this volatile, especially in a command situation. It was the Fleet—or what he thought was the Fleet—that was causing this turmoil. He had been searching so long, and now they were here, and he couldn't do anything.

He thought of having Mae and the diplomats hail the Fleet, but that would draw the Empire's attention. Maybe. Or maybe not. And there wasn't even a guarantee that Mae could contact them, given the cloaking that the Fleet was currently using.

They didn't want to be seen, not yet.

He would have to deal with them later.

He scanned the area for Boss's single ship. She had been right: he hadn't wanted her in danger, and he didn't want her on this mission now. But she was, and he couldn't change that.

He let out a sigh.

All he could do right now was observe and distract.

With that in mind, he opened a channel to Trekov.

She didn't answer immediately, but when she did, she sounded as brusk as he would have in the same circumstances.

"I'd like to offer assistance," he said. "I'm not sure what we can provide. Your medical facilities are better than ours, and we have none on Lost Souls."

That they could use anyway, but he didn't add that.

"I can send personnel if you need it," he said, thinking *but that would be like putting a thumb on a gaping wound.* "I can also—"

"We have more than enough ships and personnel," she said. "When this is over, we will discuss what happened, you and I."

And then she signed off.

He deserved that, he supposed. He had been about to ask her about the observers. But she wouldn't let him.

So he wasn't going to be able to distract Trekov by talking to her. But it sounded like she was as busy as she should have been, given the dire circumstances.

He leaned the back of his legs against the arm of his captain's chair. He was in the unenviable position of trusting his people to do their jobs, and do them well.

He wanted to be involved, but right now, he just needed to hold the pieces together. *That* is *involvement,* Captain Debbie Nisen told him way back when he was just a lieutenant. *Sometimes organizing is the most important thing of all.*

It seemed he had to learn and relearn the same lessons in his life. And he was going to have to learn this one, while standing here, watching his people work.

And hoping that they did it in record time.

64

THE RESCUE EFFORTS WERE MASSIVE. Three-quarters of the remaining Enterran Empire ships were involved, each clearly assigned to one of the damaged ships. The remaining vessels had fanned out around the entire area, as a protective force.

Cohn watched from the bridge of the *Geesi*, a bit surprised at all that happened. She had never seen that particular formation used in a battlefield situation, but then again, the Enterran Empire ships had no idea the *Geesi*, the *Sakhata*, the *Mächteg*, and the *Royk* were nearby. As far as the Enterran Empire was concerned, the battle was over.

They had survived, and, perhaps, by their lights, prevailed. Although she had no idea what the point of any of this had been.

The *Ivoire* remained in its position on the opposite side of the damage. The *Ivoire* and the other DV-Class ships did not seem to be participating in the rescue. She wasn't sure if that made sense or not. She had no idea what the relationships were.

"Life signs are gone," Vinters said.

Cohn looked at her, frowning, thinking that the life signs on all of the damaged Empire vessels were gone. Then Cohn realized Vinters was referring to the two remaining enemy vessels, the ones that had been attacked, and buried in Vinters' comment had been a question.

With everyone on board those ships dead, did Cohn still want to go to those ships? Apparently the fifteen minutes was done.

"Were you able to pull information from those ships?" Cohn asked.

"They sent a burst of information, along with an emergency signal a few minutes ago," Vinters said. "And after that, we lost the last life sign."

Someone had sent for help at the last minute, and had sent what information the ship had to share.

"I take it you intercepted the burst of information," Cohn said.

"We did intercept," Vinters said. "We were able to block it."

Cohn paused, wondering if she should let the information go out. If it did, she could track it. But she didn't need to track it. The destination would be inside the information itself.

"Good," Cohn said. "What about the rest of the data?"

"Systems are down inside that ship," Vinters said. "I have no idea if the last sending was everything or just the last few days. Or maybe some other call for help. So, no, we probably don't have the data. If their ship is anything like ours, then there is backup data storage built to survive even after massive damage, but it will take an in-person response."

Cohn had been afraid of that. She had worried that she wouldn't get all the data she wanted from a simple data pull.

"We'll need to take those ships back to the Fleet," she said.

More tethering, as they all traveled long-distance. She didn't like that, but she didn't want to leave all this knowledge behind either. Clearly something had been happening with abandoned DV-Class ships. Or these three ships—two now—were some kind of threat the Fleet wasn't even aware of.

She looked at those damaged ships, and thought for a moment. Then she said, "The Enterran Empire ships are preoccupied with rescue, so I'm not worried about them. But I have no idea what the *Ivoire* and those other ships are doing. I do not know what the plans of the Lost Souls Corporation are. So we need to tether to the ships, and then get them out of this part of space as fast as we can."

Vinters nodded. "Do you want me to contact the other three vessels?"

"No," Cohn said. "I'll strategize with them. If we're going to tether through foldspace once again, I want Captain Wihone to work with you, Erasyl, to make sure that we travel safely."

"We don't have the luxury of tether inspections or anything else," Iosua said. He'd thought Wihone had been overly cautious in his plans to get the five ships to the Scrapheap at the start of this mission.

"I'll let him know," Cohn said. "We need to get to those ships, and tether, while remaining cloaked. That'll be difficult, but I don't want to alert either Lost Souls or the Enterran Empire to our presence, until we snatch the remains of those ships out from under their noses. Do I make myself clear?"

"Yes," Iosua said. The others nodded.

"All right," Cohn said. "Let's plot a course. I'll talk to the captains. We need to get this done quickly."

She didn't give them an exact timeline because she didn't have one yet. She would once she talked with Wihone.

She was feeling pleased with herself. If she returned to the Fleet with two captured enemy vessels, even if the entire crew was gone, she would have actual evidence to back up her claims of danger coming to the Fleet from behind.

But she couldn't feel too victorious. She didn't have the ships yet.

It would be a lot of work to get them, and she didn't have a lot of time.

But she knew her team could do so.

They would have to.

THE DIVE

65

By the time I reach the rendezvous point, I am feeling better. The liquids helped, as did time away from that blast wave. I'm also feeling just a bit of adrenaline at the adventure ahead, even though I'm trying to keep my emotions under control.

We have two dangerous dives ahead of us, and they won't be timed.

Yash has brought a runabout from the *Ivoire*. And Mikk, damn him, has sent another runabout, with Orlando, Tamaz, and Nyssa on board. Mikk remains with the *Madxaf*, monitoring the Fleet vessels.

He doesn't trust them. I don't either. But if he was going to go against my orders—which he has—I wished he had done so all the way. I would have rather had him diving with me than Orlando or Tamaz. I know that Nyssa won't be diving, because she's being sent to keep an eye on me.

When this is all over, we're going to have a long talk about caretaking Boss. And by we, I mean I'm going to let everyone from Ilona to Mikk to Coop know that I can damn well take care of myself.

Yash has picked a rendezvous point on what she calls the back side of the Not-Fleet vessel. This vessel is the farthest from all of us, but she chose it because she believes she'll get a better sense of the systems on this ship than on the other one.

She's probably right.

We've been sending encrypted communications back and forth. I don't think the Empire is monitoring us, preoccupied as they are by the rescue of their own people, but we can't be too careful here. I'm also not sure what the Fleet (if that's who they are) are capable of.

I've already established that I will be in charge of the physical dive. If there's a problem that I can see, I will abort the dive no matter what. I know that Yash understands the systems better than I do, but she's a marginally experienced diver, about to enter a fraught situation.

That we have a limited period of time to do this makes the dive even more difficult.

Yash wants to do a double dive, which I hate. We do the first ship, and then go to the second. Coop wants us to take the *anacapa* drives and destroy all the evidence of them.

If our initial dive takes too long, I've already told Yash that Orlando and Tamaz are going to have to handle the second ship. She won't agree to that. Apparently, there's something about handling *anacapa* drives that's difficult for even the most trained engineer.

I don't really care. If the choice is between executing Coop's orders and saving lives, I will save lives.

We've already lost enough of them today.

Yash and I arrive at roughly the same time. Orlando and Tamaz are already there, because the *Madxaf* was closer to these vehicles than I was or than the *Ivoire* was. They've already completed their initial dive.

I figured getting into the Not-Fleet vessel would be one of the most time-consuming parts of the dive, so I assigned Orlando and Tamaz to cut through one of the exterior doors before I get there.

It's a risky maneuver, but we can't bank on those doors being easily accessible. As I traveled to the Not-Fleet vessel, I heard them discussing the entrance. They tried the door anyway, and failed to get in. So they've been diligently cutting an opening and sealing its edges so that it won't cut into our suits.

Yash wanted a door closer to the bridge, which is one of two places we have to go. But I vetoed that. We need to stay as hidden as possible.

And this location is the best one. It's out of sight of the Fleet, as well as any Empire vessel.

If they're not monitoring these ships, they won't be able to see us.

They might not see us anyway, if they're not looking for something small. They might even think we're surviving members of the Not-Fleet's crew, trying to effect repairs.

I can't think about that, though. We have two dives to complete and very limited time to do so.

Yash has sent me what she believes to be the interior map of the vessel. She's also given us a timeline, which I ignore. We're going to go as fast or as slow as the ship allows.

We only get one shot at this.

We're going to do it right.

66

THE PLAN WASN'T EXACTLY THE ONE COHN HAD WANTED, but in the end, she deferred to the expertise of Iosua and Wihone. They believed it would be better—more efficient and less time-consuming—to tether one ship to each strange enemy vessel. Those ships would immediately take the vessel into foldspace.

That way, if there ended up being a problem, at least one of the strange enemy vessels would eventually make it back to the Fleet.

The two remaining ships would fend off anything that threatened the operation. The moment both of the ships—and their cargo—made it into foldspace, though, that was the moment the other two ships would go into foldspace as well. The *Sakhata* and the *Mächteg* would take the disabled vessels into foldspace. The *Royk* would help the *Geesi* defend the area until those ships were completely gone.

Like all plans, it sounded so easy when it was being devised, but as the *Geesi* led the way toward those disabled enemy vessels, Cohn had time to reflect. She knew that this plan was flawed in half a dozen ways. She simply didn't have a choice.

If she wanted those vessels—and she did—then she had to act fast, and fast wasn't always efficient.

It was Wihone who made that point, which was why they all ended up with this plan. He said that if they got only one ship out—at the cost of three of their own—that was better than returning to the Fleet empty-handed.

He was right.

Cohn plotted a course for all four ships to get to first vessel. That vessel had been closest to the explosion that had come out of foldspace. The ship was probably the most destroyed, and she had argued that they pick it up last.

But it was Iosua who gently contradicted her.

The most damaged vessel was the one they wouldn't have to handle gently. They could get it out quickly, without worrying about causing more damage. They could tether and jump, maybe in less than an hour depending on the vessel itself.

Back to not having enough time to do things right.

Cohn stood in the middle of her bridge, rubbing her hand against the back of her neck, primarily because her hair kept standing on end, and she was rubbing it down.

She could feel each second pass as if it were a disaster averted. She knew that the legion of ships out there—both from the Empire and from Lost Souls—couldn't see her vessels. She made sure all four ships were traveling cloaked.

They would work cloaked too, although the moment that the *Sakhata* started to tether, it would only be partially cloaked. Anyone paying attention would see the tethers deploy and the work commence.

She was gambling—they were all gambling—that no one was paying attention.

She was monitoring everything else, though. The *Ivoire* hadn't moved, and neither had the other Lost Souls vessels. They hadn't even gone to help with a rescue of the damaged Empire vessels.

The Empire had sent dozens of ships to their damaged vessels. On a few, they were mounting a rescue attempt. Apparently, those ships they weren't saving. On others, the teams had boarded, maybe to help stem whatever crisis was happening on board.

Even if the Enterran Empire or the Lost Souls vessels had known her ships were here, they weren't doing anything about them. And they weren't close to the damaged vessels either, apparently no longer considering them a threat.

She glanced at the screens before her, at all of the activity. Lost Souls, the Empire, they all had more than enough to do at the moment.

They probably figured they could wait to deal with the damaged vessels. That would be how she would think about it, particularly with all of the lives at stake.

If she was lucky, she would be able to leave with both ships, and it would be a long time before either Lost Souls or the Empire knew they were missing.

The Empire did not have the capability to track her vessels through foldspace. As far as she could tell, the Empire did not understand foldspace at all.

Her concern was the DV-Class ships from Lost Souls. They had foldspace capability and they knew how to use it.

She couldn't imagine them tracking her, though, or going after those vessels. But then again, she had no idea what their real purpose was, and what they were doing.

She only had guesses.

She assigned five people on her team to monitor the Empire and Lost Souls. That would be more than enough. Everyone else would take care of the tethering, and the guarding.

She hoped all of that would go fast. She was ready to leave this place.

She didn't have all of the answers she wanted, but she had some of them.

More than enough to pass this particular flashpoint on to someone else. At the Fleet, they could dissect and recover the information off the damaged enemy vessels. They could figure out what they wanted to do about the Enterran Empire, and the Scrapheap, and the *Ivoire* in particular.

Once she was out of here, she would consider her work done.

Whether her bosses agreed would be another matter.

Then she smiled at herself. Her mind was already halfway down the road. Apparently, she didn't think that tethering the ships and carting them through foldspace was going to be hard.

Wihone certainly didn't think so. And Iosua liked the plan.

She had vowed to trust both of them, so she would.

The *Geesi* was almost to the first enemy vessel. Iosua estimated that it would take no more than fifteen minutes to tether and leave with the ship.

Fifteen minutes to get this last operation underway.

Cohn hoped that was an overestimate. But she knew enough about plans to understand that hope was never a good strategy.

The *Geesi* slipped into position—between the damaged vessel and what remained of the Empire forces. The *Royk* took its position beside her.

The *Sakhata* moved behind the damaged enemy vessel, with the *Mächteg* guarding its flank.

This was all on Wihone now.

And Cohn had to trust him to do everything right.

67

IT HAS BEEN YEARS SINCE I'VE DOCKED MY SINGLE SHIP against a dark and damaged Dignity Vessel. This ship isn't quite a Dignity Vessel. That has become clear as I attach to it.

The exterior of the vessel is composed of something like nanobits, but they're brown and not as shiny as the nanobits I'm used to. Coop had mentioned something strange about the nanobits at the old Sector E-2, and this must be more of the same.

The exterior is full of holes, but the nanobits—or whatever the brown things are—are holding. Attaching my grappler takes more time than I like.

I'm only using the grappler because I'll be outside of the single ship for a short period of time as I move to the opening that Tamaz and Orlando cut in the ship.

None of them know I'm going to do this; I'm sure Orlando would have tried to talk me out of it.

But it's easier to attach to the Dignity Vessel and move along its side than it is to attempt to travel from my single ship to Orlando's runabout, and then back to the Dignity Vessel. Not to mention the amount of time it would waste.

Still, I think about all of that as I suction the single ship to the strange brown material and hope it will hold. I'm using the grappler on its highest strength, a sign that I'm a lot more nervous than I would admit to anyone except myself.

I've checked my environmental suit, run a dozen diagnostics on it, and sent three to Mikk. I sent the same three to Nyssa, who will be monitoring my vital signs—and, I hope, Yash's. I haven't discussed that with Yash, but she does know the rules of a dive.

Those rules are going to hold no matter what the circumstances are here. If one of us is sick or injured, we're aborting the dive. I don't care what Coop promised the Empire, and I don't care what he's trying to keep from them. We're going to do the best we can to clear the Dignity Vessel of any and all trace of an *anacapa* drive, and then we're going to leave.

Using a remote hand that I've set up myself, I attach one end of a tether to the opening that Tamaz and Orlando have cut, and the other end to the exterior of the Dignity Vessel just above my single ship.

Here's the difficult part: I have to trust my equipment and the readings that come to me. I can't test the strength of the line on my own.

I only have to cross six meters from the back end of my single ship, but those six meters could be six hundred if I'm not careful.

Yash will follow me, using her runabout's docking tube. I insisted on it; I'd like to keep any danger to Yash at a minimum. She's the only one with enough expertise to figure out these systems on the fly.

There are three exits on my single ship. Two are regulation (one deemed "emergency") and one is of my design. It's near the cockpit, and it's more of a round hatch than an actual doorway.

I make sure everything is in place. I don't have my dive belt, with Karl's knife and my usual talismans. I feel naked without it, and more than a little superstitious. I don't like diving without my standard equipment.

But nothing is standard about this dive. We're not sending in a probe to see what's before us. We're not working with a large enough team. We're only guessing at the layout of the interior, and we don't really know if the entire crew is dead.

We think so because none of our systems show any life signs, but we don't know if something is blocking that information.

I wear the equipment belt that Yash designed for this environmental suit. The belt has a lot of emergency features so that I can notify someone for help, as well as some small fiddly places for tools that I'm not carrying. It does have loops for emergency liquids, though, that can be pumped into the environmental system. Considering that weird dehydration I experienced during the blast wave, I am bringing the liquids. They're wrapped in a thermal layer, so that they're protected from the cold of space.

They look tiny and barely enough, but I know they work with the recycled fluids from my own body to replenish any liquid I might need, should something go wrong.

I listen to my own thinking: I'm expecting something to go wrong.

I attach two laser pistols to the belt, one on each hip, and hope to hell all of that will be enough.

Then I open the small hatch, and float through it, using my gloved hands to pull me through.

As I emerge from the single ship, I half expect to hear the music of a damaged *anacapa* drive, but I do not. The only thing I can hear is my own breathing, even and steady.

I usually sound a lot more ragged than that at the beginning of a dive. Either I'm really calm about this one, or the gids I had when I left the *Madxaf* hours ago count to my subconscious as the beginning of the dive.

I reach the tether and test it ever so gently. It is firmly attached to that weird brown exterior. I don't like the bulky look of those nanobits or whatever they are. I'm just cautious enough to worry that they might be toxic to other materials, so I'm going to avoid them until I'm inside the ship.

That means a loose grasp on the tether, using it more like a guide than something that will anchor me and keep me safe.

I lean to the right, heading toward that cut in the exterior of the ship. Six meters sounds short, but from here, against the curve of the ship, with bits of debris floating nearby, it looks like I have to cross an entire galaxy.

In the distance, I see the *Madxaf's* runabout. Orlando and Tamaz are safely back inside. Just beyond it, I see the edge of Yash's runabout. She's waiting for me to finish this.

My heartrate has increased. I'm a lot more nervous than I expected to be. I haven't dived solo from a single ship in a very, very long time. To think I used to do this with no backup at all.

If I lose my grip now, Orlando and Tamaz will be able to capture me and pull me inside their runabout.

If I had lost my grip on any of those previous outings as a much younger woman, I would have been screwed. Just screwed.

And I never thought about that. I just did the work, more worried about what was ahead of me inside whatever wreck I was diving than I was about some kind of accident between here and there. I always worried about getting trapped inside a wreck.

I never worried about losing my grip on the way into one.

I shake off the thought and extend my left hand, moving it next to my right. I let my boots hang. I really don't trust that brown stuff, and I'm not going to put my boots on it unless I have to.

Yes, I'm aware that there will be something similar inside the ship, but maybe that something similar won't look as pockmarked and damaged as this stuff does. Maybe the unadulterated wave that hit this ship did more damage to its exterior than to its interior.

I'm hoping anyway.

My heartrate is climbing even more. I don't like diving when I don't know what's ahead of me. We should have sent a probe in while Yash and I were getting ready.

Of course I would think of that *now*. This is why I have procedures and methods and *rules*. T

hat way nothing gets missed.

I take a deep breath. The recycled air in my suit seems a bit metallic, or maybe that's the taste in my mouth from the incident earlier. I don't know, and I'm not going to worry about it (as I lie to myself. I *am* worried about it. I'm worried about all of it).

Finally I round the edge of the ship. The opening that Orlando and Tamaz cut into the side is not sealing closed, which I was worried about. Had this been a standard Dignity Vessel, the opening might have sealed itself.

Unless the ship was so damaged that it couldn't repair itself anymore. That happens to DV-Class ships like the *Ivoire*. It might have happened to this ship too.

The opening is huge, about three times taller than I am and wide enough for four people to go inside together.

There will be no airlock, no safety procedures. I just have to go around and in, and then activate the gravity on my boots as I wait for Yash.

Before I go in, though, I inspect the edges of that opening one more time. I don't have a spare environmental suit that's easily accessible. I have an ancient one in the single ship, and I wouldn't trust that suit to keep me safe on a dive this complicated.

I pause and peer, half expecting to hear Nyssa in my ear, wondering what I'm doing. Mikk would have urged me on, but he's back at the *Madxaf*, monitoring the Fleet for Coop.

Everyone has a job, and mine is to get inside this ship, so that Yash can follow me.

I let go of the tether with my right hand and reach around the opening. I grip the edge, then slide my right leg inside. When I'm half-in the opening and half-out, I activate my torso light.

The beam shows some tiny brown debris, floating like unbonded nanobits. It looks smoky inside, even though that's not smoke that I'm seeing. It's that debris.

I straddle the edge of that opening, then set my right foot on a surface. I can't tell if it's designed as a floor or a ceiling or a wall, not from this angle, and it doesn't really matter what it is, not at the moment.

I activate the gravity on that boot, then shuffle forward just enough to bring in the rest of my body. I set the left foot beside the right, activate the gravity on that boot, and turn on my knuckle lights.

There is a door straight ahead of me and it's open. It takes me a moment to realize that door is upside down.

So I'm standing on the ceiling.

"I'm inside," I say to anyone who is listening. That is Yash and Nyssa for certain. "Yash, I'll be waiting for you."

I should have brought a probe. While I'm waiting for her to get inside, I could have launched it and figure out what we're facing.

Behind me something makes the opening shake, and all of the debris shifts. The light changes, growing darker.

I turn my torso, with my feet stable, and blink, wondering if my heartrate can increase any more.

It's the tube that Yash is going to use to get in here. The damn thing looks less stable than I like.

I was going to go explore while I waited for her, but now I'm going to have to help.

That's annoying. This entire dive is annoying.

And we just have to get it done.

68

COOP RESISTED THE URGE TO PACE NERVOUSLY across the bridge of the *Ivoire*. His bridge team was already watching him sideways, knowing he was worried.

He had stood, nervously, before his opaqued screens as three members of Boss's regular diving team headed to the Not-Fleet vessel. Then he had threaded his hands together so that he couldn't worry them, as he watched Orlando and Tamaz cut an opening in the Not-Fleet vessel. The information came not from a buoy or anything else, but from a feed from the runabout Mikk had sent as a backup.

Coop was glad that Mikk went against orders and sent a backup for Boss.

Strange that Coop didn't think of it as a backup for Yash. Maybe that was because he thought of Boss as the backup for Yash.

Boss had arrived after Yash, but they both went into the Not-Fleet vessel. And now, Coop had no feed at all. He had no idea what they were doing in there, only that they were inside, seeing who knew what.

It was driving him crazy. He hadn't realized just how reliant he was on technology, on being able to see any team that was not on his ship, on knowing exactly what they were doing at all times.

He wanted to give some commands, maybe have Mikk partner the *Ivoire* onto whatever feed Mikk was watching—although Coop knew that was technically difficult. Mikk was probably monitoring Boss's movements on their old technology, not through the *Madxaf.*

If the damned observers weren't here, Coop could contact the *Madxaf's* runabout directly, and have them send him a real-time feed, but he didn't dare do that either.

And Yash, damn her, either hadn't thought to send him a feed or had explicitly not done so. Coop didn't want to take her pilot's attention away from whatever Yash was doing.

He kept telling himself that this dive wouldn't take long. Both Boss and Yash knew they had to get in and out of that Not-Fleet vessel quickly, that they didn't have much time at all.

But he had heard both of them discuss how time stretched on some dives, and he was very worried that this was one of them.

Maybe he had been wrong. Maybe he should have taken Boss's advice. Maybe they should have destroyed the ships, his promise to Trekov be damned.

But it was too late. He already had two of the most precious members of his team onboard that Not-Fleet vessel, searching for those *anacapa* drives.

He half-smiled. Boss would yell at him for his terminology. *She* wasn't a member of his team; he was a member of hers.

He glanced at the three observers in the back of the bridge. They were spread out, Honoré still trying to look at consoles she shouldn't have clearance to see, and Faifai studying something on one of the screens.

Coop didn't even try to figure out what she was looking at. His gaze met Paek's. Paek's gaze was cool, almost suspicious. Paek knew Coop was up to something, but with luck, Paek would never figure out what it was.

Coop broke away first. He slowly turned back toward the screens, but as he did, his eye caught something on one of the larger screens. He frowned, staring at the change in the formations.

Almost every Empire ship had moved. Technically, there were no formations any longer. The ships were all trying to aid the ships damaged in that blast wave.

Or to be more precise, there were formations, but they were no longer his. Now the Empire ships farthest from the blast wave had moved into a more protected position. Half of the ships faced outward, toward some incoming threat, and the rest had turned toward Odite.

He gritted his teeth. Trekov was up to something.

But the change in formation wasn't what caught his eye. He scanned to see what his subconscious had caught. It took a moment, but then he saw it.

Ten ships had broken away from the formation farthest from the blast wave. Those ships were heading away from Odite, which he thought odd. But then, as he watched them, he realized that they were making a wide turn outside of any radius he had set up.

They were in a battlefield position—one ship in front, followed by two, then three, then four. They expected something to come at them from the direction they were heading in.

He'd used that formation a million times. It allowed the lead ship to peel off if need be, and the others to find another formation or even to flank whatever was coming at them.

He almost turned back around to ask Paek what Trekov was doing. But he stopped himself. He had not received any information from his crew that Paek was in direct contact with Trekov.

Coop and Trekov hadn't directly forbidden it, but Coop had made it clear that he would be observing the observers.

And he was. If they had tried to contact her sideways, he would know about it.

There was a good chance that Paek was as clueless about all of this as Coop was. So Coop said nothing. He didn't want to let Paek know he had seen the vessels branching off.

If they were heading to the Not-Fleet vessels, they'd picked a damn roundabout way to do so. But even as he had that thought, he realized that it was a smart maneuver.

Trekov probably hadn't received all of the telemetry from her various ships—not in a way she could process. Hell, after that blast wave, not all of the captains could process what was going on inside their ships, let along what was happening to each of the one hundred vessels.

By taking ships farthest from the blast wave, she had chosen ships that were most likely the least damaged, or not damaged at all. They would have the ability to take on whatever came at them from the Not-Fleet vessels—if there was anyone still alive on board them, which there was not.

He should have given her more credit. Like him—like any commander—she could do several things at once. She was mounting a massive rescue, and dealing with her lost ships, but she also kept her eye on what she had come for.

The Not-Fleet vessels.

Coop leaned forward, did some quick calculations, and then leaned back. At this rate of speed, the Empire ships would reach the Not-Fleet vessels within a half an hour.

If the Empire ships took a direct route, which Coop doubted they would. A direct route would take them through the rescues that were going on closer to the Not-Fleet vessels.

The ten Empire ships would probably go around or below or above all of them, staying out of the way as they headed toward those Not-Fleet ships.

So a little longer than a half an hour. But not much.

He needed to let Boss and Yash know. He started to contact the pilot, then stopped himself.

The pilot wasn't who he needed to reach. He needed to talk to Mikk.

Coop silently cursed himself once again for those observers. It made communications from the bridge almost impossible.

He pivoted, then headed to his ready room.

"Captain?" Tren asked. She was surprised. Perkins probably was as well.

He didn't dare explain his behavior—and he didn't have to. He just nodded at them, then went into his ready room, and contacted Mikk.

Without preamble, Coop said, "I need you to get ahold of Boss, right now. Empire vessels are on their way, and I figure we have maybe twenty minutes until they figure out what's going on. I don't think—"

"We have another problem," Mikk said.

Coop paused. He had grown accustomed to the lack of protocol among Boss's team. And he knew what Mikk was monitoring.

"The Fleet?" Coop asked.

"They're on the move," Mikk said. "They're headed toward both vessels."

Coop felt an immediate calm fall over him. This was worse than he expected, and he needed to think clearly. Thankfully, his training made that easier.

"Tell Boss and Yash to get out now," Coop said. "We can't do it from here."

"I thought you wanted the drives," Mikk said.

"I do," Coop said, "but it might come down to a battle between the Empire and the Fleet. I don't want our people in the middle of that."

"I'll tell them," Mikk said.

"Make sure they get out," Coop said. "Make sure they understand—"

"I'll do what I can," Mikk said, but his tone was sad. It was Boss and Yash, after all. The two most independent thinkers Coop knew.

He was going to have to trust Mikk to convey the message clearly. The women had to get back to their ships, and they had to get out of the area. They had to do it fast.

"Where is the Fleet, exactly?" Coop asked.

"Almost to the other ship, not the one that Boss and Yash are on."

A small miracle, then. But still too much of a risk.

"I can tell Denby to go there," Mikk said. "We could act as a buffer—"

"A newly reconstructed DV-Class vessel against four fully armed ships?" Coop said. "No. We minimize losses. We don't add to them."

And with that statement, his heart clenched. His subconscious had been ahead of the rest of him. As a captain, as the leader of this fight, he knew that he might lose people.

He just hadn't expected to lose Boss. Or Yash.

"Yes, sir," Mikk said. He sounded shaken. He wasn't a fighter. He had probably never been in a battlefield situation. He probably didn't understand acceptable losses.

Not that losing either woman was acceptable.

But it might be inevitable.

Coop signed off, then left the ready room. There must have been something on his face, because Perkins said, quietly, "Sir?"

His gaze went from her face to the observers. Paek was still watching him just a bit too closely.

Coop didn't say anything to Perkins. Or to anyone else. He didn't trust his voice.

He thought about taking the *Ivoire* to those Not-Fleet vessels, but he would be in the same position that the *Madxaf* would have been in. And he would have to use the *anacapa* drive to get there ahead of the Fleet vessels, just like the *Madxaf*.

He could tell Trekov about them, but that would require too much explanation. Although he could let her think they were Not-Fleet ships, coming to rescue their own.

Only her ships were too far away.

There were no good choices here.

He would just have to get through the next hour, and hope that everyone else he cared about would be able to get through it as well.

69

YASH OOZES OUT OF THE TUBE, then flails her arms as if she's trying to push herself forward. I grab one arm and pull her the rest of the way into the Dignity Vessel. The tube collapses in on itself.

Yash is wearing an environmental suit of a type I don't recognize. She has large *anacapa* containers strapped to the front of her legs. I would have recommended torso, had I realized she was bringing containers. Her gloves look too thin, her hood seems a little too tight, and her eyes are wide.

She scared herself coming in here. I don't blame her. Those containers probably had an impact on her balance. She wasn't shaped the way she usually is when she's in zero-g.

I'm sure the tube didn't help.

I hate tubes like that one, which is why I prefer tethers. The collapse of the tube will be a problem when we're ready to leave, but we have at least an hour of diving ahead of us. With luck, Orlando and Tamaz will solve the tube problem with the help of whomever is piloting Yash's vessel.

"Welcome aboard," I say to her, trying to sound cheerful.

She grunts at me, then braces one arm on me as she turns on the gravity in her boots. Instantly she locks down onto the ceiling beneath us, with a force I hadn't expected.

"There's a door," she says as she looks ahead of us. "There shouldn't be a door ahead of us."

"We're upside down," I say. "We're standing on the ceiling."

She shakes her head anyway. "Use your map," she says.

"No," I say.

She looks at me. I can see her face inside the clear part of her hood. She seems startled.

"The map is a guess," I say. "You didn't download it from any systems. You just set it up the way that a standard Dignity Vessel is set up."

I use the phrase "Dignity Vessel" because I want to differentiate this ship from the DV-Class ships that Yash is used to. We're in my territory now, whether she likes it or not.

"I can tell you for a fact this is nothing like a standard Dignity Vessel," I say.

"You can't know that," she says. "You've been onboard for five minutes."

"And the exterior is made of a substance I don't recognize. The things floating around us look like unbonded nanobits until you actually get one on your suit. Then it's clear that they're bigger and denser than a regular nanobit. These ships may have used the basic shape of a Dignity Vessel, but they're not like anything I've ever seen before."

Yash glances around, then sighs. "There isn't emergency lighting," she says.

"There is," I say. "It's not working."

I went looking for any emergency system while I was waiting for Yash. I figured that there would be something near the open door, and there was, but the controls looked fried.

"Well, that could be a problem," Yash says. She taps the packet of finger-sized black bars on her belt. She has devices that can pull information from consoles—or at least, they can from Fleet ships. I saw her use one of them on a runabout just after I was injured.

Apparently, she had planned to use them here.

"Let's just get to the bridge," she says.

"If there's no emergency system, there's no map," I say.

497

"I scanned the ship from the runabout," she says. "The configuration is close enough. The bridge is in the very center of the ship."

Then she peers at that door. "I didn't expect that, though. I wonder what this room actually is."

I wonder many things about this ship, but we're not going to get answers.

"We don't have a lot of time," I remind her.

She nods, glances over her shoulder at the opening. The tube is already gone, which she probably finds unnerving. I am happy that it's gone. That means Orlando and Tamaz are working with Yash's pilot, and they will have something for us to escape into when we're done here.

Yash says, "I wanted to split up, send you for the communications *anacapa*, and—"

"No," I say. "We're not splitting up."

"Yeah, I figured you'd say that," she says. "I've been thinking about our time limits. We might have to leave the communications *anacapa* drives—if they have any—and hope that the Empire doesn't notice them. Coop wants the regular *anacapas* off both ships."

I knew that. He told me that. But we haven't talked logistics. "Shouldn't they have backup *anacapa* drives as well?" I ask.

"The Fleet had them off and on," Yash says. "I have no idea how the Not-Fleet is going to work. I've been thinking about this hard, and I think the best thing we can do is get rid of the active drive, and all the information about it. If the Empire finds the other drive, then they'll think it part of stealth tech or whatever. Because the drive won't be hooked up."

That is the historical precedent. The Empire has found loose *anacapa* drives before, but usually those drives end up killing whoever gets close to them.

But she's underestimating the Empire. They have good scientists. They'll eventually figure out what they're finding.

"Maybe we should just destroy the ship," I say.

"Coop says he promised," Yash says.

"I know what he says. But we're on the ground. We can say—"

"No," Yash says. She glances over her shoulder one more time. "I don't want to walk this, but—"

She's nervous about the opening behind us, the one we came through. She's still not used to open space. It's one of her handicaps as a diver.

"Walk to that door," I say. "I'll be right beside you."

And once I go through, I'll figure out how to close the door, so that she feels a little more secure.

Yash strides toward the door, a little off-balance. It's not the same walking in gravity boots as it is walking in gravity itself. You feel light with heavy feet, rather than someone who weighs the same throughout.

She gets to the door, and goes through it first, then squeals.

I've never heard Yash squeal before. It takes me a moment to realize that it's a suppressed scream, not a squeal.

I propel myself to her side, and peer through the door. She's blocking it, but I can see past her.

There are bodies everywhere, floating, limbs askew. Some have their arms in front, some with legs to the side, some on their backs. It's a ballet of corpses, almost lovely in its coordination, until one body bumps toward us. The face inside is grayish, but recognizably male.

That person had been alive this morning. *All* of these people had been alive this morning.

I mentally brace myself. If this ship had a full complement of crew, and that crew was similar to our DV-Class ships, then we have to go through a gauntlet of hundreds of bodies.

Yash glances over her shoulder, sees me close, and moves to one side. This has clearly thrown her.

I've dived ships with bodies still on board—dozens, maybe hundreds of ships like that. But the bodies were few and far between, and when I did find them, it was obvious that the bodies had been there for decades, maybe longer.

I've never been on a ship with the entire crew dead in front of me.

Had this been any other dive, I would have given Yash the option to quit. This is unnerving even for the most experienced diver.

But I'm not giving Yash that option. We're here at great risk to ourselves, and she has already told me twice what Coop wants. I'm not going to waste my breath telling her that we can leave, because neither of us feel like we can.

She'll just refuse me anyway.

She shuts off all of the lights on her suit. I'm about to admonish her—that's no way to get through a pile of newly dead floating bodies—when I realize she's not looking at the dead.

She's looking to my left.

I follow her gaze, and see light, spreading downward like a beam of raw sunlight.

"What the hell is that?" I ask.

"On a standard DV-Class vessel," she says, "that's where the *anacapa* drive is."

"Can it still be working when the rest of the equipment is down?" I ask.

"The drive yes," Yash says. "The equipment around it, no. At least, not on our Fleet vessels or any that we've found. But this is not the Fleet."

It's finally come home to her then, that we're in strange new territory.

She thrusts one of the long thin black boxes at me. "See if there's a working console somewhere in this area."

She's not supposed to give me orders, but we're in that gray area now, where her expertise and mine clash.

"What are you going to do?" I ask.

"I'm going to take a look at that drive," she says. She starts to move, then looks over her shoulder at me. "Are you hearing that weird *anacapa* music you hear? A malfunctioning drive?"

"No," I say.

"Well, then," she says. "Small blessings."

I don't know if it's a blessing or not. I'd go with her, but I am useless around an *anacapa* drive. She has to do that part alone. She'll call me if she needs me.

We've risen to that level of trust.

She shuts off the gravity in her boots and floats toward that light. I shut off the gravity in my boots, and propel myself toward all of the consoles lining the ceiling.

As I get close, it becomes clear that they're all powered down, maybe even useless. Still I set that black box underneath one console that's positioned where most DV-Class vessels position their captains.

Yash has explained these boxes to me before. They have their own power source, and if anything can pull information from a dead console, these things can. I've seen them do it on centuries' old vessels. I suspect they might be able to do it on a newly devastated ship.

Then I move forward and upward. Something tells me that Yash should not be alone with that drive.

It's tough moving with all of the bodies. Some of them are floating past me because Yash has dislodged them.

Apparently the mystery of the light has overcome her own squeamishness about the bodies here. Or maybe she wasn't squeamish at all, merely surprised.

When I reach her, she's wedged between a body and what looks like a wall. She's holding onto the built-in and glowing *anacapa* housing with her left hand. With her right, she's fumbling with her belt.

"Oh, good," she says when she sees me. "Get another of the backups. This housing is alive."

"What does that mean?" I ask.

"It's got its own power source," she says, "probably the *anacapa* drive itself."

"And you want me to what?" I ask.

"Put the backup inside when I tell you to." She sounds completely businesslike, completely Yash. "This person here, the one I can't seem to get past, is stuck to the equipment."

Yash does not seem bothered by this. In fact, it seems to buoy her.

"Let me move the body," I say.

"*NO.*" The force with which she expels that word startles me. "She's what's keeping this housing open."

She? Yash must have taken a good look at the person in that environmental suit.

"You don't know how to open the housing?" I ask.

501

"I'm sure there's some kind of code protecting this," Yash says. "It shouldn't be open, and it is, and my guess is, if it were opened before the blast wave hit, that wave would have had an impact on the *anacapa* drive, so it was opened afterwards."

"I thought everyone died," I say.

"Apparently not right away." Her tone dismisses me, or dismisses the idea as not important to her work at the moment.

She looks at me impatiently.

"Get close," she says, "but don't dislodge her. I need you to put that box on the edge of this built-in housing. You'll see what I mean. And then I'm going to do what I can to dislodge the *anacapa* drive. If it flares, get the hell away from this housing."

She says that without urgency, which makes me wonder if I'll even have time to get away.

"And if you're wondering if I know how this housing works, I don't," Yash says. "I'm hoping the fact that this was opened by that woman means everything is unlocked."

My stomach clenches, and my suit beeps at me. Apparently I had stopped breathing a minute or two ago.

Yash doesn't know what she's doing. We don't know what we're doing. And we don't have time to learn.

She's focused down on her task.

I make myself breathe, wondering if Nyssa has even noticed that my suit beeped. Does this mean she can't contact us in here? Or this close to the *anacapa* drive?

"This is really an innovative drive housing," Yash says, and I think she's talking more to herself than to me. "I wish I had time to study it."

I carefully avoid the body hanging over us. The woman's glove is lodged against some pulsing equipment along the side.

"There are words here," I say, "but I can't read them."

"I can," Yash says. "It's a variation of the Standard that we speak."

Which catches my attention because it's interesting, but it's not something I can deal with at the moment. Neither can Yash.

"So you know what this is?" I ask.

"That's why I want you to put the box on it," she says. "It's some kind of backup system. It stores everything the ship has done within a certain time period. And no, I do not know the time period. I don't know exactly what she did, so don't ask."

Yash is sounding even more curt than she did before. She has crouched alongside the housing, the gravity in her boots on, her boots attached to the wall. She has unstrapped one of the containers from her leg, and has the container perched on the side of the housing.

I have no idea if the container has its own gravity. I assume it does.

I can't look anymore because either I'll ask unnecessary questions or I'll see disaster where there might not be any.

I take the black box she handed me and carefully place it alongside that pulsing bit of equipment. Then I attached the box, and activate it, just like I had the other one.

Yash is bent over the *anacapa* drive, an orange glow reflecting on her hood. She has both gloved hands inside the drive casing, her body positioned right over open container.

I want to leave to get the other black box, because I know it's as done as it's going to be, but I don't dare. I don't dare leave her alone.

She might need me to—what, I don't know. But she might need me.

So I hover and wait, my heart pounding so hard that it hurts. I have to remind myself to breathe, remind myself that each patient second counts, that we will leave here in due time, but I have to give Yash the space to finish what she's started.

If I didn't feel so very vulnerable, I would search the entire bridge for a backup *anacapa* drive, or I would head to engineering to find the communications *anacapa*—if there is one.

But I don't.

I wait, hoping we will both get through this.

Because I'm really not sure we will.

70

THE DAMAGE TO THE STRANGE DV-CLASS SHIP was worse than Cohn had expected. There were holes in the exterior, as if something stronger than an *anacapa* blast wave had gone through it.

The ship looked fragile, almost as if any pressure placed on it would shatter it. The ship was also a weird brown color, and bits of that brown were sloughing off.

She didn't mention that to her team on the bridge of the *Geesi*. She just worked quietly and quickly, hoping to get everything done before the Empire or the Lost Souls ships noticed what she was doing.

She had placed the *Geesi* between the vessel and what remained of the Empire ships. She was monitoring the Lost Souls ships as well, and not seeing any movement, which still surprised her. She expected them to somehow support the Empire ships, maybe even help with the rescues.

But so far, they seemed to be doing nothing.

And all of that nothing bothered her.

The *Royk* was closer to the initial blast site, positioned similarly to the *Geesi*. The *Mächteg* had stopped beside the *Sakhata* on Cohn's orders. She had made one modification to their plan: she wanted to make sure the *Sakhata* could tether to the strange damaged ship before she sent the *Mächteg* to the next one.

Captain Wihone had moved the *Sakhata* into position on the most intact side of the damaged vessel. That side also seemed to include the bridge, which made sense.

Still, Cohn was nervous about this entire procedure. She would be happy when it was over and they were on their way.

That weird brown material bothered her. She sidled over to Iosua, and peered over his shoulder. He was monitoring the front part of the *Sakhata*. The tether had already emerged from its base, and was heading—carefully—toward the damaged ship.

"What do you make of that brown material?" Cohn asked Iosua.

"Never seen anything like it," he said, without looking up. "It's acting like nanobits, though. Unbonded nanobits."

"But it's not nanobits," she said. "Those particles are too large."

"We don't know what they are," he said, a little curtly. He clearly wanted to concentrate on the tethering.

The tether had moved closer, but still hadn't arrived.

"Do you think that material is what caused the explosion to be so much worse?" she asked.

"Honestly?" Iosua asked. "I'm thinking it's that wild *anacapa* energy that seems to surround all of those Empire ships. But I haven't had time to study any of it. I'll just be glad when we're out of here."

The tether crossed the last distance to the damaged vessel, then hooked on.

"How's their *anacapa* drive?" Cohn asked Iosua.

"The *Sakhata*?" he asked. "It's fine. It's—"

"That brown vessel," she said. "It clearly has one."

Iosua let out a breath of air. "Their drive is still active. But it's giving off less energy than any of our drives do at rest. I think they'll be okay going through foldspace."

Cohn hated the hedge. She could press him on it, but she didn't. Whatever happened, happened.

The fact that she had so many questions was one reason she had ordered the *Mächteg* to wait before heading to the second ship. If this first ship blew up or disintegrated or somehow didn't make it into fold-space, then Cohn would have preserved at least one of her ships.

"Tether secure." The voice belonged to Wihone. He was letting them all knew he had done his job. "We're heading into foldspace. See you on the other side."

Cohn hated that statement. It always sounded fake, and it made her uncomfortable.

Her shoulders tensed as she waited.

A foldspace window opened, revealing the tethered end of the *Sakhata* against the light, but not the entire ship. The tethered end went through the foldspace window and, with a rather firm tug, the damaged vessel followed.

The foldspace window held for a moment, unwavering.

Cohn held her breath.

Then the window vanished.

Cohn slowly let out her breath, but it was Iosua that loudly exhaled with relief. Apparently, he had been more worried than he had let on.

"They're through," he said, "Or at least, as far as we can tell, they are."

"No further damage to that ship?" Cohn asked.

"Not from the tether or the pull into foldspace," Iosua said. "What happened as it went through the foldspace window, well, I have no idea, and won't until we get over there ourselves."

Cohn nodded. "Tell the *Mächteg* to head to the other ship," she said to Vinters.

Then Cohn looked at the emptiness on the screen before her. Two ships had been there only a moment ago. If she could get to the other ship without incident, she would be done with this place. She would leave the strange ships, the Empire, and the Lost Souls ships in the Fleet's hands.

She didn't have a lot of time. In all of those ships, involved in a rescue or not, someone would have seen the strange damaged vessel disappear. If they were watching closely, they would have seen it vanish through a foldspace window, just like she had.

She had no idea how those ships would respond. Maybe they would do nothing.

Or maybe they would come after her ships.

They had revealed just enough about themselves. She was going to have to move faster.

They needed to get out of here as soon as they possibly could.

71

YASH IS BRACED BETWEEN THE WALL, the housing, and that woman's body. Yash is bent at the waist, her head all but invisible from where I stand. She's cursing loudly, as she works the controls around the housing of the Not-Fleet ship's *anacapa* drive.

"This damn thing is well built," she says, and I think, for the first time in a while, she's talking to me.

"You want my help?" I ask.

"Can you lift an *anacapa* drive with your bare hands?" I'm trusting that she means with my gloved hands. I'm about to answer her when I realize her tone was sarcastic.

I chose to answer her as if she's being one-hundred-percent serious.

"I've never tried it," I say.

"Then now is not the time to start." She grunts, the way people do when they're using a lot of effort.

"I can brace the container."

"No," she says. "But you can retrieve the black boxes. They should be done by now."

I have the odd sense that she's giving me make-work, that she has no real idea if those boxes have pulled all of the information from this ship's systems.

I'm beginning to think it doesn't matter, though, because we're using up a lot of time here. We still haven't figured out if there's a communications *anacapa* drive or not—and then we have the other ship to get to.

Something crackles in my ear, and for a moment, I think there's something wrong with my suit.

Then the crackle comes again.

"Tell them to go the hell away," Yash says. "I don't need nagging."

At that moment, I realize she's hearing the same crackle.

I'm about to respond, when a tone pierces my ear. It's an emergency tone, something we rarely use, and only if someone hasn't responded.

The damn sound has given me an immediate splitting headache.

I respond to whoever it is, and say, "You're not coming through loudly enough. Boost your voice. And Yash doesn't want to be nagged."

I figure Nyssa probably doesn't quite know how to use the system. I also figure that both my vitals and Yash's are completely screwed up. We're trying to hurry, we're tense, and we want to be done.

"...out of there." The voice isn't Nyssa's. It's Mikk's, and that immediately fills me with alarm.

"Mikk," I say. "We can't hear you. Please repeat."

"Those Fleet ships," Mikk says. His voice is so faint I can barely hear him. "They've already taken the second Not-Fleet ship. They're coming for you right now. You have to get out of there, as fast as you can."

A jolt of energy shoots through me.

"Yash," I say, "we have to go, now."

"I almost have this damn thing," she says.

"I don't care," I say. "Didn't you hear Mikk? The Fleet ships—"

"Yeowch," she says, and leans backwards. She curses again, and then stands upright, her arms around what looks like a solid, glowing oblong boulder.

"Boss," Mikk says. "You have to—"

"We will," I say to Mikk. "I'm getting Yash out now."

I'm not sure if that's true. Yash is hunched over the container, as she tries to fit that oblong boulder inside. I propel myself to her side.

"Go the hell away," she says.

"We have to leave—"

"I heard it all," she says. "We're taking this damn thing. And you need to get the black boxes."

She's right. If we can take these three things, at least this dive won't be in vain. I bend over the side of the housing, grab the black box, and dislodge it.

I attach it to one of the pockets in my belt, and take the extra few seconds to seal the pocket flap.

Yash is still struggling to get the drive into that container.

"Turn it slightly toward me," I say.

She does, and the drive slots in. She looks up at me, her face red inside that environmental suit, sweat dotting her skin. I hope to hell that's from the stress and not a suit failure.

"All right," she says. "Let's go."

With my right hand, I indicate that she should go ahead of me, but she shakes her head.

"Get that last box," she says. "I've got this."

I hope to hell she's right. I push myself over to the other console, grab the second box, and turn toward her.

She's got the container attached to her torso, not her leg like the other one, which is probably a good thing.

She pushes away from the housing—which means that the gravity in her boots is off—and as she does so, she grabs a laser pistol from her own belt.

"What the hell are you doing?" I ask

"Destroying the housing," she says. "If the Empire—"

"The Empire be damned," I say. "Didn't you hear Mikk? It's the Fleet that's on the way?"

She freezes—every single part of her, and there's an expression of naked longing on her face. She clearly hadn't heard that.

I can see the decision right there. She's weighing whether or not to stay on the ship, let the Fleet take her, and deal with the consequences. I need to stop that thinking right now. I can't lose her. Coop would never forgive me.

Hell, *I* would never forgive me.

"Or whatever the hell was chasing me," I say. "You know, Fleet, Not-Fleet, Guardians of the Boneyard, whatever."

My tone is lighter than I actually feel, which is good, because I don't sound like I'm trying to convince her.

Maybe it's the tone, maybe it's my words, but she moves again. She nods, head down, as if she is hoping to hide her reaction from me. She replaces the laser pistol, then pushes away from the housing, heading toward the door.

"This time, you go first," I say. I'm not sure she can get through that door, and she's going to need my help.

We're going to need a lot of help, because I'm not sure she can pull herself into her own runabout.

"They're close," Mikk says in my ear. "Boss, you have to get out—"

"We're coming now," I say. "Get Orlando and Tamaz into position. We're going to have to do a crossing."

Mikk has been with me long enough to know what a crossing means. It is, essentially, a leap from one opening to another. Maybe with a tether, maybe without. I'm not sure Yash can do it. I'm not sure I can do it anymore.

But there's no time for tethers or tubes or any of the niceties of a dive. There's getting out of here, and then getting away from here.

It has to be done quickly, and quickly is the exact opposite of a safe dive.

To his credit, Mikk doesn't argue with me. "I'll let them know," he says. "They'll be ready."

I have no idea how he knows that. He's on the *Madxaf*, far away. They're in a runabout who knows how far from the opening they cut into the door. If my single ship fit another person, I'd shove Yash that way, but it doesn't. And I don't trust her pilot to handle a crossing.

It's up to Orlando and Tamaz. I trust Orlando, but I can't remember the last crossing he's done. If any.

But he saved my life once.

Maybe he'll be able to save it again.

"Let's go," I say to Yash, trying not to scare her, but trying to force her to hurry. "We really don't have all that much time."

72

ELISSA SLAMMED A FIST ONTO THE CONSOLE BEFORE HER. The entire team in central command swiveled their heads, looking at her as one unit. The faces registered surprise.

She lost her temper occasionally, but she didn't hit things. But this time...this time, everything had gotten worse.

"What the hell happened to that ship?" she asked.

Most of the team had no idea what she was talking about. But Bahe did. Bahe's eyes had sunken into her whitish-gray skin. She looked as exhausted as Elissa felt.

Bahe moved closer to Elissa, then toggled the screen before her.

"Let's look," Bahe said, as if she were speaking to a child.

Elissa resented the tone, but didn't say anything. Everything that would come out would be justification. She had lost at least twenty vessels. Twenty more were damaged in one way or another, according to the reports that were just starting to come in.

The number of dead was in the thousands. She needed those damn enemy vessels and now one had just vanished.

She had thought those things were damaged and disabled. She had thought everyone on board those enemy vessels was dead.

"Oh, crap," Bahe said.

She swiveled the screen toward Elissa, then replayed what she had seen.

513

One of those weird lighted doorways had appeared and the ship had gone through it.

The image made Elissa feel like cold water had been poured over her head. It was bracing and clarifying and chilling all at the same time.

She pushed Bahe to one side, then slowed the images down. Elissa also raised some telemetry, looking at the data from a completely different angle.

There was something near that ship, something…

One frozen image on that screen showed a sleek vessel, with a similar shape to the damaged vehicle, but not quite the same. That vessel tugged the enemy vessel through that lighted doorway.

Elissa tapped the screen before her. "You see that ship?" she said to Bahe. "Figure out what that ship is."

"I have no idea how it got there," Bahe said, her wispy voice no longer condescending. Now it was Bahe who sounded defensive.

"Neither do I," Elissa said. "Let's figure it out."

She squinted at the ship. Its shape looked familiar.

She moved to another console, called up the silhouettes of the various ships that Cooper's people had used.

"There," she said, poking a finger at one of them. "This thing has the same shape."

"It's not the same ship," Bahe said.

"I *know* that," Elissa said. "But it's the same kind of ship."

She cursed. What kind of game was Cooper playing with her? Did he think her that stupid?

"Tell our ships to hurry," she said. "I don't see any other ships near the remaining enemy vessel, but that doesn't mean they're not there."

She sounded paranoid. She was paranoid. She had put herself into this position, and now things were getting worse. The only thing that would make this disaster survivable were those two ships, and now one was gone.

"And get Cooper for me," she said. "*Right now.*"

"Yes, ma'am," Bahe said. "Privately—?"

"What part of *right now* is impossible to understand?" Elissa snapped.

"Yes, ma'am," Bahe said.

Elissa bent over the console, staring at that lighted open door in space. Two ships, one pulling the other through the doorway.

Surely, Cooper wouldn't take the ship from Lost Souls. Would he?

Of course he would. She would.

He had betrayed her again.

And this time, it would cost them both.

73

COOP STOOD IN FRONT OF HIS CAPTAIN'S CHAIR, completely surrounded by screens. There was no way Trekov's observers could see what he was seeing, so on one screen, he was monitoring the ready vessels, Boss's single ship, and the Not-Fleet ship.

The *remaining* Not-Fleet ship.

The other ship had been tugged into foldspace by a Fleet vessel. He'd seen the vessel, outlined as the ship entered foldspace. The vessel looked like an SC-Class ship, but sleeker, slightly trimmer, and—maybe—darker. He couldn't quite tell, not with what limited information he had.

He had telemetry, but it wasn't enough, and he couldn't bring himself to study it. He had sent a private order to Perkins and Tren, telling them to figure out what the vessel exactly was. They'd assign someone else, which was what he wanted.

No. What he really wanted was to take the *Ivoire* into foldspace and position it in front of the remaining Not-Fleet vessel. It took all of his training to prevent himself from doing that.

That was impulsive, dangerous, and wrong. He no longer had enough time to execute any kind of defense, even if he arrived there before the remaining Fleet vessels did.

Then something chirruped overhead, and an announcement filled the entire bridge. A contact from Commander Trekov.

He wanted to let it go. He didn't need her right now. She was causing enough trouble.

But he couldn't ignore her, not with her own people on the bridge.

He opaqued all of his screens, brought one of his barrier screens down, and stepped slightly to the side so that he was near Perkins.

Then he accepted the contact from Trekov.

"What the hell did you do?" she said, her voice reedy with tension.

No greeting, no nothing.

"Me?" he said, surprised.

"That was your ship, pulling that enemy vessel out of here, through one of those lighted doorways. No sense denying it, Captain," she said. "We all saw it. You promised me those ships. You *promised me*."

He felt a surge of anger. He had promised her, and because he had made that mistake, two of the people he cared about the most were in danger right now.

"That was not my ship," he said, sounding calmer than he felt.

"It looks like one of yours," she snapped.

"No, it doesn't," he said. "It's similar, but not the same. Just like those three enemy vessels were similar but not the same."

She was silent for a half a second. He resisted the urge to say more.

"That ship came out of nowhere to take the enemy vessel," she said.

"It did," he said. "It was cloaked."

"How do we know there aren't more?" she asked. Her voice still had that furious edge.

"We don't," he said.

"I'm getting my vessels there as fast as possible," she said.

"I can see that," he said.

"If you know what that ship was," she said, "you need to tell me know. I've already lost too many people."

It was, perhaps, the only argument that might sway him. He empathized over the loss of life, the destruction of the ships. But the argument didn't sway him.

Still, he told her the truth. "I don't know what that ship was," he said. He had suspicions, that was all. Just suspicions, which he wasn't going to share with her.

She cursed. "If they take that ship, all this loss will be for nothing."

Not for nothing, he almost said. *You have defended Lost Souls admirably well.*

But he remained silent. He didn't want to encourage her to send more ships or divert resources from the rescue effort.

"None of this has gone as planned," he said, and that was true as well. "But remember one thing."

"What's that?" she asked.

"Don't have your ships fire on that enemy vessel or the ship around them. If they open a…doorway…we might have another explosion like the one we just had."

She cursed, and he could tell from her tone that she hadn't thought of that.

He let out a small breath. He had just headed off a disaster he hadn't even realized was possible. If Yash and Boss had gotten out of the ship, then got hit with another blast wave…

He didn't want to think about it.

"We will get there before they drag off the remaining ship," she said.

"If there is someone to drag it off," he said, trying to slow her down.

"Oh, there is," she said. "None of these ships travel alone."

And then she cut the transmission.

Coop glanced sideways at Perkins who glanced at him. They both knew that they had to double-time the rescue.

"Tell Mikk," he said as quietly as he could.

She nodded.

That was all Coop could do. He had to keep Trekov as far away as possible, and then he had to wait.

He was not built for waiting. He had used up all his patience years ago, when the *Ivoire* was becalmed in foldspace. These days, he wanted to take action.

Only now, there was no good action to take.

Without a glance at the observers, he stepped into his ring of screens, bringing up the one he had lowered, encasing himself.

Immediately, he noted the difference. The runabouts had moved. They were waiting outside the opening that Orlando and Tamaz had cut into the Not-Fleet vessel. One runabout seemed to be right in front of that opening, with the other runabout below it.

He had no idea what the strategy was, having the runabouts so close to each other.

This one was all on Boss's team. And he hoped to hell they knew exactly what they were doing.

74

I HALF-PUSH, HALF-GUIDE YASH through the door into that weird room. The bodies float past us, disturbed by us. I've brushed some, Yash has brushed some, and we dislodge them.

They almost seem alive, those bodies, and the thought makes me shiver.

Yash reaches the opening that Orlando and Tamaz cut, then spreads both arms, gripping the sides of that opening with both hands.

I have no idea if this is a Yash idea of a freeze, but I can't have it.

"There's no tube," she says, and her voice is shaking. "No tether."

I haven't told her the plan. She's nervous enough about traversing this distance with a tube or a tether. She's not going to be able to do a crossing.

I come up behind her and peer over her shoulder. A runabout is perfectly lined up, as close as it can be without bumping into the side of the Not-Fleet vessel.

Orlando stands in the open door of the runabout. He's gripping a tether with a lasso on the end. I have no idea if he was smart enough to bring one or if it had always been on board.

The lasso is a last-ditch item. If we miss, he'll try to get the loop to us. We'll be able to put it over our heads.

Maybe.

That'll be too much for Yash. I know that without even consulting her.

"Why isn't he releasing the tether?" she asks, her voice still shaking. She's trying to be strong here, but she's clearly terrified.

"Because he's not," I say. "I'm going to get you to the runabout."

"Over empty space?" she asks. "We're going to jump? I've never done that. I—"

She stops herself before she says *I can't*. Because she knows that *I can't* is an impossible phrase, one that admits defeat even before we start.

"I'm going to put my arms around you," I say as I unclip a small rope from my belt. I haven't done something like this in decades. "I'm also going to tie us together. You're going to hold onto that container."

"And then what?" she asks.

"Then you remain perfectly still," I say.

I wrap my rope around her, careful to place it under the container, around her hips. The rope isn't enough, because she'll overbalance. That's why I'm going to hold her.

"You will face away from me," I say. I have my communications link open. Orlando can hear all of this.

He's crouched in that doorway, the gravity in his boots on. He's wearing one of the new environmental suits too. I have no idea where Nyssa is. Tamaz should be piloting, at least, I hope he is.

"When I put my arms around you," I say to Yash, "you will raise your feet, and crouch in as close to a sitting position as you can."

Orlando can avoid her booted feet, but if she kicks me and dislodges me, then that'll change her trajectory and we'll both miss that opening on the runabout.

The opening looks smaller than it did a moment ago, and I know that's the effect of nerves.

I slip my arms around Yash, holding the front of the container as well, because I don't want to accidently knock it from her arms.

We get one shot at this. If we miss, it'll be up to Orlando, and that probably won't work.

Yash lifts her feet as instructed. I can hear her breath in my comm, raspy and terrified. But she remains motionless.

I lean us out of the opening Orlando and Tamaz cut into the Not-Fleet vessel, and see the other runabout below us at an angle.

Good job, Orlando, I think. That second runabout gives us something we can try to attach to if we flail free. Something that we might be able to get close to, and turn on the gravity in our boots.

Otherwise, that's too risky a maneuver, because we might lock onto the Not-Fleet vessel itself.

I bend my knees. I'm not going to give Yash any warning. I lean forward even farther, pointing us at the runabout.

Yash lets me bend her. She's doing remarkably well. I'm not sure I would have been able to do as well.

I'm giddy and terrified and grateful for the emotions, because they'll give me energy I might not otherwise have.

I stare at the middle of the runabout's opening, to the right of Orlando, mentally pointing myself at it.

And then I shove off with every ounce of force I have.

We launch. Yash makes a slight panicked noise in the back of her throat, but she doesn't move. She doesn't flail her arms, she doesn't reach for Orlando, she doesn't' change position.

The Fleet gives its team years of training in zero-g, and it paid off here. It paid off well.

At least on her side.

But I'm not sure that even with my gids and terror, I used enough strength to get us across that opening.

Then I realize I'm smiling. I'm floating in space, floating free, something I love doing. I wouldn't mind dying like this.

Yash probably would, but I won't.

We reach the edge of the runabout. Orlando steps off that edge, grabs Yash by the legs and yanks us both toward the runabout.

He's tethered inside. Someone is backing him up, pulling all three of us in.

It feels like my heart is about to pound out of my chest, through my suit, and launch itself into space all alone.

I'm grinning like a fool. Yash is making a whimpering sound.

We reach the interior of the runabout, and Orlando turns on the gravity in his boots, pulling us downward. The doors close behind us, and Orlando shouts, "Go! Go! Go!" at whoever is piloting.

He sways sideways and lets us go. Gravity has been reestablished inside even though my suit tells me the environment still isn't suitable for humans.

I tumble to the floor, letting go of Yash as I do. She tumbles as well, but somehow manages to protect the *anacapa* container.

I sprawl on myself, having trouble catching my breath. She's beside me, Nyssa hovering over us.

"Your vitals are all over the map," she says, sounding panicked, and I can't help myself.

I laugh.

Through the hood of her environmental suit, I can see her eyes. They're wide. She looks startled.

I don't want to say that we've made an impossible jump after a terrible dive, after we were hit with some kind of blast wave. *Of course* our vitals are all over the map.

"Are we clear?" Yash asks. She's struggling to sit up.

"Clear of what?" Orlando asks. He looks a little top-heavy.

"The Not-Fleet ship," Yash says.

"Yeah." That from Tamaz, who is piloting this. Thank God.

"What about my ship?" Yash asks, and it takes me a moment to realize she means the other runabout.

"He's staying with us," Tamaz says, curtly. He clearly doesn't want to be interrupted.

I manage to sit up. I'm feeling lightheaded, but exhilarated too. Close calls are thrilling and stupid and weirdly fun.

I don't dare say that to anyone, though. They're all dealing with the aftermath of panic.

I want to say, *Let's get the hell out of here*, but that's just redundant. My team is already doing that.

My suit lets me know that the runabout's environment is suitable now, so I bring my hood down. Yash does the same. Her face is red and blotchy, and either tear-streaked, covered with sweat, or both.

Her gaze meets mine.

"Thanks," she says, and I know what she means. She wouldn't have been able to make the crossing without me. Hell, she wouldn't have survived the dive without me.

I nod once. "It's always an adventure when we dive together."

She let out a choked laugh.

"That it is," she says with a smile. "That it truly is."

75

COHN STOOD WITH HER FEET APART, hands clasped behind her back. She felt weirdly calm. This was the last stage of this mission.

The *Mächteg* had been in position for a good five minutes. It had arrived just a few moments before the *Geesi* and the *Royk*, setting to work the moment it arrived.

Which was a good thing, because those ten Empire ships had sped up. Clearly they had seen the first damaged vessel disappear into fold-space, and they were going to prevent this one.

Cohn's bridge crew was ready. She would pick off those Empire ships, if she had to. She didn't want to.

There had been enough loss of life as it was.

"Captain?" Vinters sounded odd. "Look."

She was tapping the holoscreen before her.

Two small vessels, so small that Cohn saw their movement before she saw what they were, sped away from the damaged ship.

She studied the ships for a moment, frowning. They looked like runabouts.

"I thought you said everyone on this ship was dead," she said.

"They are," Vinters said. "Those runabouts have an ancient design."

Ancient design. Lost Souls.

They took something from the ship, or planted something.

"Before the *Mächteg* hauls that ship into foldspace, make sure that no one planted an active weapon on board," Cohn said.

"Already have." That was Iosua. Of course it was. He didn't want anything to interfere with a foldspace leap. "There's nothing active on that ship, except a small emergency beacon."

Cohn let out a breath. She hoped to hell he was right.

He probably was. Because there was no way Lost Souls had known she was coming—not with enough time to plant some kind of bomb.

"Captain Fjeld says they're ready." This from Gray.

The *Mächteg* was tethered then, and ready to go into foldspace. This was a moment of reckoning. Either Cohn believed it was safe to go, or she aborted.

The Empire ships would be here in less than five minutes.

"Tell her to go. We'll see her at the Scrapheap," Cohn said. They had agreed to rendezvous there, pick up their fifth ship, and maybe head back to the Fleet or reassess.

The *Mächteg* opened a foldspace window. Cohn could see it on her screens as well as in the telemetry. The *Mächteg* dragged the damaged vessel through the window faster than the *Sakhata* had with its burden.

And then the window vanished.

"Should we go, Captain?" Vinters asked with some urgency in her voice. The Empire vessels would be here quickly.

If Cohn were in charge of them, she'd just blanket the area with weapons' fire. Her ships could withstand that, but she didn't want to subject them to it.

She looked at those small ships. Once a thief, always a thief. They had taken something from the damaged vessel, and she would love to know what that something was.

If she got close, she could shut down those ships, taking their crew prisoner, learn more about the thieves. The brig was more than big enough.

"Captain?"

But she had no idea what she would learn from those thieves. She was going to learn a lot from the damaged vessels, without the hassle of dealing with actual people.

She knew that Lost Souls and the Empire was here. She knew they had some kind of conflict with each other. She was more curious about the vessels she had taken than she was about the thieves.

They were probably stealing to support themselves in the conflict.

"Tell the *Royk* we're leaving now," she said to Vinters.

"Yes, Captain," Vinters said.

Iosua grinned at Cohn, then plotted a course to send them back to the Scrapheap.

Within seconds, the *Geesi* started vibrating. They were heading into foldspace.

She maintained her balance through the vibrations.

What a strange day. What a strange journey. What a strange mission.

She had a hunch everything she learned would change policy in the Fleet. But that wasn't her concern.

None of it was.

She was bringing back ships of a type they hadn't seen before, and answers to questions the Fleet probably didn't even know it had.

A much more successful mission than she had thought it would be.

She had a hunch the Fleet would see it exactly the same way.

76

THE SECOND ENEMY VESSEL VANISHED through one of those doorways, just like the first had done. Elissa could see the outline of yet another ship, pulling the enemy vessel through that doorway of light.

She didn't curse. She didn't pound her fist on the console.

There was no point in being angry—even though everyone in the command center expected her to be. Half the team was shooting her sideways glances, wondering what she was going to do next.

She had lost—probably everything. Flag Commander Janik had given her a command reluctantly. He certainly wasn't going to back her after this debacle.

She had nothing to show for it.

"Call those ships back," she said to Bahe. "And get our people from the *Ivoire.*"

Maybe she would have some intelligence from that, although she doubted it.

She had gambled, and she had lost.

She pivoted and let herself out of the command center. They would finish the cleanup operation, and then she would take her ships back across the border.

She could almost hear Janik. The same lecture he had given her once before—how she had brought disgrace to the Trekov name, how she wasn't worthy of service in the Empire's space force, how she didn't deserve her own command.

The only difference had been then that she had believed he was wrong. Maybe he hadn't been.

She headed down to her office. She only had one choice now. As soon as the Empire left this part of space, she would tender her resignation, and of course Janik would accept it.

She would have accepted it too. She would be lucky if she didn't face actual charges for insubordination or whatever else Janik could throw at her.

She let out a breath.

Three times. Three times she had let Cooper beat her. He had outthought her, outmaneuvered her, and nearly destroyed her. Nearly, anyway, the first two times.

This time, most likely, he had destroyed her.

Or, he would argue, she had destroyed herself.

She let herself into the office, closed the door, and sank into her chair.

She was done. Everyone on this ship knew it. Probably everyone in the space force knew it.

Time she admitted it as well. Maybe, before she saw Janik, she could figure out how to atone for the lives lost.

The lives she had destroyed.

Maybe.

Or maybe there was no atonement at all.

77

COOP RAN THROUGH THE CORRIDOR TO THE SHIP BAY. He had insisted that the runabouts come to the *Ivoire*, even though the *Madxaf* was closer. He didn't care about that extra distance.

He needed the runabouts here, needed to see for himself that Boss and Yash were all right.

He hadn't said a word as he peeled away from the bridge and began his trip from the bridge to the bay.

His behavior wasn't professional. He didn't care about that either. Screw the Fleet. Screw his training. He had made it this far, and his people were all right.

He was going to have a lot of work to do after greeting them. He had to shepherd the Empire vessels out of here. He would probably let Mae and the others handle the diplomacy of that, maybe even come to some kind of agreement.

He suspected Trekov never wanted to hear from him again.

The doors to the ship bay had just closed when he arrived, and the environment had reestablished itself. The air smelled faintly of ozone and had that chill which often came from a newly arrived vessel.

Two newly arrived vessels.

They had parked near each other, each in an empty space, looking no worse for the wear.

The door to the *Madxaf's* runabout opened, and a ramp extended. Orlando got off first, his hair glistening, probably with sweat.

"Thank you," Coop said.

Orlando gave him a half-smile. "All in a day's work," he said as if nothing had happened at all.

Coop ran up the ramp, stopping when he saw Yash. Her face was red and sweat-streaked. She looked more exhausted than he'd ever seen her. She was sitting on the floor of the runabout, legs splayed, an *anacapa* container attached to her chest.

"We didn't get the communications *anacapa*," she said to him when she saw him. "But I guess it doesn't matter since the Empire didn't get either ship."

"You were amazing," he said.

"Eh," she said, waving a hand. "We don't really need another *anacapa* drive. But I learned a lot. That ship had *incredible* technology—and I suspect we got it all."

She grinned at him then, looking more like herself.

He smiled back at her, and then looked past her.

Boss was sitting slightly behind her, eyes sparkling. Boss looked more alive than he had ever seen her.

"Orlando saved us," she said, as she started to pick herself up. "We had to jump."

"Jump?" Coop asked, reaching her side. He grabbed her gloved hand, which clung to his just a bit too tightly.

"From the Not-Fleet vessel to the runabout," Boss said.

"No tethers, no tube," Yash said. "Just that crazy woman, launching us both into the void."

Then Yash grinned and Boss grinned back. Coop had never seen the two of them look so at ease with each other.

Boss let him help her up. Her legs wobbled, and as he got close to her, he realized just how spent she was.

"The only bad thing," she said, "besides losing both Not-Fleet vessels, is they got my single ship."

He had always hated that thing. He thought it dangerous, and he thought it encouraged Boss to be too reckless.

Of course, if she hadn't been the reckless type, both she and Yash would probably be heading through foldspace right now, traveling who knew where.

"Is there anything on it?" he asked.

"Just half my life," she said, sounding rueful.

"I mean, information—"

"Oh, I don't know," she said. "I don't know what it can mean to them."

Them being the Fleet or whatever that had been. They had come here, they had taken two Not-Fleet vessels and they had left.

Maybe he hadn't lied to Trekov after all. Maybe those vessels weren't Fleet. Maybe they were related to the Not-Fleet ships, and maybe they were just retrieving their missing vessels.

"We were just checking," Yash said. "It looks like we pulled a ton of information off that Not-Fleet ship."

She was still sitting on the floor of the runabout. Even her voice sounded tired. But not upset. Not angry. Maybe even slightly pleased with herself.

"What kind of information?" Coop asked.

Yash smiled. "Their entire data file. Boss did that."

"At your direction," Boss said.

She leaned into Coop. He put his arm around her. She was so thin. Or maybe he just realized how vulnerable she really was.

"I don't think I've ever been this tired in my life," she said softly.

He pulled Boss close and then extended a hand to Yash to help her up.

She shook her head.

"I think I'm moving in here," she said. "Someone just bring me food."

Nyssa came out of the galley, holding some kind of concoction. "We are not letting you stay here," she said. "I'm taking them both to the med bay, just to make sure everything is all right."

"I'll help," Coop said.

"I won't argue," Nyssa said. "They're difficult patients."

"We're not patients," Boss said. "We're just tired."

"Exhausted beyond their limits," Nyssa said.

"Now that's probably accurate," Boss said, and both she and Yash laughed.

Coop looked at both women, grateful they were alive. Amazed they were alive. Stunned that he and Lost Souls and all of the ships had survived this day.

The Empire hadn't, and he would probably have to deal with that, among many other things.

But this—the runabout, the information, the two most important people in his life—this was a victory.

An amazing victory.

One he hoped they would never ever need to repeat.

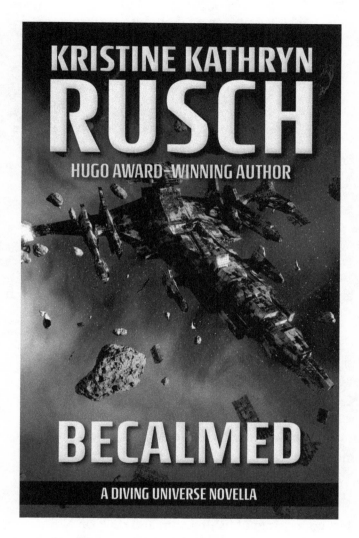

To read more about the diplomatic mission that went
awry in the *Ivoire*'s past, check out this book in
Kristine Kathryn Rusch's award-winning
Diving series, *Becalmed,* on sale now.

I value honest feedback, and would love to hear your opinion in a review, if you're so inclined, on your favorite book retailer's site.

Be the first to know!

Just sign up for the Kristine Kathryn Rusch newsletter, and keep up with the latest news, releases and so much more—even the occasional giveaway.

To sign up, go to kristinekathrynrusch.com.

But wait! There's more. Sign up for the WMG Publishing newsletter, too, and get the latest news and releases from all of the WMG authors and lines, including Kristine Grayson, Kris Nelscott, Dean Wesley Smith, *Pulphouse Fiction Magazine, Smith's Monthly,* and so much more.

Just go to wmgpublishing.com and click on Newsletter.

ABOUT THE AUTHOR

New York Times bestselling author Kristine Kathryn Rusch writes in almost every genre. Generally, she uses her real name (Rusch) for most of her writing. Under that name, she publishes bestselling science fiction and fantasy, award-winning mysteries, acclaimed mainstream fiction, controversial nonfiction, and the occasional romance. Her novels have made bestseller lists around the world and her short fiction has appeared in eighteen best of the year collections. She has won more than twenty-five awards for her fiction, including the Hugo, *Le Prix Imaginales*, the *Asimov's* Readers Choice award, and the *Ellery Queen Mystery Magazine* Readers Choice Award.

To keep up with everything she does, go to kriswrites.com and sign up for her newsletter. To track her many pen names and series, see their individual websites (krisnelscott.com, kristinegrayson.com, retrievalartist.com, divingintothewreck.com, fictionriver.com, pulphousemagazine.com).

The Retrieval Artist Universe
(Reading Order)

CPSIA information can be obtained
at www.ICGtesting.com
Printed in the USA
BVHW031628140921
616732BV00002B/23/J

9 781561 464784